Although she ... medieval romances, it seems ... sagas set in her home city due to its ... background, especially as she has several mariners in her family tree and her mother was in service. She has written twenty sagas set in Merseyside, as well as in the beautiful city of Chester and Lancashire countryside.

Visit June Francis's website at: www.junefrancis.co.uk

Also by June Francis:

A Mother's Duty
A Daughter's Choice
Lily's War

JUNE FRANCIS

A Sister's Duty

EBURY
PRESS

3 5 7 9 10 8 6 4 2

Ebury Press, an imprint of Ebury Publishing
20 Vauxhall Bridge Road,
London SW1V 2SA

Penguin
Random House
UK

Ebury Press is part of the Penguin Random House group of companies
whose addresses can be found at global.penguinrandomhouse.com

First published in 1998 as *For the Sake of the Children* by
Judy Piatkus (Publishers) Ltd
This edition published in 2016 by Ebury Press

www.eburypublishing.co.uk

A CIP catalogue record for this book
is available from the British Library

ISBN 9780091956363

Typeset in India by Thomson Digital Pvt Ltd, Noida, Delhi
Printed and bound in Great Britain by Clays Ltd, St Ives PLC

Penguin Random House is committed to a sustainable future for
our business, our readers and our planet. This book is made from
Forest Stewardship Council® certified paper.

MIX
Paper from
responsible sources
FSC® C018179

Dedicated with love and gratitude to the memory of my mother May Milburn Nelson and Great Aunt Jane, who took Mum and her sister Flo in when their mother died.

Acknowledgements

Many thanks to Mr Radcliff of the Boots' Retirement Association for help with pharmaceutical details and also to some of the staff and children of St Vincent's School for the Visually Impaired, West Derby.

'Duty is the cement which fills in the cracks in a family and helps hold it together' — *J.F.*

'Love, it is said, is blind;
But love is not blind.
It is an extra eye which shows us
what is most worthy of regard'
— *J.M. Barrie*

Chapter One

Where was she? She should have been in by now.

Fifteen-year-old Rosie Kilshaw paced the kitchen floor, arms folded across her chest, thin fingers gripping the shabby wool of her coat. Her delicate face, all planes and angles in the gas light, was screwed into a ferocious scowl.

'D'yer think she's forgotten, Rosie?' piped up Harry.

'She better hadn't have,' said Rosie darkly, glancing down at her younger brother and sisters huddling as close as they could to the smoking fire struggling for life in the black-leaded grate.

'She did promise,' said Dotty, looking anxious as she knelt up on the rag rug.

'She did. But she doesn't always keep her promises,' said Babs, the second in the family, flicking back the light brown plait which hung over her shoulder. 'Where could she be? She's always late in, lately.'

'God only knows,' muttered Rosie, impatience and concern forming a tight knot in her chest. It was going to be a big disappointment if they didn't get to the pantomime this evening. A promise was a promise and although she accepted her mother had to work odd hours doing this extra war job she had taken on, Rosie wished she hadn't accepted it. The trouble was her mother hated being at home and was blinking pigheaded into the bargain! Rosie could easily have left school and got herself a job by now. But no, Violet Veronica Kilshaw had insisted on her eldest daughter getting an education, which was stupid when they were so hard up.

Rosie looked down at the three upturned faces framed by royal-blue woolly hats which still had a crinkly appearance, having been knitted from an unpicked pullover by their nextdoor neighbour, and felt a surge of anger. Not with her mother this time but with her maternal grandfather and aunts Amelia and Iris, who lived in the lap of luxury out West Derby way on the outskirts of Liverpool.

It was more than five years since the row which had caused the newly widowed Violet to storm out of her father's house, but Rosie, like her mother, had not forgotten or forgiven that day, which had left them both shocked and resentful for different reasons.

They heard the noise of the front door opening and closing, the tap-tap of high heels on the linoleum, and the next moment Violet entered the kitchen, carrying two shopping bags. 'Hi, sweethearts.'

'You're late. I hope you haven't forgotten, Mam?' said Rosie, relieving her of the shopping bags and eyeing her flushed cheeks and sparkling eyes with curiosity and relief. Her mother's moods swung up and down like a yo-yo but this evening she looked particularly pleased with herself. 'Where the heck have you been?'

Violet laid a finger against her nose. 'We all have our little secrets. But – hell, I'm sorry I'm late, kids! Look at you, all ready and raring to go.' Her scarlet-painted mouth widened in a beaming smile as she took in their coats and wellies. 'But I'm late for a reason. I had to go and get my birthday boy his present.' She bent and kissed five-year-old Harry on the top of his balaclava-clad head and took a box from one of the shopping bags Rosie had placed on the chenille tablecloth. The boy took it from her hands, tearing eagerly at the brown paper.

'Tea's in the other bag,' said Violet, seating herself on the easy chair to the side of the fireplace and kicking off her high heels. She rested her curly dark head against the back of the chair and began to hum to herself.

'You have remembered you're supposed to be taking us to the pantomime?' said Rosie, undoing the newspaper-wrapped package. Babs, almost fourteen, pounced on the parcel. 'Is it fish and chips?' she asked eagerly.

'Of course it's fish and chips,' said Dot, her junior by a year. Her delicate nostrils quivered in her lovely face as her head turned in the direction of the table, eyes damaged by a bout of measles unable to focus on her sister.

'Lovely!' said Babs. 'I'm starving. We've only had jam butties, Mam.'

'Well, Mam?' said Rosie, knowing Babs's greed and shoving her aside to open the vinegar-soaked newspaper herself. 'You haven't answered. Can't you afford to take us now?'

'I'll keep my promise, don't you worry, but let me have a rest first.' Violet half closed her eyes, stretching sheer nylon-clad legs towards the fire. 'There's a second house, isn't there?'

'Yes. But that's at eight o'clock and there'll be a queue. And can we afford the tram fare to get there on time?'

'Mmmm. I got a bonus tonight,' said Violet, opening her velvety brown eyes briefly before closing them again and smiling to herself.

'That's great! But nobody else I know's mother goes out to work like you do. Let me leave school, Mam? Let me get a job?' pleaded Rosie.

'No.' Violet's expression hardened. 'You have your paper round and that's help enough. I want you to do well at school. I want you to get qualifications that'll help you to get a better job than I've ever been able to have. I want you to be able to cock a snook at our Amelia and say: "Look at me! I've done it without any help from you Needhams." Besides, your dad really wanted this for you. They hated him, you know that. They hated him, my two ugly sisters,' she said vehemently. 'Dead jealous of me they were – so you've got to show them.'

Rosie had heard all this before, expressed one way or another, and each time it fuelled her own rage because she could not understand anyone hating her father, Joe. He had been so good and kind and funny. Never would she forget the day his body had been brought home, all broken and bruised. Her mother had been expecting Harry's birth, and after she had recovered from the initial shock had rushed with her three daughters to her father's house to ask for financial help. None had been forthcoming.

'This is just what I wanted, Mam.' Harry was on his feet, chubby face alight with pleasure, clutching a red-painted wooden engine to his chest. He leant against her knees, throwing back his head and smiling up at her.

Violet kissed his rosy mouth. 'Aren't I a clever mam? I wasn't able to get it for Christmas but your birthday's a much better day, isn't it, sweetheart?'

'How much was your bonus, Mam?' mumbled Babs, her mouth full of chips. 'It must have been a few pounds to be able to keep us, buy Harry that train *and* take us to the pantomime as well.'

'Don't be nosy,' Violet reproved, a frown clouding her brow. 'Now pass us some chips before you scoff the lot, greedy guts.'

'What is this work, Mam?' said Rosie, sawing at a loaf. Her lovely, long-lashed eyes, so like Violet's own, were watchful. It was not the first time she had asked.

Violet clicked her tongue against her teeth. 'All these bloody questions! It's secret war work, if you must know, so don't ask again. Now make us a cup of tea, there's a love, before we have to go out into the cold, cold snow.' She shivered expressively, winking at Harry as Rosie handed her a folded slice of bread with chips inside.

'Has it really started snowing?' he asked, his eyes shining.

She shook her head. 'But Jack Frost is about and the pavements are bloody slippy. I don't know how I didn't break my leg getting here.' She cocked her dark head on one side and grimaced. 'You are all sure you want to go to the pantomime? It's freezing out. We could stoke up the fire and put on the wireless?'

Their faces fell, uncertain whether she meant it. 'But you promised!' wailed Dotty. 'And it is Harry's birthday.'

'I know, I know. Keep your hair on,' said Violet, biting into the chip butty. 'You don't all have to look like a wet weekend. I was only joking.'

'Thanks, Mam,' said Harry, looking relieved.

'You're a good lad.' She ruffled his hair. 'The spitting image of your dad.'

And he was, too, thought Rosie, biting into a chip butty herself. Family likeness – you couldn't get away from it. He had Joe's flaxen hair, blue eyes and easy-going nature. She loved the bones of him. His birth had brought the colour back into their lives after months of Violet's dark moods and living hand to mouth. Had it not been for the goodness of their neighbours, she did not know how they would have survived. He had been an adorable baby, capturing her heart from the moment he was born. His presence had gone a long way to filling the gap left by her father's death. Joe and Rosie had been close and he would have loved tonight. He would have said what were chilblains and frozen noses and them being broke for the rest of the month when it came to seeing *Mother Goose* at the Shakie? Like his four children, he would have walked through a blizzard for such escapist delight on this dark freezing evening of January 1945.

Their breath formed clouds of vapour as the children raced the tram to the stop. Violet shouted at them to slow down, slithering on the ice in a flat pair of shoes with well-worn soles.

They jumped aboard. Harry and Babs sat next to Rosie, nudging each other in their high spirits and demanding to know if there would be a beautiful princess in *Mother Goose*.

'I don't know. But it'll be fun, I know that!' Her eyes were bright with anticipation, remembering the last panto-mime she had seen. It had been *The Old Woman Who Lived in a Shoe* with Old Mother Riley before the war, and had been her last trip out with Joe.

Her father had been a carter, and according to Violet, Grandfather Needham had considered Joe not good enough for her. Yet Grandfather Needham himself had pulled himself up by his boot straps to become a pharmacist. Perhaps he was ashamed of his beginnings and that was why he hung on to his money despite having his own shop and a four-bedroomed semi-detached house. Snobs of the first order, Violet had called him and her sister Amelia, and Rosie could only agree.

'What's with the face?' said her mother now, startling Rosie.

'I was thinking of Grandfather and the ugly sisters,' she blurted out without thinking.

'Well, don't!' Violet twinkled. 'It's not *Cinderella* we're going to see, you know. We're going to have fun this evening, so fix your face.'

Rosie smiled and committed her relatives to oblivion.

The tram rattled on down London Road, approaching the Paramount cinema which was across the road from Fraser Street where the Shakespeare Theatre was situated. They all stood up, Rosie holding Babs and Harry by the hand, Violet with Dotty in front. To their surprise and dismay, the tram went rattling past the stop.

'Hey, mate, where yer goin'?' demanded a youth standing at the bottom of the stairway. 'I wanted that stop!'

'So did we!' chorused the children.

The driver ignored them, pulling desperately on the brake handle as the tram hurtled like a rocket towards William Brown Street, screeching as it went, and straight on past the bomb-damaged Liverpool Museum. Dotty screamed, clinging to her mother's arm. 'It's going too fast!'

'Of course it bloody is,' muttered Violet as they all swayed and pitched with the tram as it thundered towards Dale Street.

'It's getting away from him,' shouted the youth.

'Let's jump!' said his mate. 'I don't bloody like this.'

'Sweet Jesu!' The words were torn from Violet as the tram leapt the points where Dale Street met Byrom Street.

People screamed and yelled as all the lights went out and the tram toppled over. Rosie lost her grip on Babs and Harry and was flung against a seat before rolling over and vanishing between two of them as the tram went skidding along the ground with a noise reminiscent of a knife scraping a tin plate. The next moment, they hit something, making a horrible grinding noise. Rosie clung to one of the seat supports, praying the tram would stop, but it carried on sliding. Then the tram hit something else before shuddering to a halt.

For a moment, she dared not move and could only think how quiet and still everything had gone. Then, just as the first chirp of a lone bird signals the dawn chorus, came the tinkling of falling glass and shifting bricks, followed by the moans and groans of the injured.

'Rosie!' screamed Dotty. 'Mam's gone!'

Gone where? she thought, stupefied but beginning to think about moving. The trouble was the floor was not where it should be. But she managed to drag herself painfully upright and took several deep breaths. 'Harry! Babs!' she yelled.

They both answered. Using the seats for support, she was able to move in the direction of their voices. Her gloved fingers touched a bare leg. 'Who's that?'

'Me. Wasn't that fun?' Harry's teeth were chattering as he clung to her arm. 'Are we upside-down?'

'Something like,' she said, hugging him.

He trembled in her arms and she could just about make out his face. 'Where's Mam?'

'Here somewhere.' She tried to sound cheerful, subduing her own anxiety. Carefully, she put him down, ordering him to stay put.

'Don't want to,' he said, clinging to her coat.

'You *have* to while I find Mam and the others,' she said, coaxingly. 'Now do as you're told, please.'

'What a bloody mess!' said a woman somewhere behind. 'I've been cut.'

Rosie touched her own forehead where it hurt and the discovery that she was bleeding too made her feel sick, but at least she was walking wounded, she thought. How would it be with those who weren't?

'Rosie, help me,' shrieked Dotty. 'I can't get up.'

'Coming.'

'I'm stuck,' came Babs's calm voice somewhere to Rosie's left. 'One of me plaits is caught on something and it doesn't half hurt when I pull.'

Stretching her arm in the direction of the voice, Rosie touched a face. 'Is that you?'

'Yeah.' Babs rubbed her cheek against Rosie's hand. 'Can you get me out?'

Dotty sobbed, 'Rosie, Rosie!'

The same female voice which had spoken before said, 'You go and see to her, luv. I'll deal with these two.'

Rosie thanked the woman and made her way to the front by dint of dragging herself from seat to seat. She found Dot wedged under the stairwell by the groaning, prone body of the youth she took to be the one who had been standing at the foot of the stairs. He was barely conscious but she managed to drag him out of the way, realising by the look of the mess about her that the tram had ploughed into a shop window. Her heart began to thump heavily as she wondered if her mother was under all that rubble.

Dotty's fingers searched Rosie's face. 'It is you but your face is all wet!' she said, voice trembling with relief.

'It's blood, but I'm OK. Can you get up?' Rosie touched her sister's arm but withdrew her hand swiftly, aware of shards of glass penetrating the wool of her glove. Ordering Dotty to lean on her, she levered her sister upright.

Suddenly, Rosie was blinded by the glare of headlights as a vehicle squealed to a stop. There was the sound of male voices.

'Here comes the cavalry,' drawled the woman who had offered to take care of Babs and Harry. 'The Yanks, by the sound of it.'

A cheer went up and a voice said, 'A bit of light on the subject. That's a relief.'

'I want me mam,' wailed Dotty. 'I want me mam!'

'Shut up!' said Rosie fiercely. 'Don't be such a baby. You're thirteen and you're making a show of us.'

'But Mam's gone! She nearly yanked my arm off,' whimpered Dotty, breath catching on a sob.

'When was that?'

'When the tram jumped the points.'

Rosie almost choked with relief. A broken arm or leg, she thought, remembering what Violet had said about slippery pavements.

A head popped into view above a shattered window. It was male, wearing a helmet with 'MP' on it. A large capable-looking hand shone a torch into their faces. 'Anyone want out of there?' asked its owner cheerfully.

'Ask a daft question,' murmured the woman, who had Harry and Babs in tow. She thrust the boy forward. 'Could you get these kids out, mate?'

'Sure, ma'am!' He touched his helmet with the side of his hand, telling them to step back, and got rid of the jagged pieces of glass remaining in a side front window pretty sharpish.

In no time at all, the four Kilshaw children were standing on the road. Several firemen, civilian policemen and transport workers were now on the scene, their offices in Hatton Garden a short distance away having been swiftly alerted.

The headlights of the US jeep lit up a scene reminiscent of the Blitz and there was a smell of brick dust and hot metal in the air. A live cable swung dangerously above two trams lying on their sides and Rosie realised that the other tram must have been the first thing theirs had hit.

She took Dotty and Harry by the hand, telling Babs to stick close, and began walking back to where the tram had jumped the points. Suddenly, a constable, past middle age and plump, loomed up in front of them. One of those, she presumed, who had been called upon after retirement when younger men had gone to war. Rosie could see where he had cut his chin shaving as, lowering his head, he gasped, 'Where are you off to, kids? You've got a few cuts that'll need seeing to. Wait for the ambulances. They'll be here soon.'

'We're looking for Mam. She fell off the tram when it jumped the points.' Rosie's voice trembled despite all her efforts to stay calm.

'Well then, I think I'd better come along with you,' he said, taking Babs's hand and falling in beside them.

People were hurrying past towards the scene of the accident but one man was crouching over a figure sprawled on the pavement. Instantly, Rosie left the others and ran.

'Take it easy now,' said the policeman, catching up with her and placing a hand on her shoulder as she knelt on the pavement.

Scarcely aware of him, Rosie gazed down at her mother's ashen face. There was blood coming out of her nose, which made Rosie feel sick all over again. She was scared, just as she had been on the night of Harry's birth.

Removing her woolly hat and swallowing back tears, Rosie placed it beneath her mother's cheek. Then, taking one of her hands, she chafed it, pretending not to have seen the blood staining the hoary pavement.

'An ambulance'll be here soon,' said the constable in a would-be comforting voice, taking off his cape and covering Violet with it. It was true. Rosie could hear bells clanging as if to say, *Make way! Make way!* He picked up a handbag lying on the pavement. 'Is this your mam's?'

'Yes!' Rosie almost snatched it from him, looping it over her shoulder. Violet never allowed anyone to look in her handbag. She made jokes about keeping her secrets in there. She watched the policeman taking out a notebook and pencil, and was irritated. Surely he wasn't going to start asking them questions now?

But he was. 'Now how about giving me some details about yourselves while we're waiting?'

'It's my birfday,' said Harry, breathing noisily through his nose while sucking his thumb.

Babs said crossly, 'Stop that. Only babies suck their thumbs.'

Harry took his thumb out of his mouth and looked up at the policeman. 'I'm five today, and we were going to the pantomime.'

'To see *Mother Goose*. Mam was treating us,' said Dotty in a shaky voice. 'We won't be able to go now and I was looking forward to it even though I wouldn't have been able to see it. I'd have enjoyed the jokes and the music.'

'Shut up about it,' snapped Rosie. 'What's a pantomime when Mam's bad like this?'

'Now don't be getting yourself upset,' said the policeman. 'Give me your mam's name and address and, tell me, is your dad in the Forces?'

The four Kilshaws shook their heads. 'He was killed before he could go and fight,' said Babs. 'Crushed by a truckload of scrap iron on the dock road.'

The policeman clicked his tongue against his teeth. 'Shame! Any other family? Grannies, aunts, uncles?'

Before they could reply, a man appeared, carrying a small black bag. Hastily, Rosie moved out of his way, holding her breath as he bent over Violet, willing him to be able to do something. But his inspection was brief, and he asked the policeman to direct the ambulance over to them before giving the children his attention. 'You'd all better go to the hospital along with your mother and have those lacerations seen to.'

'Mam?' said Rosie.

'Too early to tell.' He rested a hand on her shoulder a moment and then left.

An ambulance came and Violet was slid on to a stretcher. Rosie thought how lovely it would be if suddenly she regained consciousness because of the movement, just like in *Snow White* when the poisoned bit of apple had been dislodged and the heroine came back to life.

'I'm frightened,' whispered Dotty, her hand creeping into Rosie's as they climbed into the ambulance.

'"Don't think it and it won't be,"' muttered Rosie. 'Remember Mam saying that? Now smile or you'll worry Harry.'

'I'll try. Honestly, I'll try. But it's not easy, Rosie. What'll happen to us if—'

'Don't say it,' she said fiercely, squashing her sister against Babs and putting an arm round Harry.

The policeman joined them, asking the little boy about his birthday, going on to talk about steam locomotives and a journey to Yorkshire before the war with his own son.

Within minutes, they'd arrived at the Royal Infirmary in Pembroke Place and once inside, Violet was whisked away. Rosie would have gone with her but was told to be sensible and look after her brother and sisters. There followed an unpleasant half hour while glass was dug out of faces and abrasions dealt with. Then the policeman asked them if there were any female relatives who could stay with them that night.

'I'm not going anywhere,' said Rosie, expression defiant, folding her arms. 'I'm staying here until I know Mam's OK.'

'There's the aunts,' said Babs. 'And Grandfather.'

Rosie glared at her. 'Have you forgotten?'

'Forgotten what?'

Rosie continued to glare at her and Babs rolled her eyes. 'Oh, that! I bet half of it was Mam's fault. You know how she gets.'

'How can you say that? She's only the way she is because of them!' cried Rosie, her fury ready to erupt.

Babs shrugged. 'Aunt Iris was OK. Remember how she took us in the garden and played with us?'

'Her? She'll be no help! She was under their thumb. Remember Mam telling us that?'

'What's it matter now?' Babs rested her chin on one hand. 'It's years ago. The war's probably changed everything.'

'I don't believe it,' muttered Rosie, tapping her foot on the floor.

'Give us the address of one of them,' said the policeman, coaxingly.

Rosie said grimly, 'Don't you dare, Babs!'

'Come on, Babs,' said the policeman persuasively.

'Having trouble?' A woman dressed in the uniform of the Women's Auxiliary Peace Corps stood at the policeman's shoulder.

Rosie nudged her sister in the ribs. 'Not a word,' she hissed. 'Or it'll be the worst for you when Mam comes to.'

'You think she will?' whispered Babs.

'Just keep your mouth shut.'

The policeman looked down at the two sisters and they stared woodenly back at him. He sighed. 'I need someone to stay with these kids tonight. Their mam's not too good,' he explained.

'Sure, I'll look after them,' said the woman, expression sympathetic. 'What an evening it's been for you, hey, kids? I bet you're worn out. Shall we be off?'

'I want to stay,' insisted Rosie, scared all of a sudden that if she left the hospital she might never see her mother again.

'I understand how you feel,' said the woman brightly. 'But think of your sisters and brother. They need you and their beds. Leave your mam to the experts.' She placed a firm arm round Rosie, ushering her unwilling body to the exit.

At home, the cat was mewing on the step. Rosie scooped him up, pressing her face against his fur a moment

before thrusting him into Babs's arms. She hurried ahead
to light the gas mantle, tears threatening, remembering
how they had been so looking forward to the evening a
few hours ago. She rushed out of the room, not wanting
to disgrace herself by giving in to her tears, and ran down
the yard to the lavatory.

It was almost pitch black with the door closed because
the storm lantern placed there to prevent the pipes from
freezing had gone out. Placing her mother's handbag on
the wooden seat, she allowed the tears to fall. She remembered Joe hanging that very same lantern here year after
year when she was a child and wished fervently he had
not died. Her father had had eyes which could change
from sadness to humour and devilment as quickly as you
could say 'Flash Harry'.

They had never had much money, though their house
had been a happy place with him in it. But she knew little
about his family background, she realised. He had seldom
mentioned his mother who, Violet had told her, had been
as against the marriage as her own family and had cut her
son out of her life after he set his will against hers. As
for his father, Joe himself had said he remembered there
being a row and his sailor father Walter Kilshaw leaving
in a hurry. His mother had told him Walter had gone to
join his ship, but he had never returned and Joe, only a
small boy at the time, had mourned his passing, believing
him lost at sea.

Rosie felt doubly sad now, regretting she had never
got to know any of her grandparents. Violet had been
convinced Joe's mother, Maggie Kilshaw, was dead. She

had lived not far from the docks where the city had been heavily bombed. The houses there were a far cry from the one in West Derby. Rosie found herself thinking again of her Grandfather Needham and aunts and of that visit after Joe's death.

Her mother had been quite cheerful, convinced she could persuade Grandfather Needham to give them money. After all, she had said, she had once been his favourite daughter. That was why it had hurt him so much, her marrying against his will.

Rosie shivered, remembering the humdinger of a row with Aunt Amelia's angry contralto voice joining in. They could be heard in the garden where Aunt Iris had taken the children to play. Rosie had immediately rushed to press her face against the French windows and been scared almost out of her wits by the sight of her grandfather's face. His eyes were bulging, his cheeks scarlet, and she had moved away quickly, thinking he might explode. But not before Amelia had spotted her and given her a furious look.

Within minutes, Violet had come searching for them, hurting their wrists as she seized hold of them, storming out of the garden, yelling she would never return and that they'd better never darken *her* doors, ever! And they never had.

Footsteps sounded in the yard and a voice called, 'You haven't fallen down, have you, luv?'

'No, I'm coming.' Rosie dragged automatically on the chain but it did not release a torrent of water. The pipes had frozen and in the morning they would have to carry a bucket of water down to flush the lav. It was enough to make her weep all over again.

'You OK?' said the woman cheerfully, meeting her at the back door and hurrying her inside.

'Fine,' she said tersely, realising in an almost heart-stopping moment that the woman must have used nearly all the coal to have stoked the fire so that it glowed deep red. Babs was making toast before it.

'Where's the kids' night things?'

'We don't have any. Just underpants and vest or knickers and vest,' said Rosie, embarrassed.

'No problem,' said the woman, still cheerful. 'It'll save warming them up. I'll bunk down on the couch.'

'You could have Mam's bed,' said Dotty eagerly, turning her face towards her. 'Me and Babs sleep in her room in a single bed.'

'No, you're OK, luv. The couch is fine.'

'I sleep with Rosie,' said Harry, pushing his new engine back and forth on the linoleum. 'We couldn't afford another bed when I got too big for me cot.'

'Shush,' muttered Rosie. 'You don't have to tell everyone. It would have been difficult getting one anyway with shortages.'

'That's true,' said the woman, adding casually, 'Does your mother have any family?'

Before Rosie could prevent her, Dotty said, 'Two sisters and a father.'

'And where do they live?'

Rosie shot a warning look at Babs and said swiftly, 'We're not going to tell you! We'll manage without them.'

From her perch on a sagging easy chair, Dotty said, 'I've only met them once. When Dad died and Mam took us to see Grandfather. I was only eight. It was a lovely house with a huge garden. I remember the flowers smelling all spicy and sweet.'

'I was nine,' said Babs, forking another slice of bread.

'It was just after I caught measles and my eyes went funny,' said Dotty. 'Mam went there for money. D'you think—' She turned her face in Rosie's direction.

'I think you should shut up,' muttered her eldest sister, scraping margarine on to the toast.

Harry looked up at her and without a word left his engine, resting his head against her thigh. 'Don't get upset,' he said, patting her arm. 'Don't get upset, Rosie. You know Mammy doesn't like it when we get upset.'

Rosie placed her cheek against his hair. 'You're right, love. But she'd like it even less if her sisters set foot in this house. So let's have no more said about them, Dotty. It's time we were all in bed, anyway.'

The woman looked at her but said nothing more about the aunts, and after having a slice of toast each and a hot drink, they went upstairs.

Rosie woke early, slipping out of bed cautiously so as not to wake Harry, dressing and creeping down the wooden stairs.

In the kitchen she found their local bobby, drinking Camp coffee with the WAPS woman. He stood up immediately Rosie entered, a solemn and unhappy expression on his face. Clearing his throat, he said, 'I'm sorry, Rosie. But they said she didn't suffer at all.'

Although half expecting the bad news, it knocked her sideways and if she had not sat down hurriedly, she would have fallen. Rosie sank her head into her hands, struggling with tears.

'You cry if you want to, luv,' said the woman, standing at her shoulder and patting it.

Immediately, the girl lifted her head. *What was the point in weeping?* she thought. It wasn't going to bring her mother back. She rose and made herself some tea, drinking it piping hot. But even the heat did not melt the icy lump inside her chest.

'These aunts, Rosie.' The bobby straddled a dining chair, gazing at her with a whole world of sympathy in his eyes. 'You'll have to tell me where they live.'

'No! I can look after us,' she said desperately. 'I'll leave school and get a job. I've been used to caring for the others when Mam's been out evenings.'

'It's not on, luv. You need your aunts if there's no one else.'

Rosie was silent, twisting a handful of the chenille tablecloth between her fingers. 'You're wrong. I could look after us with Mrs Baxendale next door's help. She's very respectable, sings in the choir.'

He sighed. 'She'll do for today, luv. But you're going to have to tell me where those aunts live. What are you going to do for money, like? You couldn't earn enough to keep you all.'

Rosie jumped to her feet, dark hair flying about her shoulders, a wild look in her eyes. 'The last thing they'll give us is money! They wouldn't give it to Mam. They're not going to care about us. You don't know that family. Mam said . . .' She stopped, sinking on to her chair, knees shaking, realising she would never hear her mother saying anything ever again.

'Families do fall out. There could be reasons you don't know anything about,' said the bobby with careful patience. 'So where do they live?'

Rosie stared at him, full lower lip pressed against the thinner upper one. Then she swallowed. 'You're not going to wear me down.' She rose to her feet, adding loudly, 'I've got to get the kids' breakfast ready before we go to school. I've had the oats in soak.'

'You're not doing yourself any favours. Whether you like it or not, you're going to have to tell me,' said the policeman, exasperated. 'With your mam dead, yer don't have a choice.'

From the doorway a thin voice said, 'They live in West Derby.'

'Don't say another word!' yelled Rosie, incensed.

Dotty came further into the room, padding on the lino-leum in her bare feet, clutching a disreputable golliwog in one hand and wearing her underskirt and liberty bodice. She collided with the chair which the bobby had pulled out, yelping, 'Who moved that?'

'Serves you right,' said Rosie coldly. She turned to the policeman. 'She won't remember. She was only a kid.'

'It smelt of lavender and beeswax polish,' said her sister, sitting down. 'It's in Honey's Green Lane, Babs said.' Dotty's face turned in Rosie's direction. 'She said if Mam died we could be put in an orphanage and I don't want to be put into an orphanage, Rosie, so what else can we do? Aunt Iris was OK.'

Rosie made no reply, her own face pinched and drawn. Placing the trivet over the fire and putting on the porridge pan, she said, 'I'm going to wake the others and then we're going to school.' She walked out of the kitchen, head held high.

'Stubborn, isn't she?' marvelled the woman.

'She's like Mam.' A tear escaped to roll slowly down Dotty's left cheek. 'Poor Mam. But they will help, won't they? They're family. They'll have to. They live in Honey's Green Lane. It's a pretty name, isn't it?'

'Do you know the number?'

'No. But Babs said the house is called "Eden". It's interesting, isn't it? It's out of the Bible. Mrs Baxendale next door read the story to me. It's where Adam and Eve lived.'

'Hmmph!' The bobby wrote down the name, thinking all had not been lovely in the Garden of Eden either. Then he got up. 'You staying?' he asked the WAPS woman.

She shook her head. 'I'm whacked. I think the girl can cope with making porridge and getting them off to school.'

They left the house together, he to visit the next-door neighbour to ask her to keep her eye on the Kilshaw children before making the house called 'Eden' his next port of call.

Chapter Two

Amelia Needham checked the standard measures on the back of the NH card against the side of the bottle and handed it to the woman on the other side of the counter. 'That'll be tuppence.'

'Tuppence?' she exclaimed, sounding scandalised as she reached for the bottle. 'My husband's supposed to get this free. It was Lloyd George who said—'

'I don't care what Lloyd George said. You know what the tuppence is for, Mrs Rothwell,' said Amelia, holding the bottle of cough mixture just out of reach. 'Your husband might be on the panel but if you don't want to pay the tuppence again, bring the bottle back next time.'

'It's a bloody disgrace,' muttered the woman, fumbling in her shabby purse. 'Tuppence! I could put that in the gas meter.'

Amelia remained unmoved, wishing not for the first time she could afford to give the darn bottles away but knowing that if she did, none would ever be brought back, and bottles had to be saved. Counting the cost of the war was something the whole country still had to do.

The elderly woman pressed a penny and two ha'pennies into Amelia's palm and almost snatched the bottle from her. Turning away, she collided with a younger woman. 'Watch where yer going!' she snapped before hurrying out.

'Tess, are you all right?' Amelia came out from round the counter and steadied her friend.

'Don't fuss, Lee!' Tess's voice shook as she thrust a prescription into Amelia's hand.

She glanced at it. 'What's this? Sleeping pills?' Amelia had known Tess Hudson since they had attended college in Blackburn Placc thirteen years ago to study the theory part of their secondary certificate in pharmacy. She noticed that her friend's lipstick was smeared halfway up her thin cheeks and the metal-framed, thick-lensed spectacles nccdcd cleaning. Her auburn hair dangled untidily and the buttons of her coat were fastened through the wrong holes so that it hung lopsided.

'It's getting worse, isn't it?' said Amelia, guiding her to the chair used by customers needing a rest. Tess was a diabetic and had ulcerated feet. Amelia wondered if she was eating properly and taking enough insulin.

'I don't want to talk about it,' muttered her friend, dropping her head.

Amelia's face tightened with concern. 'I wish I could help you. Are you worrying about Peter?'

Tess avoided her eyes. 'If he had gone to Burma, maybe, but we worked out a code and he's in Norway. The war's as good as over there.'

'Then what is it?'

Tess clasped her hands tightly in her lap. 'You should know,' she said wearily. 'I can't keep up with the twins and the place is always a bloody mess. I can't see well enough to do anything properly – and I can't bloody sleep!'

'But you've got Chris. He's a good lad, and he's got a job now. His wages must help? Although I never thought Peter would agree to his working on the land.'

'Why not? Besides, have you forgotten? Chris isn't his son.'

Amelia bit her lip. 'I had. Peter's always behaved like a father to him and I put what you told me all those years ago out of my mind. Have you ever heard from the real father?'

'No. And it's unlikely I ever shall. He married someone else.'

'You never told me that.' Amelia slanted her a puzzled glance.

Tess made a queer little noise in her throat which could have been a laugh, before saying in a breathless kind of voice, 'I don't think he even loves his wife. Listen, Lee, are you going to give Mr Brown that prescription or not? I haven't got all day.'

'Of course, keep your hair on.' Amelia squeezed her shoulder, hating to see her friend going downhill so fast. 'I wish I could help you more,' she repeated, about to add that what with the shop and the house to see to, she didn't get much of a chance for anything else.

Tess lifted her head. 'Do you mean that, Lee? Do you?' There was an almost hysterical note in her voice. 'That you'd really like to help me?'

'Of course I do.'

'Thanks.' Tess smiled, the smeared lipstick making her face appear clown-like. 'Now, that prescription, if you don't mind?'

'All right! I'm going, I'm going.' Amelia returned her smile and went into the dispensing room to the rear of the shop.

It was a place she had always loved ever since her father had first brought her here when she was only a child just after the Great War. When old enough, she had started her training as a dispenser but had never completed it because her mother had died and her own life had been turned upside-down. 'Be quick with this, Brownie. Mrs Hudson's waiting for it,' she said to the man her father had trained before her.

She returned to the shop, only to be brought up short by a navy-blue-uniformed figure. Of Tess there was no sign. Amelia wondered where she had gone.

'Can I help you, Constable?' she asked, raising well-shaped eyebrows interrogatively.

'You are Miss Amelia Needham?' he said solemnly.

'Yes. That *does* sound official.'

'Perhaps you'd like to sit down, miss?' There was gingery stubble on his chin and where he had taken off his helmet she could see a red mark caused by the strap.

'What is it?' she said, heart beginning to thump.

His expression was compassionate. 'Your sister – I'm afraid she's met with an accident.'

Amelia gripped the counter with both hands. 'Iris! Is it serious? But no—' Uncertainty appeared in her face. 'They wouldn't tell me like this. Iris is in Canada.'

'It's Mrs Violet Kilshaw who's dead,' he said heavily.

Amelia stared at him, shocked. But almost instantly she was remembering the last time she had seen Violet, could hear the harsh words echoing in her head. Now all that defiance, all that vitriol, was wiped out. Violet was dead. She thought of the pain and suffering they had all gone through after Violet had stormed out with her daughters, and the memory left a sour taste in her own mouth.

'Are you all right, miss? Do you want to sit down?'

Amelia stiffened and flung back her head, pale green eyes as hard as glass. 'I'm perfectly all right, and I'm not going to shed any crocodile tears if you expect that! Thank you for telling me. Now, if you don't mind, I've got work to do.'

His expression was one of disbelief. 'But what about the children?'

'Pardon?'

'Your sister's children. They're all alone. They need you,' he said urgently.

'I don't know my sister's children.' Amelia's voice was dismissive. Yet she was remembering a girl's face pressed to the window, gazing in just as Father had suffered his stroke. 'My sister kept them away from us. She let my father die without ever seeing him again.' Amelia's voice was passionate. 'Don't expect me to grieve for her!'

'That's as may bc, miss,' he said, looking uncomfortable. 'But the children . . . they need someone.'

'Then find someone,' she urged, leaning across the counter, cheeks flushed. 'Someone else!'

He looked shocked.

There was silence broken only by the voice of the pharmacist. 'Miss Needham, prescription's ready.'

Amelia turned and took the drugs from Mr Brown with a murmur of thanks, and then she did what she should have done earlier and filled in the prescription book.

'Excuse me, miss, but you don't really mean that, do you?' said the constable.

'I do.' Amelia's voice was carefully controlled now, though her heart was pounding painfully.

'But they're all alone and there's a funeral to arrange. You can't expect them to do that.'

Amelia plucked the eldest girl's name out of the air. 'Rosie – how old is she?' she said, glancing up from the book.

'Fifteen. Sixteen in a couple of months, so the neighbour said.'

'Almost a young woman.'

'Aye. But not old enough to cope with this kind of thing. Doesn't want to believe it's happened. That's how it can take people. Throws them right off their stride.'

Amelia finished writing and fixed him with a stare. 'You don't have to tell me anything about grief, Constable. It's only a year since my father passed away, and my mother died in childbirth when I was eighteen, along with the baby boy we'd all been hoping for. I had to break off my engagement and my studies to take care of my father and younger sister, who was eight at the time. Violet, the eldest, decided she had her own life to live and left me to pick up the pieces while she waltzed off with her latest boyfriend, marrying him against my father's wishes.'

'Aye, well,' he murmured, looking even more uncomfortable. 'I'm sure you have your reasons for feeling the way you do, but are they good enough to split up the family and let your own kith and kin go into a home? Because that's what'll happen to the younger ones if you can't help out. I mean, where's your conscience?'

'You take too much on yourself, Constable!' Her voice was like a whiplash. 'There's nothing on my conscience. I've done my duty by my family. Who's with the children now? What about their father's mother?'

'Don't know anything about her. Never mentioned her. A neighbour's with the one they call Dotty but the other three went to school. You can't really expect a neighbour to see to the funeral and everything. That's family business, miss,' he said firmly. 'So are you going to come?'

A heaviness seemed to descend on Amelia and she felt chilled to the bone. She did not need a cocky little policeman to tell her where her duty lay. Duty was what had killed all her hopes and dreams; her romance with Bernard, which in the end had turned sour on both of them. It was as if once more Violet was mocking her for doing what she had, except this time instead of across a table it was from beyond the grave. *Where's your sense of duty now, Lee?* She could almost hear her sister saying it.

Well, she wasn't going to have it! Why should she have to look after Violet's children? Why? It wasn't fair! Then she caught the policeman's eye and knew she would at least have to make the funeral arrangements.

'I'll go,' she said, resentfully. 'Now, if you don't mind, I've work to do.'

He thanked her and turned to leave the shop. Tess collided with him on her way back in and he begged her pardon. She waved him away and headed for the counter. 'Is that prescription ready, Lee?'

'Yes.' Amelia brought her thoughts back to the job in hand. 'Give me your bag and I'll put it in. But you'll be careful with these sleeping tablets, won't you? Don't ever take more than two.'

'I'll be careful.' Tess went to hand her the money.

'No. This one's on me,' said Amelia, folding her friend's fingers over the coins.

Tess gave a twisted smile. 'You're very good to me, Lee. Thanks for everything. Goodbye.'

'I'll see you soon,' called Amelia. Then she turned and went into the dispensing room to tell Brownie he was going to have to hold the fort for the next few days.

It had been a difficult day for Rosie. School had seemed so normal that despite the painful stitches in her face and aching ribs where she had fallen against a seat on the tram, she had wondered several times if she had dreamt the policeman sitting in the kitchen saying her mother was dead. She wanted it to have been a nightmare. She certainly felt strange, limbs leaden and head woolly, as if she had just woken from a deep, deep sleep. Stupidly, she pinched herself, knowing all the time it was no dream.

A gust of freezing wind blew up the skirts of her school mackintosh and, shivering, she broke into a run, humping the satchel of books over her shoulder.

'Hey, Rosie!' A delivery bicycle came to a skidding halt in the gutter beside her. 'Give us your satchel?' said its rider, balancing his heavy machine with one foot set against the kerb.

'Is that a joke?' She gave him a hostile stare. Davey lived next door, Mrs Baxendale's only remaining son, the eldest having been killed in the war. She had always been kind to the Kilshaw children but Davey had been the bane of Rosie's life for as long as she could remember.

'I'm trying to be neighbourly,' he drawled, flicking back the curling lock of dark hair that dangled over his forehead. 'I've heard about your mam.'

'And that's supposed to make me trust you? No, thanks!'

'Give us a break.' He drew together eyebrows like sooty slashes, slanting upward at the outer corners. 'Worms turn. So do leaves.'

'Leopards don't change their spots, though.' Rosie's tone was scornful.

'You're cutting off your nose to spite your face,' he warned, a mite impatiently, stretching out one hand. 'Give us it here, I'll drop it off at yours. Then you can go straight off and do your paper round. No need to worry about the kids. I dropped in on Ma and she tells me your aunt's there.'

Rosie's heart felt as if it had suddenly taken a ride on an helter-skelter. She decided to take a chance on him, dumping her satchel in the wicker basket at the front of the bicycle. 'I can't afford to replace those books, you know. So don't be losing them. Or else!'

'Trust me.' His sky-blue eyes were guileless as they met hers. 'Anything else I can do for you, you only have to whistle. See yer!' He pushed off from the kerb and cycled away.

Rosie watched him a moment before hurrying in his wake. Davey was a year older than she and from the moment he had pushed her off their front step when she was a toddler, grazing her knees and dirtying her frock, he had infuriated her. He had pulled her plaits, dragged off her ribbons, stolen her sweets, and mimicked people with such wicked talent she had laughed until it hurt. He'd taught her card tricks and diddled her out of the few ha'pennies she had ever possessed. He'd tickled her unmercifully until giggles turned to tears. He had sung alongside his mother in the C of E local church choir until his voice broke, but he was definitely no angel.

Could she trust him with her satchel? She broke into a run, praying he would not dump it in some garden and then drop exasperating clues as to where she could find it. The thought worried her as much as the idea of one of her aunts waiting at home. But she had to do her paper round first because she needed that money.

When she was finished, Rosie found Babs keeping her eye on Harry, who was sliding with some other small children on the icy road. Their cheeks were flushed and eyes bright with enjoyment until they saw her. Then Harry and Babs left the others and came plodding towards her in their too-large wellies, faces solemn now. 'Aunt Amelia's in the house. She told us to scram,' said Babs.

'What's she up to?'

'Nosing in the sideboard.'

Rosie swore under her breath. Harry tugged on her mackintosh. 'I showed her me engine and told her about me birthday but she didn't give me anything.'

'She just looked at him dead hard,' said Babs. 'Like this!' And she fixed Rosie with a basilisk stare before relaxing her features and wiping her nose on her coat sleeve. 'I don't think she likes kids.'

'That doesn't surprise me.' Rosie set her jaw and marched into the house. Babs and Harry followed, stepping in unison and leaving wet footprints on the linoleum. But Rosie did not find Amelia in the kitchen, where a covered pan simmered on the trivet, nor in the scullery.

'Where is she?' Rosie demanded of Dotty, who was sitting in front of the fire, singing 'We'll Meet Again' in a melancholy voice.

'In the parlour,' she whispered, wriggling her stockinged feet on the brass fender. 'I didn't know what to say to her. She frightened the life out of me, asking questions I didn't know the answers to and searching through everything.'

'What about Aunt Iris?'

'She doesn't live with her any more.'

'What?' said Rosie in dismay.

She left the kitchen in a hurry, trailed by Babs and Harry. The parlour was as cold as an icebox. Only at Christmas was a fire lit in its tiled and cast-iron grate. A faint smell of gas issued from the meter cupboard next to the bay window, and in front of the sideboard, opposite the fireplace, knelt a woman.

She was wearing a thick tweed coat and plain green felt hat, rather like a man's trilby. The hair that curled in a roll beneath it was golden-brown. She glanced over her shoulder and Rosie caught a glimpse of a high-cheekboned profile with a short tiptilted nose and skin the pale colour of ice cream. The fact that she was not ugly as Violet had always said did not make the girl feel any warmer towards her.

'What are you doing nosing around in there? That's where Mam keeps her private papers.' Rosie's voice was taut with suppressed anger and nervousness.

'Exactly why I'm looking.' Amelia put her head down, continuing to root through the contents of the narrow pullout compartment between the cupboards. 'Do you always get home from school this late, Rosie? A youth dropped off a satchel. I don't know what you think you're playing at, flirting with boys when everything is in such a mess at home. You're just like your mother.'

Rosie was about to deny any flirtation vigorously but changed her mind. 'Why shouldn't I be like my mother? I am her daughter.' Her tone was defiant and laced with dislike.

Amelia straightened up. 'You're stating the obvious. I suppose you have no sense of responsibility either where your younger brother and sisters are concerned?'

'Definitely not. I'd rather be out gallivanting.'

Amelia's eyes swept over her and the younger children from head to foot. 'Wellington boots should be taken off at the door. You are dirtying the floor.' Her tone was icy. 'Tell me – our Violet, did she keep all her documents in here?'

'Yes!' said Rosie through gritted teeth, determined not to be intimidated.

She left the room and her brother and sister followed her to the front door where they kicked off shoes and wellies, hanging their coats on the hooks in the lobby before going into the kitchen where Rosie had set the table. She looked into the cooking pot and asked Dot whether Mrs Baxendale had made the soup and how much did they owe her for getting in coal. Dotty said their aunt had sorted that out.

Rosie felt unreasonably irritated about that but no sooner had she cut bread and spooned pea soup into bowls than Amelia entered the room.

Before the girl could demand how much she had given to Mrs Baxendale, her aunt said, 'I've found what I was looking for.' She shrugged off her coat. 'I'm glad our Vi didn't lose all her wits when she lost Joe. She kept up her payments to the clubman, which shows more sense than I'd expected from her. It also proves she wasn't as broke as she made out.'

'Mam had plenty of sense,' said Rosie, voice rising. 'And you have no right to—'

'What's that uniform you're wearing?' Amelia's words cut through hers like a knife through stone.

Rosie told her in a stiff voice and her aunt's eyebrows rose. 'Not a school I would have chosen but at least it shows you've got brains. It must have cost, though.'

'I won a scholarship,' said Rosie impatiently. 'But I'd have left by now, if Mam would have let me, and found work.'

'You surprise me. Because scholarship or no, Violet would still have to pay something, plus need money for uniform and the rest. I suppose Joe's mother relented and helped her out?'

'We haven't seen head nor tail of Dad's mam. We always presumed she was dead,' said Rosie, sudden hope in her eyes.

'I wouldn't know. I haven't set eyes on the woman since she came storming up our path, demanding Father do something to stop his daughter from marrying her son. Mother had just died and everything was at sixes and sevens.' Amelia's face darkened. 'Cheek of her! It was a better match than she had any right to expect. She was a Mary Ellen with a stand in town selling flowers. Did you know that?'

'No! But I always knew you were a snob.'

Amelia's eyes flashed green fire. 'And Joe's mother was an inverted one! As for you – you're impudent. And if you had any sense at all, you wouldn't be trying to provoke me. The last thing I want is to be here.'

'Then why stay? I can look after us,' retorted Rosie, a flush on her cheeks.

'If only!' said Amelia, rolling her eyes. 'As it is, our Violet's doubly amazed me.' From her pocket she took a sheet of paper and waved it in the girl's face. 'I never thought she'd consider the possibility of her own death but she did and . . .' She paused, giving a wry smile.

'No!' cried Rosie, backing away from her. 'She couldn't have. She wouldn't. She hated you!' The girl could scarcely believe what her aunt was hinting at.

Amelia's laugh lacked mirth. 'Oh, yes she could. She's asked me to be your guardian. She certainly hated me, all right!'

'Rip it up! Nobody need know. You can go away again. I'll get a job. I'll look after us,' said Rosie desperately.

The laughter died in Amelia's face as she folded the paper, replacing it in her pocket. 'Don't tempt me. But she's done this deliberately, not lightly. She's thrown me a challenge.'

'What d'you mean?' Rosie's expression was puzzled.

Amelia's eyes met hers. 'Think about it, kid.'

Rosie could only think that her mother had betrayed them.

Her aunt's gaze wandered over to the table. 'Is there any soup left?'

Rosie nodded absently, seeking to unravel the mystery of why her mother should ask the sister she hated to take charge of them.

'How did Violet manage financially?'

Rosie gazed at the slender figure silhouetted against the fire, blackened saucepan in hand. 'She worked.'

'At what? She's got some lovely clothes upstairs.'

'I don't know!' The girl's voice rose. 'War work. She never talked about it. Have you been nosing up there, too?'

'I'll ignore that last remark.' Amelia sat at the table, spoon in hand. 'You never asked what she did?'

'Yes, but . . . I think it was some kind of hush-hush work. Perhaps for the government?'

'The government?' Amelia's laugh was genuinely amused. 'She'd need some kind of qualification and our Violet was never one for studying.'

'She never got the chance,' said Rosie, temper rising again.

'Is that what she told you?' Her aunt's mouth curved into a derisory smile. 'She had more chances than soft Joe – and I don't mean your father.'

'I don't believe you.' Rosie's voice was harsh.

Amelia raised her eyebrows. 'Do you think I care? She had looks and a certain charm and used them to get what she wanted.'

Rosie sprang to her mother's defence again. 'She'd have to, wouldn't she? She knew she wouldn't get any help from Grandfather or you. I mean, where is he now? He doesn't care about us at all, does he?'

Amelia's face went blank. 'He's dead. And it was your mother who killed him.' Her voice sounded hollow.

Rosie was stunned. She gripped the back of Harry's chair. 'How could she? She hadn't seen him for years.'

'That last big row when she brought you all to our house for the first time . . . He suffered a stroke – was more than three years dying.'

'That wasn't her fault! You were all at it except for Aunt Iris,' cried Rosie. 'Where is she, by the way?'

'Married. Left Liverpool.' Amelia sighed, rubbing the spot between her eyebrows.

Babs, who was sitting across the table from her, exchanged looks with Rosie. No help from that quarter then, the look said.

Amelia reached for the crusty loaf in the middle of the tablecloth. 'Where will we live?' asked Babs. 'Will you come here or— ?'

'You're joking! I'd be mad to move in here when I've four bedrooms at home and the shop to see to in Kennie.' Amelia sawed herself a slice of bread, dunking it into her soup, one elbow resting on the table. She chewed deliberately, staring at Babs. 'Besides, it's not exactly Buckingham Palace here, is it? Anyway, I haven't made up my mind yet whether to rise to our Vi's challenge.'

'You – you wouldn't put us into an orphanage?' stammered Dotty.

Amelia frowned as she glanced at the girl. 'I can't understand our Violet. That woman next door tells me she's kept you at home since your eyes were damaged. Stupid and utterly wrong! You're scared of your own shadow. You need to mix. Learn to look after yourself.'

Dot squeaked a protest. 'I couldn't see the blackboard! It was no use me going to school.'

'She can read, you know,' said Rosie belligerently, hand on hip. 'And write. Even though her nose almost touches the paper because she can only see close up. She knows some history and geography, I taught her them, and Mrs Baxendale next door is teaching her to knit.'

'That's something at least,' murmured Amelia. 'But can she make her own bed? Does she do any cooking? Can she wash her own things and light a fire? Does she go out on her own and shop?'

'No, but—'

'There you are then. She needs to be a little more independent. I suppose our Violet found it hard to accept that her child wasn't perfect.'

Tears of fury started in Rosie's eyes. 'Do you have to criticise her? Don't you care at all that she's dead?'

Amelia stared at her. 'Actually, I do care. I'd like nothing better right now than to have her in front of me so I could tell her *just* what I think of her.'

Rosie gasped. 'That wasn't what I meant.'

'I know what you meant! And you know there was no love lost between our Vi and me.' Amelia's voice was hard. 'But we knew each other well enough for her to be sure I wouldn't shirk my duty.'

'Duty! Is that all you care about?' Rosie's voice broke. Turning her back on her aunt, she struggled for self-control while seething with hatred.

'Someone has to,' said Amelia in a tired voice. 'Our Vi never did.'

Harry slipped down from his seat and pressed himself against Rosie. Her arm went round him and she rested her cheek against his mass of golden curls, finding comfort in the act.

'Very touching,' murmured Amelia. 'He reminds me of that painting, *Bubbles* – but it's time he had a haircut.'

Rosie lifted her head. 'You wouldn't! Mam loved—'

'I would,' said Amelia, a glint in her eyes, remembering how angelic her twin godsons had seemed when their hair was that length and how deceptive appearances could be. Not only that but . . . 'I bet he gets teased at school. You'd like a haircut, wouldn't you, Harry?'

The boy fingered one of his curls and nodded vigorously. 'They call me cissy.'

'Right.' Amelia made up her mind there and then. 'Doubt I'll have time tomorrow so I'll do it tonight.' She dunked the last of her bread into the soup.

'You're going to cut his hair tonight?' gasped Rosie in disbelief.

Amelia nodded, finished the soup and dusted her hands against each other. 'Get me the scissors.'

Rosie did not move but Babs slid off her chair and shot over to the fireplace where a pair hung on a nail above the mantelshelf. She handed them to Amelia. 'Towel? Basin?'

'Thank you,' said her aunt, smiling.

'Sucker up,' hissed Rosie as Babs brushed past her. Her sister only stuck out her tongue and marched into the back kitchen.

Rosie could not watch but turned her back as Amelia knotted the towel at the nape of her brother's neck. The girl could not shut out, though, the snip-snip of the scissors as each golden curl fell on to the linoleum.

'You can look now,' said Amelia, voice smooth with satisfaction.

Rosie turned and could have killed her aunt because gone was her sweet angelic-looking baby brother and in his place stood a replica of a basin-cut street urchin, preening himself as he stood on a chair to gaze at his reflection in the sideboard mirror. 'I like it,' he said. 'And I'll swipe anyone who calls me cissy now!'

'You do that,' said Amelia. 'Boys have to learn to take care of themselves and protect the weak. Now bed, you three younger ones.'

'You're not staying?' said Rosie bluntly.

Amelia stared at her. 'Wash the dishes, then I think you and I'd best have a talk.' She pulled a sagging easy chair in front of the fire and began to go through a pile of papers she had brought in from the parlour.

The last thing Rosie wanted was a tête-à-tête with her aunt. 'I always take Harry to bed and tell him a story,' she said.

'Not tonight you don't,' said her aunt, without looking up. 'He can go up on his own. Can't you, Harry?' She smiled at the boy. 'You're not frightened of anything, are you? You're a big boy now.'

'Don't like the yard in the dark,' he said after a brief cogitation, bottom lip thrust out.

'Babs and Dotty can go down the yard with you then,' she said reasonably. 'And don't forget, girls, take a bucket of water with you to flush the lavatory.'

Rosie watched them go, boiling with frustration, wanting to tell Amelia to go to hell. Who did her aunt think she was, coming into this house, rooting through cupboards, giving orders and taking over? How could her mother have left that note? How could she, after all she had said about her sister?

'Dishes, Rosie,' said Amelia, a hint of warning in her voice.

Rosie felt like throwing the crockery at her but instead made as much noise as possible as she gathered plates, bowls and cups together, singing defiantly as she took them out into the back kitchen.

'Night, night, Rosie,' said her sisters and brother as they trooped past her.

'Night,' she muttered, not looking up from the sink.

When Rosie had put away every dish and piece of cutlery, she entered the kitchen and tiptoed across the room towards the other door, only to be stopped short by her aunt's voice.

'You can't escape. Sit down.' Amelia waved her to the green and black moquette chair on the other side of the fireplace. 'We have to talk about the funeral.'

Reluctantly, Rosie sat down, hands resting on the wooden arms of the chair. 'When is it?'

'I don't know yet. I'm going to sort things out tomorrow. But I'm sure the best thing would be to have Violet's body taken to my house and the funeral to go from there.'

'No!' The word burst from Rosie. 'This is her home. She'd want to be here with us! She never wanted to set foot in your house ever again.'

'Well, she won't be doing that, will she?' retorted Amelia, a spark in her eyes. 'I wonder if you realise what it's going to be like?'

'I know it'll be upsetting. I'm not a fool.' Rosie slouched way down in the chair, as if it could provide her with shelter and comfort.

Amelia was silent a moment. 'All right. We'll bring her body here, if that's what you want. We will lay Violet out in the front parlour and I'll provide the candlesticks and black crêpe. As her eldest daughter, I expect you to keep vigil with me the night before she's buried.'

'What about Aunt Iris? Have you told her?'

'I've dashed off a note but don't be looking for her to be here. There's a war on, remember.'

'But she's Mam's sister!'

Amelia fixed Rosie with a stare and said in bored tones, 'You're stating the obvious again. She lives in Canada. She can't possibly get here.'

Rosie's heart sank even further. Definitely no help from that quarter.

'Now you can go to bed. I've had enough of you.' Amelia picked up that evening's *Echo* and began to read the front page.

Rosie opened her mouth to say, '*I feel the same about you,*' but before she could utter a word, Amelia said, without looking up: 'You'll catch flies like that. Shut your mouth and the door on your way out. There's a helluva draught in here.'

Rosie slammed the door and stormed upstairs, half expecting, half wanting her aunt to come flying after her. She would know then she had got to her. But there was no movement from downstairs.

When she went into her bedroom it was to discover that she was not even going to have the comfort of Harry's warm little body snuggling up to hers. Their bed was empty and when she looked in on her sisters it was to find the crowns of three heads showing above the bedcovers. She whispered their names but there was no response. Feeling rejected, angry and miserable, she made her way to her own lonely bed.

The next day, Rosie did not want to get up. Her head and heart felt chock-a-block with a dragging, heavy sadness. Reluctantly, she threw on some clothes and went downstairs, expecting to have to confront Amelia. To her relief, there was no sign of her aunt, only a note propped against the teapot, saying she had gone to sort things out and would Rosie stay in and tidy the place because there would be lots of other things to do later on that day.

'Blast, blast, blast,' she muttered, noticing a fire burning in the grate. She pouted, not wanting to think any good of her aunt at all. The oats had been put in soak, too, and that did not please her either. She placed the pan on the fire then went upstairs to wake the others.

'What's a vigil?' asked Harry, picking up his empty porridge bowl and licking it after Rosie had told them what had been said last night after they went to bed.

'Don't do that,' she said automatically. 'Amelia'll say you've got the manners of a pig.' She gave him more porridge.

'A vigil means keeping awake and watching,' Babs informed him from her position on her knees in front of the grate where she held the toasting fork to the fire.

'What's our Rosie going to watch for?' He spooned up the rest of the porridge, smacking his lips.

She shrugged. 'The Holy Ghost? Or maybe we're there to keep evil spirits away?'

Dotty shivered. 'Rather you than me. Aren't you scared?'

'It's for Mam, isn't it? And it'll probably be the last thing I'll be able to do for her.' Tears caught her by the throat and she lowered her head so the others could not see her face.

'I miss Mam,' said Harry, bottom lip trembling. He scrambled off his chair and climbed on to Rosie's lap. She held him tightly, kissing his cropped hair.

'What are we going to do?' sighed Dotty.

'Stick together, whatever happens,' said Rosie. 'That's what Mam would want.'

Dotty stammered, 'You don't mean Aunt Amelia'll try and separate us?'

Rosie did not think that at all but she wanted the others on her side, not sucking up to Amelia, so she remained silent.

'You think she will!' Dotty's voice was shrill, blue eyes apprehensive.

'It's as I said last night: I just wonder if she might think there's too many of us for her to cope with.'

There was a dismayed silence and Rosie felt horrible for scaring them so said cheerfully, 'I could be wrong. Let's pray the old gorgon will have second thoughts. Now, we've got to get the house tidied up before she comes back.'

She set them various tasks. When they had done theirs, Babs and Harry wrapped themselves up warmly and went out to play.

Before Rosie started scrubbing the front step, she took Violet's handbag from the sideboard cupboard, intending to go to the corner shop for a loaf and milk. But there was no bulging purse inside nor the brown envelope that had been there yesterday; there was only a lipstick, a pot of Pond's vanishing cream and a half bottle of Evening in Paris.

Surely she couldn't have dropped them in the cupboard? Rosie searched among the clothes there but found no purse. Then she sat back on her heels, clenching and unclenching her hands, face screwed up in thought, remembering how surprised she had been at the amount of money in that purse. Now it had gone and she could only believe Amelia had found it in her search of the sideboard and taken it. The thought filled her with fury. A thief! Her aunt was nothing more than a common thief. When she came, Rosie was going to say something to her, even if it meant getting a clout for it.

Amelia returned at two o'clock, carrying a large leather holdall and a shopping bag. She looked tired and her face was pinched with cold but that did not stop Rosie from flying at her. 'You took Mam's purse! That money belongs to us.'

'Oh, do shut up,' said Amelia, in no mood for an argument. She took a couple of tarnished candlesticks from the holdall, placing them on the sideboard. 'Get polishing them. We're going to need them.'

Rosie did not move. 'Us kids need Mam's money.'

Amelia sat on a chair, stretching shapely rayon-clad legs towards the low-burning fire. '*I* need, Rosie. For all that has to be made ready to give our Violet a decent send-off and to keep you lot for the next few weeks.'

'But you're rich!'

Amelia made a noise in her throat which could have been a chuckle. 'Father mortgaged the house to renew the lease on the shop just before he died. There wasn't enough insurance or money in the bank to pay off all the mortgage. I have to work hard just to keep a roof over my head.'

'But Mam said—'

'Stop telling me what our Vi said as if she was some blinking oracle!' groaned Amelia.

'But I wanted to give Harry his birthday treat,' said Rosie, cheeks flaming from the force of her emotions. 'To take him to the pantomime as Mam intended.'

'Sorry, Rosie,' said Amelia, not sounding a bit sorry. 'But there's no money for treats.' She delved into the holdall again and, pushing a duster and a tin of metal polish along the floor in Rosie's direction, ordered, 'Now get cracking. The funeral's on Tuesday, weather permitting. And they'll be bringing Violet's body here later today. I took one of her gadabout frocks from a cupboard upstairs for them to dress her in.'

'Mam didn't gad about,' said Rosie in a choked voice. 'She had to look nice for her job. As for the money in her purse, it was a bonus.'

'Is that so?' murmured Amelia, taking a pair of dressmaking shears out of the holdall on her knee and snipping the air with them before dropping them to the floor.

Rosie watched her, fascinated, resisting the urge to argue with her further. 'What are they for?'

Amelia's smile was grim as she dragged a tape measure out of the bag. 'I've come to measure you up. I've some very nice material left over from when we made the blackouts. It'll make good mourning frocks.'

'This year's latest fashion? *Just* what I wanted to wear,' said Rosie.

Amelia took out paper and pencil. 'I'm glad you've a sense of humour, Rosie. You're going to need it in the months to come. Dotty, come over here.'

The girl got up swiftly and Amelia began to run the tape measure over her trembling figure. 'There's no need to shake so much. I'm not going to eat you. Keep still or this frock will fit someone the size of Thumbelina instead of a tall girl like you. Wouldn't spectacles have helped?'

'Rosie!' There was a note of panic in Dotty's voice.

'If glasses could have helped, Mam would have seen Dotty had a pair,' said Rosie without a hint of doubt, rubbing at a candlestick with a duster.

Amelia glanced at her. 'I have a friend who's half-blind. Glasses *do* help.' She jotted down figures on a scrap of paper but the girls were silent. When Amelia was done with Dotty, she told her to go and call Babs in.

'Me?' Dotty's voice was startled.

'That's what I said,' murmured Amelia. 'You now, Rosie.'

But she was already making for the door to fetch Babs. Amelia was across the room in seconds, pulling her back. 'I said, Dotty can go. Dotty, you're quite capable of finding your way up the lobby, I'm sure. After all, you manage to get yourself upstairs and down. It's time your sister stopped smothering you.'

'I don't—' began Rosie, only to fall silent at the expression on Amelia's face. Reluctantly, she moved out of the doorway and stood stiffly as her measurements were taken.

'I want to go to the funeral,' said Harry, having accompanied Babs indoors. 'I want new clothes and to meet the Holy Ghost. He's coming to take Mam to Heaven.'

'Oh, aye!' said Amelia, measuring Babs swiftly.

'And angels, lots of them,' he said with relish. 'All singing and playing harps.'

'That I'd like to see,' said his aunt, straight-faced. 'If they turn up, I'll let you know, Harry. But I think you're much too young for funerals.'

He jutted out his chin and looked ready to argue with her but she seized him by the shoulders and marched him out of the room, telling him to play out. Then she commandeered the table and, taking out a brown paper-wrapped parcel, cut a pattern out of the paper before spreading a swathe of black material over the table and setting to work pinning and cutting.

By four o'clock, Amelia had the three frocks tucked away in the holdall, ready to sew on the machine she had at home. Next she entered the parlour and set about moving furniture about, so that two straight-backed chairs faced each other in the bay.

Rosie entered with the candlesticks. 'It had to be done, before you say anything,' said Amelia.

'I know. They put Dad's coffin there,' said the girl, a tremor in her voice.

'I spoke to the priest at St Michael's, by the way, and he only vaguely remembers our Vi. I know Joe had no religion when he met her, but I thought she would have managed to change his mind by the time Babs was born.'

'The church didn't do *her* any favours. It refused to marry them,' said Rosie defensively.

Amelia looked scandalised. 'Are you saying they weren't married? I know Joe wasn't your normal barrow boy. He had some unusual ideas about love and marriage, having read a lot of modern stuff, but . . .'

'Of course they were married!' Rosie's voice was angry. 'What d'you think Mam was? They were married in the good ol' C of E. It's perfectly legal. The priest wanted Dad to sign a paper saying we'd be brought up Catholics. He refused.'

Amelia frowned but only said, 'You mustn't mention any of this to the priest when he comes.'

'I wouldn't. I'm not in the habit of talking to priests.'

Amelia got to her feet. 'You're trying to get me going. But faith can be a great comfort at a time like this. I'll arrange for you all to have instruction as soon as I can.'

Rosie determined to resist with all her being. 'I was baptised C of E and confirmed, and that's good enough for me. I'm not taking instruction from no priest,' she said, whisking herself out of the room without waiting for her aunt's reaction.

They brought Violet's body home at dusk when Rosie was out delivering the evening papers. When she returned, it was to find the curtains drawn in the parlour and the coffin placed on the two dining chairs.

With due ceremony Amelia inserted candles in the silver holders and set them in place at the head and foot of the coffin. She had draped the sideboard mirror and mantelshelf with black crêpe, placing a crucifix on the sideboard. Then she knelt on the linoleum, silently beckoning the children to follow suit.

Rosie glanced at her mother's still face and felt lost and lonely. She gripped Dotty's hand and tugged on it, bringing them both to their knees beside Harry and Babs, who had their eyes closed and hands together.

Amelia, with a black veil over her head, prayed concisely for mercy and compassion for Violet's soul, as well as for her children in the days to come. The three younger ones crossed themselves obediently at her command, and at a 'Stand up now, children,' scrambled to their feet. 'Now, kiss your mother. Then into the kitchen. We'll have some supper then bed for you younger ones.'

Rosie's lips barely brushed her mother's face. The parlour had suddenly become a place of which nightmares were made. Dotty drew back swiftly as her fingers touched Violet's cheek. 'She's freezing!'

'Like marble,' said Amelia, clearing her throat. 'But there's nothing to be scared of. Your mother wouldn't hurt you.'

'But it's not Mam! She's not here!' cried Dotty, bursting into tears.

That set the others off and without a word Amelia hustled them out of the parlour and into the shabby, comforting warmth of the kitchen and put on the kettle. She stared at her nieces and nephew, sitting on the sofa. A sobbing Harry was on Rosie's knee. Tears rolled silently down her cheeks. A weeping Dotty and Babs sat to either side of her.

'I shouldn't have given in to you, Rosie,' said Amelia, vexed. 'I should have taken her home. But what's done is done and tomorrow is Sunday. Let's hope you – we – can all find some comfort in church.'

'No church,' said Harry lifting his head. 'Stay here with Rosie.' He buried his face against his eldest sister's breast.

'Someone'll have to do the washing tomorrow,' said Rosie, eyeing her aunt defiantly. 'I'll be at school on Monday. I certainly can't go to church.'

'I'll go to church,' said Babs on a hiccup. 'I like church.'

'We'll all go,' said Amelia firmly. 'The big wash can go to the nearest laundry. You mustn't let your mother down. The priest will be expecting us in church. Now, I think we'll have some supper. How does spam fritters and scrambled eggs sound? That's one meal I can cook well.'

The three younger children's faces brightened. 'Real eggs?' asked Babs.

'Be realistic, girl!' Amelia ordered Rosie to get out the frying pan. She switched on the wireless. Dance music flooded the room and the Kilshaws looked at their aunt, expecting her to switch it over or off. But she left it on and they all felt less sad.

They were just finishing supper when the letter box crashed shut. 'Now who's that?' muttered Amelia, toasting her toes on the fender while enjoying a second cup of watered-down tea.

'I'll answer it,' said Rosie, pushing back her chair. 'It'll probably be one of the neighbours asking about the funeral.'

But she was wrong. Before her stood a man in the uniform of the US Air Force. He was small and slightly plump, with a young, chubby-cheeked face. When he removed his cap he revealed mousy hair that was already receding. Rosie was completely taken aback.

'Is this the home of Mrs Violet—?'

'She's dead,' interrupted the girl, hoping to God none of the neighbours was looking out of their window. 'What d'you want?'

'I'm not here to cause trouble, little missy. Just to pay my respects and ask when the funeral is,' he said in deep rumbling tones.

Rosie cleared her throat but her voice still came out as a squeak. 'Tuesday, St Michael's church at one o'clock.'

Thanks.' He hesitated. 'You must be one of Violet's children?'

She could not speak, thinking they must have been close for him to know her mother had children. Suddenly, she was remembering how glamorous Violet had looked, going out in the evenings in sheer nylon stockings and high heels. Had those stockings been courtesy of the US Air Force and not the black market? *Oh, hell!*

'Who is it, Rosie?' called her aunt. There was the sound of footsteps.

Rosie panicked and did the only thing she could think of. She slammed the door in the Yank's face.

Chapter Three

Amelia pushed open her own front door and hurried inside, putting her foot on the paper before she could stop herself. It was Sunday afternoon and she had left Rosie and Gwen Baxendale in charge of the younger Kilshaws. Placing the milk bottle on the occasional table, she dropped the holdall on the rug and peeled the paper off the damp sole of her shoe.

Carefully, she unfolded the single sheet and read the scantily worded page: *Aunt Lee, something terrible has happened. Mum's dead. Could you please come as soon as you can? Chris.*

Amelia's arm curled round the newel post and she hung on tightly as if needing to anchor herself to something solid in a world that seemed to be rocking beneath her feet. Tess dead! How? She could not believe it. She had only seen her a couple of days ago. She couldn't be dead. Tears filled her eyes, blurring her vision. She could see her friend's face in front of her, hear her voice saying how bloody everything was.

'Purrrr!' The cat stropped his head against Amelia's legs. He walked round her, forcing his way between her ankles, purring heavily. She picked him up and walked slowly through the hall and the morning room into the kitchen. She switched on a ring on the electric cooker and placed the kettle on it. Then she poured milk into a saucer, watching Sooty lap it up, as if by focusing on the commonplace everything would feel normal again.

She could not believe it. Maybe she had misread the words? She leant against the sink and read the note again. *Dead! Tess dead*! She repeated the words over and over as if by doing so their meaning would become real to her. How could she be dead? Had she gone into a diabetic coma and not come out of it? Or— Suddenly, Amelia remembered the sleeping pills.

Oh, Jesus! She crossed herself and straightened with a quick jerky movement. She would have to go right away. The sewing could wait. She switched off the stove and rushed to the shed, wheeling out her bicycle. She pedalled swiftly past Leyfield Farm and the Carmelite convent before turning and heading in the direction of West Derby village.

'It had to have been an accident, Aunt Lee,' said Chris, a cigarette smouldering between his fingers. One long arm rested on the mantelshelf; the other hung limp at his side. He looked completely lost and bewildered.

'Of course it was an accident.' Amelia's voice was soothing as she patted the fifteen-year-old on the shoulder.

'There – there's talk of it being suicide. Although there's no note. They asked me had she been worried about anything – about Dad and the war and all that.' He rubbed his left eyebrow with the back of his hand. 'The doctor had prescribed sleeping pills. But you'll know about that. They're doing a post-mortem.'

'But you told them she wasn't worrying about Peter?'

'Of course I did! She always said she believed Dad would come through.' He drew on the cigarette so deeply the end glowed a fiery red, paper and tobacco burning swiftly. 'They're getting in touch with the Army. It'll be OK when Dad's here. He'll know how to cope with things.'

Amelia felt certain Peter Hudson would. He was a capable man, steady, reliable and kind. Only once had she known him to lose control and she had been intensely grateful for his actions then. Since that time, her feelings towards him had been a mixture of warmth, confusion and regret. In her opinion, Tess had possessed the best of husbands, though perhaps she had not appreciated him enough.

'The twins are running wild.' Chris flicked ash into the fire.

Amelia gave him her full attention once more, wondering as she had not done for a long time just who his father was. 'Where are they now?'

'I chased them out. They were sliding down the stairs on a tray. When I told them off, they started bouncing on the sofa and hitting each other with cushions. Generally acting crazy.'

Amelia made no comment. Her godsons' behaviour did not surprise her. Tess had let them get away with murder. Not that that was completely her fault. As she had said the other morning, her eyesight had been getting worse. 'I suppose there'll be an inquest as well?' she murmured, half to herself.

Chris nodded, rubbing his eyebrow again.

She squeezed his arm. 'Let me know if there's anything I can do. Unfortunately, my sister's just died and I'm having to see to her kids and arrange the funeral, but I should be clear in a couple of days. Even so, don't let that stop you asking for help,' she said rapidly. 'I'll give you a hand with the arrangements.' It was not something she was looking forward to, already being in the middle of such arrangements. *Oh, Mary, Mother of God!* she thought. *How am I going to cope with all this?*

Chris looked relieved and escorted her into the back yard, wheeling out her bicycle for her, pausing outside the gate. Noisily, he cleared his throat. 'Mum never had a sister but she always said you were as good as one,' he said huskily.

Words were beyond Amelia so she just reached up and kissed his cheek and held him close a moment. Then she climbed on to her bicycle and rode off.

For the rest of the day, she sat at the old Wellington machine, which had belonged to her mother, stitching the three frocks for the girls, thinking of Tess and feeling angry with herself that she could not have done more for her friend. Then she caught the last tram to take her back to the children.

Monday was taken up with making the final arrangements for the funeral and Amelia also managed to put in a couple of hours at the shop and go to 'Eden' to tidy up and check her cupboards for food and drink. It was then she found the letter on her doormat, addressed to her in Tess's handwriting. The contents almost swamped her in misery and dismay. She destroyed the letter, tearing it into tiny pieces before burning it.

By Tuesday, the temperature had risen and the frozen pavements were slushy underfoot. Amelia led the three girls into church, looking neither left nor right. There were shadows beneath her eyes and her mind was taken up more with that final letter from Tess than Violet's funeral.

It was on the way out that Amelia noticed the Yank sitting in a pew behind Gwen Baxendale. Rosie stopped dead and received Amelia's knuckles in her back. 'Keep in step,' she hissed. The girl quickened her pace almost to a run until Amelia's exasperated voice told her to slow down.

It was not until the car began a dignified crawl behind the hearse that Amelia noticed they were being followed by a US jeep. The three sisters were squeezed on to a long seat facing the way they were going, while she sat on a pull-down one facing the way they had come. She kept a weary eye on the vehicle, considering the contents of the brown envelope she had found in Violet's handbag. *So many secrets*, she thought.

'This isn't the way to the cemetery!'

She started at the sound of Rosie's loud voice.

'Don't be stupid,' said Amelia in long-suffering tones.

'It isn't!' insisted Rosie. 'Anfield's north.'

'We're not going to Anfield.'

'But that's where Dad's buried! They'd want to be together.' There was a wild look in her eyes.

'You didn't mention it,' said Amelia, exasperated. 'So naturally I arranged for her to be buried in the Catholic cemetery with Mother and Father.'

'But you can't do that!' Rosie's expression was anguished. 'Stop the car!'

'Be sensible, Rosie, and sit down,' ordered Amelia.

But the girl would not sit down. Instead she leant forward, almost knocking her aunt off her seat. 'Driver, driver, stop!'

'Get a hold of yourself!' Amelia's face screwed up with effort as she tried to drag Rosie away.

'It's not right! It's not right!' Her face crumpled and tears rolled down her cheeks as they struggled. 'They'd want to be together. They would! They would!'

'It's too late now,' said Amelia fiercely. 'The arrangements are made. I'm sorry, Rosie, but we can't change them now.'

She was visibly shaking, eyes full of hatred. 'You've done this deliberately. You never wanted them to be together. You were against them marrying in the first place because you were jealous,' she said scornfully.

Amelia felt a stab of pain but only gave the girl one of her basilisk stares. 'You don't know what you're talking about. And now is not the time to be saying such things. You're getting hysterical.'

'Yes, shut up, Rosie,' hissed Babs, nudging her sister in the ribs.

'I won't! She was jealous because Mam got a man and she didn't.'

'I could have had two—' Amelia bit off the rest of the words she was tempted to say, continuing to stare the girl down. Babs dug Rosie in the ribs again. Rosie dug her back but subsided into a brooding silence, arms folded, black tammy-clad head bent, trying to think of some way of getting back at her aunt.

It was as they were walking away from the grave towards the tree-lined avenue that divided the cemetery into two that Rosie glanced over her shoulder and saw the Yank. He was clutching a bunch of violets which, as she watched, he let fall into the open grave. She stood rooted to the spot.

Amelia noticed her actions. Turning, she saw the American and immediately retraced her steps to the graveside.

Rosie's stomach did a backward flip as she watched them talking. But the last thing she'd expected was for the Yank to accompany her aunt back along the path towards them.

They stopped in front of the girls. 'Rosie, Babs, Dotty, this is your stepfather, Sam Dixon,' said Amelia, a tremor in her voice and a devilish glint in her green eyes.

I hate her! I hate her! Rosie seethed as she handed round plates of sandwiches to complete strangers who had once known her mother. Why couldn't her aunt have told them her mother had married again? The marriage lines had been in that brown envelope in Violet's handbag, apparently. Rosie was mortified that her mother had married such a young man, and she was convinced Amelia was revelling in her discomfort.

How could her mother have done this to her? Rosie ground her teeth. How could she have married this man who was at least ten years her junior, without a word to them or him of the other's existence? He had told them that it was not until he had read the report of the accident in the *Echo* that he had discovered Violet was the mother of four children.

Oh, she could scream! How she wished her mother was in front of her so she could demand an explanation. But the trouble with the dead was they got out of accounting for their behaviour. Rosie wanted to weep and wail and stamp her feet but instead was stuck handing out sandwiches and having to put up with remarks about her hair and eyes, even her shape, because people said she was so like her mother when Violet had been that age.

At last Rosie managed to escape with some food and, accompanied by Babs, went in search of Dotty, who was sitting on a pouffe in a corner of the parlour, out of sight alongside the piano. 'Let's get away. I've had it up to here,' muttered Rosie, making a movement with her hand to her throat.

'Who'd have believed it of Mam?' said Dotty, allowing herself to be pulled to her feet by her sisters.

'Twenty-three he is and Mam was nearly forty,' said Babs, shaking her head.

'She'd have to be, wouldn't she? If I'm fifteen,' said Rosie tartly.

'Aunt Amelia's thirty-one and on the shelf. I heard some woman saying that,' said Dotty. 'Although someone else said she'd had her chances.'

'They'll all be gossiping about Mam and him now,' muttered Rosie, dragging Dotty halfway up the stairs. 'I don't know what she thought she was doing.'

'You don't think he'll want to take us to America?' said Dotty with an anxious expression.

'Don't be daft! The last thing he'll want is the responsibility of four stepchildren,' said Rosie.

'You can say that again,' said Babs, plonking herself
on the step below the one where Rosie and Dotty had
perched. 'I'm surprised he said yes to Aunt Amelia's
invitation. I'd have thought he'd have made a run for it.'

'She didn't give him any choice. She was hellbent on
rubbing my nose in it,' said Rosie, taking a savage bite
out of a sardine sandwich.

'What d'you mean?' said Dotty.

'She hated Mam and I stick up for her, don't I? So by
bringing him here she's saying, "Look, your mother wasn't
all you thought she was! She deceived you."'

There was no answer to that so Babs and Dotty
remained silent. Their mother had kept things from them
as well. Rosie wasn't the only one suffering from shock.
Sometimes, thought Babs rebelliously, she took too much
on herself.

People began to disperse, standing in the hall below,
putting on coats and hats. 'It's awful about her friend
Tess Hudson, isn't it?' said one woman in a low voice.
'There's that many rumours going round the village.
Comas, overdoses . . . They say she would have been
blind in three months, you know. I bet Amelia's feeling
it. They've been close for years despite Tess Hudson
being a Proddy.'

'As if Amelia didn't have enough on her plate with
Violet's children,' said another.

'You can bet she'll be running along to the Hudsons,
though, seeing what she can do to help there.'

'I believe they've sent for the husband, but he'll not get back in a hurry. He's the other side of the North Sea and the war's not over yet. The poor Southerners are still getting buzz bombed.'

'Surely he'll get compassionate leave? The twins are only eight and there's only that brother to look after them.'

'I don't envy Amelia. They're real scallywags. She's going to need all our prayers. And so is Peter, poor man.' The front door opened.

'How'll she manage with the shop?' said the first voice.

The door closed so the girls never got to hear the answer to that. But before they could move or speak, their aunt had come into the hall.

'Then you'll ask the Mother Superior for me?' she said.

'Of course. I'm certain St Vincent's have free places for special cases.' It was the priest's ponderous voice. 'Dorothy is an orphan and your father was always most generous so her prospects are good. She'll have to board, of course, but you know that, my dear.'

Dotty clutched Rosie's sleeve and made to speak but her sister clamped a hand over her mouth, intent on listening to the priest. 'About the boy – have you considered sending him overseas?'

'I haven't given much thought to what to do with Harry. Violet's death was such a shock. Then my friend . . .'

'Well, do consider it, my dear. There's a scheme for sending orphans to the colonies. Plenty of opportunities in Australia for boys if they're trained properly. They can make a good life for themselves there.'

'But Harry's only five years old!' Amelia sounded slightly shocked at the idea.

'They like them young, can mould them better.'

'I see that. Have a child 'til it's seven . . . But it seems so cruel.'

'Sometimes you have to be cruel to be kind, my dear. You think about it and I'll make the arrangements. Now, my hat, if you would be so good?'

The girls stared at one other, faces blank with shock. Rosie took a couple of deep breaths before whispering, 'Let's get out of here.'

'But she can't send Harry away, can she? And what about me? Where's this St Vincent's place?' wailed Dotty.

'Sshhh! Wait until she's gone back into one of the rooms,' whispered Rosie.

They waited then crept downstairs, lifted their coats and hats from the newel post and were through the front door in a flash. It was a good walk to the village where the tram started but Rosie made her sisters run, determined Amelia was not going to catch up with them.

'What are we going to do?' panted Dotty.

'I need to think.'

'That St Vincent's place is only up the lane from the house. I noticed it when we passed in the car,' said Babs, clinging on to the black pom-pom hat which threatened to slide from her shining ringlets.

'If it's that close then why do I have to board?' said Dotty. 'I'll run away,' she gulped, hanging on to Rosie's arm.

'Don't be dotty, Dotty,' said Babs, giving her younger sister an impatient look. 'You'd be falling over your feet. Besides, it wouldn't be sensible at this time of year.'

'I don't care. If I end up frozen and dead like the Little Match Girl, it'll serve Aunt Amelia right!'

'We don't want you frozen and dead. Isn't it enough we've just buried Mam?' said Rosie wrathfully.

'I'm sorry. Oh, why did she have to die?' moaned Dotty.

'Shut up. Crying's not going to help,' gasped Babs, putting a hand to her side. 'I'm getting a stitch. Can't we walk now?'

'OK. But let's shut up and do some thinking,' said Rosie. They all fell silent but it was not until they were almost home that she had her idea.

The girls found Harry playing in the street and quickly Rosie drew him away from his playmates. 'Did you see the Holy Ghost?' he said, jiggling on the spot, gazing eagerly up at Rosie.

'No. But never mind that now.' She was overwhelmed by love for him and hugged him convulsively.

'You're hurting me,' he said, wriggling out of her grasp and slanting her a reproachful look. 'What's up, Rosie?'

'Clever lad. Can't hide anything from you.' She ruffled his short hair. 'Come on. We've got to get cracking. Don't take your coats off.'

She opened the front door with the key on the string. Once inside, she began to empty the food cupboard, glad their aunt had stocked up yesterday. 'Go upstairs, Babs, and bring down a change of clothes and a blanket each. Put the clothes in a pillowcase.'

Babs stared at her and sighed heavily. 'Are we running away?'

'Shut up and get upstairs,' ordered Rosie, scowling at her. 'I'm going to give Aunt Amelia the fright of her life. She'll see she can't split us up.'

'What do you want me to do?' said Harry, raising himself up and down on his toes with excitement. 'Can I take me engine?'

'If you can carry it. But hurry!'

Rosie went down the yard, taking a claw hammer and an axe from the shed. She felt beneath the sideboard runner where Violet always put the rent money, smiling when she found it untouched. With the paper-round money she had been paid on Saturday, it meant she had seventeen shillings and eightpence. There were several other necessary items to remember before, heavily laden, Rosie led the others up the back entry to the rear of the bomb-damaged houses they had passed on the way home.

It was a relief to find a back gate unlocked. At least Davey was useful for something, she thought, having remembered hearing him talking about this house a while ago. She set to with the claw hammer, prising out the nails fastening the wooden boards over a window.

Dusk was falling so as soon as they had climbed over the window sill and were inside, Rosie lit a candle and led the way out of the scullery into a front room.

'It's cold,' said Dot, hanging on to her sleeve. 'And d'you think there's mice?'

'What would they live on?' drawled Babs, glancing around with a resigned expression.

There were holes in the ceiling where broken lattice-work showed through, wide cracks in the wall where the paper had peeled off. The floor was littered with chunks of plaster and all kinds of rubbish.

'Look at that,' said Harry, running over to a tatty sofa, setting springs squeaking in protest and sending clouds of dust into the air as he jumped on it.

Rosie placed her burdens down and left the room. When she returned it was to chop up a couple of the wooden boards and make a fire. That done, she told the others to stay put while she did her paper round. Babs was ordered to make jam butties and to keep the fire going.

It was the swiftest Rosie had ever delivered her newspapers. On the way back, she narrowly missed colliding with Davey, cycling without lights up the entry. 'Idiot!' she gasped, banging her funny bone on the wall as she stepped back. Her face screwed up with the agony of it as pain tingled up and down her arm.

He backtracked and lowered his dark head so their faces were level. 'What are you doing here?'

She caught the gleam of his eyes and could feel his warm pepperminty breath on her face. 'None of your business.' She tried to brush past him but he grabbed her arm.

'What's up?' His voice had softened and for a moment she thought he sounded as if he really cared. Then she dismissed him as being incapable of such emotion.

She flung back her head so that the dark ringlets bounced on her shoulders. 'Nothing! I'm on a message, that's all.'

His mouth curled up at the corners in a sardonic smile. 'I don't believe you. And you shouldn't be going down jiggers in the dark.'

'I know. One never knows who one might bump into.'
She kept her voice light.

'No, one doesn't, does one?' he mocked.

She felt a surge of anger. 'Let me go, Davey.'

'Sure.' He released her. 'How was the funeral?'

'A barrel of laughs.' She forced her way past him
and ran.

Davey watched her a moment, thinking she was getting
to be a real handful. Interesting. But no doubt about it,
she considered herself a touch above him. He rode slowly
home, wondering what she was up to.

Amelia was not in a good mood. She had planned on
having the girls to stay at her house that night and had
telephoned the corner shop, requesting the proprietor to
tell Gwen Baxendale so and ask her if she could take care
of Harry until tomorrow. Amelia had planned on checking
if Chris and the twins were all right, then writing a couple
of letters, one to Canada and one to Norway, before finally,
thankfully, getting into her own bed.

Instead, here she was standing in the middle of a kitchen
that was cold, dark and eerily silent, having let herself
into the house with the key on the string. She could not
light the gas mantle or the fire because she could not
find the matches and in her search had also discovered
the kettle was gone and all the food that had been in the
cupboard. She turned on her heel swiftly and went and
knocked on Mrs Baxendale's front door.

It was opened by Davey.

'The children?' said Amelia without preamble.

'Not here.' He rested one hand on the door jamb, gazing down at her, face expressionless, but she had caught something in his eyes a second before. An alertness, an on-his-guard look in the second he realised who it was.

'Have you or your mother seen them?' She kept her voice calm, determined not to give vent to her anger.

'Can't you find them?' He allowed himself to show some interest.

'They're not in the house and I know the girls found the funeral upsetting. Particularly Rosie. Do you have a bobby on the beat?'

Davey shifted position, bringing down his arm, placing his hand in his pocket. 'Are you that worried?'

'Of course I'm worried! Why do you think I wouldn't be? What's Rosie been saying about me?'

He looked surprised. 'Why should she say anything to me about you?'

'You're her boyfriend.'

His eyes gleamed with amusement. 'You say that to her and she'll knock your block off!'

Amelia stared at him, then nodded. 'If they turn up here, tell them they don't have to worry about the Yank.'

'Sure,' said Davey, asking no questions, and closed the door.

Harry snuggled against Rosie. The four Kilshaws were huddled together on the sofa with a blanket beneath them and several covering them. The wood in the fireplace crackled, sending billows of smoke swirling round the room, making them cough occasionally.

'I'm worried about this sofa,' moaned Dotty. 'It's probably full of fleas and there's a smell in here I don't like.'

'Oh, you and your nose! Probably a dead bird in the chimney,' yawned Rosie, thinking she had made a mess of things, not having given a thought to whether the water would be on in the house or not. It wasn't.

'I've never eaten roasted bird,' said Harry, his high-pitched voice echoing round the room.

'It's probably only a skeleton,' said Babs.

'Spooky and smelly!' sniffed Dotty.

'D'you think there's a ghost?' asked Harry.

'No.' Rosie's tone was definite.

He sighed. 'Then tell us a story, Rosie?'

Before she could start, Babs said, 'The skeleton fights the Germans! The smelly spy! I spy with my little eye something smelling like . . .'

'Evening in Paris. Can I have the half-empty bottle in Mam's handbag?' said Dotty.

'Aunt Amelia has it,' said Rosie.

'She's probably hopping mad right now,' said Babs. 'And who can blame her?'

'Whose side are you on?' said Rosie crossly, remembering the quarrel between her mother, aunt and grandfather. The three furious voices and faces. Had her mother's behaviour really caused Grandfather's death? And why hadn't he left much money?

'My own,' said Babs frankly, stretching out her legs. 'I don't want a clout – and I don't think this was a very good idea.'

'It's a bit late to say that now,' muttered Rosie. 'Why didn't you say so before?'

'Because you hustled us out of the house. You're always bossing us.'

'Oh, shut up,' said Rosie, physically uncomfortable and feeling utterly fed up.

'I want a wee,' said Harry.

A groan issued from his sisters. 'You'll have to do it in the grid outside,' said Rosie, pushing back the blankets.

'What if we want a pooey?' asked Dotty.

'You blinking can't have one,' she said, exasperated, dragging Harry to his feet.

They had all got settled again when Dotty whispered, 'I can hear a noise.'

They held their breath as the door creaked open. Dotty squealed. Trembling with excitement, Harry clutched at Rosie, who brushed off his hand and shot to her feet. 'Come out, come out, whoever you are,' she yelled.

'I am the ghost of the midnight rocket . . .'

Rosie picked up the kettle and threw it at the figure in the doorway. 'I suppose you think that's funny, Davey Baxendale?'

He caught the kettle with one hand, passing the beam of a torch over them. 'Snug as a bug in a rug,' he said, walking over to Rosie. 'Your aunt's getting the local scuffer on your trail.'

'What!' It was the last thing she expected or wanted.

'And you're shooting sparks, did you know that? It's a good job the Luftwaffe have gone home. And this place is dangerous, by the way.'

'What do you mean, dangerous?' she said, convinced he was just trying to frighten her. 'You used to come in here.'

'That was when I was a stupid kid. Everything's a bit shaky – that's how bombs affect buildings close by when they explode.'

'OK, OK!' she said, nervously rubbing her nose with a knuckle.

Davey brought his face so close to hers she could have counted his long, almost feminine eyelashes if she had wanted to. 'I know it's been a lousy day,' he said softly. 'But this is no way to deal with things.'

'What would you know about it?' she said, dropping her hand and stiffening her backbone. 'You haven't lost your mother.'

'I lost my dad when I was younger than Dotty, and my brother a couple of years ago. And I've a mother who's that scared stiff of losing me it drives me crazy sometimes.'

She felt herself flushing. 'I was sorry about your dad and your Frank. I know I didn't say so at the time.'

'I know you were. But we're not the only ones to lose family. There's thousands feeling as miserable as you are right now. So chin up.' He punched her chin lightly.

Rosie felt ashamed of herself. 'It's not only losing Mam,' she said in a low voice. 'Aunt Amelia is planning on sending Harry to Australia.'

'You're joking!' He glanced at Harry. 'What have you been up to, fella?'

'Nuthin'. Where's Australia?' said the boy, scrambling down from the sofa.

'The other side of the world,' said Babs. 'They have kangaroos there.' She rose from the sofa, dragging blankets with her. 'Aunt Amelia said she did think it was cruel, with him so young.'

'Right, Harry! If she feels like that—' Davey sat back on his haunches in front of the boy. 'You, fella, are going to have to put on the act of your life. Spinster ladies like a bit of the old soft soap. I know, I've got a couple of aunts meself. Think you can do it?'

'What's soft soap?' asked Harry, wrinkling his nose.

'Be nice, be friendly, give your aunt a cuddle a day.' Davey winked. 'Even a kiss. I know it's soppy but you don't want to go to Australia, do you?'

'Dunno. What's it like?'

'Never mind what it's like.' Rosie's voice broke on a tearful laugh. 'You'd be away from us and we couldn't bear to be without you.' She held him to her. 'Although I'm not sure soft soap will work on Aunt Amelia.'

'It's worth a try.' A smiling Davey picked up a blanket that had fallen on the floor. 'Let's get you home. And I'll be right behind you, kiddos. Just in case she's got the knives out!'

Chapter Four

Amelia stared fixedly at the fire she had lit after buying matches from the newsagent's round the corner. Her whole body was weighed down with a sense of failure: she was thinking not only of the Kilshaws but of the contents of that letter from Tess. Her friend's words rang in her head.

Lee, you said you wanted to help me – look after the boys and Pete. He deserves someone better than me. You're so controlled, you'll make a much better job of it than me.

What did she mean by that? Amelia pushed back a strand of hair which had come loose from the roll on her neck.

The trouble is, I never loved him and the thought of his coming home and things going back to the way they were – the long silences after him trying so hard, and me going slowly blind – fills me with horror. Even now I can't tell you the extent of it all so I'm saying no more. Forgive me. I've written to him explaining things.

Forgive her? Tears clogged the back of Amelia's throat and prickled in her eyes. If only she hadn't been so busy with the shop, she would have seen this coming. She had thought everything was OK with the marriage. Tess and Peter had appeared to be close, to complement each other, he so strong and dependable and Tess so delicate and needing someone to look after her. It just goes to show you never know what happens behind someone's front door once it is closed, she told herself.

Amelia had written to Peter without knowing what Tess had said in her letter to him and without mentioning she had received one too. She had wanted to reassure him that she would keep her eye on the twins and Chris. How she was to do that and cope with her own nieces and nephew and the shop was beyond her at the moment, but somehow she had to.

That Rosie and the others would turn up again, she had no doubt. That girl was Violet all over again. The way she stood, with one leg in front of the other, knee crooked, head tilted to one side as she spat out her insults. For a moment, Amelia's grief was speared by a dart of hurt and anger. Then she suppressed it, deciding the other three wouldn't be a quarter as difficult to handle. Besides, she had plans for them. Even as she considered them she heard the key on the string being pulled through the letter box and was up in a flash.

Rosie, who had been in the act of turning the key, lost her balance as Amelia pulled the door open from the other side and a shopping bag became entangled between the girl's legs. The kettle fell out and went clanging down the step. Rosie would have fallen if Davey had not grabbed her. She looked up at her aunt and blurted out, 'Now see what you've made me do!'

'What *I've* made you do?' Amelia drew a sharp breath and raised her hand. Rosie flinched but stood her ground.

Harry, though, turned and ran, his beloved engine clutched to his chest, a half-empty pillowcase bouncing on his shoulder.

'Where on earth does he think he's going? I haven't laid a finger on you yet,' cried Amelia, exasperated. 'Although, believe you me, I'm tempted!'

'He's scared of you sending him to Australia,' cried Dotty. 'And I don't want to go to any blind school!'

'So that's what this is all about?' Amelia frowned, shaking her head at Rosie before her gaze fell on the youth at her side. 'Do me a favour, Davey, and run after him?'

'Me?' He grinned. 'I've already done my Good Samaritan act for the evening. Not that the two of you see it like that, by the looks on your faces.'

'You disappoint me,' said Amelia, and took off after her nephew.

Rosie and Davey gazed after her. 'She's going to catch him,' said the girl. 'She can't half run.'

'She's good!' There was a hint of admiration in Davey's voice. 'I wonder if she ever ran for the Liverpool Harriers when she was young?'

'She's not that old now,' said his mother, taking them unwares as she came out of the house next door. 'I admire her. It can't be easy for her, taking on you lot. I bet it's put the kibosh on any wedding plans she might have had once the war's over.'

'Who'd marry her?' said Rosie, flushing.

'I wouldn't be surprised if there was someone,' said Gwen, resting one bony shoulder against the door jamb. 'Missed her chance earlier with having to take care of your grandfather when he ended up in a wheelchair. It happens to a lot of eldest daughters. Duty's a cold bedfellow, though.'

The thought that it was her own mother who had been the eldest passed through Rosie's mind, but she kept silent. It would have been a betrayal of Violet's memory. Besides, she bet Amelia had only nursed Grandfather to get her hands on his property, mortgaged or not.

Amelia returned with a struggling Harry. 'In!' she ordered them all in a voice which brooked no argument. The younger two hurried indoors but Rosie would have lingered if her aunt had not thrust the kettle against her chest, saying with a grim expression, 'Don't push your luck! Put that on and make me a cup of tea.'

Rosie took one look at her face and decided not to argue this time.

A quarter of an hour later, the younger three were in bed and Rosie had made the tea and was about to pour it out. She was tense, waiting for the storm she was sure would come. So far, her aunt had not asked where they had been and now, having drunk her tea, she was sitting back in a chair with her eyes closed. Even so, the girl felt as if every move she made was being monitored.

'Tomorrow you'll move out of here,' said Amelia, startling her so much she dropped the cup.

'That was careless.' Amelia gazed down at the broken fragments. 'You'll sweep that up.' Her cat-like eyes rested on Rosie's face. 'I can't be doing with all this going backwards and forwards.'

'Tomorrow, though!' protested Rosie, shocked. 'What about schools and packing and everything?'

'There's nothing here I need but the food you've already packed and the kettle and some other bits. I have enough beds and furniture for all of us. I'm sure your landlord here has a long waiting list with I don't know how many bombed-out families eager to take this place over, lock, stock and barrel.'

Rosie's mouth had gone dry. She had to swallow before she could speak. 'But what about Mam's things and our clothes?'

'We'll take the good stuff, of course.'

'OK, I can accept that,' said Rosie, clasping her hands in front of her, the muscles of her face stiff with strain. 'But you've no right to send Harry away. That paper Mam wrote, it can't be legal?'

'Oh, I'm sure it would be admissible in any court of law,' murmured Amelia, tapping her fingers on the arm of the chair. 'I'm your closest relative and I'm sure they'd be only too happy to hand full responsibility for you all over to me. Anyway, I'll be seeing a solicitor in the next day or two.'

'But you can't do it!' cried Rosie wildly, leaning heavily on the back of the chair. 'It's cruel. How can you do something like that? You're wicked, just like Mam always said.'

Amelia fixed her with one of her stares. 'You're pushing your luck again, Rosie. Go to bed. It's been a long day for both of us. I had no sleep last night and I've loads to do the rest of this week, sorting things out.'

'I won't sleep,' said the girl, straightening up. 'How can I sleep, worrying about Harry? He's too young to be parted from us and sent to Australia.'

'Don't go on,' said her aunt wearily. 'You've said what you wanted to say and I don't need to hear it a second time. Now get to bed.'

Rosie opened her mouth and Amelia half rose in her chair. For a moment, there was a battle for supremacy. Then the girl shot out of the room and Amelia sank back in her chair and closed her eyes, letting her body go limp. She must be mad. What had she taken on?

'You're going to have company, puss,' said Amelia, tucking the cat under her arm and going upstairs in her own home the next morning. She could not see her way clear yet but last night had made a start by setting the alarm clock for six. This morning, she had left a note for Rosie, telling her to make sure she packed the rest of the children's clothes and anything else they might want to bring with them. They were not to go to school but to stay in the house and await her return.

On the way home, Amelia had slipped into the shop before it was open, leaving a note for Mr Brown saying she wouldn't be in until the next day. Then she had called on the rag and bone man who hired out his horse and cart, arranging to meet him at the house in Everton. After that she made an appointment with the man who had been her father's solicitor.

She entered the main bedroom, which was spacious and clean-looking, being the most recently decorated just before the war. She had moved into the room after her father's death, but now the double bed would be of more use to the three girls so would have to be moved out because she would be damned if she would let them have the best bedroom as well.

She placed the cat on the linoleum, warning it of the invasion soon to come, and proceeded to strip and dismantle the double bed. She had the frame stuck in the doorway and was cursing herself for having started single-handed when she heard a hammering on the front door. She squeezed past the frame and ran downstairs, wondering who it could be.

'Chris!' He was the last person she wanted to see right now but she could hardly say so. 'What is it? Peter? He's not—?'

'No, he's OK. Although they won't let him come home just yet.' Chris's square-jawed face wore a strained expression and he dropped his eyes and mumbled, 'I thought you might come to the inquest with me? It's today.'

She felt a rush of guilt. 'I'm sorry, Chris. I've my nieces and nephew coming. Have you time for a hot drink, though?'

He looked grateful. 'Thanks. I'm freezing.'

'I'll put the kettle on. Then, if you can spare a minute, you can help me move a bed.'

He looked at her as if she had run mad. 'A bed?'

'Yes, I've got it half in, half out of the bedroom.'

'Oh.' He followed her into the kitchen and then upstairs, thin wrists showing beneath the too-short sleeves. The jacket, she knew, had once belonged to her father.

'How are the twins?'

'They're another reason why I came,' he said, attempting a smile. 'I've got to make up the hours I'm taking off.

I wondered if you could look after them for a few hours this evening?'

'Isn't there a neighbour?'

He pulled a face. 'You know the twins. And Mam wasn't one for making friends in the street. People aren't exactly volunteering. It's a mess. I don't know what to do.'

Unexpectedly, Amelia felt angry with Tess. A white-hot anger, as if she had just been stabbed with a poker. How could she have done this to her own children? How could she have done this to *her*? Then the feeling vanished as quickly as it had come, leaving her drained and filled with guilt again. She licked her lips. 'They'll have to come here,' she said. 'Now let's get this bed moved. I've got to get back to Everton soon.'

The children looked up as Amelia entered the room, leaving the door open to a breeze that blew right through the house.

'Everything packed?' she said briskly.

'Yes. I had to use pillowcases, though, because we haven't suitcases,' explained Babs.

'That's all right. I've a horse and cart waiting outside. You'd better douse that fire. We don't want the place going up in flames.' Amelia surveyed the four of them, noting they were all looking glum. 'And cheer up! Or I *will* send you to the orphanage. You can see your friends here again if that's what you want.'

'It won't be the same,' said Babs, getting up and slinging a pillowcase containing her few possessions over one shoulder. 'We won't be seeing them every day so we'll just drift apart.'

'You'll make new friends. Look upon this as an adventure.'

'Did you say a horse and cart?' said Harry, face brightening.

'I did. And stop kicking that chair before you break it.'

He slid to the floor, engine under his arm. 'Can I go and see the horse?'

She nodded. 'Take your bundle with you.'

'What about the cat?' said Dotty, lovely face drawn with anxiety.

'Mrs Baxendale's having it. Now stop looking like a wet Whit weekend and accept things as they are, Dotty,' said her aunt Amelia with a touch of impatience.

'You're going to send me to that blind school, I know you are,' muttered the girl.

'I haven't got you in there yet. Anyway, it's a very good school.' She turned to Babs, determined not to have a confrontation with Rosie. 'Is there any coal left in the cellar? We could do with it if there is. I think it's going to turn cold again.'

'A few shovelfuls.'

'Right, it can go in the cart too. Now get your things and let's go.'

Reluctantly, the three girls did as they were told. For no matter how humble, this house had been their home all their lives.

Amelia spoke to the rag and bone man and he went inside, but before the girls could climb up into the cart,

an unfamiliar voice said, 'And where d'yer think yer goin'
with them kids?'

As one, Amelia and the children turned and looked at
the dumpy figure wearing an ankle-length black serge
skirt, woollen jacket and black shawl. There were hob-
nailed boots on her feet and gloves with the fingertips cut
off on her hands. The old woman leant heavily on a stick.

'Do I know you?' said Amelia, clamping one hand on
Harry's shoulder, thinking the woman looked vaguely
familiar.

She made no answer, dark button eyes sliding from
Babs's face to Rosie's. 'Yous the eldest?' she demanded.

'Yes.' Rosie's expression was curious.

Her answer did not seem to give the old woman much
pleasure. 'Yer the picture of her but I hope yer not like
her,' she grunted. 'The lad, though, he's the spittin' image
of our Joe when he was that age – and I've a proper
studio photo at home to prove it. I'm Maggie Kilshaw,
yer grandma, and I've come to see what I can do for
yous all.'

There was an astonished silence.

'You've chosen your moment,' said Amelia, ice in her
voice. 'We've had the funeral and everything's sorted out.'

'We thought you were dead,' said Rosie in wonder,
trying to take in that this old woman, who somehow
reminded her of a dame in a pantomime, was really her
dad's mother.

'I could have been for all anybody cared,' sniffed
Maggie. 'As it is I've dragged meself out of me sick bed
to come and do me duty by yous kids.'

'You don't have to bother. I'm in charge of these children,' said Amelia, fingers tightening on Harry's shoulder,
remembering that confrontation on her own front step
years ago. 'I'm their aunt, Amelia Needham.'

A scowl brought Maggie's bushy brows together. 'Aye!
I thought I recognised yer. And still just as hoity-toity as
ever yer was. I haven't forgotten yer pa keeping me waiting
on the step, telling me my Joe wasn't good enough for
his daughter.'

Amelia's eyes flashed. 'And who was it who said my
sister wasn't good enough for her son?'

'She wasn't!' Maggie rapped her stick on the pavement.
'A right flibbertigibbet! Thought she'd get her hands on
me money through our Joe, but I wasn't having it!'

'You don't look like you've two farthings to rub
together,' said Rosie, ears pricking.

'Well, you shouldn't go by appearances, girl,' said
Maggie. 'My Joe should have taught you that.'

'Dad did. But even so.' She pursed her lips. 'Mam
wouldn't have cared if you'd looked like a duchess or
owned the Bank of England. She married Dad because
she loved him.'

'Ha!' Maggie's expression was disbelieving. She leant
heavily on her stick. 'Sez something, I suppose, that yer
loyal to her memory. And yer dad, what did you feel about
my Joe?'

'I loved my dad. It was awful when he was killed.'
Rosie blinked back unexpected tears.

Maggie made a noise in her throat. 'Glad yer feel like
that,' she said gruffly. 'Strong, are yer, girl?'

'What's that got to do with anything?' said Amelia, deciding the conversation between the two of them had gone on far too long. 'If you think you're going to take this girl and use her as a skivvy, you've got another think coming!'

'Perish the thought,' said Maggie, little button eyes rounding, one hand going to her bolster of a bosom. 'Use me own flesh and blood as a skivvy? Not bleeding likely! I was thinking what I could do for the girl.'

'You do surprise me.' Amelia raised her eyebrows in that way Rosie was becoming familiar with. 'Going to spoil her, are you? Give her everything you've got?'

Maggie pursed her lips. 'Maybe.'

'I don't believe it,' said Amelia, eyes glinting. 'Our Violet said once you were an old Scrooge and I've seen no reason to doubt it. Come on, children. The only thing your grandmother will pass on to you is bad language and bad ways.' She lifted Harry into the cart but Rosie stayed where she was, eyes darting to the dumpy figure of her grandmother before returning to her aunt. 'Wait! I can't just walk away. She's my gran. Don't I have a duty to her?'

'Give me strength!' cried Amelia, rolling her eyes. 'This woman has ignored your existence all these years, Rosie. You don't owe her a thing. She was rude about your mother and cut your father off without a farthing. Did he ever talk about her, you tell me that?'

'No. But—' The girl gnawed on her lip. 'But she's still Dad's mam and she's not going to send Harry to Australia, is she?'

'I'm not. And I'm your aunt who came as soon as I was called. Despite our Violet cadging plenty of money from Father for you lot when times were hard in the Thirties.'

Rosie began to tremble inside. 'I don't believe it!'

'Why else d'you think he had to mortgage the house? She used to go to the shop when Father was there on his own and give him her sob stories. Brownie told me.'

'Nobody called me, not even when our Joe died,' said Maggie, tapping Rosie's arm with her stick to gain her attention. 'It wasn't until I saw yer ma's death in the newspaper that I gets to know our Joe's dead too. Broke me heart, I did, crying. Almost bust me stitches. So I gets up off me sick bed and goes along to the cop shop to find out where yous kids live. And, blow me down, don't I find out that yers have been living only five minutes away all this time. So I came right away. Family's family, after all.'

'Family didn't matter to you in the past when your Joe was struggling,' said Amelia, staring at her with distaste. 'This has gone on long enough.'

'Now you just watch it,' said Maggie, shaking one leathery-looking finger, face flooding with dislike. 'Family's always mattered to me. It was yer sister getting her claws into my Joe that made me do what I did. But he was besotted and put her before his poor old mother. Still, that's all in the past now he's dead, poor lad. But one thing's for sure: he'd want me to look after his kids.'

'Don't make me laugh! He had more sense than that.' Amelia tugged Dotty's hand, urging her up into the cart. 'Come on now, Babs. And you, Rosie.'

She hesitated. 'Wait! Gran, we thought you lived down by the docks?'

'And so I did, girl.' She chomped on toothless gums. 'But I was bombed out, wasn't I? So I moved in with me friend Emily, but she kicked the bucket a few months ago. Fair ol' shock, that was. Now I'm on me own.' She sighed gustily. 'There's room for yous all. But I wouldn't deprive yer aunt of the pleasure of all of yer company. Just yous, girl, would do me. I'm real lonely these days and mightn't have long to live.'

Rosie did not know what to make of this grandmother of hers, and was still stunned by what Amelia had said about her mother taking money from her grandfather. Still, there was one thing her grandmother could give her that Aunt Amelia definitely could not and that was information about her father. 'I'd like to go with her,' she said, gazing up at her aunt.

'I'd let you,' said Amelia, 'only I wouldn't be doing my duty by our Violet if I did. This woman is working on your sympathy. You can't trust her. Think of your father. And I'll remind you, Rosie, that you have sisters and a brother who have more of a claim on you and will need you in the coming months. Also that I'm your legal guardian. Now, in the cart! And that's an order, not a request.'

Babs scrambled up into the cart but still Rosie hesitated and the atmosphere became tense. 'Where do you live, Gran?' she asked.

The old woman told her.

'Right!' The girl smiled and flung her bundle into the cart, climbing in after it. 'I'll come and see you, then. If that's OK?'

'I'm disappointed in yer, girl.' Maggie's expression had turned ugly. 'I thought yer were one of me own and would do what I asked, but yer just like yer father. No backbone.' And without another word, she turned and stumped away.

'You all off then?' Suddenly Gwen was there, taking their attention from that solitary figure.

'Yes, Mrs Baxendale.' The children smiled at her.

'You'll come back and see us?' she said, scooping up their cat in mid-lick as it cleaned itself on their front step.

'Of course we will,' they chorused.

'Thanks for everything,' said Rosie, resting her chin on the side of the cart, thinking Davey's mother was someone who had been there for them for as long as she could remember.

'Well, don't you forget.' Her thin face with lines crisscrossing it, as fine as a spider's web, creased into a smile. 'Our Davey'll be looking out for you, Rosie.'

The girl flushed and murmured something indistinct, thinking Davey's mother was just daydreaming.

The driver flicked the reins and the cart jerked forward. The children continued to wave until the skinny figure in the flowered pinny and headscarf turban turned and went indoors.

Chapter Five

'I'm going to need your help, Rosie,' said Amelia. 'And yours, Babs.' She smiled at this middle niece of hers, regarding her as the least troublesome of the three girls.

Rosie looked up from contemplating the cobbled road which was taking her away from the place that held all the dearest memories of her parents and childhood. 'What kind of help? You never mentioned help before.' There was an edge to her voice.

'I am now,' said Amelia firmly, gripping the side of the cart as it took a corner too sharply. 'Surely you don't expect coming to live with me to be a joyride? I have to be at the shop all day, and so until you leave school, we're all going to have to pitch in with the housework and everything else. As well as that, there's the Hudson twins.'

'Who are they?' asked Babs, looking interested.

'You'll be meeting them later. And I'm expecting you all to put yourselves out to make them welcome. They've lost their mother too.' Amelia saw no need to explain further.

The Hudson twins were identical except Tom had a tiny scar at the corner of his left eye from where he had walked into a wall. They each had their father's thick tawny hair, slate-grey eyes and well-defined nose. When they smiled, dimples formed in their cheeks. But there the likeness to their father ended because the vicissitudes of life had not left a mark on the boys' freckled faces, nor had the years slimmed their short stocky bodies into the tough, lean fitness of Peter Hudson, who even before he had gone to war had been an active member of the Territorials.

They had also to learn the arts of dissembling and of thinking before they acted. They had not been in Amelia's house an hour before getting into mischief. They stood before her now, hands behind their backs, feet slightly apart, clad in similar navy-blue jumpers and black serge shorts, trying to look as if half-drowning her cat and then attempting to put it through the mangle to dry had not endangered its life.

'We wouldn't really have put it right through,' said Tom, the elder by half an hour, in his most beguiling voice.

'We were just trying to squeeze some of the water out of its fur,' said Jimmy helpfully. 'And that seemed the quickest way. We didn't want it catching cold.'

Harry snorted. 'It was wicked!'

Two sets of eyes swivelled in his direction as the twins calculated how best to get revenge.

'Look at me!' ordered Amelia, tapping each on the shoulder with the bamboo cane she held. 'You must think I was born yesterday!' She had hoped it was not going to be like this. Why she had been so optimistic she didn't know.

Tom eyed the cane uneasily. Telling the truth had always worked fine with their mother. 'Tell the truth and shame the devil' had been one of her favourite sayings and it had served them well. She had caught them with the back of her hand occasionally but that had been more by luck than anything. He felt a soreness in his throat just thinking of his mother and shifted so that his shoulder touched his brother's, the warmth of it bringing some kind of comfort.

'We didn't mean to hurt Sooty. We like cats,' he said. 'We're very, very sorry.'

'Yes. We're sorry,' echoed Jimmy.

'I'm glad to hear it but you're not getting off without punishment. Sooty's tail will never be the same. Now, left hands out.' One swift stroke each, enough to sting and make them think twice before doing such a thing again, thought Amelia. 'Now go and play. There's a game of Snakes and Ladders in the cupboard over there. You can teach Harry.'

Thomas plonked himself down on the rug in front of the fire. 'We don't want to play stupid Snakes and Ladders with him. He's a telltale tit!'

'Don't use that expression.' Amelia frowned down at him. 'Rosie, you watch them. I have to see to supper.'

'Do I have to?' she groaned. 'I've homework. Anyway, I think they're a pair of horrors and should have got six of the best.' She whisked out of the room carrying an armful of books.

'Babs?'

'I'm setting the table.'

'I don't *want* to play with them,' said Harry, wheeling his engine on the floor.

'That suits us,' said Tom, eyes fixed on the toy.

Silence reigned, lulling Amelia into thinking matters would get better between the two lots of children, but all the time lines of defence and attack were being drawn up.

Chris came to pick up the twins around eight o'clock. By then Harry and Dotty were in bed and the twins were drooping. Amelia took him into the kitchen and made him a cup of tea, asking how the inquest had gone.

'They said she took her own life while the balance of her mind was disturbed,' he whispered unhappily. 'Do you think people imagine and say things that aren't true when they're like that?'

Amelia did not know how to reply. She faced sick people every day in her work, as well as the dying and the bereaved, but she knew little about the mentally ill. She would have liked to have had a ready answer for him but didn't. There was something obscene about suicide. It said dreadful things about more than one person's failure.

'She couldn't face the blindness, that's all I know,' said Amelia in a low voice, not wanting to hurt him by saying any more.

'But she might not have gone blind! Didn't she care about us at all?' he said bitterly.

Amelia looked at his young, bruised-looking face. Shock and not enough sleep had marked him. Gazing at him, a memory stirred. 'I'm sure she loved you.'

He was silent and she guessed he found that hard to accept. She did herself. If you loved, how could you deliberately do something which you knew would hurt those closest to you? The mind had to be unbalanced. Yet hadn't she herself given up Bernard, knowing that would hurt him? But the thought would not help the boy or herself. For now, there was nothing she could think of to say that would help him but there were things to do. 'The funeral?' she murmured.

Chris nodded. 'They won't allow her to be buried in consecrated ground, will they?'

Amelia shook her head. The thought hurt her. Even though Tess had not been a Catholic, Amelia believed she had a soul worth the saving. Surely God in His mercy knew that as well and would have pity on a life which had been spoilt by an illness not of Tess's own making?

'She will be buried, though. And we'll pray for her.'

Chris nodded, knowing that the two women had never let their religious differences affect their friendship.

Amelia gave him the remains of the soup she had made and went to get the twins' coats.

Tess's funeral was the most trying of all the events she had gone through in the last couple of weeks. Very few people attended the graveside service but the boys were stoic, bearing themselves well, and Amelia thought Tess and Peter would have been proud of them.

The next day, she visited the Mother Superior of St Vincent's and, not without a great deal of persuasion and reference to the girl's background, arranged for Dotty to be allowed into the school. Amelia had already initiated a course of instruction for her in the Roman Catholic faith. Tears were shed, almost enough to fill a bucket on the day she was parted from her sisters and brother, but Amelia remained firm in her conviction that St Vincent's would be the making of Dotty.

Babs and Harry were also to take instruction but as Babs was nearly fourteen and would be leaving school soon, Amelia thought there was little point in her moving from the school she already attended. Harry was enrolled at a small local Catholic school where he seemed happy enough. At least, he did not complain to his aunt.

Rosie would be sixteen in March before taking her school certificate in the summer. She insisted she would not take instruction. Amelia decided to leave things as they were for the moment.

An uneasy month passed in which the twins' aim to get back at Harry was thwarted time and again by his sisters. So Tom and Jimmy took to wandering, not only on Lord Sefton's Estate, where Chris worked on the farm, but much further afield. They were a constant worry to Amelia and were it not for that letter from Tess, there were times when she would have cheerfully washed her hands of them.

One day they walked as far as the Pierhead and were brought home by a policeman. Another time they played darts and one put a dart into the other's head. Their welfare caused Amelia many a sleepless night. Two families! How could she possibly amalgamate them if anything should happen to Peter? The house seemed overcrowded to her, having become used to her own company during the last year. So many things about having children in her home drove her crazy. But most of all it was just having more of everything to deal with. More wet towels, more washing, ironing, shopping, cooking. More noise. Even the wireless no longer seemed her own.

Then in March, when the first of the crocuses were opening their purple and yellow petals beneath the apple tree, two letters arrived for her. Having no time to read them immediately and with a certain amount of trepidation concerning their contents, she crammed them into her handbag and placed it in the basket in front of her bicycle as she set off for work, wishing not for the first time as she passed the chemist's on the corner opposite Alder Hey Hospital that her father could have held the lease on that shop. As it was, theirs was in Kensington, nearer the town centre, because that was where he had lived as a boy. Amelia had been born in the rooms over the shop and it was not until Iris arrived that the family had moved out to West Derby. Iris . . . What would her letter say?

As soon as Amelia reached the shop, had donned her overall and greeted Mr Brown, she took her sister's letter from her handbag and began to read:

Dearest Lee,

I hate to think of what you must be going through, having to deal with Violet's funeral and everything. It must bring back memories of that terrible quarrel and Father's stroke. I think you're noble taking on Vi's kids but is that really fair, I wonder? Bill and I would dearly love to lighten your load. It is a

great grief to us that due to his wounds we'll never
be able to have children of our own.
*   Dearest Lee, could you see your way to sending*
one of each sex to us? There's plenty of room here
and we're not short of a bob or two. Write me times
of sailings and everything as soon as possible.

With much love,
Your loving sister, Iris

With careful fingers and an uncertain expression, Amelia
folded the letter and returned it to its envelope. Oh, Lord!
What was she to do about such an offer? Poor Iris, not
to be able to have children. It was a generous proposal
but Rosie would not like the idea one little bit. Even so . . .
Amelia stared into space, thinking of all the material things
Iris and Bill could give two of the children that she could
not. What was she to do? Then she remembered the other
letter in her handbag and reached for it, glad to delay
making a decision.

For a moment she hesitated, apprehensive about the
contents of Peter's letter. Then, abruptly, she slit the envelope with one finger and spread the sheet of paper on the
counter.

Dear Lee,
*   It was good of you to write so quickly and*
although you make no mention of a letter from Tess,
I know she sent you one because she wrote of it in
her one to me. This is a difficult letter to write. You

*must be feeling as stunned as I am by what she did
but I have to pull myself together and think of the
children. I don't know what you feel about her idea
of us taking care of the boys? She doesn't mention
the words 'a marriage of convenience' but that's
the only way I can see us managing it.*

Amelia stopped reading and put a hand to her breast as
if she could contain the sudden heavy thudding of her
heart, which seemed to be threatening to break out of its
confines of skin and bone. Marriage! Was that what Tess
had meant?

Amelia bit on her lower lip so hard she tasted blood
and hastily resumed her reading.

*I know it needs some thinking about. You would
have to give up much more than I would. Your house,
the shop. Perhaps it's too much to ask when all I
can offer is my name, a limited income and three
lads to mother? As well as that there's the question
of me being a Proddy and you a Cattywak. It is too
much! Forget it. I don't know what else to say except
thanks for always being a good friend to us both.*

*Warmest regards,
Pete*

Amelia had to sit down because her legs were trembling
so much. To give up her independence, house and shop
and marry Pete whom she had liked for a long time? To

be a married woman at last! The thought gave her a certain
amount of pleasure but was liking enough? And all for
the sake of Tess's children. She did not know what to
think. Then she remembered Pete did not know yet that
Violet was dead and that Amelia had her children to take
care of too. She would have to write and tell him it was
impossible. Although there was Iris's offer to take two of
the children . . . But would it be right to separate them?
Besides, there was still some danger from German U
boats. She just did not know what to do. She needed to
think and would do that better after she had seen the
solicitor dealing with Violet's affairs. She had a meeting
with him that afternoon. Perhaps she could ask him for
advice?

Amelia left the solicitor's office full of hope. Hours on
her feet, back at work having to deal with several difficult
customers and a mistake with a prescription, meant she
had little time to consider just how she was going to word
the letters to Iris and Pete. So it did not help or improve
her mood when she arrived home to be told by Rosie that
the twins had stolen Harry's engine.

'I don't know why you don't just wash your hands of
them Hudsons,' said the girl, hands on hips, scowling at
her aunt. 'They're always picking on our Harry.'

'You've got proof, have you, that they've taken his
engine?' said Amelia, pulling off a glove.

'Who else would have done it? They know he loves
that engine and they've been determined to get their own
back after the episode of the cat and the mangle.'

'So you accused them?'

She shrugged. 'Harry accused them. We just backed him up and they shot out of the house. We've been to theirs but got no answer.'

'Does Chris know about this?' said Amelia, pausing in the act of taking off her hat.

'No. You don't think we were going to go looking for him on the farm?' said Rosie with an incredulous expression on her face.

'One of the neighbours told me the twins have been seen in the street during school hours, eating scraps thrown to the birds,' said Babs, licking jam off her fingers. 'She's going to report them to the school board. She thinks they should be taken into care until their dad comes home. Said Chris wasn't doing a good enough job.'

Amelia was silent, wondering what to do. Rosie sat down and picked up a pen which she dipped into a bottle of ink. She glanced at her aunt and saw she looked tired and, annoyingly, felt guilty. 'I'm sorry if you think we should have gone to the farm. But it was getting dark and it's a heck of a walk. Besides, I've work to do, Aunt Amelia – you told me I've got to do well in these exams. And we had to see to the tea – and Babs has been doing the ironing – and there was our Harry—'

'OK, you don't have to give me any more excuses!' Amelia put her hat and gloves on again and walked out the back to get her bicycle out. *Why couldn't that woman have helped?* she fumed. Just because the twins were little devils, it didn't mean they didn't deserve some help.

She cycled down the path and almost collided with Chris, wheeling his bicycle as he pushed open the gate. 'Have you seen the twins?' she said.

'Yeah! I told them to go home but they're not there. That's why I'm here, just in case they'd come to bring the engine back.'

'So they *do* have it?'

'They told me all about it.' He groaned. 'They'll be the death of me! Where can they have got to now?'

'They don't have a den anywhere? You know what kids are like.' She was thinking of Rosie and the others running away.

His eyes widened. 'Of course! I know where they'll be. It's a bit of a way, though.'

'Let's go. And when I find them, I'm going to kill the pair of them,' she said vehemently. 'Worrying us both like this.'

Amelia had to climb over piles of rubble in a street off Prescot Road. She had to duck under cracked and broken lengths of wood and remnants of brick wall before finding the twins. They were huddled in front of a miserable, crackling apology for a fire. 'You pests!' exclaimed their brother wrathfully. 'D'you know how much trouble you've caused?'

'Shut up, Chris,' said Amelia, noticing the boys were not only filthy but shivering. 'That can wait. Let's get them home.'

'Don't want to go home,' muttered Tom, poking a stick into the fire. 'Nothing there.'

'I meant my house. Come on, you can't stay here.' Her voice was firm, although inside she was trembling. What if something had happened to them? What if they'd fallen into the Mersey or accidentally gassed themselves at home? Then *she* would be to blame. Tess had asked her, almost literally on her death bed, to take care of them, and she was failing them, just as she had failed her friend.

Jimmy glanced at Tom. Neither of them moved.

'I know what you're thinking,' said Amelia, crouching until her face was on a level with theirs.

Jimmy's eyes shifted to his twin. Tom whacked the ground with the stick. Amelia kept a hold of her temper. 'Now, Tom.'

'D'you hear Aunt Lee? Move, you two!' yelled Chris. 'Or I'll clout you one.'

Tom darted past him, just out of reach.

Amelia seized his arm. 'Come on,' she said. 'Everything will be all right.'

'You'll take their side,' shrilled Tom. 'I want Mum. I want me mum!'

Amelia hugged him to her, thinking of her friend and wishing things could be different. The boy struggled a moment then sagged against her shoulder, sobbing his heart out. Jimmy rapidly joined in. Chris turned his back on them but Amelia was aware that his shoulders were shaking too. What was she to do? The extent of their pain and inability to understand their mother's death only intensified her own sense of loss and pain. 'Come on, you can ride on the bikes. We'll be home in no time,' she managed to say, even forcing a cheery note into her voice.

'Where were they?' asked Rosie, standing in the bathroom doorway watching her aunt supervising the twins.

Amelia raised her eyes and said wearily, 'Does it matter? What *does* is that you make them feel welcome here. They can't stay in their house any more. Chris can't manage.'

'So we have to put up with them? I tell you, Aunt Amelia, if they start on our Harry again—'

'Enough!' she shouted, throwing a sponge into the water. 'They have lost their mother. You should know what that's like! They don't have an elder sister to care for them, or a real aunt, just Chris and me. So be kind . . .' Her voice broke. Horrified, she turned her back on her niece.

Rosie backed away, not only alarmed by Amelia's vehemence but uncomfortably aware she herself had not been kind to the twins and still did not want to be. They seemed even more like intruders now they had come to stay than they had been before, and she did not doubt they were going to cause her more work.

Amelia tucked them up in her own bed then sat in a chair, wondering if she had run mad but knowing now exactly how she was going to respond to Iris's and Pete's letters.

The next few weeks were hectic with Amelia having to visit both a shipping agent and her solicitor. The twins seemed more settled and, although there were squabbles, the cane which Amelia kept handy under the sideboard ensured a degree of discipline. She cleared out the sewing room and the twins moved in there, sharing a bed from their old home. The noise of young people filled the house and Amelia had no rest at all. Her hands were also full at the shop because everyone seemed to have colds or else was demanding tonics. Finally, she received answers to her letters and dithered for only a few hours before finalising the arrangements for Babs and Harry to join Iris and Bill in Canada.

It was early one Saturday morning towards the end of April, when the newspaper headlines announced the probable end of the war in Europe, that Chris dropped in before work to inform Amelia that Peter was home and would be calling in to see her later that day. She was filled with trepidation. Writing to him had to be a lot easier than speaking face to face. Despite having known him almost as long as she had known Tess, Amelia felt she had only really got to appreciate him after she had broken off her engagement to Bernard. Then only Peter had seemed to understand the difficulty of her situation and the pain of having to choose her family above the man she had loved. Although he had never said so, she had also known he had no time for the kind of man Bernard had been in those days.

At least Amelia knew Peter was unlikely to go off the rails over Tess's suicide. She found herself remembering the past and how once he had been besotted with the beautiful, delicate girl that Tess had been. Besotted enough to accept a mystery man's child and Tess's story of how she had been taken advantage of.

They had married young and Peter had supported his wife and the baby, born supposedly prematurely, by working as a clerk in the Post Office – a job which Amelia guessed bored him to tears. He had joined the Territorials not long after his marriage but resigned when the twins were born.

When war broke out he had volunteered and been assigned to the Pay Corps for Western Command in Chester, where Tess had been able to visit him with the children. Amelia had wondered at the time whether he had joined up to get away from his wife. Something had definitely gone out of the marriage by then. Had she finally told him who Chris's father was? Amelia had no idea. Tess had always kept mum about the man's identity. Probably she had taken that secret to the grave with her.

The last time either woman had seen Peter was when Amelia had accompanied Tess and the twins to a transit camp in Newcastle after he had been called up for overseas service late in 1944. By then, Tess's eyesight had been failing and the twins had been too much for a woman in her state of health to cope with alone.

Amelia decided she had to get rid of the children for this first meeting. It was Saturday so Rosie was helping out at the shop and Chris was at work. She gave Babs money to take the boys to the pictures.

Wanting to look her best, Amelia tried on various frocks before deciding to wear one of Violet's. It was made of oatmeal crêpe-de-chine with padded shoulders and a calf-length skirt, fluttering about her long slender legs.

The weather had turned cold again. The skies were heavy, threatening rain. Not the best of days, she thought, sitting in the parlour, an accounts book in front of her, wondering what time Peter would come.

She saw him before he saw her but made no move, watching him come through the gate, glance up at the house (noticing the woodwork needed painting, she thought), and walk up the path. Her heart was already pounding before he rattled on the letter box and rapped the door with his knuckles.

She dropped her fountain pen, ink blotching the page. *Damn!* She almost tripped over the cat as she made for the door. 'Coming!' she croaked as the letter box rattled again.

He was gazing upwards, the line of his jaw and throat taut, profile etched against the dark sky, trilby pushed way back on his head, threatening to topple off. She was reminded of heads on coins, of Jesus saying to the Pharisees, 'Render unto Caesar the things that are Caesar's', and wondered whether to hand the twins straight over to him and say she had changed her mind.

Then Peter lowered his head and his slate-grey eyes met hers. It was the most peculiar feeling, seeing that likeness to the twins. She had no time to put up her defences and felt as if her inner self had been stripped bare and inspected. He removed his hat and smiled. She felt she had almost forgotten how to smile in the last few weeks but he made her remember. He had a lovely smile.

'Hello, Lee. That's a nice frock. And you've done something different with your hair. It looks good.'

She did not know whether he really remembered how her hair used to be but so unaccustomed was she to compliments that a blush flooded her creamy skin. 'You look very presentable yourself.'

He was wearing a collar and tie, beige corduroy trousers and a brown hairy-looking jacket with elbows patched with leather. He was not really handsome, but when he smiled he gave the impression of being very good-looking indeed.

'I had a job finding something decent to wear,' he said ruefully. 'The house was a bit upside-down.'

She resisted the urge to say it had been worse before she and the girls had scrubbed and polished it from top to bottom a week ago. 'Come in. I've sent the kids to the pictures so we can talk in peace.'

He wiped his feet on the coconut mat and said almost casually, 'You haven't changed your mind?'

'Have you?' She rubbed her bare arms, feeling cold all of a sudden. 'Written down, it sounded so sensible.'

'But in the flesh I'm a bit too much to take, perhaps?'

She made no answer, leading the way into the sitting room, hesitating in the middle of the room, unsure what to do next. 'Would you like a drink?'

'What are you offering?' His eyes met hers briefly.

'I've some whisky.'

'Lucky me.'

She went over to the drinks cupboard and poured them a double each. 'It was Father's. I was saving it for the end of the war. But what the hell? Your war's as good as over, isn't it?'

'Catterick for a few weeks and then hopefully I'll be home for good. I've explained how things are to my commanding officer. He has children of his own and is trying to be as helpful as he can.'

'Good.' She smiled and handed him a cut-glass tumbler.
Their fingers brushed. His were cold, the skin rougher
than she expected.

'To us!' he said, raising the glass.

She was silent, nursing the drink between her hands.

'Cold feet?' He put down his glass.

Amelia took a sip of her whisky. 'I'm not sure.
Everything feels so strange.'

'It would be odd if it didn't. We've never been in
this situation before.' His voice was pleasantly masculine. If he sang, he would probably be a tenor, she
thought. And there was a certain scent issuing from him,
compounded of a masculine smell, shaving soap and
tweed. She liked it.

'Why don't you show me over the house?' he said.
'Tell me the arrangements you've made.'

'OK.' Amelia put down her glass but he picked it up
again, handing it to her. 'You might as well drink it if
you're feeling cold.'

She did not argue, thinking a bit of Dutch courage
wouldn't go amiss. She hoped he would not grow bored
and led him quickly through the morning room to the
kitchen and then into the parlour. He had only been in the
house once before and that was thirteen years ago.

'You do your own accounts?' he said, glancing down
at the open pages of her ledger on the arm of a chair in
the parlour.

'Saves money.'

He nodded. 'Isn't that partly what this is all about?
Two households can live almost as cheaply as one.'

She did not question what *this* was. 'Not just money.' Her voice was firm as she closed the book. 'It's about the children mainly, isn't it?'

'Yes, of course. And Tess and you and me.' There was sadness in his face. 'A dying wish is a dying wish.'

'From a suicide?' she burst out, and immediately needed to take a large sip of her whisky.

His expression froze. 'Don't ever say it aloud again. You can't blame me any more than I blame myself.'

'I *don't* blame you,' she said, mortified. 'I blame myself. I was here at hand. You weren't. And I blame her, if I'm honest.'

'She was never strong. I used to think sometimes that I could snap her between my hands.' He looked down at them, flexing his fingers, turning the palms over and gazing at the backs.

They were strong hands, thought Amelia. There was a moment's silence before he added, 'We had to round up the Jerries, you know.'

Amelia accepted the change of subject with gratitude. 'You had to fight? I thought they'd surrendered by the time you got there?'

'There were pockets of resistance. Norwegian girls in love with Jerry soldiers who didn't want to go home.' His voice had softened and she could tell from his expression that he was seeing it all in his mind. 'It was hard. Most of them were younger than I was. Love or lust – it sweeps you off your feet at that age.'

Amelia could not argue with that, remembering Bernard, feeling again the pain of parting from him. She decided they would have another whisky and, picking up their glasses, left the parlour.

Peter did not follow her. When she returned to the parlour, he was not there either. 'Peter!' she called.

'Upstairs.'

He was in the main bedroom. Her mother had been a real homemaker and her taste still prevailed in the heavy Edwardian furniture, homemade curtains and patchwork quilt. 'This is my room,' said Amelia, as if staking a claim.

'I guessed that.' His eyes washed over her face. 'I'm looking at your books.'

She went over to where he stood in front of one of the alcoves next to the fireplace and handed him his glass. She glanced over the bookshelves, scanning titles. *The British Pharmaceutical Codex, Culpeper's Herbal, Flora and Fauna of the British Isles, Little Women, Jane Eyre, Pride and Prejudice, The Black Moth* and others.

Peter gulped at the whisky. 'What a mixture! You're a romantic. I never realised. Tess always said—' His voice trailed off.

What had she said? That I was controlled and tough-skinned? Amelia wondered. She felt cold and took a cardigan out of her wardrobe. She drained her glass then held the door open, needing him to get out of her room right now. Feeling that his being there was an invasion of her privacy. 'I'll show you the other rooms.'

He did not look at her but lingered behind. Impatiently, she left the room and he followed her into the small front room. 'I've put the twins in here for now but they could move into the larger room the girls share at the moment, with Chris.'

'Rosie's the eldest? The one you want trained as a dispenser?'

'That's right. She's got the brains for it.'

Amelia left the room and he followed her along the landing. By now, she had her hands tucked inside the sleeves of her cardigan like a Chinese mandarin.

'You're not enjoying this, are you?' he said.

Amelia made a noise in her throat that might have turned into sardonic laughter if she had let it. 'I'm not exactly loving it, no.' She led him into the second largest room.

His eyes took in its size. 'It'll take the three boys nicely. But what about me?'

'Come!' she said imperiously, cocking one finger at him.

He followed her down a step past the bathroom and toilet and along to the final bedroom. She flung the door open. 'At the moment, Harry's sleeping in here, but he'll be gone in a few days.' She was starting to feel light-headed so sat down on the bed.

He sat next to her. 'Does he know yet?'

Amelia did not answer him, hugging herself and staring out of the window. It was not a very big room and she felt swamped with guilt. But it had been Peter's idea that they should have separate rooms.

'Is it fair, Lee? Sending him – and Babs, is it – away?'

Again that overpowering guilt. 'They're not your worry,' she said stiffly. 'It was Iris and Bill's idea. He owns a canning factory – fish.' She fiddled with a strand of hair. 'His wounds . . .' She made a sketchy indication of his nether regions. 'He can't have children.'

'I see.' Peter grimaced. 'Poor bloke.'

She nodded and forced a smile, skin feeling taut. 'Life'll be easier anyway when Harry goes.' She turned her empty glass round and round between her fingers. 'He and the twins don't get on. I think I told you?'

He nodded. 'How are the twins? Tess was forever complaining she couldn't manage them. They played tricks on her, apparently. All the time.'

'They're no angels,' said Amelia abruptly. 'But I'm hoping you'll take them in hand if—'

For what felt like an age they stared at one another, each trying to read the other's thoughts, but neither was giving any more away. 'So-oo!' he said at last, rubbing the back of his neck. 'Shall we stick to what we decided in our letters and give it a whirl?'

His choice of words reminded her of roundabouts and swings, making the idea of marriage with him sound fun. Even so, she was not going to kid herself that any of it would be easy. She took a deep breath. 'OK. Thank you.' She did not know why she thanked him.

Peter smiled and bowed. 'Thank you!'

As Amelia made cheese and pickle sandwiches and cups of Camp coffee, she thought back over the last hour or so. They had got through it without too much difficulty. Thanks to the whisky, she decided. She took the tray into the sitting room. Peter was looking at the pictures the twins had crayonned.

'I'll take over the mortgage payments,' he said, accepting a cup from her.

She nodded. 'I'll still have to go into the shop for a while.'

His eyes were thoughtful, estimating how long she would stretch that while. 'You'll be needed here.'

'I know, but I can't give up just like that!' She snapped her fingers. 'It's been my life. And, besides, I'll have to see Rosie settled in.'

Privately, Amelia hated the thought of giving up the shop. It was going to be difficult, just as it was to imagine him as her husband, not Tess's. A marriage of convenience, they had both agreed, but for how long would he be satisfied so easily? She would face that when it came, she decided. Just as she would face telling Rosie – after Babs and Harry had gone off to Canada.

Chapter Six

Amelia had packed most of Babs's and Harry's things and even managed to sneak down his engine that morning. She was all on edge, not having told them or Rosie that today the two children would be sailing on a ship of the Canadian Pacific Line to Montreal. She would be glad when she got them down to the docks and waved them off. She had kept them off school on the pretence of having made dental appointments for both of them. She did not like telling fibs but told herself the parting would be easier for them this way.

She sighed, thinking she had taken so much time off lately that Mr Brown was complaining he didn't have two pairs of hands, asking when Rosie would finish school for good and saying the girl showed a real aptitude for the work. He was willing to teach her all he knew.

'Soon,' Amelia had soothed him, pleased that he felt like that. She wanted the girl to get on but did not want her knowing what she was up to right now.

'Are you two ready?' she said, straightening the collar of Harry's grey flannel jacket.

'Yes.' Both of them pulled faces but followed her out, dragging their feet.

Babs stopped short at the sight of the taxi waiting at the kerb. 'We're not going in that, are we?'

'Yes! Get in. I've a lot to do today and can't waste time.'

'I've never been in a car before,' said Harry excitedly.

'I've only been in a funeral car,' said Babs, stroking the seat as she would a horse. 'It makes going to the dentist not so bad.'

Amelia felt dreadful but decided to wait before telling them the truth about their destination.

When they passed the dental hospital in Pembroke Place, she decided she could delay the moment no longer. Clearing her thoat, she said, 'You're not going to the dentist. You're going on a lovely adventure to Canada.'

Two pairs of astonished blue eyes stared at her.

'Canada!' said Babs. 'But that's thousands of miles away. You can't send us there. What about Rosie and Dotty?'

'They'll be OK and so will you. You'll be living with your Aunt Iris and Uncle Bill. It's not as if you're going to strangers,' said Amelia, squeezing Harry's hand.

'But we hardly know Aunt Iris,' cried Babs, anger and dismay causing her voice to quiver as she fumbled with the door handle. 'You've got to let us out of here!'

Amelia leant across Harry and prised her niece's fingers from the handle. 'D'you want to be killed?' The driver's head swivelled and the car slowed. 'Drive on!' she ordered.

Babs wrenched her hand away from Amelia's, glaring at her as she put an arm round Harry. 'I knew you were up to something. It's to do with the Hudsons and their father, isn't it?'

'It's nothing to do with them. Iris asked to have you. She has no children of her own and thought it only fair, as she is your aunt too, to share the responsibility of bringing you up.'

Babs was silent, thinking about that.

'Where's Canada?' asked Harry. 'Is it a long, long way away?'

'Not as far as Australia,' said Amelia, taking his hand and patting it. 'And I haven't forgotten your engine. It's in the boot. You and Babs will be going on a big ship and will be met in Montreal by your other aunt. My sister and her husband Bill.'

'A ship?' His face brightened then fell again. 'But you said Rosie's not coming?' His bottom lip wobbled and tears filled his eyes. 'Want Rosie.'

'She has to sit her exams. It would be wrong to move her now. Maybe later she'll come and see you. When you're settled.'

Babs, who had been sitting very still, said, 'Are you just saying that to keep us quiet?'

'Don't you think she'll want to come and visit you?' parried Amelia.

'Yes, but where will she get the money?'

'We'll find it. You just think how lovely it'll be on the ship.' And having got to know Babs's weaknesses in the last few months, she added, 'And when you get to Canada, there'll be lots of food: cakes, sweets and lovely Canadian apples. Aunt Iris'll take you shopping and buy you new clothes.'

'And toys?' asked Harry, tears evaporating.

'Of course,' said Amelia, relief colouring her smile.

'Are they rich? Richer than you?' said Babs, a calculating expression on her face.

'Much richer! You're going to have a marvellous time,' promised Amelia, crossing her fingers as she began to tell them what she knew about Canada and her sister's life there.

When they reached the docks and saw the Mersey gleaming in the sun and the liner at its berth, she felt a rush of longing to join them on their voyage. To leave Liverpool, with its expanses of blighted wasteland and damaged buildings. But she had had her chance after her father died and had not wanted to get rid of the shop and house for which he had worked so hard.

'You're very lucky kids,' she said, accompanying them to their cabin.

'They are that,' said the stewardess appointed to look after them. 'You're going to have a lovely time.'

Babs's face brightened. 'Will there be games to play, books to read?'

'We've all sorts,' said the stewardess, and began to reel off the pleasures in store.

Amelia crept out of the cabin, deciding it might be best not to say goodbye. On the dockside, she gave the liner one last look, thinking that a day's work lay ahead for her and then later she would have to break the news to Rosie. It was a task she was not looking forward to.

Rosie flung her satchel on the floor in a corner of her room, wondering where Babs and Harry had got to. Her sister was generally home before her with the tea on by now.

Could Harry have persuaded her to take him to Lord Sefton's Estate to play? There had been no sign of them outside or in the garden. In fact, the house was unusually silent. The twins had gone home for a few days because their father was home for a week. Then he would be going to some Army camp in England, so her aunt said. The war in Europe was as good as over now Hitler had killed himself.

Rosie went upstairs and checked Harry's room, noticing his engine was not in its usual place. She stared at the empty space and for some reason the thought popped into her head that the terrible twins had stolen it again because Harry did not normally take it out with him. Perhaps Babs and he had gone tearing off to the Hudsons's house now their dad was home, to complain, and he might not be at all pleased. She hesitated only a moment before going out again and heading for the village.

Against her will, Rosie liked Peter Hudson at first sight despite it being obvious where the twins got their looks from. She did not know what it was about him. Maybe it was the smile that reached his eyes and his lovely even white teeth.

He asked her in and no sooner did she set foot in the untidy kitchen with its unpolished brass fenders and books on the hearth than he asked her if she would like a job as she looked a strong fit girl. That made her smile and feel right at home. He was obviously in the middle of ironing and everyone knew it wasn't a man's job. There was an art to it.

'No, thanks,' she said. 'I'm looking for Harry and Babs. And I've the tea to put on and homework to do.'

There was a pause before he said, 'Your aunt's told me about you. Says you've plenty of sense.' He placed the iron on the glowing coals and gave her a glimpse of that heartwhirling smile.

'It's more than she's said to me,' murmured Rosie, cheeks glowing. 'She makes me feel an idiot sometimes.'

'That you're not. She wouldn't be thinking of helping you towards being a dispenser if you were.'

'She said that to *you*?' Rosie was amazed.

'We've known each other a long time,' he said gravely, thinking now was obviously not the right time to say he was going to marry her aunt.

'Of course.' She blushed. 'I wasn't thinking. Your wife and she were close friends.'

'Yes.' His smile vanished and he rested one elbow on the mantelpiece. 'Anyway, Babs and Harry aren't here, so is there anything else I can do for you?'

She hesitated. With those wonderful eyes on her, she felt embarrassed about revealing why she had come. 'Oh, I just wondered if the twins had brought an engine home with them?' she said as casually as she could.

'Ah! Harry's is missing, is it?' He gave her a quizzical look as he took up the iron with a singed cloth and spat on its flat bottom. 'Try asking your aunt where it is.'

'She's not in.'

'Try waiting until she is.'

Rosie did not know what to say to that. She had a feeling he was trying to tell her something. But that was ridiculous; he had not said anything at all really. 'Perhaps I'd best go home then?'

'I would,' he said, without a smile, and saw her out.

There was still no sign of Harry or Babs when she arrived home. So Rosie switched on the wireless because the house was so quiet and found some liver in the meat safe in the larder. She peeled an onion and put on the frying pan. When she heard the cat mewing she ran to let him in and gave him a cuddle.

She put the liver and onions in a casserole dish in the oven, then tried to settle to studying, but could not concentrate. Where could Harry and Babs be? It was not their evening for instruction at the priest's house.

Closing the book on Elementary Chemistry, she ran upstairs and into Harry's room. She opened a drawer. It was empty. She opened another and that was empty too. A search for Babs's clothes came next. They were all gone.

Rosie felt panic rise inside her. Where had they gone? What had Amelia done to them? She raced into her aunt's room, turning over things on her dressing table, opening drawers. Then she saw scribbled on a notepad the name of a ship, a date and a time. It was today! She threw the pad at the wall, wishing it was her aunt's face, and dashed downstairs as she heard the key in the lock.

As soon as Amelia had the door open, Rosie pounced on her. Seizing the lapels of her jacket, the girl shouted in her face, 'You've sent them to Australia, haven't you? You've sent them to Australia!'

Amelia jerked back her head. 'Let go, Rosie. I haven't done anything of the sort.'

'I don't believe you. I saw the name of the ship,' she yelled, tears already streaming down her face.

Amelia dropped her bag and seized hold of the girl's wrists. 'I have *not* sent them to Australia,' she said emphatically. 'Now let go of my collar before you break my brooch. It's very precious to me.'

'Where are they?' Rosie panted, eyes wild, still holding on to her. Amelia wrenched the girl's hands away and she yelped. 'You've cut me!' She gazed at her finger, which was oozing blood.

'It's your own fault,' said Amelia crossly, glancing down at the silver brooch on her lapel. 'What d'you think you're doing, acting like a mad thing? There's ways of asking people if you want a quick answer.'

Rosie wiped her finger on the palm of her other hand, leaving a streak of blood. 'Where are they?'

'On a liner bound for Canada. There, I've told you.' She let out a breath. 'What a relief! It's been blinking hard keeping it from you.'

'Canada?' Rosie's face was aghast as she sank on to the bottom stair.

'I've sent them to Iris. Two each, that's what we've agreed.'

'Two each?' gasped Rosie, gazing up at her with a horrified expression. 'We're not a pound of apples that you can divide between you. We've got feelings!'

'And so have I,' said Amelia, exasperated. 'And I'm not in the mood for this.' She felt exhausted, wanting nothing more than a cup of tea, a bath, a good book and bed. She picked up her bag and walked to the kitchen.

Rosie rushed after her. 'Tell me what happened?'

'I don't want to talk about it now.'

'But you *must*. I need to know. It's my brother and sister you've sent away. Just because you hated Mam and have no feelings, you can't treat us like a bundle of rags!'

Anger flashed in Amelia's eyes and she felt the throb, throb, throb of pain behind her left eye. 'I should have sent *you* but I didn't want our Iris to have that burden.' As soon as she said the words, she wished she hadn't.

'So I'm a burden, am I?'

Amelia made no answer but poured milk into a cup and the cat's saucer.

'Don't ignore me!' yelled Rosie, smashing a plate against the sink.

Amelia stepped over the broken crockery.

The girl opened the cutlery drawer and pulled out knives and forks, flinging them on the floor. She stared at her aunt. Amelia returned her stare but did not speak, opening the oven and taking out the casserole. Inside she was quivering, but she could see no sense in having a fight. She made some tea and went upstairs.

Rosie did not follow her. She put her head down on the table and wept. After a while, she wandered into the sitting room and huddled on the sofa, arms clasped about her knees, thinking of Harry and Babs. They would be feeling as miserable as she was. The thought brought a lump to her throat and tears to her eyes. She snuffled like a baby, wanting her mother. Then, suddenly, she decided she would go to the cemetery and visit her grave. She got up and put on her blazer and went out again. As she passed St Vincent's, she thought of Dotty and sympathy for her mingled with her own misery and anger. Perhaps tomorrow she would try to get to see her.

Dotty had made up her mind that she had to get out of St Vincent's. They had cropped her long silvery hair because there had been a lice scare and she could not bear the feel of it. She grieved for her mother and the easygoing routine of her old life. She missed the outings to the shops and being spoilt by Gwen Baxendale when Violet was working. She missed the chatting and playing with her sisters and brother at the end of the day; she yearned for the shabby cosiness of the home she had left behind and the comfort of Babs's warm body snuggling up to hers in their old bed.

At St Vincent's, she had to share a dormitory with seven other girls, and although one of the nuns slept in a small room nearby, Dotty was scared at night because some of the older pupils had whispered of a ghost called Betty Eccles who haunted the building, watching for any child who misbehaved. Dotty was desperate to behave well but she was frightened in bed, nervous of the staircases and the playground outside. The other girls shrieked and shouted, touching her face and clothes when she spoke. She had been told this was because most of them were blind and sound and touch was their way of drawing attention to themselves. But there was something else that bothered her far worse, which she had not voiced to anyone.

A gate post loomed right in front of her nose and she drew back her head and felt her way round it. She was

out! Terrified and exhilarated at the same time, Dotty
began to walk.

'You OK?' said a male voice.

She spun round, attempting to see through the fuzziness
that plagued her. 'Who is it?' Her voice trembled.

'Are you from St Vincent's?'

'No!' she denied emphatically, and said the first thing
that came into her head. 'I'm – I'm looking for the cemetery. My – My mother's buried there and I've forgotten
exactly where it is.'

'I'll show you.' Instantly, he was much more than a
voice and a misty outline as his face came into focus. He
had brown eyes, a long narrow nose with delicately flaring
nostrils and untidy chestnut hair. 'Have I seen you before?'

She fell back a pace, aware of an overpowering smell
of manure, peppermint and carbolic soap, and almost tripped
over a dog. He took her arm, steadying her. 'I'm not from
round here,' said Dotty swiftly. 'You've made a mistake.
After I've been to the cemetery, I'm going to my aunt's.'

'Well, if you're going to the cemetery, you're going in
the wrong direction.' Turning her round, he fell into step
beside her, close enough for her to know he was gazing
at her.

She knew she was pretty, having been told so often in
the past, but did she look like a person who was almost
blind? The thought terrified her and Dotty, who for so
long had accepted her reliance on others and relished the
attention, now knew she had to act as if there was nothing
wrong with her. 'I'm Dotty Kilshaw. My aunt lives just
up the road. I've been to visit her.'

'Kilshaw? You're not related to Rosie and Babs, are you?'

'You know them?' she said in a startled voice.

'Of course I know them. My dad's going to marry their aunt. Your aunt, too, by the sound of it.'

For a moment, she could not think what to say. Then she stammered, 'Who are you?'

'Chris Hudson.' He laughed. 'It looks like we're going to be related but I don't know what that makes us.'

'Me neither!' She bit her lip. 'I had no idea.'

'It's only just happened. Dad's been away in the Army. They're marrying for the sake of us kids. A marriage of convenience, he called it. We're going to move into her house because it's bigger. He said that's the sensible thing to do.'

'I see,' she said forlornly.

'You don't like the idea?'

She shrugged her shoulders. 'What's it to do with me?'

'You're her niece.' His face swam into vision again and he touched her shoulder. 'Look, here's the cemetery. Are you sure you'll be OK? Only I'm on a message.'

'I'm fine,' she said, and to prove it walked straight through the cemetery gates, not stopping until she blundered into a headstone and went sprawling.

'Hey there, little missy, are you OK?' The voice had a Transatlantic twang and the hands that lifted and steadied her were strong.

She clutched at his jacket, thinking what an outing this was turning out to be. 'You're American!'

'My, you're quick.' There was a smile in his voice.

'It's the way you speak,' she stammered. 'Just like at the pictures. I've never met a Yank before. Although Mam married one.'

'Is that a fact now?'

'Honestly,' said Dotty, brushing herself down. 'I'm visiting her grave now.' She peered about her. 'The trouble is, I'm not exactly sure where it is.'

'Does she have a headstone? What's her name?'

'Violet. I don't remember her married name or whether they even put it on the stone.'

He drawled. 'It was Dixon. Sam Dixon. And this sure is some coincidence. I am that American and I was just visiting your mom's grave.' He thrust out a hand. 'I think I remember you now from the funeral. Weren't you sitting in a corner, just by the piano?'

Dotty's mouth fell open but before she could say what a good memory he had, a more familiar voice spoke. 'Dotty, what are *you* doing here? I was just thinking about you! Oh, I'm so glad to see you. Something terrible's happened!'

Dotty gave a cry and fell into Rosie's arms. It really was turning out to be some outing. She was glad she had escaped.

The two sisters hugged each other, rocking from side to side. 'Fancy us meeting like this! This is the first time I've been here since Mam died and I wouldn't have come now if I hadn't had a row with Aunt Amelia,' said Rosie, eyes clouding.

'Aunt Amelia? Why did you?'

'You'll never guess what she's done. I feel like never going back there again.'

'Oh, don't say that,' said Dotty in a scared voice. 'What would happen to me if you weren't there? Besides, where would you go?'

'I'd think of somewhere, don't you worry!' Rosie's tone was savage.

There was the sound of a throat being cleared. 'Excuse me, ma'am?'

Rosie turned. She had forgotten the man standing there but now she gave him her full attention. 'You're Mam's Yank!'

'Widower, ma'am,' he said, removing his cap.

'Ma'am? I'm only sixteen!' Rosie laughed, eyeing him with interest. He looked even younger than the last time she had seen him, despite the thinning hair. She wondered anew what had got into her mother to put him in Joe's place. 'You can call me Rosie. After all, you're our stepdad, aren't you?'

'Oh, Rosie, I forgot your birthday!' burst out Dotty, hand going to her mouth.

'That's OK. I wasn't there to remind you. I won't forget yours, though.' Rosie's head swung in her sister's direction. 'What on earth's happened to your hair? I've only just noticed your plaits have gone.'

'They chopped them off!' Dotty's face crumpled. 'My hair looks terrible, doesn't it?'

'I think you look kinda cute,' said Sam.

The two girls stared at him as if he had run mad. 'I loved my hair long,' said Dotty in a sad little voice. 'Mam always said it was a woman's crowning glory.'

'Veronica Lake put hers up for the war effort as an example,' said Sam, turning his cap round and round between his hands. 'Women working in factories could catch it in the machinery. Doesn't bear thinking about, does it?'

They agreed.

There was a lull in the conversation, none of them knowing what to say next. The two girls waited for the man to speak first.

Sam cleared his throat again. 'You're not really thinking of leaving your aunt's?'

'Sure I am,' said Rosie instantly.

'But where would you go?' said Dotty, concerned.

'I'm thinking about it.'

Sam shook his head at them. 'Your aunt seemed kinda nice.'

Rosie looked at him pityingly. 'You don't know her. And I'm surprised Mam didn't tell you about her.'

'She mentioned no sisters, nor kids. Only an elderly pa who hated Yanks.'

'I'll never understand why she did it,' said Rosie, hurt and sad. 'Anyway, to get back to Aunt Amelia – she's gone and got rid of Babs and Harry! She's sent them to Aunt Iris in Canada, and *without a word to me*.' Her voice rose indignantly on the last few words.

Dotty gasped, placing a hand on her narrow chest. 'That's awful!'

'I hate her!' said Rosie, folding her arms and digging her nails into the fabric of her blazer.

'You know why, don't you?' said Dotty. 'She's getting married.'

Rosie laughed. 'You've lost your marbles. Why should you think that?'

'Someone called Chris Hudson just told me.'

Rosie stared at her and thought she saw it all. 'The cow! That's why she got rid of Babs and Harry.'

'And me!' said Dotty. 'She'll probably want you to stay to help with the housework and everything.'

Sam, who had been listening with interest, said, 'So what are you gonna do? Where'll you go?'

'I know where I'd go,' said Dotty thoughtfully.

They looked at her. 'Mrs Baxendale's. She was good to us and she has a spare room.'

'She was Violet's next-door neighbour,' said Sam, nodding his head sagely.

'She told you that?' said Rosie.

'Said she was good with her pa. Looked after him when she was at work.'

Rosie shook her head, still scarcely able to believe her mother could dissemble the truth in such a way.

'If you do decide to go, will you come for me?' said Dotty, slipping a hand through her sister's arm. 'I could bear St Vincent's for a few more days if I knew I wasn't going to be there for ever.'

'Of course,' said Rosie, thinking that if Mrs Baxendale took her in, she would be living under the same roof as Davey and she didn't know about that.

Sam glanced at his watch. 'I'll have to be going.' He fumbled in his trouser pocket and brought out a slab of chocolate. He handed it to Rosie. 'It's been a pleasure meeting you again. You're very like your mom, you know.'

'So they say.' Her eyes had lit up at the sight of the chocolate. Impulsively, she leant forward and kissed his cheek. 'Thanks, Stepdaddy!'

'It's nuthin'!'

'It is! You Yanks – don't you know we're always hungry?' She kissed his other cheek and he blushed.

'Maybe I'll see you again some time, girls?' He saluted and strolled away in the direction of the gates.

'Chocolate,' breathed Rosie, breaking the slab. 'Here, Dotty.' She handed her sister half.

'Lovely, lovely,' said Dotty, putting several squares into her mouth all at once and closing her eyes in ecstasy.

'Hmmm!' Rosie let the chocolate melt in her mouth. When they had finished it all, she said, 'Shall we visit Mam's grave?'

'We're here, we might as well. She might have been a liar but she's still our mam.'

The girls made their way through a maze of angels and crosses and when they reached the grave saw there were fresh flowers on it. 'One thing,' said Rosie with a sigh. 'Mam certainly knew how to pick nice men.'

There was silence but for the sound of the wind in the trees. 'This Mr Hudson . . .' said Dotty tentatively. 'Is he a nice man? Only his son said it was a marriage of convenience.'

Rosie chewed on a fingernail, eyes thoughtful as she gazed unseeingly at the grave. 'He's the father of the twins, isn't he? How can he be nice? Let's go. I've had enough of cemeteries.'

They went, stopping when they came to the entrance to St Vincent's. 'You're going to have to go in,' said Rosie. 'I won't be going anywhere tonight.'

'I'm going to have sneak in,' whispered Dotty. 'I hope I won't be caught.'

'You can come up with some excuse. Anyway, I'll see you soon.' Rosie kissed her and slowly walked home.

The next day was the first of May and in another lifetime Rosie, Babs and Dotty would have dressed up in old frocks of Violet's and waltzed out into the street to join a May procession. Rosie's heart ached as she wished Babs and Harry could come bouncing into the room as they had on so many other mornings. She ignored Amelia's presence across the table from her, although there were in fact several questions she would have liked to put to her.

'They reckon that a declaration of peace is imminent,' said her aunt, voice extra loud in the quietness. 'There'll be celebrations and you'll probably get a couple of days off school. As long as it doesn't interfere with your studies, it should be fun. There'll be a party here. I want you in the shop full-time as soon as you leave school, Rosie.'

The girl remembered what Dotty had said. 'I'm surprised you want me around at all. This house is going to be full enough without me, isn't it?'

Amelia lowered the newspaper. 'What's that supposed to mean?'

She leant back in her chair, raising the front legs off the floor. 'Mr Hudson. You're going to marry him. Another little secret you kept from me,' she said bitterly, bringing the chair down with a crash.

'Don't do that,' said Amelia automatically. 'I intended telling you this week. Today hardly seemed the right time with you already upset.' She folded the newspaper. 'I can imagine how your mind's working but it's not true. I didn't get rid of Babs and Harry because I'm marrying Mr Hudson. Nor do I want to get rid of you. I appreciate your good points. You work hard and you've been very helpful to me.'

'Work hard! Helpful! Is that the best you can say to keep me here?' Rosie's voice cracked and she got to her feet hurriedly, fearing she might give way to tears. 'You're so cold,' she whispered. 'I feel sorry for Mr Hudson, but then, I suppose all he needs is a housekeeper.'

'That's enough!' Colour flamed in Amelia's face as she sprang to her feet, resting her hands on the table. 'You're very rude. And I didn't ask your opinion. Now get to school. I've a busy day ahead of me.' She click-clacked furiously out the room.

I'll kill her, thought the girl. *I've read in that herbal book of hers about different potions and Brownie's told me about the dangers of overdosing. I'll poison her tea. Then she won't be* able *to get married.*

The cat miaowed and stropped Rosie's leg. Suddenly, all the anger seeped out of her. 'What do you want?' She bent and lifted Sooty, resting a cheek against his fur, finding comfort in his warm purring body. 'What am I going to do, puss?' Her voice was melancholy.

Of course, Sooty made no reply, only rubbed his head against her chin in a way that was infinitely soothing, almost like a kiss. Rosie remembered their old cat and

thought of that day they had left their home and her
grandmother had turned up. She froze. She had scarcely
given Maggie a thought since then because life had been
so full since they'd moved. Now she smiled. Perhaps this
was the time to visit her.

Chapter Seven

Rosie turned into the street where she had once lived to see a scene that was being duplicated all over Britain. Women were decorating windows with red, white and blue bunting; youths were piling up wood for a bonfire to be lit that evening. The war in Europe was over and people's relief knew no bounds. The King had announced a three-day school holiday.

'Rosie!'

She glanced up and saw Davey's mother hanging out of a bedroom window, holding a large Union Jack. 'Wait there, lovey! I've got something for you.'

Rosie waited, wondering what it could be.

Gwen Baxendale appeared at the front door with the Union Jack draped over her shoulder, carrying a box.

'What is it?' Rosie lifted a flap and gazed inside. Then she lifted her head and stared at Davey's mother. 'It's food!'

'Your mam's Yank brought it. Seemed to think he might be able to get in touch with you here.'

'Sorry!' Rosie grimaced. 'I need to get away from my aunt and Dotty suggested your house in front of him as somewhere for me to stay.'

Gwen looked upset. 'I'm sorry, lovey, but I've taken in a lodger. Come this time next year our Davey will have had his call-up papers and I'm going to feel it. Besides, I could do with the money. What's wrong?'

'Oh, it's nothing. We just don't get on,' Rosie said brightly, reluctant to explain because the subject was still too painful for her to talk about. 'Anyway, as it is I thought I'd look up my grandmother.'

Gwen's expression altered. 'Are you sure about that, lovey? She's been round here a couple of times. Sharp as a knife she is. You'll need to watch she doesn't put too much on you. Now this box – can you manage it?'

'Oh, yes,' said Rosie quickly. 'Although I suppose I shouldn't accept it. He's almost a stranger. But I'd be daft not to, wouldn't I, the way rationing is?'

Gwen agreed. 'Make the most of it while you can, lovey. With the war in Europe over, the Yanks'll be moving out of Burtonwood. You count your blessings. There's thousands who'd like to be in your shoes. And this is nicely timed. I suppose there's a party out where you are?'

'Mmmm. I've heard talk of a party tomorrow and the decorations are going up.' Rosie took a tin of salmon and one of peaches out of the box. 'I'd like you to have these, Mrs Baxendale. You've been good to us.'

The woman's face lit up. 'Now that's kind of you. They're a real treat. And if you have any time later, why don't you call in on us this evening? You'll know every-body – except the ones that have moved into your house. Our Davey'll be pleased to see you.'

'I'll probably hang around Gran's this evening but I'll come if I can.' Rosie wished Davey's mother would stop making out he had his eye on her. 'I hope you have a nice day.'

'Well, it'll be a testing time.' Mrs Baxendale took the Union Jack from her shoulder, tears glistening in her eyes. 'I wasn't going to put this up but our Davey said Frank gave his life for the peace and he deserves to have a flag flown in his memory.'

Rosie agreed, thanked her old neighbour again and hurried away. She found her grandmother sitting in an armchair on the front step, watching a couple of lads making an effigy of Hitler. 'You're making a right hash of that,' grumbled the old woman. 'In my day we knew how to stuff a Guy.'

'There on the first Guy Fawkes Night, were yer, Granny?' said one of the lads.

'Don't you give me any old lip or I'll box yer ears for yer,' she growled.

'You and whose army?' he retorted.

'I'll do it on me own with one hand tied behind me back,' said Maggie, bristling, half rising from her seat.

'Hello, Gran. Remember me?' Rosie placed the box on the step.

The old woman sank back into her chair and eyed her granddaughter up and down. The youths wolf-whistled and Rosie did a twirl, pleased that the time she had put into her appearance was paying dividends. From the garments which had been her mother's, Amelia had given her several. The frock Rosie was wearing was scarlet with white piping round the neckline and hem. It was also short on her so showed a good expanse of shapely leg.

Maggie sniffed. 'Haven't gone gaga yet, girl. Warra yer doing here?'

'Came to see you, Gran. Thought I might take you up on your offer,' she said boldly.

'And what offer would that be? Refresh me memory, girl.'

'The one to come and live with you?'

'Oh, that one!' Maggie's eyes narrowed and she thrust her head forward like a snake about to strike. 'And why should yer think I'd want yer when I haven't seen yous for love nor money in months?'

Instinctively, Rosie went on the defensive and what better way than to blame the woman whom she knew Maggie disliked? 'It hasn't been easy for me to get away. Aunt Amelia keeps my nose to the grindstone. I've been working in her shop most Saturdays, and when I wasn't doing that I was looking after the others and cleaning her house for her.'

Maggie cackled and rocked herself. 'Not spoiling yous then? At least she shows some sense. But why should yer think life would be any different living with me? I'd expect yous to work too. Can't keep yous for nowt.'

'I wouldn't expect you to,' said Rosie, perching on the cardboard box. 'I'd leave school straight away and get myself a job, help you in the house and everything. But I thought most of all you wanted somebody who was family living with you?'

'Hmmmph!' Maggie's expression was cynical. 'D'yer think I was born yesterday? There's more to it than that.

But yer can tell me later. Help me up now and let's go into the house.'

Rosie heaved her grandmother out of the chair. Maggie prodded the cardboard box with her stick. 'And what's this? All yer worldly goods? Cast yous off, has she? Been misbehaving have yer, girl? Cos I tell yer now, I don't want any disgrace brought to my door!'

Rosie looked shocked as indeed she was. 'Give me credit for some sense, Gran. It's food. I thought you might need some luxuries.'

The old woman's mouth fell open. 'Now yous *have* surprised me. It's the sort of thing my Joey would do.'

Rosie smiled. 'Well, he was my dad. Is it that surprising I should be a little bit like him?'

Maggie stroked her chin, where several hairs sprouted from a wart, looking thoughtful. Then she seemed to come to a decision and signalled the girl to bring the box inside.

Rosie was about to get a grip on it when one of the lads lifted it. 'I'll carry it in for yer, luv. And how's about a date?'

'Don't yous be talking like that,' said Maggie belligerently, whacking him on the back of one knee with her stick. His leg gave way and he nearly fell. Rosie just managed to save the box from crashing to the ground.

'Sorry,' she murmured.

He did not look at her but beat a hasty retreat.

'Why did you do that?' said Rosie, frowning at Maggie. 'He was only trying to be helpful.'

'Helpful my foot,' she growled. 'When yous been alive as long as I have, girl, yer learn who yers can trust. He'd be casting an eye over what I've got. Now in with yous.'

They went inside. Maggie lowered her bulk into a chair in front of a grate much in need of blackleading. 'Let's get me breath back,' she gasped.

Rosie placed the box on the table, glancing round and seeing no sign of all the money her grandmother was supposed to have. 'It's not so different from our old house,' she said, unable to disguise her disappointment.

'What did yers expect?' Maggie's bushy eyebrows met angrily. 'Gold plate and Persian carpets?'

Rosie could not help smiling.

'Take that smirk off yer face! Think I couldn't afford such things, hey?'

'To be honest, Gran – no. But that doesn't mean to say there's anything wrong with this room, and I loved our old house. It was home.'

'And home is where the heart is, eh?' said Maggie, surprising her again. She hoisted herself up unaided. 'Come through and I'll show you something. Give us yer arm.'

Rosie helped her and they walked slowly across the kitchen and out through the other door. The girl stared at the sight that met her eyes. Here was a counter with scales and weights, knives and a cutting block, sheets of grease-proof paper and paper bags – as well as a biscuit tin with CASH written on it. On shelves there were loads of tins, packets and jars; on the floor blocks of salt, packets of soda, soap and bottles of disinfectant.

'It's a shop!' said Rosie.

'That's right, girl.' Maggie rested one hand on the counter where a well-thumbed ledger hung by a length of string from a nail. 'When me rheumatism got real chronic, the doctor said I had to quit the streets, but I couldn't just sit back and twiddle me thumbs.'

'But wouldn't it be better at the front of the house?'

'Them that needs to know knows!' Maggie tapped her nose before ushering Rosie back into the kitchen. 'Now how's about a spot of something to eat? There's a quart of brawn in that there 'fridgerator and some leftover bubble and squeak yer can heat up in the frying pan.' Rosie hesitated. 'Well, jump to it, girl! I'm not going to be carrying yous around.'

'I don't expect you to, Gran, but the fire's not lit.'

'There's a two-ring thingymebob in that cupboard.' She pointed her swollen, twisted hand. 'Yous sticks it on the gas outlet and Bob's your uncle. I couldn't be doing with lighting fires all the time once Emily went.'

Soon Rosie was setting in front of Maggie a plate of crispy potato and cabbage with slices of melting brawn on top. The old woman rubbed her hands together and smacked her lips. 'It looks good. Not that yous can go much wrong with bubble and squeak.'

Rosie agreed, fetching her own plate and sitting down at the table. After they had taken the edge off their hunger, Maggie said, 'And now I'll ask a question of yer, Rosie girl. Have yous any idea why my shop's at the back of the house?'

She remembered a time when Violet had taken her to a yard where a large van had been parked. In a room to the rear of the house, frocks, skirts and coats had hung from curtain rails while shelves were packed with other garments. Rosie had tried on several frocks before her mother signed a piece of paper before coming away with the one she had chosen. It was not until later Rosie realised why they had gone in the back way. 'You allow people to buy on tick,' she said slowly.

'Clever girl!' Her grandmother looked approving. 'Some people see shame in it and that's why they comes up the back jigger. But there's lots of folk who go through hard times, and if there weren't people like me around to help them, they'd be in a worse state.'

'But isn't it wrong to encourage people to get into debt?' said Rosie mildly.

'No need to look at me like that, girl.' Maggie's tone was disapproving. 'I makes sure they pays me something regular and don't get in over their heads.'

'But you must charge interest?'

'Can't be doing with working out percentages,' mumbled the old woman. 'A farthin' here, a ha'penny there. It's always up front on the goods so there's no unpleasant surprises. They knows exactly how much they owes and I'm satisfied with what I makes. As me old mother said, "Look after the pennies and the pounds'll take care of themselves." That's the way money grows. I've been bit once or twice but I'm not a bad judge of character.'

'You don't look like you've got money,' said Rosie frankly.

Maggie stared at her unblinking. 'I've got enough to see me out. Now polish off that food and take that look off yer face. I'm no Scrooge nor Shylock. Tell me instead how me lad met his fate? In the Forces, was he?'

Rosie told the tale of how Joe had been crushed by a lorryload of scrap metal. Maggie shook her head and wiped away tears but recovered quickly, asking the girl what treats were in the box.

'In a moment, Gran. Now you tell me a bit about me dad when he was young. And how about *his* dad? Dad only told me he was lost at sea.'

'Lost at sea?' Maggie smiled grimly. 'I only told him that tale because I didn't want him upset. Walked out on me, did Walt. Men! You can't always trust them, girl. Now how about seeing what's in this here box?'

Feeling stunned by this news, Rosie's mind was elsewhere as she did as she was told. So her granddad hadn't been killed at sea! 'Where is he now?' she demanded.

'Who?'

'My granddad?'

There was a short silence before Maggie, not looking up, grunted, 'How the hell should I know? Did yers pay for all this, girl?'

Disappointed, she said absently, 'Do me a favour, Gran. I earn a pittance working in Aunt Amelia's shop on a Saturday. No, this was a present.'

Maggie chewed on her gums. 'I hope yous isn't carrying on with the Yanks?'

'Of course not, Gran!' Rosie did not even consider telling her the truth, guessing the old woman would only pull Violet's character to shreds. 'It's from a friend.'

'Nice friends yous have! In the black market, are they?'

Rosie raised her eyebrows as if in horror but was silent. Let her grandmother think what she liked. Rosie suspected from a couple of things she had noticed under the counter in the shop that Maggie had dealings with them herself.

Her grandmother nodded her head slowly, a smile on her wrinkled face. 'I bet that aunt of yours finds you a handful.'

'We have our differences,' said Rosie, lacing her fingers and twiddling her thumbs.

'What kind of differences? It wasn't fellas, was it? Cos I tell yers now, I won't have them hanging around yer like wasps round a jam pot.'

'It wasn't fellas, Gran. If you want to know—' She hesitated, wondering just how much to tell her. 'Aunt Amelia's getting married and he's got three lads of his own.'

'Well, well, well. Who'd have thought it?' mumbled Maggie, forking the last of the food into her mouth. 'What about yer sisters and brother?'

'Gone. She's got rid of them all. Dotty to the blind school and—' Rosie swallowed, 'Harry and Babs have been sent to Canada, to Aunt Iris. I tell you, Gran, I could have killed Aunt Amelia when I found out! But there's nothing I can do at the moment except get myself a job and save some money. But if you could put up Dotty as well, so we could be together, that'd be marvellous.'

'Why?' said Maggie, dropping the fork and pulling her shawl more securely about her shoulders. 'I don't want her and that's the truth. What use would she be to me?'

'But she hates it at school, Gran!'

'She'd probably hate it here. She's better off where she is. They'll teach her to look after herself. So forget her, girl, if yous want to come and live here with me.'

For a moment, Rosie did not know what to do, could only think, *Poor Dotty! Nobody wants her.*

'Take it or leave it, girl,' muttered Maggie, hand shaking as she poured herself another cup of tea. 'Yous don't have to make up yer mind straight away. There's the street party. We'll go to that and yer can tell me what yous have decided later.'

With that Rosie had to be satisfied, but she felt uncomfortably as if she would be deserting her sister if she came and lived with her grandmother. On the other hand, if she did not then she would have to do what she was even more loath to do and continue living under Amelia's regime, sharing a house with the terrible twins. If only she had some money, she would quit Liverpool and head for Canada, taking Dotty with her so the Kilshaws could be reunited once more. But she didn't. So what was she to do? It needed some thinking about and attending the street party would give her time to do just that.

Rosie marvelled at how much food there was, aware of mothers and grandmothers hovering, making sure their offspring got their fair share. Children were already seated round well-spread tables drawn up in a long line down the centre of the street. Plates were piled high with sandwiches and homemade cakes. There were bowls of jelly and blancmange, jugs of soft drinks made from watered-down orange juice and lemonade powder. Rosie thought of Harry and sadness and resentment dragged her spirits down. It wasn't fair! She had to get to Canada somehow.

An upright piano was brought out, and a bald man with a drooping moustache struck the keys, launching into 'Run, Rabbit, Run'. Crates of brown ale made their appearance and Maggie told Rosie to move her armchair closer to the piano. The next moment the old woman was supping brown ale and conducting the music with a sandwich in her other hand. Rosie watched and listened as everyone began to sing along, faces flushed and happy. Finally, she resisted no longer but joined in.

The effigy of Hitler was hoisted aloft and the bonfire lit. Wood crackled, sending sparks flying into the sky, to the cheers of children. Some capered around daringly close to the flames. Women gossiped or admired sleeping babies. More than one middle-aged man reminisced about the last war. There was lots of laughter and couples began to dance. Homemade peppermint lumps made the rounds as did more bottles of brown ale.

'Wanna cut a rug?' drawled a familiar voice in an assumed American accent, causing Rosie almost to drop her cup of lemonade. 'Unless, that is, you're ashamed to be seen with me in your glad rags?'

She turned and looked at Davey. He wore a shirt and tie today and looked quite different; his hair was slicked back with Brylcreem in a way which made him look older. 'What are you doing here?' she asked.

His eyes scanned her face, ran down over her throat and the swell of her breasts beneath the tight-fitting bodice of the scarlet frock. 'I almost didn't come but Ma insisted. Enjoying the goodies? Nice of the Yank, wasn't it?'

'Very nice,' she said, cheeks pink, aware that he was seeing her in a different light. 'You know he was married to Mam?'

'So I believe. Bit young to be your stepdaddy, though.'

'That's what I thought.'

'There's a law against it, you know?' he said laconically.

'Against what?'

'You can't go marrying your ma's husband.' His expression was deadly serious.

'D'you mind?' gasped Rosie. 'What d'you think I am?'

'I'm thinking you've got a soft heart and the Yanks have had their wicked way with too many of our women!'

'*Our women?*' Rosie laughed. 'You're mad! I'm not a woman.'

'Aren't you?' He swept her into his arms. The pianist was playing 'Jealousy' and Davey whirled her round and down over his arm.

'You are mad!' She gazed up at him, heart racing. This was fun. He brought her back against him with a jolt, squashing her breasts against his chest, pressing his cheek against hers. He shot out their arms and took her forward at a glide. '"It's all over my jealousy,"' he sang.

'I don't know what's got into you,' she marvelled.

'It's you, changing overnight. I knew where I was when you were a scruffy, dirty-faced kid, straight as a board with plaits. Now you go in and out and it's driving me crazy!'

'I was never scruffy,' said Rosie indignantly. 'Poverty-stricken, yeah!'

'That as well. But, honestly, I remember you having
to turn your socks inside-out to make them last out the
week because you didn't have another pair. You've
forgotten now you're living with your posh aunt.'

'She's not posh. Just hard and cruel,' said Rosie, her
expression hardening. 'As for me, I'm just the same as
ever I was.'

'No, you're not. You've grown up.' His voice was a
caress. And he kissed her right on the mouth before she
could do anything to stop him.

'Hey, hey, hey!' said a voice, loud as a ship's foghorn.

'Hey, hey, hey,' echoed Davey's voice in Rosie's ear.

'What did you do that for?' she hissed, affected far
more by the kiss than she wanted him to know. 'Gran
already seems to think I'm a handful.'

'You are. A lovely handful. Now let's ignore her and
dance.' So they danced some more and when the music
stopped, swayed as if still hearing the piano play.

'Hey, hey, hey! That's enough, I said,' shouted Maggie,
hoisting herself from her chair and making her way over
to them.

'It was nice while it lasted,' said Davey, and pressed
his lips against Rosie's again. He punched her lightly on
the chin. 'Take care of yourself, kiddo. See you around.'
He blew Maggie a kiss and was gone.

'Cheeky monkey,' growled the old woman. 'Dancing
like he was Jimmy Cagney.'

'He was just messing, Gran. You know what lads are
like.' Rosie linked her arm through the old woman's. 'Are
you tired?'

'Aye, me bones are weary and I'm ready to go up the dancers.'

'Then let's go in. We've still got things to talk about.'

'Not tonight, girl. Me head's full of noise,' she grumbled. 'I'm in need of a bit of peace.'

Rosie wondered whether to go back to Amelia's or not. In the comfort of her own bed, she would have time to think and work out what best to do.

But it appeared there was no doubt in Maggie's mind that Rosie should stay the night. 'We'll discuss things in the morning, girl,' she gasped, dragging herself upstairs by the banister rail. 'Unless yous have to go rushing off like a lap dog to Miss Toffy Nose in West Derby?'

Rosie thought of Amelia looking at the clock then her watch, going to the door and gazing up at the night sky, seething because she had no idea where her niece was. 'No, Gran,' she said. 'But I'll have to go tomorrow, what ever I decide.'

'Aye. Yous'll have to fetch yer belongings. Yous can take the middle room. There's a bed in there. But yous'll have to make it up.' She patted Rosie's arm. 'Yer can bring me up breakfast in bed. There's a nice piece of saltfish in that 'fridgerator. Put it in soak now and it'll be ready to boil first thing in the morning with some nice bread and butter. See yous then.' The door closed in Rosie's face.

She turned and ran lightly downstairs, found the saltfish and put it in soak, mind still in a whirl. It was not until she went back upstairs and was undressing that she thought of Davey and the kisses that seemed to linger on her mouth

still. 'See you around,' he had said. But he wouldn't if
she wasn't living here . . .

She made up the bed and slid beneath the covers: 'To
sleep, Perchance to dream'. Would she dream of dancing
with Davey? How quickly her feelings had changed
towards him. She pressed her cheek against the pillow,
prayed for Harry, Babs and Dotty, and after the day she
had had, fell asleep immediately.

Rosie woke early and made Maggie's breakfast and took
it up. The bedroom was full of heavy dark furniture. 'Oak,'
said her grandmother, already sitting up in bed with a
multicoloured shawl draped round her shoulders. 'I had
some nice stuff before. Went up like that matchstick factory
out past Bootle during the Blitz. Don't burn any different
in the end, however much it cost. This lot was Emily's.
Yous made up yer mind yet, girl? I'll tell yer what I'll
expect of yous: yer'll leave school as yous said and work
for me in the shop.'

'Will you pay me?'

'Yous'll have yer keep.'

Rosie frowned. 'Not good enough, Gran. I have to have
some money for myself. I need to save.'

'Ah, well, perhaps I can spare five bob a week,' she
said mildly.

Rosie realised the old woman was testing her. Aunt
Amelia had only given her a shilling for working all day
Saturday, saying she was getting valuable training which
some would give their right arm for. 'And my keep still?'

'Aye. But I'll need help in the house, as I've said.'

Rosie thought she would be able to save if she was careful and maybe there would be other ways of earning money. It was a waste of her education but when Gran died . . . She did not think further than that because it made her feel uncomfortably like a gold-digger. But it would be worth working her fingers to the bone if her grandmother had money and left it to her.

'OK,' she said. 'I'll come and live here.'

Maggie's wrinkled face, almost as brown as a russet apple from all her years of working in the open, split into a smile. 'Now yer talking! Yous go off now and tell Miss Toffee Nose what yous have decided.'

Said like that it sounded simple, but Rosie knew it was not going to be easy at all. Still, at least she would have the pleasure of seeing the anger and chagrin in her aunt's face when Rosie revealed she was going to go completely against her wishes.

Chapter Eight

'In!' said Amelia with a jerk of the head, flinging the door open before Rosie could knock. Her aunt was wearing one of Violet's dresses in a deep lavender-blue with a low-cut neckline. The girl had never seen her dressed in anything which suited her so well and it annoyed her no end. 'I'm not even going to begin to play your game by asking why you stayed out all night,' said Amelia. 'Dotty's here and the—'

'Dotty? You didn't tell me she was coming!' said Rosie.

'I would have if you hadn't gone trolling off dressed to the nines. The Hudsons are expected any minute. Now move yourself!' Amelia shoved her in the direction of the kitchen.

Rosie dug in her heels. 'What did Dotty tell you?'

'I'm not going to discuss this now. I'd appreciate it if you would start thinking of other people instead of yourself. Find out what's worrying her for a start, before she slips down a grid.'

'I know what's worrying her,' said Rosie fiercely. 'She hates St Vincent's.'

'She might have told you that but I don't believe it. Mother Superior says she's doing very well, and soon she'll be fitted with a pair of spectacles. She gets on all right with the other girls. It's true she's a bit timid still, but she has made a friend. Going anywhere strange can be hard at first.'

Rosie frowned. 'She didn't tell me she'd made a friend.'

'*You* didn't tell me you'd met her and Sam Dixon in the cemetery.'

'She told you *that*?' Rosie groaned, wondering what Dotty was thinking of, telling Amelia their secrets.

'And why shouldn't she? What have you to hide?' She stared down into her niece's cross face but when Rosie did not say any more, said only, 'It can wait. You can help me in the kitchen. I'm cooking a proper meal.'

'But what about the victory party? I thought we'd just be having a snack.'

'You can forget the party. I told you, the Hudsons are coming. Peter and I have a lot to discuss before the wedding.'

'When's that to be?'

'June. And if you behave yourself, you can be a bridesmaid along with Dotty.'

Rosie was stunned. Then she pulled herself together. 'Why should I want to be your bridesmaid?' she said with a look of disdain.

Amelia raised one eyebrow. 'You ungrateful little madam! Don't, if you feel like that then. I can always bring someone in off the street to accompany Dotty down the aisle.'

'If you put it like that, I suppose I'll have to,' said Rosie, flushing, thinking that so far she had not been able to say one word she had rehearsed.

'How gracious of you,' said Amelia. 'Go and help your sister set the table.'

Rosie went into the morning room, knowing that now was hardly the time to mention her grandmother.

'Where have you been?' whispered Dotty, sidling up to her. 'Did you go to Mrs Baxendale's? I told Aunt Amelia that's where you might be.' She glanced through the open doorway at her aunt, who was taking a roasting dish out of the oven.

'What did you have to tell her anything for?' said Rosie irritably, trying to come to terms with Amelia asking *her* to be a bridesmaid.

'Because she was talking about going to the police station and I was made up with her thinking to include me in this dinner with the Hudsons.' Dotty's eyes shone in a face made more elfin by the cropped hairstyle. 'And guess what? I'm coming to stay for the whole of the summer holidays and when I go back she said she'll arrange with Mother Superior that I can come here weekends because it's so close.' Her voice was dreamy. 'Isn't that good, Rosie? We'll see each other regularly then. That's unless Mrs Baxendale said she would take you in?'

'No, she's got a lodger,' murmured Rosie, feeling sick to the stomach. How dare Aunt Amelia be nice to Dotty when Maggie wouldn't have her?

Dotty sighed happily. 'That's OK then.'

'No, it isn't,' said Rosie, taking the smile off her sister's face. 'I'm going to live with Gran.'

Dotty peered at her in dismay. 'You can't!'

'I can!' Rosie's eyes glinted with annoyance. 'Have you forgotten what Aunt Amelia's done to Harry and Babs?'

'She said it was for their own good.' Dotty was eager to reassure Rosie. 'And she knows how we both feel. She said it was really hard saying goodbye to Aunt Iris because she'd looked after her since Grandmother died.'

'I don't care what she said, Aunt Iris was grown up! You've let her get round you.'

Dotty's face fell and Rosie felt guilty. She was about to apologise when her sister squared her narrow shoulders in their new plaid frock with a lace collar, and said, 'So what? I feel happier now. Although I wish you weren't going to live with that old woman. Have you told Aunt Amelia yet? Has she said you can go?'

'I don't see how she can stop me,' said Rosie, tossing back her dark hair. 'I was sixteen a few weeks back, remember? But don't you go saying anything to her. I'll tell her in my own good time.'

'What are you two yapping on about?' said Amelia, poking her head through the doorway. 'The Hudsons will be here any minute and the pair of you haven't even set the table yet. Hurry!'

They hurried, Rosie realising she did not have to help her sister as much as she would have in the past. Which meant, little as she liked to admit it, Amelia was right and St Vincent's was doing Dotty good. Still, that did not make up for her sending Harry and Babs to Canada.

Rosie was just draining the potatoes when a rattling at the letter box heralded the arrival of the Hudsons. Without

thinking, she raced Dotty and Amelia to the front door and
beat them to it, untying the strings of her apron on the way.

'I hope we're not too early but I forgot if you said one
or two o'clock,' said Peter, caught in the act of polishing
the toes of his shoes on the back of his trousers. He
looked harassed. 'You can blame these two. They wouldn't
come in.'

'We were playing a game,' said Tom. 'Anyway, we're
here now.' He smiled, hair slicked down with water, face
scrubbed shining clean.

'You've come at exactly the right time,' said Amelia
softly. 'Come in.'

The girls stood aside as the Hudsons stepped over the
threshold. It felt like an invasion, thought Rosie.

'Peter, I don't think you've met my eldest niece.'
Amelia urged her forward.

'But I have.' They shook hands, Rosie unable to
disguise the pleasure she felt at seeing him again.

'You never said,' said Amelia, feeling slightly put out.

'I thought she'd have told you?'

'I forgot,' said Rosie, hanging on to his hand.

Amelia nudged her. 'Dotty, you definitely haven't met
Mr Hudson, have you?'

'No. Hello, Mr Hudson,' said the girl shyly.

'Hello, Dotty.' He smiled, shaking her hand.

'I've met you,' said Chris in a teasing voice. 'And you
told me a fib. You *are* at St Vincent's.'

Colour flushed Dotty's pale skin. Glancing at Amelia,
she said, 'I didn't want anyone to know. I thought he'd
take me back.'

'You've embarrassed the girl, Chris,' said Peter.

'I didn't mean to.' The youth coloured to the roots of his hair.

'Well, think next time.'

Chris looked sulky.

'Let's eat,' said Amelia, leading the way.

They were all soon seated round the table except for Amelia, who was busy forking succulent moist ham on to their plates. Rosie was handing round potatoes and tinned peas.

'Have you got a wishing wand?' said Peter, smiling. 'Where did you manage to get such ham?'

'A farmer I know – and I'll say no more than that except that I had to barter for it,' said Amelia. 'Everyone needs a treat now and then.'

'Hear, hear,' said Tom, chin on the table, eyeing his plate at close quarters.

Rosie thought of the box of goodies Sam had given her and wished she had not given them all to her grandmother.

As if Dotty had read her mind, she said, 'Sam gave us chocolate.'

'Who's Sam?' asked Chris, gazing at her.

She avoided his eyes and addressed Peter. 'He was married to Mam. Did you know Mam?'

Peter looked towards Amelia. 'I thought she was married to a Joe?'

'She was,' put in Rosie, placing the serving dish in the middle of the table. 'He was my dad. Sam's a Yank. He was Mam's second husband.'

'He's stationed at Burtonwood,' said Amelia. 'Younger than Violet and a well-kept secret. He comes from Chicago.'

'You see much of him?'

Amelia smiled. 'Once since the funeral. We were both putting flowers on the grave.'

'*You* never said!' said Rosie, put out.

Amelia sent her a cool glance as she slipped into a seat opposite Peter. 'I forgot. Now shall we say Grace?'

The twins nudged each other but at a look from their father subsided and put their hands together.

Prayers said, everyone began to eat and no one spoke for at least five minutes. Then Rosie, feeling sorry for Chris, who still looked downcast, asked him to tell her something about Lord Sefton's ancestry.

He went red with pleasure and said eagerly and with assurance, 'Oh, the Seftons have been around for hundreds of years. The present one was Lord in Waiting to the King's brother before his abdication.'

'I never realised we had a lord that close. Did you, Dotty?' said Rosie, seeking to draw her sister into the conversation and get her over her embarrassment.

'I know his family used to own the land where the Grand National's run,' ventured Dotty, picking at her food and not taking her eyes off her plate. 'I heard one of the Irish girls saying so. Her father owns a race horse.'

'The family name is Molyneux and they're supposed to have crossed over with the Conqueror,' said Amelia.

'That doesn't exactly endear them to me,' murmured Rosie. 'His lot pillaged, raped and burnt half of England.'

'Well said,' said Peter, looking amused. 'I know they owned huge tracts of land.'

'The Seventh Viscount was a Jesuit priest who renounced the estate in favour of his brother,' said Amelia, determined to get the conversational ball back in her corner, away from Rosie who was reminding her more of Violet by the minute. 'That was in the eighteenth century. It was his son whose wife persuaded him to desert the true faith and curry favour with one of the Georges. By doing so he ended up an earl and entertained a king of France.'

'That would be before the revolution, I take it?' said Rosie.

'Of course,' said Amelia, frowning at her niece.

'What's a revolution?' asked Jimmy.

'It's when the peasants revolt. In France, they chopped the heads off the king and queen,' said Rosie.

'Perhaps it was a ghost we saw, then,' said Tom, arm going round his twin's neck. 'Maybe he haunts the Hall?' he added with relish.

'Don't say that!' Dotty shivered.

Rosie winked at the twins. 'Dotty's been told St Vincent's is haunted.'

Thomas paused in the act of trying to cut off all the blood to his brother's brain. 'Have you seen it? Does it wail and drag its chains like this?' He threw back his head and howled, waving his arms about. Jimmy followed suit. Dotty put her hands over her ears.

'Stop it, you two,' ordered Peter, frowning. 'Or Aunt Lee won't want us to come and live here.'

'Fat chance of that,' murmured Rosie.

Her aunt glared at her and Rosie hurriedly went to fetch the blancmange for the next course.

For the rest of the afternoon, Rosie watched Peter and Amelia, but as time wore on she could see nothing of the lover in his behaviour. *What kind of marriage of convenience would it be?* The thought that they *mightn't* sleep together somehow made her feel better about the whole thing.

The Hudsons left shortly after five and it was then Rosie told Amelia about her plan to live with her grandmother.

'You're what?' demanded her aunt, slamming the cutlery drawer shut and leaning against it. 'Have you run mad?'

'I don't know why you should say that.' Rosie twiddled her thumbs, resting her back against the stove, not meeting her aunt's gaze.

'Then you *are* mad. And look at me when I'm talking to you.'

Rosie lifted her head. 'You're always preaching duty to me. So I thought it *was* my duty to go and look after her.'

'You're a liar! You're just trying to get back at me for sending Harry and Babs away.' Amelia flicked at a fly with the tea towel. 'But it won't work. You go. As long as you turn up for work on Saturday.'

'I can't do that. I'm sorry, Aunt Amelia, but—'

'You're not sorry at all.'

'I am! But I won't be going to school any more. I'll be working for Gran in her shop.'

The muscles of Amelia's face tightened and her eyes were as hard as flint. 'And what and where would this shop be?'

'Not far from where I used to live,' said Rosie, tilting her chin. 'She sells groceries.'

'I see. Pack your things.'

That startled her. 'But—'

'But nothing. Do it! I'm coming with you.'

'Coming with me?' squeaked Rosie. The last thing she wanted was her aunt setting eyes on her grandmother's poky little back-room shop.

'Yes. You've no objections, have you?' Amelia's eyebrows elevated in that speaking way which Rosie hated.

'Gran will,' she said. 'You know you don't get on.'

'Well, we'll just have to try, won't we?' said Amelia sweetly. 'Now, move!'

Rosie swore under her breath. Not one thing had gone as she had planned.

Maggie was in the shop, tidying shelves and muttering to herself when they arrived. Immediately, she turned on Rosie as she entered a little ahead of Amelia. 'And what time's this to be coming in? I expected yer hours ago.'

'Sorry, Gran, but I've brought a visitor,' said Rosie with a grimace.

'A visitor?' growled her grandmother. 'I don't want any visitors.'

'Good evening, Mrs Kilshaw.' Amelia stood in the doorway, filling the shop with her flowery perfume. 'Rosie, leave us.'

Maggie looked taken aback but made a fine recovery. 'Here now, who do yer think yous are, telling her to go?

Under my roof she does what I say. You want to speak to me? Be sharp about it, Miss Hoity-Toity.'

Amelia's nostrils flared as if scenting something distasteful and a muscle quivered in her cheek. 'Rosie is to stay on at school. I'll let her come and live with you but she works for me full-time once she leaves school. Is that understood?'

Rosie stared at her dumbfounded. Maggie spluttered, 'No, it bleedin' isn't! What good is she to me under them terms?'

'I'd have thought it was obvious. But if that's all you've got to say, we'll say goodbye now. Come on, Rosie,' said Amelia.

'Hang on! What is this? What right have yous to keep my granddaughter from me?' said Maggie.

'I told you last time – and I'll not have her wasting a good education in this dump.' Amelia's gaze swept disparagingly over the shelves and counter.

'Dump?' Maggie's tone was scandalised. 'Who are you to be calling my little shop a dump?' Her eyebrows bristled and she clenched her fists as if ready to square up to Amelia. 'A little goldmine this is!'

'Fool's gold more like. Rosie, come.'

'Hey, hey, hey!' Maggie seized hold of the girl's sleeve. 'Yer not going to walk out on me, girl. Yer not going to let her talk to your old gran like that? Yer know how bad I am on me pins. Tell her yer want to work here!'

'It's no use talking to her like that. She only stays on my terms,' said Amelia firmly.

Maggie looked at her with dislike. 'I suppose she could help me in the evenings – when me legs swell up like balloons because I've been on them all day.'

'Excuse me while I get out the violin.'

'I don't mind doing that.' Rosie managed to get in a word edgeways.

'That's up to you. But you have to get through your exams and do well.' Amelia picked off an invisible thread from her coat sleeve. 'Mrs Kilshaw has to understand that. I'll be keeping in touch with the school to make sure you keep your head down.'

Rosie was horrified. 'Don't you trust me? I'll do it if I say so.'

'See that you do. Now I'm going. I'll expect to see you the Sunday after next, Rosie. That'll give you time to settle in and see how things go. Good evening, Mrs Kilshaw.' And Amelia inclined her head and walked out.

'Bleeding cheek!' said Maggie, stomping into the kitchen and lowering herself into a chair. She dropped her chin in her hands, gazing broodingly at the fireplace.

Rosie thought it best not to speak and tiptoed across the room to the other door with the suitcase which Amelia had overseen her packing.

'And where are yous going?' growled Maggie.

'To unpack, Gran.'

Maggie muttered something under her breath but before Rosie could creep out a bell jangled. 'You come back here!' ordered her grandmother, hoisting herself up out of the chair and beckoning Rosie to follow her.

In the tiny shop stood a woman dressed in a shabby winter coat and wearing a headscarf. There were shadows beneath her eyes and she had a child in her arms and another clinging to her coat-tails. She cast a furtive glance at Rosie, who recognised her and immediately felt ashamed for her.

'I'll come back another time,' whispered the woman, turning about.

'Don't be a fool, Gertie,' chided Maggie, clawing her back. 'This is me granddaughter who's come to live with me, so yer'd best get used to her being around. She knows to keep mum.'

'I didn't know . . . I didn't realise,' muttered the woman, hanging her head. 'I was sorry about your mam, girl. She was a right laugh. She'll be missed.'

Rosie thanked her and would have retreated as far from the counter as she could, but Maggie seized her arm. 'Now take note, Rosie girl. I'll want yous here every evening so I can rest me carcass. Right now yer going to be me hands and feet.' She turned to Gertie. 'Give us yer list and we'll get cracking.'

Rosie was to get cracking several times that evening and was kept so busy she began to wonder how she was to fit in cleaning, polishing, cooking, working in the shop, school *and* homework. Would she be expected to do the washing as well? Maggie eased her mind on that score, telling her the big wash went to the laundry every Monday. But Rosie was glad in a way that Amelia had laid down the law. Working in the little shop day in, day out, would soon have bored her to tears. It was a relief to think that come summer she would be back in the chemist's shop, learning pharmacy from Mr Brown.

In the days that followed, Rosie often felt disorientated and tired. When she came in from school she cooked the evening meal, washed up and helped in the shop, which stayed open until ten o'clock. Saturday was taken up with scrubbing the front step and the back yard and being available to help in the shop. She wondered what Maggie would say when it came to Sunday, expecting her grandmother to kick up a fuss at the idea of her seeing her aunt.

On Sunday morning, Rosie was weighing out sugar and sealing it in blue bags, wondering how best to broach the subject, when her grandmother told her she had done enough and handed her a shilling. 'You've worked well, girl, and without complaint. That pleases me. Don't come back until suppertime. I've a visitor coming.'

Exhilarated by the sudden freedom, money, and not having to mention where she was going, Rosie tore out of the back door, racing down the entry past the laundry which Mondays to Saturdays filled the air with billows of steam and the gorgeous smell of fresh washing, to catch the tram.

At 'Eden' the front door was opened by a tousle-haired Amelia wearing slacks and a Fair Isle jumper. She looked so different from the last time Rosie had seen her that for a moment the girl was tongue-tied, not sure how to react.

'So you remembered?' said Amelia. 'Come in quickly. I've the twins in the back and I want to measure you up for a frock. Later we have to go to St Vincent's.'

'St Vincent's? A frock?'

'Bridesmaid! You haven't changed your mind again.'
There was a hint of the old Amelia in her tone of voice.

'No,' said Rosie. 'Is Mr Hudson here?'

Amelia gave her a sharp look. 'No. He's at home. He's
got a lot of sorting out to do before the wedding.'

Rosie was disappointed. 'Does he need any help?'

Amelia glanced over her shoulder at her and did not
answer immediately, leading the way into the sitting room
where the French windows were open and the sounds of
the twins playing Cowboys and Indians wafted through
on the still air. 'I think he'll manage on his own now the
twins are out the way.' Amelia dragged a tape measure
from her sewing basket.

'It's a good job he's marrying you, isn't it? I mean, having
you take the twins out of his hair is so *convenient*.'

Amelia's eyes searched her face. 'I think he realises
that. Come over here.'

Rosie submitted to having her measurements taken,
wondering how Amelia could be so dispassionate about
her remark. She *must* like Peter a lot to have agreed to
marry him. After all, her aunt had her own house and the
shop bringing in an income. The girl wondered whose
idea it was to have a marriage of convenience.

'You're shaping up nicely,' murmured Amelia. 'Dot is
so much thinner. That's why I want you to come to
St Vincent's with me once Evensong is over. Chris should
be here by then. I've mentioned this before but I'll say it
again: get Dotty to talk to you. Her work's fine but she
seems to be withdrawing into herself. Find out what's

wrong – and don't tell me she hates the place. It's more than that. It's something deeper.'

'We have lost our mother and our sister and our brother,' said Rosie. 'Don't you think it might be that?'

'Maybe. We'll see.'

Rosie was silent as they walked along the lane and up the driveway to the school; mentioning her mother and thinking of Babs and Harry had brought the early months of the year vividly to mind. Since she had lived with her grandmother, she had not had time to feel miserable, but now she felt down again.

St Vincent's was a red-brick building with a statue of the saint set in a niche high up in the wall. Rosie could hear children playing and wondered how they coped with being blind. Dotty had said many of them were far from home and family. If they could cope, why couldn't she?

While Amelia was speaking to the Mother Superior, Rosie was escorted to the playground. She was amazed to see the girls pushing, shoving, chatting, playing tig – but could not see Dotty anywhere. The nun who had accompanied her called over one of the girls.

'Margaret, would you be so kind as to find Dorothy? This is her sister come to see her.'

'She's probably in the orchard. Shall I show her the way, Sister?'

The girl wore spectacles with lenses so thick her eyes appeared huge behind them. She indicated Rosie should follow her. 'I'm partially sighted like Dotty. And, like her, I can find my way to the orchard. She's lucky! Most of us never have visitors and seldom go further than a walk to the shops.' She sighed. 'We're not allowed to mix with the boys here, either.' She sighed. 'Lackaday! Here's the orchard. Doesn't it smell lovely?' She breathed in deeply and danced away over the grass back to the playground.

It *was* lovely. Hearing bees, Rosie glanced up at the pink blossom-laden branches of the apple trees and felt sad for those children who could not see how beautiful the world was when it was like this. She held up her arms as if in supplication. Then, catching sight of her sister sitting in the grass with her back against a tree trunk, went over to her, feet making no sound on the turf.

'Go away!' shouted Dotty.

'It's me, Rosie!'

'I know it's you. I heard your voice. I'm not deaf,' she muttered.

Rosie sank on to the ground next to her. 'What a lovely little orchard. It's a bit different from our old street, isn't it?'

'I was happy there.' Dotty's chin rested on her bent knees.

'Me too, most of the time. But we can't go back.'

There was silence, then Dotty began to hum tunelessly.

'What's wrong?' said Rosie gently.

'I hate this place.'

'Aunt Amelia says that's a lie.'

'What does she know about it? She's never been blind or had to stay here.'

'No, but—'

'How's the old granny? Tell me how you're getting on?'

'It's hard work and she's a grouch.'

'I don't know why you want to live with her.'

Rosie thought of Maggie's alleged fortune but was not going to mention that to her sister. It would seem mercenary. 'I told you why. Are you looking forward to the wedding? The material for our frocks is nice, isn't it?'

'It's only pink cotton,' said Dotty. 'Have you seen *her* frock yet?'

'No. Have you?'

'I asked her about it but she said she hadn't sorted anything out yet. It seemed funny to me.'

Rosie was silent, thinking how nice it would be to have a new frock.

'I suppose I should go and see the old granny?' burst out Dotty.

'Why? You said she was an old witch.' Rosie rolled over on to her stomach and gazed up into her sister's thin, strained face. She suddenly felt terribly sorry for her. 'What is it, honeybun?' she said gently. 'Tell your big sister and I'll do my best to help. Things mightn't be as bad as you think.'

Dotty opened her mouth, closed it, swallowed, opened it again. 'I'm going blind,' she said baldly.

For a moment, Rosie could not speak, shocked to the core. 'Who says?'

'Nobody says but I know,' said Dotty in a choking voice. 'Mary! Sh-she's partially sighted like me but they're training her on the Braille machine for when she loses her sight. So it's better I go and see the old witch now before I can't.'

'Of course you can come and see her,' said Rosie hurriedly, not sure what to make of her sister's words. Surely Aunt Amelia would know if Dotty was going blind? She squeezed her sister's hand. 'I'll ask Aunt Amelia about it. She'll sort it out.'

'Thanks. And you will come and see me again?'

'If I can.' Rosie kissed and hugged her, holdly her tightly.

It had gone nine o'clock by the time Rosie arrived home. Her grandmother was waiting for her, black shawl over rounded shoulders, arms akimbo across her sagging bosom. 'And what time d'yer think this is to be coming in, miss?'

'Sorry. But you told me not to come back until supper,' said Rosie. 'Shall I put the kettle on?'

'I can bleeding put me own kettle on. Where've yer been?'

'You know where I've been. I saw Dotty. She wants to come and visit you next Sunday.'

Maggie appeared mollified by that but said, 'Not Sunday, girl. I have me visitor coming again and I don't want yer hanging around. As soon as Dotty gets here, yous can go and have a nice walk to the Pierhead.'

'But she wanted to see you,' said Rosie patiently.

'Well, she can say hello and go.'

Rose gave up. 'If that's what you want.'

'And how's Miss Toffee Nose?'

'Preparing for the wedding – which I'll have to go to, Gran.'

'Humph! As long as yous don't start looking down on me, comparing me to her.'

'You're Dad's mam. We're part of each other.'

Maggie grunted. 'Just as long as you remember, girl, I'm doing yer a favour letting yous live here. Yous treat me with respect, d'yer hear?'

'I hear,' she said, wondering how her grandmother worked out all the favours were on her side.

Rosie was thinking about that and the wedding when she bumped into Davey a few days later on the way home from school.

'Long time no see,' he said, braking in front of her. 'I thought you might have been round by now.'

'I thought you might have been round to me,' she said with a toss of the head, heart fluttering at the sight of him. 'You know where I live.'

'I called but your gran wasn't very welcoming. Even when I came bearing gifts.'

Rosie slid her satchel off her shoulder and leant against a garden fence. 'She never said.'

'Honest?'

'Cross my heart and hope to die.' She genuflected. 'Anyway, what gifts are you talking about?'

'The Yank. Set Ma's pulses racing, I can tell you. Not much to write home about, *I* think, but *she* reckons he's got charm.'

'When was this?'

'Monday.'

Rosie's face registered annoyance. 'The old faggot! I bet she's put them in the shop. How dare she? I could have given something to Dotty.' She clenched her fists, seething with anger. 'I'm going to have words with her.' She hoisted the satchel back on her shoulder. 'Thanks, Davey. Be seeing you.' She marched off as if to war.

'Anytime,' he murmured, taking a cigarette from behind his ear and putting it in his mouth.

Rosie bounced into the house and found Maggie in the shop, leaning over the counter, her head close to that of a customer. The girl wondered whose reputation they were tearing to pieces this time.

'Go and put the kettle on, girl,' said Maggie, shooing her away.

'I'd rather wait here.' Rosie's voice was cold.

The customer stared at her. 'The cheek! I know what I'd do, Maggie, if one of mine dared speak to me like that.'

'Well, I'm not one of yours, am I?' said Rosie. 'Thank God.'

The woman raised her eyes ceilingwards. 'College education! It does them no good. I'm going, Maggie. I'll see you tomorrow and tell yer the rest then.'

Even before she had closed the door, Maggie turned on Rosie. 'Don't yous ever make a show of me like that again, girl! Or yous'll be wishing the final trump had already sounded.'

'You don't frighten me,' she said scornfully, folding her arms. 'I've got a bone to pick with you, Gran. Why didn't you tell me Davey had called and brought a box of goodies?'

Maggie's eyes blinked rapidly and she put her hands beneath her large bosom and heaved it up like an enormous jelly. 'Box of goodies! Aye. Fine goings-on, my granddaughter having relations with a Yank.'

'I am not!'

'Arrh, don't you be lying now. Yerra dark horse. Not a word to me about him. Making out instead yer carrying on with that lad when all the time it's a Yank yer seeing.'

Rosie was incensed. 'Sam was Mam's Yank, so there!'

Her grandmother gasped and put a hand to her bosom. 'So you think that makes everything fine and dandy? Yous is your mother's daughter, all right! And a highty-flighty flibbertigibbet she was!'

'Don't you speak of Mam like that! She loved us and Dad. She'd never have cut us off like you did Dad, whatever we did!' blazed Rosie, sweeping tins off a shelf. 'And I'm not surprised Granddad left you if you treated him like you did Dad. I just wish he was here now. I'd give him plenty of love. Anyway, Mam was married to Sam so put *that* in your pipe and smoke it!'

Maggie's expression was ugly and for several moments she did not speak. Then her features relaxed. 'Well, you *are* in a paddy. I'd have had a smack around the chops if I'd dared speak to my elders and betters like that. But maybe yer get yer temper from me. I used to enjoy a good barney and so did Walt, but I can't take it the way I used to. Let's be forgetting what we've both said. You make a cuppa and we'll have a tin of tongue from the box.' She limped out of the shop. 'Luv!' she muttered. 'What does someone your age know about life and luv?'

'More than you,' called Rosie. 'And I want to give Dotty some cookies,' she said firmly. 'And Aunt Amelia a tin of salmon to help with the wedding breakfast.'

'A tin of—' Maggie clamped her mouth shut, then cleared her throat. 'So yer mam was married to the Yank?' she said. 'Well, I suppose in that case her side of the family's entitled to something. Yer've a kind heart. But the next time that Yank calls on that boyfriend of yours, tell him he's welcome to visit here. I'd like to pay my respects.'

Over my dead body, thought Rosie, eyeing her grandmother with suspicion. She would stowaway to Canada first.

Chapter Nine

Amelia shuffled forward along the wooden strut, the beam of her torch lighting up the tea chest wedged next to a box of yellowed, dog-eared copies of *Lady* and *Queen* magazines. She thought of how her mother had shown her the illustrations of fashionable Edwardian ladies when she was a girl and had told her about her own wedding day.

Agnes Needham had been a June bride in 1907, and once upon a time Violet and Amelia had dressed up in Agnes's old clothes and played Let's Pretend. Violet had been six years older than her sister, their mother having suffered three miscarriages in the years between the births. Amelia had adored her elder sister in those days. She had been so full of life and laughter – it had not struck Amelia then that it was generally at someone else's expense.

Even so, when her sister had gone off with Joe, she had left a space which not even Iris had been able to fill. She had been too young to have shared in her elder sisters' activities in the years just after the Great War when they had lived in the rooms over the shop. It had been a different kind of life altogether there with the streets as their playground and lots of other children to play with. From babyhood, Iris had been spoilt and their mother over-protective and Amelia had carried on where Agnes had left off. Now she realised that perhaps Iris had missed out on something important: seeing how the other half lived. It would have been interesting to observe how she managed Babs and Harry. One thing Violet had never been was a snob.

Amelia sighed. Pulling herself up, she balanced precariously on the beam as she flashed the torch into the tea chest. Peter might not be her Prince Charming but she would be damned if she didn't make the best of her big day. She stuck the torch down the front of her blouse and delved into the chest, carefully peeling back sheets of tissue paper interleaved with crumbling sprigs of lavender to reveal fold upon fold of ivory-coloured crêpe-de-chine, which she knew to be trimmed with yards of lace made by Irish nuns. Her mother had been an accomplished needlewoman and had made the gown herself, although before marrying William Needham she had earned her living as a typist in a shipping office down by the docks. An avid follower of fashion, she had made her own 'waists' from muslin and broderie anglaise, which she had worn with long black serge skirts to the office.

Amelia held the gown against her. It was cut in a waterfall style, with tucks around the hips. The skirts brushed the dusty rafters of the loft as she swayed, humming a Viennese waltz. Then she sobered and stood perfectly still, head bent, wondering whether she was a fool for wanting to wear such a gown. A quiet wedding with a few carefully selected guests, they had both agreed. It was, after all, only a few months since Tess's death. A neat little lavender suit had been her original choice, having found such an outfit among Violet's clothes. But yesterday Amelia had found herself rebelling. She was getting married and wanted to celebrate climbing down from the shelf. She was fed up of people calling her a spinster. She wanted to knock them all dead!

She flung the gown over her shoulder and delved into the chest again, searching for the undergarments that Agnes had worn beneath her wedding gown that never-to-be-forgotten day in June. If she was going to fit into the dress, she would need the corset and petticoats to go with it. She would also need someone to help her dress and supposed it would have to be her eldest niece in the absence of her sister. She had never made another friend as close as Tess. She needed to get in touch with Rosie anyway. Two letters had arrived yesterday from Canada. One was from Iris, addressed to herself, and the other was for Rosie and presumably from Babs. Amelia only hoped it said all the right things to reassure her prickly niece that all was well with her brother and sister. She would redirect it tomorrow and ask Rosie to visit on Sunday.

Amelia gripped the board at the bottom of the bed and held her breath as Rosie pulled the corset laces tighter. 'Can you still breathe?' she asked, enjoying having been given permission to perform what she could only think of as torture on her aunt.

'Just about,' gasped Amelia, slowly exhaling. She felt as if she was encased in steel. Beneath the corset she wore a chemise tied with a drawstring ribbon over her bustline. 'I'll just have to starve myself from now to the wedding.'

'Why are you doing it?' asked Rosie, finding it hard to equate this woman with the aunt she had clashed with so often over the past few months. 'The pair of you aren't exactly love's young dream, are you?'

'You don't have to remind me,' said Amelia, frowning at her own reflection. 'And that's cheeky. Why is it the young think they're the ones with a monopoly on love? Pass me that camisole and tell me, are you happy now you've had a letter from Babs? Iris wrote to say that they're settling in very well.'

'She would, wouldn't she?' said Rosie, picking up a pair of knee-length drawers trimmed with ribbons and lace. 'Grownups always see things differently from children.'

Amelia turned round slowly. 'You mean, Babs says they're not?'

Rosie felt uncomfortable with her aunt staring straight at her because her own emotions had been in a turmoil ever since she had received the letter from her sister. It had been full of the exciting life she and Harry were leading, telling of shopping expeditions for clothes, toys, books, and about how spacious the house was and how plentiful the food. Rosie could not understand her own feelings because the letter had made her feel miserable instead of relieved that they weren't pining away for her and Liverpool. She did not know how to answer Amelia, not wanting to admit that perhaps she had done the right thing in sending them away. So instead she held up the drawers.

'Are you going to wear these? You'll have a job going to the lavatory if you do.'

Amelia continued to give her one of her basilisk stares but did not repeat her question. The girl's silence told her all she wanted to know. Suddenly, she felt sorry for Rosie, knowing what it felt like to be left behind.

'I've got a perfectly decent pair of cami-knickers,' she said, fastening the last button on the camisole with difficulty over breasts which were pushed upwards and out by the corset. She felt like an opera singer: all bosom. 'Petticoats?'

Rosie recovered her composure and picked up a blue taffeta one off a chair. There was also a white cotton one trimmed with blue bows and a red silk. 'All the sewing that must have gone into them,' she marvelled. 'And think of the ironing and washing!'

'They didn't wash everything. And those who had money, like Lord and Lady Sefton, for instance,' gasped Amelia, resting a hand on the back of the chair while she hoisted the petticoat over her hips, 'had servants to look after their clothes. Your grandmother told me white silk was never washed but cleaned by rubbing it with bread crumbs. And to get stains out of some materials, a mixture of Fuller's earth, ammonia and benzine was used.'

Rosie grimaced. 'They must have smelt pretty awful!'

Amelia managed a laugh. 'You can say that again! Mother said they'd hang the clothes out in the fresh air afterwards, but I should think the smell would still linger.' She straightened, breathing out cautiously then in again. 'Now help me with the gown.'

Almost reverently Rosie lifted the wedding gown from its hanger, trying to imagine the first time the dress had been worn. 'You're going to roast if it's a hot day,' she murmured.

'If Mother could do it, so can I,' said Amelia, as between them they eased the dress over her hips. She slipped her arms into the three-quarter-length sleeves, frilled at the elbows with lace. The neckline was high and had a mandarin-type collar. 'Now button me up.'

'This is some job,' said Rosie, starting on what appeared to be a couple of dozen tiny mother-of-pearl buttons. Every now and again, she peered over her aunt's shoulder into the mirror. When she had finished, neither of them spoke for several seconds.

Amelia, who was breathing shallowly in case any of the buttons should pop, was stunned by the vision which was herself. Rosie was equally impressed. 'You look . . .' She searched for the right word.

'Not a bit like myself?' murmured her aunt.

'No,' said Rosie frankly. 'You'll need to do something with your hair to match the look, though. Will you wear a veil?'

Amelia toyed with a loose strand of hair, wondering what Peter would make of her appearance. Probably think it too much, perhaps, but she did not care. 'No, I'll wear Mama's hat. It's that pale straw.'

Rosie picked up the hat, the brim of which was covered in artificial gardenias and cream roses. She was about to place it on Amelia's head when there was the sound of footsteps on the path below, then a rattling of the letter box.

'See who that is,' said Amelia, taking the hat from her.

Rosie went over to the window. 'It's Mr Hudson.'

'Oh – bother!' The words burst from Amelia and she dropped the hat. 'He can't see me like this. Rosie, undo me.' The girl came over to her. 'No!' Her aunt warded her off with a hand. 'You'd best let him in, in case he goes away again. We need to talk. Then come up here straight away and get me out of this dress. No lingering, and no making eyes at him,' she said rapidly.

Rosie gave her a look. 'I do not make eyes at men old enough to be my father,' she said in as dignified a manner as she could.

Amelia gave a strangled laugh and clasped her hands together. 'Oh, yes you do! And you're very pretty and I'm not blind. I remember your mother at your age, testing her charms on a friend of Father's before she met Joe.'

That was news to Rosie and it annoyed her. She had not needed to know that. Her eyes glinted. 'Don't start on Mam! You know how I feel when—'

There was another banging at the door. Amelia shoved her in the direction of the landing. 'Don't you start! He'll go away and I've told you, I need to talk to him. Hurry or he'll think I'm out.'

'I'm going, I'm going,' muttered Rosie, scowling as she left the room.

Peter was turning away even as she opened the door. 'Hello, Mr Hudson. Sorry to keep you waiting.'

'Oh, it's you, Rosie.' He gave a hint of a smile as he stepped over the threshold. She thought he looked harassed. His hair was untidy and he was not wearing a tie. 'I take it your aunt's around somewhere?'

'Upstairs, trying on a frock.' She twinkled up at him, knowing just how to get back at Amelia for starting on her mother. 'Come into the kitchen and I'll make you a cup of tea. She won't be long.'

'Good! I was dreading her not being in. I've left the twins playing out and I never know what they're going to get up to. Last week they put a ball through one of the neighbour's windows.'

'Chris at work?' She put on the kettle and leant against the sink.

'At this time of year he seems to work all the hours God sends.' Peter fiddled with a knife on the oilclothed table top. 'I don't know where he gets it from, wanting to work on a farm.'

'Nobody in your family in farming?'

He hesitated. 'Generations ago in Ireland. But that wasn't so unusual in the days before the Industrial Revolution. It was Tess's idea, though. Which surprised me because I thought she'd want him following in her footsteps.'

Rosie prodded him gently. 'In what way?'

'She studied for her secondary certificate, just like Lee. I thought she'd have wanted him to be a pharmacist.' He rasped a finger across his chin. 'But perhaps she knew what she was about after all.' His tone had altered.

'Is that how your wife met Aunt Amelia?' said Rosie.

'Yes. They should have been awarded their certificates in Pharmacy at the Apothecary Hall in Colquitt Street.'

'Your wife finished the course?' She flushed when he did not answer. 'Sorry. I'm being nosy. I know Aunt Amelia didn't because of family reasons.'

'Strong sense of duty, Lee,' he murmured. 'It wasn't easy for her breaking off her engagement, but your mother had married Joe, their mother was dead and Iris was only eight. But in the end I reckon she had a lucky escape.'

Curiosity overwhelmed Rosie. 'Did you know—' She clicked her tongue against her teeth, making out she had forgotten the fiancé's name when she had never known it. 'Whatshisname?'

'Bernard Rossiter? Oh yes, I knew him all right,' he said grimly. 'He used to come into the Post Office where I worked. He was a salesman for one of the big pharmacy suppliers in town; believed himself God's gift to women.'

'What did he look like?'

Peter did not answer but rose abruptly. 'What's Amelia doing up there? Trying on her whole blinking wardrobe?'

Blast! thought Rosie. *I've annoyed him now. And completely forgotten Aunt Amelia.* She dashed out of the kitchen and flew up the stairs.

'I could slay you,' said Amelia, eyes smouldering as she turned from the bookcase in the corner. 'Get me out of this quickly!'

'Sorry, Aunt Amelia. I didn't do it on purpose,' said Rosie, starting to undo buttons. 'We just got talking and I was so interested I forgot all about you.'

'I don't believe you. You think Peter's a bit of all right, don't you? That's why you lingered. If it wasn't that you sorted out that business of Dotty for me, I'd find someone else to fill your bridesmaid's shoes.'

'It doesn't bother me.' Rosie shrugged. 'I wonder, should I leave you in the corset?'

'Don't push me too far! I have enough on my plate at the moment without you getting even more uppity than usual. Now hurry up before I faint.'

Rosie grinned. She began to unlace the corset. 'What happened to your ex-fiancé?'

'He married someone else within the year,' muttered Amelia. Then she tried to twist round. 'How d'you know about him? Have you been talking to Peter about me? Or did our Violet tell you about Bernard?' She glanced over her shoulder at the girl. 'No, she wouldn't, not having an ounce of shame.'

Rosie's eyes glinted. '*Mr Hudson* seems to think you had a lucky escape.'

'Mr Hudson would.' There was a flush on her cheeks. 'Hurry up, Rosie. He's waiting.'

Rosie took her time, humming a martial air.

Amelia simmered but at last she could breathe freely and told Rosie to get out while she changed. 'In fact,' she added, 'you can go back to your grandmother's and leave us in peace.'

Rosie did not need telling a second time; there was a look in her aunt's eye that told her she was in danger of exploding.

Amelia found Peter in the garden, seemingly fascinated by a huge clump of sage. She felt vexed with him for having discussed her and Bernard with Rosie but tried not to show her annoyance. 'Do you know there's an old wife's tale that where sage flourishes the woman rules the roost?' Her tone belied her mood.

'Is that what this is?' He touched the plant with the toe of his shoe.

'Yes.' She gazed at him. He looked dishevelled and tired. Her annoyance evaporated. 'What's wrong?'

A dimple in his cheek made a brief appearance. 'Tess always said you were perceptive.'

'Not always perceptive enough, wouldn't you say?'

He stared at her. 'I need your help.'

'In what way?' She laced her fingers behind her back, wanting to know what he had told Rosie about Bernard, but uncertain how to bring the subject up. 'I really should get Chris to come and help me with this garden,' she commented. 'The weeds are getting out of hand.'

'I'm sure he'll help. Rosie and I were talking about him. Do you know why Tess encouraged him to become a farm labourer?'

'No.' She hesitated. 'I believe you discussed me and Bernard with her?'

'I wouldn't call it a discussion,' he said, frowning. 'She asked did I know him. I said he used to come into the Post Office.'

'You told her I had a lucky escape.'

'It's the truth,' he said harshly, digging his hands in his pockets. 'I hope you're not still carrying a torch for him, Lee. Because if you are, we might as well—'

'How can you think that after what happened?'

'OK! Forget I spoke. Anyway, we've more important things to talk about.'

'You've changed your mind about us getting married?'

'No! Would I have said what I've just said if that was it? It's Tess's clothes. I have to get rid of them.'

'I see.'

'And I'm starting at the Post Office in Tuebrook on Monday. It's not what I want but it's what I know.' His eyes, dark as rain on slate, rested on her face.

She was aware of a restlessness in him. 'What do you want?' she said softly. 'I know the war's caused lots of people to want things different.'

'I've responsibilities. I have to earn a living the best way I know how. The boys' stuff!'

He hadn't answered her question but she let it go. 'Have you sorted it out?'

Peter's expression lightened. 'They've all kinds of rubbish they want to hang on to. Cigarette cards, birds' eggs, cotton reels, bits of old blanket.' His smile faded and he dug his hands into his pockets, jingling the loose change. 'Will you come and sort Tess's things out for me? I can't face it.'

Amelia did not feel like facing it either but she had not been married to Tess, sharing her life intimately. She remembered what her friend had written in that last letter. Had she told Peter that she had never loved him? Could she have told him who Chris's father was? How much had Peter cared for Tess at the end when her letter had arrived? She wished she knew but could not question him about such things.

'Perhaps we should do it together?' she asked lightly.

He was still, only his eyes moving to meet hers. 'Remember that scent she used to wear?'

'Devonshire Violets.' Amelia only had to think of it to see Tess's face. Her heart felt sore. Despite everything, she could almost wish her friend alive again, laughing over a shared joke. Tess had loved flowers and had often said she wished she could afford a house like this one.

'It lingers,' muttered Peter, 'and I hate it.'

Amelia stared at him and knew Tess had been brutally honest. *Oh, Tess!* she thought, angry now. She touched his arm. 'I'll come right away. Best get it over with.'

When they arrived at the house the twins, who had been swinging from a lamp post, followed them indoors and upstairs. Amelia knew it would not do. It would surely upset them, seeing their mother's clothes being sorted out.

'Out of here, I'll see to it,' she said softly.

Peter's relief was obvious but still he said, 'Are you sure?'

'Go and help the twins pack.' She pushed him towards the door but he turned, expression warm as he gripped both her arms. 'Thanks, Lee. You're one in a million.' He brushed her lips with his own before closing the door behind him.

Amelia stared at it. She had not expected that. Although there had once been a time, after she'd finished with her fiancé Bernard and before Peter had married Tess, when their eyes would meet across a room and they'd smile. She had known there could have been something between them if things had been different. She gnawed on her lip, considering how much she liked Peter but also remembering how she had felt when she had found him in her bedroom. Holy Mary, Mother of God! She was all mixed up, wanting but not wanting at the same time some of the changes marriage to him would bring.

She went over to the wardrobe and began removing Tess's clothes. As she got on with the task of separating clothes for the ragman from those she could give to Mrs Wilcox, who rented the flat above the shop, she was remembering Tess wearing a certain frock, and knew that until her friend became a distant memory – instead of the ever-present ghost she seemed to be now – any intimacy with Peter was out of the question.

'Where's my clean knickers? I remember distinctly putting them down on this bed,' said Dotty, gazing at Rosie through thick pebble lenses.

'Don't look at me!' Rosie was carefully drawing lines up the back of her legs. She wished she had thought to remove the nylon stockings from that first box of goodies Sam had given to her, knowing now that Maggie must have sold them. If he should ever shower gifts on her again, she was going to make sure her grandmother did not get her hands on them. She had been down to Davey's house and told his mother exactly how the land lay and they had come to an agreement.

'Then where are they?' said Dotty, scratching her head.

Five months ago, Rosie would have looked for her. 'Feel under the bed.'

'They shouldn't be under there,' said Dotty, getting down on her knees and feeling round. She had put on weight since Mother Superior had assured her she was not going to go blind. Yet still Dotty was a little uneasy. She had told Rosie she could not understand why Mary should be going blind when she wasn't. The nun had not explained so there were still times when her old fears returned to haunt her.

She brought out a pair of white cotton knickers from under the bed and dragged them on beneath her petticoat. Then she put on the blush pink bridesmaid's frock, a pair of white cotton socks and black shoes with a bar strap. She gazed at her eldest sister. 'Have you noticed there's still only a single bed in Aunt Amelia's room?'

'I'm not blind,' murmured Rosie, going over to the fireplace and sticking a finger up the chimney. She stroked soot on to her eyelashes just as she had seen her mother doing in the past. 'You told me it's a marriage of convenience.'

'I know, but I wasn't sure exactly what it meant.'

'They aren't marrying for love. Uncle Pete is going to sleep in the back room that used to be Harry's.' Rosie slipped her feet into shoes identical to her sister's, still feeling that ache when she thought of her brother. She picked up a hairbrush and handed it to Dotty. 'Brush my hair for me. It's soothing having someone do it.'

'You're not having ringlets. I wish I could have had ringlets,' mused Dotty, fingering a strand of Rosie's dark hair. 'But do you think she might have a secret pash on him?' She wielded the hairbrush.

'I shouldn't wonder. She gets real annoyed if I even speak to him.'

'Perhaps she's marrying him for his lovely smile.'

'Don't be daft! Unless she knows something we don't and he's smiling because all the time he's a secret millionaire.'

Dotty giggled, nose almost touching Rosie's head. 'Anyway, they're going to be sleeping in separate rooms so there won't be any babies. Pity. I like babies.'

Rosie threw back her head and gazed up at her. 'Who's been talking to you about having babies?'

'Keep your head still!' ordered Dotty, dropping the hairbrush. 'The girls talk. It all sounds a bit horrible, what you have to do.'

'It can't be that horrible otherwise there wouldn't be so many people in the world. Anyway, why should they want babies when they've us and the three Hudson lads on the scene? We're enough for anyone,' said Rosie, smiling.

Dotty did not agree and said so.

A few moments later, Amelia came into the room. She looked bothered and her cheeks were flushed. 'You two ready yet?'

'Just about,' said Rosie, smoothing her skirts.

'You look very nice, both of you. Now you can come and help me dress, Rosie.'

'Where are the Hudsons?' asked Dotty, facing her aunt. 'Their things are here but they're not.'

'They're at the best man's house. Dotty, you can go downstairs and give Mr Brown a buttonhole and make him feel at home. You know where the flowers are. You don't have to be shy of him. He's a very old friend and knew your mother. Mrs Brown's down there, too, putting the finishing touches to the table. Make friends with her.'

'Did she make the cake?' asked Dotty.

'Yes. She works for Sayer's. I was lucky. Friends, neighbours, even customers turned up trumps by giving me their points so I was able to get enough dried fruit to give to her for the cake.'

'Neighbours can be good like that,' said Rosie, thinking of Mrs Baxendale.

'Yes, a good neighbour is worth their weight in diamonds,' said Amelia, following the girls out of the room and into her own.

'Now, no messing, Rosie,' she said in a mild voice. 'This is my day and I'm determined to enjoy it.'

'Give me some credit, Aunt Amelia. I want you to knock their eyes out,' she said, surprising not only herself.

Amelia stared at her and cleared her throat. 'Well, that's a change of tune for you. Are you sure you're not sickening for something?'

Rosie's smile faded and she tossed back her hair. 'I must be,' she muttered. 'Shall we get cracking? You don't want to be late.'

Amelia stood gazing at her own reflection. Had she gone too far? Her stomach rumbled. She had eaten hardly a thing that morning and very little in the last week. What would Peter think? Trepidation welled up inside her. Perhaps she should change into the lavender suit that had been Violet's? It would take time but people expected the bride to be late. She opened the door and called down to Rosie.

'She's gone, Miss Needham,' shouted up Mr Brown. 'Are you ready yet? Only the car's here.'

Holy Mother of God! thought Amelia. *Too late! Deep breaths.* She used the dress clips she had found in the tea chest to lift her skirts and went slowly downstairs.

Mr Brown's expression was a treat. 'Well, Miss Needham, your father would have been proud of you. Who'd have thought you could look so lovely?'

His mention of her father brought tears to her eyes as she picked up the remaining bouquet from a chair in the hall, only for the moment to be spoilt by him adding, 'He wouldn't have liked you marrying a Proddy, though.'

'He's a good man!' retorted Amelia, blinking back the tears.

She swept out of the house to gasps of astonishment from the few neighbours in the vicinity who had not gone to the church. She felt like a queen as people waved as the car went past. She returned the compliment, spirits high when eventually she descended from the car to the 'oohs' and 'aahs' of those who had come to watch. A camera clicked and Rosie and Dotty took up position behind their aunt. The organ launched into 'The Wedding March' from *Lohengrin* and the three of them seemed to glide down the aisle.

Oh, it really is worth it, thought Amelia, noting with deep satisfaction the whispers and dumbfounded expressions on faces around her. Then she became aware of Peter staring at her as if electrified and her knees went weak. He was wearing his demob suit, tawny hair slicked down with Brylcreem. There was a tiny cut on his chin which he must have done shaving. He looked very presentable and she was aware that her heart was racing as she came to a halt beside him.

'Bloody hell!' murmured Richie, his best man, catching sight of her for the first time. The priest fixed him with a stern eye and he apologised.

Amelia could not prevent a smile but Peter was looking woodenly ahead, a nerve twitching in his jaw. What was he thinking? she wondered, hoping her appearance made him feel the bargain they had struck was worth far more than he had expected.

'Dearly beloved . . .' began the priest, who had not been pleased about her marrying a Protestant either, but had at least got Peter's signature on the form saying he agreed that any children from the union would be brought up in the Roman Catholic faith. Easily done, thought Amelia, when they did not intend having any. Unexpectedly, the idea caused her a moment's regret. Then she squared her shoulders. Whatever the outcome of this marriage, it was too late now for either of them to change their minds.

Chapter Ten

Rosie scraped the leftovers on to a plate and watched the cat gobble them up, thinking it had been quite an enjoyable day, although it had been a pity Davey had not been there. Instead she had danced with Chris, and the best man, and Uncle Pete.

'Have you finished the dishes?' Amelia entered the kitchen, still wearing her wedding finery.

'Yes. Has everyone gone?' Rosie stifled a yawn, wondering what mood her grandmother would be in when she got home.

'I've just closed the door on the last.' Amelia rubbed her eyes. 'I'll be glad to get to bed. It seemed to go off all right, though, didn't it?'

'Fine. There was just enough food and everyone seemed to be enjoying themselves. Even you put on a good act.'

Amelia stared at her. 'What do you mean by that?'

'Ooops, sorry! I don't know why I said it.' Rosie wiped her hands on the tea towel. 'It's time I was going.'

'No, wait!' Amelia seized her arm. 'I'll need your help to get me out of this dress.'

'No, she can go,' said Peter in a tone which caused them both to turn and stare at him, standing in the doorway.

'But I need her,' insisted Amelia.

'I can do anything you need doing,' he rasped, hands in his pockets. 'It's been a long day for Rosie as well as us.'

The girl did not argue. He had worn that tight expression when she had asked him questions about Aunt Amelia's ex-fiancé in the garden. It was definitely time she was going. 'I'll see you next Sunday.' She brushed past him, lifting her coat from the hook in the hall.

'No, wait!' cried Amelia, rustling after her, but Peter grabbed her hand.

'We'll see you out,' he said, compelling his new wife to slow down.

Amelia knew then there was nothing for it but to let Rosie go. They stood on the doorstep waving until she was out of sight. 'Why did you do it?' said Peter, ushering her back inside.

'Why did I do what?' Amelia attempted to free her hand but his grip tightened.

'You know what I mean. That dress you're wearing.'

'What's wrong with it? It was my mother's.' She glanced down at herself. Her ribs and breasts were aching and she was still hungry, having eaten little of the wedding breakfast.

'You mentioned that on the way back from church,' he said with careful patience. 'What I mean is, why wear such a dress?'

'To save money.'

'Amelia, stop playing games!' He dropped her hand, a pained expression on his lean face. 'I thought we'd agreed it wasn't going to be that kind of wedding?'

'You told me to arrange things the way I wanted and that's what I did,' she said, trying to sound casual.

'I know, but—' Peter eased a finger round the inside of his collar. 'I thought there would be just a few people with you in a—'

'Little frock? Well, that wasn't what *I* wanted. It might have been your second time around but—' She stopped abruptly, remembering his first time and how young and sparkling he and Tess had appeared. That had been a sham, too, if Tess had been telling the truth in her farewell note.

'I'm sorry,' said Amelia in a low voice, fiddling with the lace on her sleeve. 'I didn't mean to bring it all back to you.'

He stared at her and then suddenly started removing his collar studs. 'I don't begrudge you your day. It's just that people seemed to think—'

'That I've been out to catch you all these years?' Her laughter contained a bitter note. 'They've short memories!'

'Tess committed suicide just as the war was nearing its end and she knew I'd be coming home,' he said, dragging off his collar. 'You know what people are like. And you processed down that aisle as if all the trumpets voluntary were playing. It was like the song – "This Is My Lovely Day".'

Of course she knew it. 'I *will* always think of today as a lovely day,' she said defiantly. 'So don't spoil it, please. I thought it would be obvious to them all why we were getting married.'

'Well, I reckon it wasn't to some.' He sounded irritable. 'Hasn't there been enough gossip about Tess's death? What with you providing her with the pills!'

Amelia gasped. 'You can't be serious? You can't think people believe I had anything to do with her death? You're imagining things.'

'Am I?'

She was silent, remembering what one of her school friends had said about her being clever and a dark horse only a couple of hours ago. She might not have said it if she had not been drinking. 'I'm sorry,' Amelia said stiffly.

Peter's expression softened. 'Let's forget it. It's done now. And isn't it time you got out of that frock? Perhaps then we'll both behave like normal people again.'

'What's normal?' she said tartly.

He did not answer, placing the studs in his trouser pocket. 'You'll need my help.'

'Yes, because you chased Rosie away and it's a really fiddly job.' Amelia headed for the stairs, holding up her skirts.

'Shhh!' he murmured. 'The twins are in bed.'

'And Chris is out,' she said. 'Do you think he went out deliberately?' There was a fluttering in her breast as Peter followed her into her bedroom.

'He's a sensible lad,' said Peter, taking her by the shoulders. 'Here, stand under the light. Imagine the poor dressmaker slaving away with a guttering candle to sew all these on.'

She was glad to present him with her back so she did not have to see his face. 'The dressmaker was my mother and my grandparents had gaslight.'

His fingers were warm against the nape of her neck and she hoped he was unaware of the shiver his touch sent right through her as she rushed into speech. 'I do remember reading, though, that buttons were sometimes handmade by dairy maids in Poland.'

'I bet they received a pittance.'

'Most women were desperate to help feed their families.' She realised they were both making conversation to cover up the awkwardness of their situation.

'Not just women,' he muttered, working his way down the back of the dress, all fingers and thumbs. 'You only have to read Dickens to realise working-class men had a hard time of it, too. And not only manual workers but white collar as well. My great-grandfather was a clerk in a mill up in Lancashire.'

'I thought your family came from Ireland?'

'In Wellington's time. My great-great-great-whatever followed the Duke to England. Not that he was a duke then.' Peter's hair brushed her back as his fingers went lower and lower, tickling her so that she wriggled. 'Keep still,' he said. 'Fought in the Peninsular Wars, had a soldier mate from Bolton who died in his arms, and later married the bloke's sister.'

'You could write a book about a life like that,' said Amelia, standing rigid now as she held the slack bodice against her.

He paused and his arm went round her waist, pressing her against him, taking her completely by surprise. 'You think so?' he said against her ear. 'I thought about it when I was in the Army. Money was always tight for us, with

Tess's illness. I put some of the story down on paper but she thought I was wasting my time.'

Amelia was interested. 'You must carry on. People need to escape their lives and live someone else's for a while. Maybe you could make us rich?' She glanced over her shoulder at him.

He grinned. 'That'd be the day. But you wouldn't mind if I had a go?'

'Why should I? It'll keep you out of mischief,' she said lightly.

'Then I will,' he said positively. 'It'll make a difference, having someone who believes in me.' He continued undoing the buttons.

Amelia almost fell as he released her and clutched at the bed post before lowering herself on to the bed. The corset dug into her ribs and she drew in a sharp breath.

'You OK?' He looked concerned.

She straightened her back, thinking she would rather die than mention the corset. Besides, she did not want him seeing her wearing just a chemise. 'Fine. Goodnight.'

'Goodnight.' He smiled and dropped a kiss on top of her head. 'And thanks, Lee. You've been really encouraging.' He closed the door and she eased herself further on to the bed and lay flat, imagining herself still encased in the corset next Sunday when Rosie arrived. His touch had made her feel all peculiar.

Her stomach rumbled and Amelia rolled off the bed and hung up the dress, padding back downstairs in her petticoats and camisole – only to stop short in the doorway of the morning room at the sight of Peter, sitting at the table, a doorstep-sized sandwich in his hand. 'I thought you'd gone to bed?' she said.

'I was hungry. Besides, I thought you might still need my help to get out of that armour.'

Suddenly, the whole thing seemed ridiculous and Amelia laughed, feeling younger than her thirty-two years. 'The latest in chastity wear!'

He put down his sandwich and smiled. 'I can understand modesty but have a bit of commonsense, woman.'

'I've loads of commonsense, as you should know.'

'You should have said.'

'I was shy and embarrassed. And I'm *starving*.' She eyed his sandwich hungrily.

'I was feeling a bit nervous myself.' He got up and offered her his sandwich. She took a bite of it and closed her eyes in ecstasy. 'It's only plum jam,' he said, eyes dancing. 'You don't have to look like it's best chicken! But you finish it and I'll make another.'

'I'll put the kettle on,' she said, a warm feeling inside her.

They ate and drank in companionable silence. Then he said suddenly, 'Remember that picture on the dangers of VD?'

She looked at him in surprise and he flushed. 'I know you saw it because Tess told me.'

Amelia nodded. 'The sexes were segregated because it was considered too shocking. It's still a scourge, as is TB. Is that why you're mentioning it? Or—' She blushed. 'You haven't got it, have you?'

'Hell, no!' He looked shocked. 'I was just thinking, it reminds me of our situation. You go one way and I go another upstairs.' He stood up. 'Come on. I'll undo your stays.'

Amelia shook her head in bemusement and followed him upstairs.

It was pure joy once she was free from the corset and she kicked it into a corner. 'My mother was heroic.'

'I'm glad I'm not a woman,' said Peter, shaking his head at her. 'I wonder if my great-great wore one like that.'

'Not if she had any sense. It was torture!' She winced as she felt her ribs beneath the chemise.

'Yet you still wore it. You're crackers!' He grinned. 'I hope you sleep well. Goodnight again.' Quietly he closed the door behind him.

Amelia dragged the chemise over her head and took a pair of pyjamas from beneath her pillow, wondering how many women were still virgins the morning after their wedding night. It was hardly a subject for gossip so she guessed she would never find out. She pressed her cheek into the flock pillow and fell asleep – to dream she was planting potatoes while a soldier in a red uniform stood at the bottom of the garden watching her. Then he pulled her to her feet and kissed her passionately and they made love on the soil.

Sunday was a quiet day. She went to early Mass on her own and then made breakfast. The dream was very much with her as she weeded the garden after Sunday lunch that afternoon. Chris had gone to the farm and the twins were rearranging their room. Peter was writing. There was a peculiar feeling to everything she did that day because she was unsure how to behave towards him.

The only example she had of how married people acted towards each other in the home was that set by her parents.

Her mother had always called her father 'William' and he had called her 'my dear'. He had always read the morning paper at the table and none of them was allowed to talk during that first meal of the day.

Her parents had always been polite to each other and Amelia had never overheard them exchange a cross word. When they had lived in the flat, her mother had helped in the chemist's below. It was only when they had moved out to West Derby that she had stopped working there.

Amelia wondered how long she could get away with putting most of the day in at the shop. She guessed she would have to wait and see how things went.

'You going to the shop this morning?' said Peter, breaking the breakfast silence on Monday.

Amelia glanced across at him. 'You haven't changed your mind?' she said defensively.

'No.' He looked surprised. 'I just wondered if you'd be home for lunch.'

'Father always came home for lunch. I'll be here if you want me to,' she said, prepared to bend a little.

'No. A sandwich will be fine,' he said amiably. 'I ask because I've our ration books and I was wondering how you're going to manage shopping with queuing and everything when you're going to be in the shop. I found it hell. In fact, if it hadn't been for Chris and the corner shop, we'd have lived solely on—'

'I'll ring and they'll deliver,' interrupted Amelia. 'It's what I did when I had Violet's children here and when Father and Iris were around. I don't always get what I'd like but it works fine most of the time.'

'Doesn't it cost to have things delivered?'

Amelia had never thought about it. She had taken the delivery boys on their bicycles for granted but of course their wages had to be paid. 'It's worth it,' she murmured.

He did not argue. 'We're going to have to talk about money, Lee. Work out costs and figures. Do a little book keeping.'

She put a hand to her mouth. 'You've reminded me! I didn't do the weekly accounts, what with the wedding.' She glanced at the clock on the wall and hurried into the kitchen, placed the breakfast dishes in the sink and hurried back to the table.

Peter was slicing bread. 'I cut my finger once,' said Tom, chin on hand.

'Elbows off the table,' said Amelia automatically, nudging them off.

'When was that?' said Peter.

'Mam wasn't feeling well and had gone to bed. There was blood everywhere,' said Jimmy with relish.

'I thought it was never going to stop,' said Tom. 'But I put a bit of newspaper on it and that stuck.'

'Sounds hygienic,' murmured Amelia, aware of Peter's stare but glad of the boys' chatter because it made it easier for her to manage the situation somehow. 'I hope you washed it first.'

'The newspaper?' said Tom, smiling in a way that reminded her of Peter.

'Don't be silly,' she said, returning the smile. 'Now eat up. The two of you need to be on your way soon.'

'I could do the accounts for you?' said Peter, putting on his jacket.

'Oh, they're no trouble,' she said, handing him a packet of sandwiches, wrapped in newspaper.

'Don't you trust me, Lee?'

'Trust?' Her brow creased. 'What's that got to do with it? It's just that I've always done them, even before Father died.'

'But you've got me now. Let me help?' he urged. 'I deal with figures all day, and you're going to have a lot on your plate until Rosie finishes school. Then there's the school holidays and Dotty coming here. You can't leave the twins to their own devices. You heard them.'

'Of course I heard them. But I like doing the accounts myself. I'll do them this evening. Besides, you'vc got your story to write.'

'Please yourself,' he said roughly, and left without saying goodbye.

Amelia stared after him and then turned to see the twins watching her. She frowned, thinking she had hardly any privacy at all now. 'What are you two staring at? You shouldn't be hanging around.'

'What are you going to do when it's school holidays, Aunt Lee?' said Jimmy, looking slightly anxious. 'Will you be here or at the shop?'

She hesitated, wondering about Dotty. 'I'll sort something out so don't be thinking you can run wild. Now hurry up and get your blazers on or you'll be late for school.'

*

Amelia stumbled bleary-eyed into the bathroom. Then drew back hastily when she saw Peter in vest, trousers and bare feet, shaving in front of the mirror. 'Sorry! Wrong place.'

'You're OK.' He wiped off the remains of the shaving soap with a flannel and brushed past her pyjama-clad figure.

She went out after him and into the toilet, remembering to shoot the tiny bolt. With eyelids barely open, she eased herself down on to the lavatory – only to jump up again at the cold touch of porcelain. She groaned and gingerly put down the wooden seat. There were some things she was never going to get used to!

A minute later someone tried the handle of the door before hammering on it. 'Please, I want to go. I'm desprite!'

'You'll have to wait. Go away, twin.'

'But—'

Amelia opened the door. The twin ducked under her arm fumbling with his underpants as he went. Too late she realised she had not put the seat up. 'Oops,' she heard, along with a pattering sound on the linoleum.

'Blast!' she muttered. Another job to see to.

She went into the bathroom and splashed cold water on her face. 'Don't forget to wash your hands!' she called, as she heard the lavatory door opening and closing. A twin sidled round the door and she guessed it was Jimmy. Tom would just have marched in. 'Use the bath tap,' she said.

Jimmy did as told and crept out again.

Amelia washed and made for her bedroom just as she had every morning for the last month. She closed the door and lay face down on her bed, wishing it was Sunday. Yet even on the so-called day of rest she was up early. There would be meals to cook and dishes to wash and she would have to go to Mass, having missed last Sunday. But should she confess the lurid thoughts and dreams she had been having? The priest would not approve, especially if she told him she was not sleeping with her husband. No, she would have to keep quiet about everything. At least she would not need to get the twins' school clothes ready because the school holidays had started.

There was a knock on the door and a voice said, 'Aunt Lee, I've wiped up the mess.'

'Thank you,' she murmured, wondering whether he had used the flannel like last time. And why was it that when the twins were going to school she had to wake them up and when they weren't they were always up early?

She asked Peter his thoughts on the subject when she met him in the kitchen later. 'Never thought about it,' he said, opening the *Daily Post*. 'I only know I was the same. What are you going to do about the school holidays and the shop?'

'Rosie's starting today full-time but I'll still have to go in for a while. I'll take the twins with me. They can play in the yard. Dotty'll be all right here on her own.'

'That's OK then,' he murmured, not looking up from his newspaper.

Amelia wondered about the kind of conversations other newly married couples had over the breakfast table. Did they whisper sweet nothings and play footsie? It was proving much harder sharing a house with him than she had reckoned, but at least having the children to talk about cut down on the awkward silences that sometimes rose between them. Even though they also caused some of the awkward silences.

'Liverpool's got its first woman MP,' said Peter.

'All the votes in from overseas, I take it?'

He lowered his newspaper. 'Yes. Eight Labour and three Conservative. Sir Maxwell got in at West Derby as you'd expect.' He dropped the newspaper on the table and spread jam on a slice of bread. 'It says the people are saying something by voting in a Labour government.'

'Of course they are.' She sipped her tea. 'They want change. They expect miracles. They want their dreams to come true.' Her tone was more vehement than she'd intended.

Peter stared at her. 'You reckon it won't happen?'

'The country must be bankrupt. We've been through two wars in less than thirty years. They don't come cheap. But at least now the working-class women of Liverpool will have a woman speaking up for them. I presume bouncing Bessie Braddock got in at Exchange Ward?' He nodded. 'Good. I'm sure she'll fight for any money there is.'

Peter eyed her with interest, leaning back in his chair so that the front legs lifted. 'I know plenty of women who don't have any trouble speaking up for themselves.'

His words surprised her. 'Are you referring to me? I thought I'd been very restrained, lately.'

'Because you haven't reminded me this week that this is your house?'

She reddened. 'Do I do that? It's not intentional. And it's ours now.'

'I know. I'm paying the mortgage.'

'Sorry.'

'I'm sorry too. I know how hard it is to kill off a habit.' There was a glimmer of that smile in his eyes which had not been so noticeable lately.

Her legs suddenly seemed to turn into India rubber, such was its effect on her. She rushed into speech. 'Toilet seats being left up annoy me,' she murmured.

'Now that's more serious than who owns the house. I'll speak to the lads.' There was a tremor in his voice.

'Thank you.'

He picked up his newspaper. 'If you've a minute, perhaps you could change my sheets this week or they'll be walking?'

'Has it been that long?' Her voice rose on the last two words and she felt guilt-ridden. 'It's probably because I don't go into your room. And what with being behind with the housework, I just forgot.'

'My room's not out of bounds, you know. I'm not your lodger, Lee,' he said mildly.

'No, of course not.'

'We are married.'

'Yes.'

He lowered the newspaper and she saw that he was frowning. 'Yes! No! Why don't you add "three bags full, sir"? Why are we always so polite to each other? For God's sake, it's not natural!'

She was so surprised by his outburst that she was startled into saying, 'Isn't it?'

'No!' he said with even greater vehemence.

That took her aback and she stood up, resting both hands on the table. Somehow that made it easier for her to give more emphasis to her words. 'If we're not polite to each other, what will happen?'

'You tell me?' His eyes were dark and unfathomable, like pebbles in a peaty stream.

'I should think we would argue,' she said. 'And that's not good for children. My parents were always polite to each other.'

'I can imagine.'

'What do you mean by that?' She bridled, not liking what she saw as implied criticism of her parents.

'You don't know how to relax, Lee! All work and no play . . .'

'Makes me a dull girl? Is that what you're saying?' She could hardly contain the anger that erupted so unexpectedly. 'Well, you try being me for a day – or better still for a week or a fortnight. This year hasn't exactly been easy for me, you know!'

'I wouldn't argue.' He threw down the newspaper and stood up.

'And you said you were happy for me to work as long as you had a clean shirt and there was a meal on the table when you came in.' She flung the words at him like darts.

'I was a fool! You're not managing. The shop, the house, the twins . . . And it'll be worse now the school holidays are here.'

'I managed perfectly well before you came along when I had Violet's children,' she said through gritted teeth.

'So it's me that's the problem?' He drummed his fingers on the table. 'We shouldn't have married. It was a daft idea. I should have known it wouldn't work.' He reached for the jacket slung over the back of his chair and put it on. 'I've got to get to the Post Office. Did you do my sandwiches?'

'No, I was tired last night.' *Tired with not sleeping thinking of* you. *Or when I did fall asleep, dreaming of you. It's not fair*, she thought rebelliously.

'You're overstretching yourself.' He shrugged on his jacket.

'You make me sound like a piece of elastic.'

'Now you're being silly. Accept you can't do everything and remember why we married.'

'I know why we married.' She folded her arms. Her blazing eyes were at variance with the coldness of her voice. 'We did it for Tess and for the children. I haven't forgotten.'

'You've made that clear.' He made for the door.

She thought that was the end of it but it was not. 'The twins will need watching, with having hours on end to fill. You can't just ignore them like you can the housework.'

Amelia was hurt and angry. She forgot how his smile made her feel, the urge to please him. 'I do not ignore the housework! And you don't have to tell me my duty,' she said passionately. 'That is something I know about.' She did not wait for him to answer but stalked into the kitchen to lean against the sink, gazing unseeing out of the window, struggling against tears. She would be damned if she would give up working in the shop altogether. It had kept a roof over her head and food in her stomach for years. Somehow, with Rosie's and Dotty's help, she would show him.

Chapter Eleven

Rosie eyed the twins, standing side by side, arms behind their backs, dressed in identical pale blue short-sleeved shirts and navy-blue shorts. Both had a question-mark-shaped curl dangling on their forehead and looked as if they had just arrived with a stamp of approval from Heaven.

She hung up her coat and reached for her overall, aware their eyes were following her every move. 'Who are you staring at?' she snapped, thinking of Harry being sent away and them being in his place.

'We were wondering why you didn't like us?' said a twin.

She presumed it was loudmouthed Tom. 'Because you're pests,' she muttered.

They both looked injured. 'We don't mean to be pests,' said the other twin, hunching his shoulders before letting them sag.

'Ha!' exclaimed Rosie disbelievingly, buttoning up her overall. 'You'll be saying next you can't help yourselves.'

'We've always had to help ourselves,' said the first twin.

'Mam expected it of us,' said the second one. '"Help each other", she said.'

'And "get out from under me feet",' supplied the first. 'She used to say we drove her mad.'

'Sometimes she didn't know which one of us was which,' said the second.

Rosie felt quite dizzy as her eyes went from one to the other, wishing she knew for definite which was which without always having to look for the scar.

'And she'd clout us both just to make sure she'd got the right one when we did something wrong,' said Tom.

'When she managed to catch us,' said Jimmy.

'I know the feeling,' muttered Rosie. 'Well, don't think you're going to run rings round me.'

'We haven't done anything to you. Haven't played any tricks,' said Tom. He was thinking of the spider he had seen in the corner of his bedroom where it was dusty. It would have given her a lovely fright if he'd put it in a match box and showed it to her. Girls were scared of spiders. They screamed and ran away just like Miss Muffet. 'Dad says you're family and we've got to be nice to you,' he added, with obvious regret.

'You don't have to bother being nice,' said Rosie, fixing them with a glare. 'Now go and play with your ball and don't be nuisances!' She shooed them into the yard and went in search of Amelia to be told her duties.

Rosie found her aunt in the dispensing room with Mr Brown. 'So there you are!' she said, looking relieved. 'The twins are behaving themselves, aren't they?'

'They're in the yard. But whether they'll—'

'I'm sure they'll be OK.' Amelia's firm voice cut through her words. 'I'll serve in the shop until lunchtime, Rosie, while you help Mr Brown. Then I'll have to go and you can take my place serving.'

'Yes, Aunt Amelia.' That suited Rosie down to the ground because it meant she was getting the best of both worlds, working and learning and meeting people and helping them. There was only one thing upsetting Rosie that morning and that was that she had had no word from Davey for weeks.

'And you can keep an eye on the twins for me, too,' said Amelia in a sweet voice. 'Thank you, Rosie. I think everything is going to work out perfectly.'

She smiled, wondering why her aunt was being so nice. The girl gazed around Mr Brown's tiny kingdom where a wooden bench with a linoleum top took up most of the space. On it were mortars and pestles and a marble slab for making up pills. Next to the slab stood the all-important scales made of brass with a central balance and supports of agate. The scales were checked at least once a year by Avery's. Mr Brown had told her how important it was to get the weights exactly right. It was the same with measuring vessels. They had a government stamp. Exact measurements could make the difference between life and death.

Rosie stared at the glass jars of all shapes and sizes displayed on the shelves. Powder containers were curved with wide necks, whereas liquid ones were narrow. Acid or poison bottles were green and ribbed so you could tell the difference between an ordinary jar and one containing a dangerous substance in the dark. Poisons were kept in a special cupboard to which only Mr Brown was allowed to hold the key.

'Here you are, Rosie, this is what you can do for me today,' he said, and showed her how to work the folding machine, which tidied up the edges of the greaseproof papers that would contain powders.

She set to work and he watched her for a moment before getting on with making up the prescription Amelia had brought in. He talked as he worked, explaining different things to Rosie. How there was a pharmaceutical weight which pharmacists used and an imperial weight which was used the other side of the counter. He talked of grains and drams, scruples and fluid ounces. Of doctors' marks on a prescription and how TDS meant three times a day.

That morning Rosie regarded herself as a very fortunate girl being taught by someone of Mr Brown's experience. Amelia had already told her that lots of people came into the shop asking for his advice. The poorer people could not afford doctors and he had a great deal of experience in treating all kinds of minor ailments.

The hours went by swiftly and Amelia came into the dispensing room several times with prescriptions. But it was only when her aunt said they would be closing for lunch in half an hour, and asked Rosie if the twins were OK, that the girl gave a thought to the boys.

The yard was empty.

For a moment, she could not believe her eyes. She walked down to the door at the bottom of the yard but the bolt was firmly shot and the padlock still attached and locked. She looked round for any hidey-holes and saw the twins' ball. It had been holed and was now deflated. She frowned, casting an eye over the outside lavatory, next to which stood a cardboard box with bits of wood and other rubbish in it. That was in front of the pullout bin set in the wall. A wall which was surely too high for two eight-year-olds to climb. Or was it?

'Boys will be boys,' Rosie had heard Mrs Baxendale say on more than one occasion, the last time being when Davey and a couple of his mates had climbed on to the roof of that bomb-damaged house in Everton where she and her sisters and brother had hidden for a few short hours in January.

I'll kill them! she thought, and took a running jump at the gate, determined to find them before Amelia realised they were missing. Surely the twins would not have gone unnoticed in their bid for freedom?

It was a pleasant day, warm if a little overcast, but the sun was managing to peep out from behind picture-book fluffy white clouds in a way which made Rosie suddenly glad to be out in the fresh air. She raced up the entry, pausing a moment to ask a man sweeping the large stone slabs if he had seen the twins. He pointed her in the right direction.

Rosie ran up Butler Street, pausing again to ask two women leaning on yard brushes, gossiping. Again she received a positive answer and carried on into Boaler Street, where an elderly woman set her on what was hopefully the last lap of her journey. She was thinking she deserved to be congratulated on her detective work as she passed the lodge on the corner of Gardner's Drive, only to be stopped in her tracks by a familiar voice calling her name.

'Davey!' She had intended to be cool and distant but could only smile because she was so glad to see him.

He cycled towards her. 'Where are you going, dressed like that?'

Rosie had forgotten she had on her overall, which did exactly nothing for her, and pulled a face. 'I've had to rush out of the shop. I'm working there full-time now I've finished my exams and left school. But those blinking Hudson twins have escaped from the yard and I've got to find them.'

Davey knew of the twins from his mother because she had spoken to Rosie a month ago. 'Want me to come with you? I've finished the morning deliveries.'

'What about your lunch?'

'Sandwiches.' He patted his pocket. 'That's why I'm here. I thought I'd have them in the park. No point in going home. Ma's in hospital.'

So that was why he had not been round. 'What's wrong with her?'

'Fell off a chair changing curtains and broke her leg.'

'Your poor mam! Is there anything I can do?'

'If you could look in when she comes home, I'm sure she'll appreciate that.'

'Of course I will. No wonder I haven't seen you.'

'I know. It seems ages since we last met.' He cast her a sidelong glance as they walked side by side. 'I called last Sunday but your gran sent me away with a flea in me ear because I hadn't heard from the Yank.'

'She never said! I'll have a word with her when I get in,' said Rosie, vexed.

'I had a feeling she had someone with her.'

Rosie stopped and stared at him. 'You didn't see them?'

He shook his head and a thick hank of dark hair flopped on to his forehead. 'Why? Is it important?'

'She spoke of "he" weeks back but she's dead keen for me not to set eyes on him.'

'You think your gran's got a fancy man?' He grinned. 'She couldn't have. Not at her age. And she's a cantankerous old faggot!'

'I know! It makes the mind boggle.' They had reached Newsham Park and Rosie glanced around. 'I should be looking for the twins.'

'Any idea where they'll be?'

'They told an old lady they were going to float their boats. I said they didn't have boats but she said imagination's a wonderful thing. They had two pieces of wood with nails in them.'

He grinned. 'They'll have headed for the pond then. Should be safe enough. There's plenty of people about.'

Rosie had no idea if the twins could swim or not but it was true there were plenty of people out today so they should be safe. Children were playing rounders or just running about. Some had flopped on to the ground and were lying on their stomachs, parting blades of grass and gazing intently at something only they could see. Rosie remembered doing the same kind of thing when she was little. Watching insects scurrying about their business had fascinated her.

She stepped round a couple, noticing they were lying on an American Air Force jacket. 'You say you haven't seen Sam?'

'Yes. Do you think I'd lie?' said Davey, dark brows meeting as he frowned.

'Of course not!' She wondered why he had to be so touchy over Sam.

'He might have been sent overseas. It's all systems go in the Far East to try and get the Japs to surrender,' he said, looking mollified.

Rosie had not thought of Sam going East. 'Do you think the Japs will surrender?'

'Suicidal idiots, aren't they? I've got a cousin out there. He's only two years older than me.' Davey looked suddenly serious. 'Come this time next year, I could be out East. India maybe.'

'Don't talk about it.' She slipped her arm through his and he squeezed it against his side. They were silent for quite a while, each thinking how strange it was that life could change so suddenly.

They found the twins kneeling on the edge of the circular pond, surrounded by the like-minded and their supporters, for whom launching bits of wood across a span of water held a fascination. Davey stood at the back of the crowd, a hand on the saddle of his bike, a smile on his face as he watched Rosie creep up on them. She grabbed both of them simultaneously.

'Gotcha!' She seized a handful of their shirts but one of them wrenched himself free, overbalanced and slipped into the pond.

'Trust you!' she groaned as the boy rose, gasping, from beneath the water which was only a couple of feet or so deep.

Davey dropped his bike and pushed his way through the crowd to her side. Together they seized the twin and dragged him out of the pond. He stood dripping on the gravel. 'Well, that's another fine mess you've got yourself into,' Rosie said.

'Not only me,' said the boy, shivering as he flicked back his hair, sprinkling her with water. 'Your overall's got slime on it.'

'Damn!' said Rosie, annoyed, gazing down at her front. 'Aunt Amelia's going to have a fit.'

'D'you want me to take this one home on the bike?' asked Davey.

'What about me?' said the other twin, jutting out his lip.

'The name's Davey, not Charles Atlas. You can go with Rosie.'

The boy's face fell. 'But I don't want to go back to the shop! Why can't we catch the tram? We could walk along Orphan's Drive to West Derby Road and get one there. Please, please?' he said in a coaxing voice, pulling on Rosie's arm. 'Perhaps *he's* got money,' he added, indicating Davey with a jerk of the head.

Rosie wanted to be rid of them both and looked at Davey, hoping he could read her thoughts. He responded instantly. 'I'll take them to the tram stop and have a word with the conductor. You'd best get back to your aunt. She'll be going spare. And here, kid, you'd best put this round you.' He took off his jacket and draped it over the dripping boy.

'It's more than he deserves,' said Rosie, gazing up at Davey with such warmth in her expression that he felt he could have conquered Everest for her. 'Thanks.' She kissed his cheek and before she could draw back again he seized her hand and brought her tight against him.

'Call at ours tomorrow at eleven. Bring some butties and we can go somewhere.' He kissed her on the mouth before releasing her then turned to the twins. 'Come on, small fry. Let's be having you.'

A dreamy-eyed Rosie stood watching them go. Once they turned and waved and she raised a hand. Then she went back the way she had come.

Needham's, like the rest of the shops along Kensington, was displaying the CLOSED sign and there was a noonday stillness about the thoroughfare. She rattled the brass latch and instantly hurrying footsteps approached.

Amelia flung open the door and dragged her inside. 'Where the hell have you been? And where are the twins?' Her face was tight with anxiety.

'I've sent them home,' gasped Rosie, who had run most of the way. 'Can I sit down?'

Amelia let her go and the girl collapsed on the customers' chair. 'What happened?' said her aunt, exasperated. 'Why couldn't you keep your eye on them for five minutes?'

Rosie made no answer. Surely it was obvious why she had not kept her eye on them?

'OK, so you were busy and forgot. Where did they get to?'

Rosie told her without mentioning Davey. Amelia groaned and went into the back of the shop, returning with a cup of water which she handed to Rosie. When the girl had drunk it, Amelia said, 'You'll want something to eat.'

'I brought sandwiches. They're in my jacket.'

'Get eating then. I'll have to be going. See you tomorrow.'

'No,' said Rosie swiftly. 'I can't come tomorrow.'

Amelia looked positively put out. 'I was hoping for your help. And Dotty's going to be disappointed.'

'I'll see her soon. It's just that I'm going somewhere tomorrow.' She avoided her aunt's eyes.

'OK. But next Sunday you'll come?' said Amelia, pulling on a white glove.

'Next Sunday,' said Rosie, wondering what she would say if Davey wanted to see her again then.

'See you Monday then – and don't forget to wash that overall,' ordered Amelia. 'Wear mine this afternoon.'

She was assured of the twins' safety as soon as she arrived home. As she unpacked the box of provisions left by the delivery boy, she chided the twins. 'Bread and water, that's what you're on today, my lads,' she said severely.

'But they've already had something, Aunt Amelia,' said Dotty, blinking rapidly behind her new spectacles. 'I didn't know they weren't supposed to eat.'

'And Davey gave us a butty to share, too,' said Jimmy.

Amelia's hands stilled and her eyes fixed on his face. 'Davey?'

'Rosie's boyfriend,' explained Tom, pressing his finger into a greaseproof-covered slab of butter. 'He gave us the pennies for the tram and told the conductor not to let me catch phew-monia.'

'Pneumonia,' corrected Amelia automatically, slapping his hand away from the butter. 'And where did you meet him?'

The twins exchanged looks and were silent.

'It doesn't matter,' she said, thinking reticence was something new for the twins. 'I can guess. But how do you know he's her boyfriend?'

'Cos he got all sloppy and kissed her,' said Tom, pulling a face.

'She kissed him first,' said Jimmy swiftly. 'It's girls that are sloppy.'

'OK, I've got the picture,' said Amelia, starting to put things in cupboards. 'If you both help me, you might get off without being punished. Go upstairs and take the sheets off your bed – and do the same for your dad's as well. And bring them down.'

The twins stared at her. 'But that's girls' work,' wailed Tom.

'Do it!' she said, raising her voice. 'Or it really will be bread and water for the two of you – for the rest of the week!'

They scurried off, leaving Amelia wondering if Davey was the reason why Rosie was not visiting tomorrow. And why had she kept quiet about meeting him? Not that Amelia had anything against the lad. Only she did not want anything preventing Rosie from accomplishing what she herself had failed to achieve. Still, perhaps she should not say anything yet. Rosie might get awkward and do exactly what Amelia did not want her to do. After all, they were only young and it mightn't be serious.

Even so, she found herself worrying about Rosie and Davey as she prepared a pilchard, leek and potato pie for tea. She placed it in the oven and then went upstairs, wondering what was taking the twins so long.

Their room was empty, sheets on the floor. She opened the door to Peter's room and the blood seemed to rush to her head. 'You fiends!' she cried, taking off her slipper and grabbing the first twin to hand. She whacked him on the bottom. The other yelled at her to let him go, pulling on her arm. She turned and seized hold of him and smacked him across the legs with her bare hand.

He shrieked 'That hurt! I'll get Dad on to you!'

'And I'll get him on to you, too,' she shrieked back.

'We didn't mean to do it,' said the other twin, face crumpling, tears in his eyes. 'It was only a game.'

'A game?' Her gaze swept the room and she groaned and put her hands to her head. 'Get out! Go on out, both of you!' Amelia forced them out of the room and slammed the door.

She rested her back against it and a deep sigh escaped her. She accepted it might possibly have been worse if it had been feathers, but flock was bad enough. She wanted to kick the torn pillow out of the window but instead she

began to pick up the stuffing which had spilt from its
striped cover, tears of rage and frustration rolling down
her cheeks.

When Peter came home it was to a house that was
strangely silent. There was a slight smell of burning in
the air which he traced to the cloth-covered pie on a
cooling rack. There was washed lettuce in a colander in
the sink and a handful of radishes on the chopping board.
But no sign of the cook.

'Lee!' he called. 'Tom! Jimmy! Dotty!'

No answer.

He went into every room downstairs and out to the
garden, but there was no one visible. So he went upstairs
to his room and there he found Amelia sitting on the floor.
She had her back to the wall beneath the window and her
legs were outstretched. She held a pillow in one hand and
was wielding a needle and cotton with the other.

'Where are the twins? And what are you doing in here,
sitting on the floor?' he asked.

'I'm sewing,' she said in a tight voice, not looking up.

'I can see that. Why in here?'

'Isn't that obvious? This is your pillow which your
charming sons just burst. I gave them *one* job to do and
you should have seen the mess.' Her voice cracked.

There was silence as he surveyed the room. 'It looks
tidy enough.'

'That's because I've spent the last two hours picking
up every single bit of flock. They had a pillow fight, didn't
they?'

His fingers curled. 'Where are they?'

'They've gone to the cemetery with Dotty. Don't ask me which one. She just called up and said they were going out. Probably gone to tell their mothers how wicked I am.'

'Come off it, Lee. They can't believe that.'

'I hit them. Hard.' She rested her head against the wall and looked up at him. There was a stricken, blank look about her face.

'Then they must have deserved it,' he said firmly.

'I lost my temper. I hate losing control. It frightens me.' She bent her head to her sewing again.

'I see,' he said softly, noticing there was flock among the fine golden brown strands of her hair and on the bare skin above the collar of her cream blouse. In that moment, she seemed vulnerable and he was so mesmerised by the idea of taking her into his arms and comforting her that suddenly he felt tongue-tied. Then she moved her head to bite off the thread.

He sighed and took off his jacket and loosened his tie. 'You're not getting much out of our agreement, are you, Lee?'

'I'm a married woman,' she said, refusing to look at him. 'I'm Mrs Hudson.'

'It hasn't changed anything for you, though, has it? Or not for the better. I should be keeping you!' His voice sounded strained, hoarse almost. 'You should be able to relax at home, see your friends, have time for cups of tea and a chat.'

She glanced up, wondering where this was leading. 'I have no friends like that. Tess was my only close friend, though Iris and I were close once.'

'Poor Lee,' he said, noticing the tearstains on her face. 'I never realised you were so lonely.' He knelt and stroked her cheek. 'You need a break, woman. A good day out.'

'I need . . .' she began and then stopped.

'What do you need?' His slate-grey eyes were intent on her face.

Her throat moved as she struggled to get words out but while he was looking at her she could not say them. She cleared her throat. 'I need exactly what you said. A day out!' She caught hold of his hand. 'Pull me up. Tomorrow could be that day. Rosie isn't coming.'

For a moment, Amelia thought he looked disappointed, but all he said was, 'Tomorrow and every Sunday during the kids' holidays we'll go somewhere. All work and no play isn't good for anyone, Lee.' He pulled her to her feet and, with him holding her hand, they walked out of the room together.

Chapter Twelve

Amelia hurried Dotty and the twins off the ferry and ran with them across the landing stage. They panted up the open passenger walkway where the slap-slap of the oily waters of the Mersey could clearly be heard below. They emerged just opposite Edward VII's statue. Although Amelia had expected to see crowds down at the Pierhead on such a fine day in August, she had not expected so many and in such high spirits.

'I wonder what's going on,' said Tom, eyes bright with curiosity.

Amelia caught the arm of a passing woman. 'Has something happened? Have the Japanese surrendered? Is the war over?'

'Where've you been, luv?' The young woman's face was alight with happiness. 'Didn't you see it in the papers this morning? Didn't you hear the ships' hooters going off?'

'No!' Amelia laughed with delight. Typical! The one morning they had overslept because she had decided not to go to the shop but to take the children out for the day. Somehow the excitement had passed them by.

'It was them atom bombs that finished them off. Killed thousands and thousands all at once. It makes you think, doesn't it?' said the woman.

'It's frightening,' said Amelia, almost in a whisper, unable to stop smiling, though, thinking what a difference this would make to so many of her customers.

'Yeah. But it was them or more of our men and allies getting killed.' The woman's face hardened. 'My man's out there. I reckon it's saved his life so I'm not crying for them Japs. Nor for the Jerries, who they're saying now are near starvation. Have you seen the pictures that were in the papers of them prisoners in the concentration camps? Beasts! That's what they are who did that. They're not human!'

Amelia agreed that it was truly terrible, then thanked the woman and headed for the tram stop.

'Will there be a party?' asked Dotty.

'Oh, yes. There'll be parties,' promised Amelia.

And there were. The fighting was over now. People wanted to celebrate and look to the future again, rebuild lives that had either been on hold or shattered altogether by the war.

It would not be easy for some, thought Amelia, reading the letter from her sister which arrived in September after the twins and Dotty had gone back to school.

'What is it?' asked Peter, glancing across the table at her as she refolded the sheet of notepaper.

She smiled faintly. 'How do you know it's anything?'

Things had been easier between them over the last few weeks. She was going into the shop later and leaving earlier, which meant she was not so tired. He had taken over the garden and seeing to the vegetable patch. She had also handed the accounts book to him and all the additional paraphernalia to do with household bills, and they had had the occasional day out with the children. Even so, there were things that did not get easier. She found his masculinity disturbing still and no longer knew exactly what her feelings were towards him. She was confused, one minute wanting to keep him at a distance and the next longing for nothing more than to be held in his arms.

'It's Bill,' said Amelia, resting her elbows on the table. 'You know he was badly wounded in the war?'

'Wounds giving him trouble?'

She nodded. 'He's got to have an operation and it's dicey.'

'Poor bloke.'

'And poor Iris. She sounds like she doesn't know where she is.' Amelia sighed. 'I wish I could help her but I don't know what to do except pray.'

'Do that. And write. It helps to know people are thinking about you when you're far from home.' His eyes held hers a moment and she thought of the last letter he had received from Tess. It did not make their situation any easier, her remembering that. But she took his advice and wrote to Iris, prayed and waited.

Rosie had also received a letter from Canada. Babs, who had always had big ears, had overheard Aunt Iris talking to her brother-in-law.

She doesn't say in so many words that Uncle Bill
could die but if he does, what's going to happen to
Harry and me? There's talk of what will happen to
the factory but not us! Who knows? Maybe we'll
all be home for Christmas. Not that I really want
Uncle Bill to die. He's been very good to us, much
nicer than Aunt Iris actually. I don't think it's her
that really likes kids but him, and I could cry when
I see him in pain.

The letter gave Rosie a lot to think about. If Aunt Iris, Babs and Harry came back to Liverpool, where would they live? Housing was in short supply after the Blitz, and manpower and materials were impossible to come by. Rosie was aware most grown-ups expected things to improve now the war was over, but shortages and rationing were still in force.

At the beginning of December, letters arrived for both Rosie and Amelia, bringing news of Bill's death. Iris had been left a half-share in the factory. Bill's brother held the other half. Iris did not know what to do. Could Amelia and Peter give her advice? Should she sell her shares to Cecil and come home or try and make a go of things in Canada? The trouble was the children. What was best for them?

'We don't interfere,' said Peter positively, lowering the newspaper which was full of the trial of Rudolf Hess. 'The brother's in a better position to advise her than us.'

'He'll be biased,' said Amelia, who would dearly love to see her sister again.

'Aren't you? Besides, if she came home, where would she and the children live?'

Amelia avoided meeting his gaze, murmuring, 'She'd have money. She could buy a house.'

His eyes narrowed and he tapped a fork on the table. 'Even with money she'd have difficulty finding a place. And what's she coming home to? Bomb sites and rationing.'

'She's British. She'll manage,' said Amelia, lifting her chin and giving him a challenging stare.

Peter's smile was sardonic. 'Tess always said you spoilt Iris. She hasn't got your bulldog spirit. You know, there's an article here in the paper saying five hundred Canadian brides will land in Liverpool any day now. They're in for a shock!'

She smiled sweetly. 'We must have something over here that attracts them.'

'I said brides, which means they've husbands, Lee. Met them when they were doing flight training over there probably. I knew a bloke from Chester who did that.'

She bit into a slice of toast. 'I'm getting the impression you don't want my sister here.'

'You've put your finger on it. I don't want her, Lee. What's she going to think, me and you having separate rooms?'

Amelia stared at him and for a moment was transfixed by the expression in his eyes. It was as if he had thrown down a challenge now and was waiting for her to rise to it. But she did not know if she was ready for what he might be suggesting. Did he want to move into her room? If so, why didn't he say so outright? After what he had said on the evening of their wedding, about her sweeping down the aisle in triumph, she was very reluctant to make any move in that direction.

Suddenly he laughed, folded the newspaper and got to his feet. 'Tell her how it really is here, Lee, I mean in Liverpool, and leave it at that. If she comes, I suppose we'll have to make room for her and the kids.' He shrugged on his overcoat and clapped a trilby on to his thatch of tawny hair. 'You going into the shop today?'

'Yes,' she murmured. 'Rosie needs to spend more time with Mr Brown after putting in so many hours behind the counter. She has to serve a full two-year apprenticeship before she goes to college and does the theory. I want her to achieve what Tess and I never did.'

'She won't if she carries on seeing that Davey, and you'll have wasted your time,' he warned. 'You should say something to her. Tell her we're missing her on Sundays.'

Amelia nodded, wondering whether *he* missed her particularly and feeling a brief stab of jealousy. There had been quite a number of Sundays when Rosie had not visited recently. Perhaps Peter was right about her saying something about Davey, although times were changing and many married women had worked during the war. Life was uncertain and there was still fighting going on around the world, with the British forces playing their part. A woman could be widowed very easily. Better Rosie had something to fall back on to earn her a decent living if the worst came to the worst. Yes, far better, thought Amelia. She would have to say something.

*

Rosie would have been amazed if she had known what her aunt was thinking. Her thoughts were all for Harry and Babs in Canada. She had no qualms about writing a letter encouraging her brother and sister to work on Iris so she would come home to Liverpool.

In a few years' time I should be able to earn some decent money and I'm sure you'll be able to get a job over here with no trouble, Babs. Then we'll be able to find a place where we can all be together. Until then I'm certain I could persuade Gran to take you two in as well. There's room enough. So see what you can do.

Your ever-loving sister,
Rosie

She sent off the letter and awaited its outcome.

The weather turned even colder. Pavements were slippery and Rosie was reminded of that day in January when they had intended going to the pantomime with their mother. As she shivered in the dispensing room, trying to keep warm by the oil heater, she was reminded that it was her mother's birthday by Mr Brown's mention of it being the King's birthday. Rosie decided to visit the cemetery and lay a holly wreath on the grave, wondering whether she would see Sam there or whether he had gone home yet.

It was a murky day and she had a scarf pulled well over her mouth to keep out the damp foggy air. There was a hole in her shoe and even the cardboard she had put in as an extra inner sole was damp and crumbling as she trudged up Yew Tree Lane.

There was someone at the grave before her and Rosie's eyes lit up. 'I was wondering if you would be here, Sam. I wasn't sure if you'd left. It was kind of you to send me the food parcels.'

He looked uncomfortable, shuffling his feet and gazing down at the grave. 'I like giving presents.'

She liked giving and receiving and wished there were more things in the shops to buy for Christmas and that she had more money. 'Were you hoping to be home by now?' she said softly.

'Sure. And there's still a chance.' He lifted his head and smiled. 'The folks back home'll be planning a real humdinger of a party. There'll be a tree and we'll have carols and a turkey.'

Rosie sighed. 'It sounds marvellous. Gran's talking about corned beef hash for us.'

There was silence, Rosie deep in thought. 'Sam,' she said, looking him straight in the eye, 'Chigago's up by the big lakes in the north, isn't it?'

'Sure is.'

'D'you ever go across the border into Canada?'

'Have been.' He pursed his lips. 'Why you asking?'

'My aunt and sister and brother live in Canada. I was wondering if you could look them up?' It did not seem likely now, despite all her prayers, that Harry and Babs would be home for Christmas.

Sam's jaw dropped. 'Have you any idea how far it is across the Lakes?'

She shook her head, the pom-pom on her red woolly hat bobbing. 'Don't you have a car? I thought all Yanks had cars.'

'Sure! Pop has an automobile but—'

'If I give you their address, will you go and see them and persuade them to come home?' she said eagerly, slipping her hand under his arm and pressing it. 'Tell them how much I miss them. How I long to see them. Please do this for me, Sam?' she said softly. 'Or, if you can't do it for me, do it for Mam.' She glanced down at the grave. 'You are our stepfather, after all. Please?'

He cleared his throat. 'Can't promise, but I'll do my best.'

She smiled and kissed his chin. 'Your best is good enough for me. Happy Christmas.'

Rosie did not see Sam again but on the Sunday before Christmas, when she was on her way home after visiting the family in West Derby, she saw Davey standing on the corner of Rothwell Street near the bombed hollow. He was in conversation with a bloke in Army uniform so she did not stop, only waved.

She had not gone far when he caught up with her. 'I want a word with you. Got another parcel,' he said, shoulder brushing hers.

'That's nice,' she said, cheeks warming.

'From guess who?'

'Sam?' She felt a mixture of pleasure and shame because she had given her stepfather a big enough hint that her Christmas would be a bit bleak. 'How kind of him,' she said lightly. 'It'll be the last, though. He's on his way home.'

'How do you know? Have you seen him?' Davey was frowning now.

'I met him at the cemetery. He mentioned turkey and I mentioned corned beef hash.'

'Said the right thing then, didn't you?' Davey smiled unexpectedly, his hand touching hers. He linked her little finger with his.

'I should feel guilty,' Rosie said soberly.

'Don't be daft! Thank God the bloke's got a conscience. That he didn't forget you at Christmas.' Lowering his head, Davey kissed her in such a way she almost forgot about Sam. But she knew his present was going to make several people happier this holiday.

Her grandmother for a start. 'Well, girl,' she said, rubbing her hands and smiling, 'you've come up trumps! Pity he's gone back home. But just to show there's no hard feelings, I've got a Christmas present for you.'

Rosie was astonished. Until that moment she would have sworn her grandmother did not go in for frivolities like presents. She was even more amazed when Maggie brought from upstairs a delicately carved wooden box and opened it. Out spilt jewellery – such riches as Rosie had never expected to see in this shabby house.

Maggie took out a ring, forcing it over a fat knuckle, sharp button eyes fixed on Rosie as she watched the light catch the facets in the cluster of gems. Then the old woman removed a brooch from the gleaming pile and pinned it to her shawl. That was only the first of many brooches with which she adorned herself. Next came two bracelets, of gold and silver. After that she unravelled several necklaces. One string was made up of black stones, the other amber, and the last was a double row of pearls.

Rosie stared in bedazzled amusement. The jewels were so pretty, sparkling and glowing, that they gave her enormous pleasure. 'You make a fine Christmas tree, Gran. We should stand you in the window and you'd brighten the place up.'

'Aye, I would that! But don't I look like I'm worth something now?'

'You look a million dollars.'

'I do, don't I?' Maggie preened herself in front of the mirror. 'Some of these have seen the inside of the pawn-shop more than once, girl. I've had it hard.' She bowed her head a moment as if in prayer before beginning to remove her precious trinkets.

The girl watched and waited. When Maggie removed the black-stoned necklace and looped it around Rosie's neck, she thanked her and tried her best to look pleased.

'Yer granddad brought me that home from Africa,' said Maggie, a wistful note in her voice.

'My granddad!' Rosie fingered the necklace. 'Tell me about him, Gran?'

Immediately, Maggie's expression changed. Her lips tightened. 'I've said enough. Now put the kettle on and we'll have a cuppa with some of them there cookies the Yank's given yous.'

Rosie saw there was nothing for it but to accept what her grandmother said. The necklace, though, had now grown in value in Rosie's eyes. It did not matter what it was worth moneywise because it had come from her granddad. She would regard it as a family heirloom and pass it on to her daughter, if ever she had one. One thing was for sure: she would wear it on Boxing Day when she went to West Derby, her grandmother having already told her she was going out that day to visit old friends.

'Now yer'd better behave yerself if that lad comes round,' said Maggie, dusting her nose with a pinky-orange shade of face powder. Rings sparkled on her fingers and she was wearing an astrakhan coat with a fur collar which smelt of mothballs.

'Davey's not coming round, Gran. He's been roped in for a family celebration. His cousin's home from the war. So how about going to the pantomime tomorrow night as a treat?' asked Rosie.

'What? Spend money on seeing people make fools of themselves,' said Maggie, her mellow expression vanishing.

'It's George Formby at the Empire! I thought you liked him?' Rosie was doing her best to see the old lady enjoyed herself this Christmas. After all, she mightn't be here the next!

'Yeah, I do.' Maggie pinned a butterfly brooch on to her coat. 'But we'll see.' She bustled out.

Rosie waited ten minutes and then left the house too.

Amelia opened the door to Rosie wearing a harassed expression. Her hair was wispy and there were dark rings beneath her eyes. 'We'd almost given you up. Have you eaten?'

'Yes, with Gran. But I could eat more,' said Rosie hopefully.

'Well, you can wait for tea now. I'm going to put my feet up. Your Uncle Pete's taking the twins and Dotty out for a walk. You go with them. I need the house to myself for an hour.'

Dotty made an appearance, wearing her red and green plaid frock. Her barley-white hair had grown and as she wasn't wearing her spectacles she looked quite pretty. 'I don't want to go out for a walk,' she said. 'I'm getting a cold.'

'I haven't noticed you sneezing. Anyway, the fresh air'll kill off any germs,' said Amelia firmly.

'It'll probably kill me and then you'll be glad,' muttered Dotty, a sulky expression coming over her face.

Amelia exchanged glances with Rosie and threw up her hands. 'She's been like this all morning! Tell her, Rosie, you'll dose her with nice big spoonfuls of nasty-tasting medicine. That'll soon have her dancing around with a smile on her face.'

Dotty glared at her aunt, and if looks had the power to dispatch people to Timbuctoo, Amelia would have gone flying straight through the front door.

'Is it OK for me to take my new ball?' asked Jimmy, bouncing it into the hall.

'Stop that!' said his father, catching the ball in mid-air. 'You'll carry it until we get to the estate. Then you can have a good kick around.'

Rosie wished him Happy Christmas with a kiss.

'Happy Christmas to you too.' He hugged her. 'We thought we'd walk to meet Chris, who's had to go in just for a couple of hours to milk the cows.'

Amelia, watching them, felt that familiar stab of jealousy again.

They set out, Dotty complaining it was a waste of time because it would be dark soon. Rosie decided not to show her sister the necklace. The mood she was in, she would probably have a good moan about not getting anything off her grandmother.

When they reached Lord Sefton's estate, the twins and Peter began to kick the ball around on the white-rimed grass. The girls huddled together, watching them. 'Has Aunt Amelia mentioned anything about Babs and Harry coming home?' asked Rosie.

'Not to me. I wish I lived in Canada. Everything's better over there,' said Dotty moodily.

'Here's our Chris!' shouted Tom.

Rosie noticed the colour rise in Dotty's face and kept an eye on her as Chris came up to them. 'Hi!' he said.

'Hi!' said Rosie, nudging her sister. 'Here's Chris.'

'I know! I'm not deaf as well as half-blind,' muttered Dotty, cheeks scarlet.

'You're not going on about going blind again, are you?' groaned Rosie.

'Why should you?' said Chris, bringing his face close to Dotty's. 'It's not as if you're diabetic like my mam was, is it?'

Dotty said in a queer voice, 'Your mum was diabetic?'

'Yeah. Not that all diabetics go blind. Most just have trouble with their eyes. But Mam was going blind and it really bothered her,' he said, suddenly looking strained.

'There's a girl at school who has diabetes but I only discovered that the other day. I haven't got it, have I?' said Dotty, turning to Rosie.

'Of course not!' She raised her eyes heavenwards. 'Is that what's been worrying you?'

'A bit. But it's OK now.' Dotty sounded relieved and beamed up at Chris. 'Thanks for mentioning it. I feel so much better.'

'Good. Does that mean we're friends?'

'I didn't know we were enemies,' said Dotty, slipping her arm through his. 'Let's go home. It's freezing here.'

So they all went home to be welcomed by a smiling Amelia, who was feeling better for a bit of peace and quiet.

Rosie showed her necklace to her aunt as she helped her with the dishes. Amelia pleased her by saying, 'It could have more than sentimental value, Rosie. The beads look like jet to me. I'm not saying they're worth anything like rubies or diamonds, but they're not rubbish.'

It was Amelia, too, who lingered in the doorway when the family came to wave Rosie off, not Dotty. 'I just wondered if you'd had any news from Babs since the beginning of the month?' she said.

Rosie shook her head. 'You haven't heard from Aunt Iris?'

'No.' She hesitated. 'I was wondering, if Iris, Babs and Harry do come over, whether your gran could have the children to live with her?'

'I've already thought of it,' said Rosie. At least in this they agreed.

Amelia smiled. 'Great minds think alike. Have you mentioned it to Mrs Kilshaw?'

'Not yet.' Rosie rubbed her cold nose with the back of one gloved hand. 'I'll have to get Gran in the right mood.'

'Perhaps if I write her a note? Offer her some money to help towards their keep?'

Rosie nodded. 'Money would help. Do the letter tomorrow and I'll see how she takes to the idea.'

The next day, Amelia wrote a note to Maggie and handed it to Rosie. Amelia was feeling so pleased they'd both had the same idea that when Peter came home from work she wanted to share it with him and followed him up to his room. 'Before you start writing,' she said, 'I've something to tell you.'

'Sounds serious,' he murmured, twirling a pencil between his fingers. 'Someone sick?'

'Oh, no. Nothing like that.'

'OK.' He smiled encouragingly. 'Something funny the twins have done?'

She shook her head, returning his smile, and began to tell him what she and Rosie had decided. She did not get far before his smile vanished. 'You're joking? You're expecting that grouchy old woman you've told me about to take on an extra two kids? One of them a boy of five!'

'Nearly six,' said Amelia, her smile fading. 'What's wrong with that? I'm going to give her some money.'

'And where's that coming from? Sorry!' He pulled himself up immediately, his mouth set grimly. 'I shouldn't have asked. You'll take it out of the shop's profits, I suppose.'

She was so upset he could not see any good in her plan that she flared up. 'And if I did, so what? They're *my* profits! But as it is I've money available for such a contingency.'

'What money? Some your father left?'

'No.' She toyed with the door knob. 'It's compensation for Violet's death. It belongs to the children. I saw a solicitor and—' She was prevented from going on by the incredulity in his eyes.

'I see.' His expression was bleak and he threw down the pencil. 'I wonder if you would ever have told me if it weren't for the fact you want Iris home and living here with us.'

'I didn't intentionally keep it from you. And this *was* her home,' Amelia retorted in a flash.

He dragged off his tie. 'I can see the way your mind's working. She'll be able to stay home and look after everything while you carry on at the shop.'

Now it was her turn to look incredulous. 'That wasn't my idea at all! She's my sister and I miss her. She's all the family I've got. I just want her home.'

'And you're my wife! And aren't I and the boys your family too?' The anger in his voice made her wince. 'Or is our marriage such a sham that we don't count as real family?'

Emotion caught her by the throat and she had to swallow before she could speak. 'This has got out of hand.' Her voice was low. 'I didn't intend to say half of that. All I was thinking was that if Babs and Harry could live with the grandmother, we wouldn't be overcrowded.'

'And what does the grandmother think?' he said stiffly, running the tie round and round his hand.

She fixed her gaze on that, rather than look into his eyes. 'I don't know. I gave Rosie a note to hand to her this evening.'

'You've what?' He almost choked on the words. 'You haven't even the good manners to go and see the woman yourself and ask her?'

'Mrs Kilshaw and I aren't exactly on the best of terms,' said Amelia, temper flaring again. 'I don't see what's wrong with a note!'

'Well, I do. You must go and see the woman and talk to her properly about this if it's what you want,' he rasped.

Amelia lifted her head and looked straight into his eyes. They were the colour of flint and just as hard. 'Right!' she said. 'I'll go now. Your dinner's in the oven. The twins were hungry so I gave them theirs. 'Bye!'

She ran downstairs, pausing only to put on her outdoor things and pick up her handbag. She slammed the front door behind her. Her high heels made an angry click-clacking noise on the path. She felt like never seeing him again. Suddenly, the thought occurred to her that their marriage had not been consummated. So what was stopping her getting it annulled? But first she had to see the old granny.

Chapter Thirteen

Rosie decided to wait until tea was over and the dishes washed before giving Amelia's note to her grandmother. But the advent of several customers, even shorter of ready cash than normal after Christmas, delayed the moment further. It was getting on for eight o'clock when she broached the subject and handed over the note.

Immediately, Maggie's face turned a shade that was almost beetroot. 'What does that bloody woman think I am – taking on a family at my age? Selfish, that's what she is. Selfish! Just like yer mam was. Does she think I'm made of money?'

'Gran, read the note. She said it'll explain everything, including money. She—'

'*She's* the cat's mother,' said Maggie, panting as she attempted a swipe at Rosie. 'Yer know what yer trouble is, girl? Yer haven't been brought up properly. That mam of yours so-cken-fun—'

'What?' Rosie rested her hands on the counter. 'What did you say, Gran?'

'Haz's mock . . .' The words were slurred and didn't make sense. Then Maggie collapsed against the counter and slid out of sight.

Oh, hell! thought Rosie, rushing round to the other side where her grandmother lay slumped on the floor. 'Oh, God, mustn't panic!' she said aloud, feeling for a pulse and sighing with relief when she found one. Even so, Maggie did not look at all well.

Somehow Rosie managed to get an arm beneath the old woman, placing her arm about her neck. But Maggie's arm seemed to have no life of its own, dropping down heavily again. Rosie struggled on, managing to get her grandmother into the kitchen and on to the sofa. There she propped her up with cushions, unsure what to do next. It seemed wrong to leave her but she had to get help.

'Sorry, Gran, but I'm going to have to leave you for a few minutes. I won't be long.' She hesitated before kissing the old woman's cheek.

Rosie went next door but there was no answer to her frantic knocking. The woman on the other side had no time for Maggie so the girl decided not to bother her. Instead she thought of Mrs Baxendale and raced along the street.

'Keep your hair on, I'm coming,' called Davey in response to her hammering on the front door. Rosie sagged against the wall of the house, getting her breath back.

His eyes narrowed at the sight of her. 'What's up? You look done in.'

'It's Gran! She's had a funny turn,' gasped Rosie. 'Will your mam come and look at her?'

Davey pulled Rosie inside and ushered her into the kitchen where his mother was sitting, feet on the fender.

'Rosie's gran's gone funny,' he said without any preamble. 'You're needed, Ma.'

Mrs Baxendale got up awkwardly. 'What happened? Have you phoned a doctor?'

Rosie sank on to a chair. 'I don't know her doctor. I wasn't sure what to do so I came here.'

'Is she conscious?' said Mrs Baxendale, looking serious as she took her coat from her son.

'Not when I left she wasn't. Her speech went all funny, though. If we need a doctor, perhaps we should telephone the one Mam had? Not that we ever saw much of him. Couldn't afford him.'

'He's the same as ours. You phone him from the corner shop, Davey. It sounds like a stroke to me,' said his mother grimly. 'Come on, lovey. Let's go and see how she is.'

Maggie's eyes were closed and she had not shifted from the position in which Rosie had left her. For a moment, the girl thought she was dead, but when Mrs Baxendale spoke the old woman's eyes opened and she tried to speak, spittle dribbling from the corner of her mouth.

'Poor old dear,' said Mrs Baxendale, tutting. 'But at least she's showing signs of life.'

'She's a tough old bird,' said Rosie, a sound escaping her which veered between a laugh and a sob. She had not realised she cared about her grandmother that much but seeing her like this upset her. She sat on the corner of the sofa, taking one of Maggie's hands in hers and squeezing it, but there was no response.

'I'll put the kettle on,' said Mrs Baxendale, limping over to the sink. 'We won't know anything for sure until the doctor comes.'

Davey arrived just as his mother was pouring out tea. 'He's on his way.'

'Good,' said his mother. 'You sit down and cheer Rosie up. It's been a shock to her.'

Davey pulled a raffia-topped stool close to the sofa and took her hand.

The letter box went and the girl sprang to her feet. To her amazement, Amelia stood on the doorstep. 'Don't look so shocked,' said her aunt in her old abrupt manner. 'I'm not the devil incarnate. I've just had a row with Peter. He's utterly against our idea. Said I should speak to your grandmother myself, not send a note.'

Rosie's mouth trembled. 'She got very angry. We think she's had a stroke. I thought you were the doctor.'

Amelia's hand tightened on the door jamb. 'It's my fault,' she whispered. 'I didn't think she'd take it like that.'

'It's mine as well then,' said Rosie. 'I wanted it, too.'

Amelia pulled herself together. 'Let me see her. I know something about strokes.'

'Do you think that's a good idea?' stammered Rosie. 'You know how you and she feel about each other.'

'She mightn't even know me, Rosie. So don't be worrying about that.'

Rosie hurried up the lobby and Amelia followed her into the kitchen, nodding a greeting when she saw Davey and his mother.

Rosie's concern as to how her grandmother might react to Amelia's presence soon vanished because Maggie did not appear to recognise the visitor at all. The doctor arrived a few minutes later and immediately addressed Amelia, who stepped forward to greet him. He asked was she a relative of the sick woman and Amelia surprised Rosie by saying yes. He dismissed the girl and the Baxendales from the room.

'Why did she do that?' said Rosie, irritated, as she led the way to the parlour. '*I'm* Gran's nearest relative. They don't even like each other, and they're not related the way Aunt Amelia made it sound.'

'She's related by marriage,' said Mrs Baxendale, patting Rosie's hand. 'And listen, lovey – he'll tell her more than he'll tell you.'

Reluctantly, she realised that was probably true, though it annoyed her.

It was not long before they heard footsteps in the lobby and the murmur of voices. Rosie opened the parlour door just in time to see Amelia closing the front one. 'What about his fee?' she said hastily.

'I've seen to that,' said her aunt, rubbing her eyes. 'Your grandmother can reimburse me when she recovers.'

'Then she's going to get better?' said Rosie, starting forward, relieved.

Amelia lowered her arm and stared at her. 'The doctor's cautiously optimistic. One thing's for sure, Rosie – your grandmother's going to need someone with her constantly for a while. You won't be able to go into work while she's like this, more's the pity.'

Rosie's face fell and Davey took her hand and squeezed it. 'We'll help as much as we can.'

'I won't be able to do as much as I'd like, though, lovey,' said Mrs Baxendale. 'Breaking my leg's slowed my gallop.'

'If only she hadn't fallen out with my granddad,' said Rosie, sighing. 'I'm sure he'd have been prepared to help me.'

Amelia stared at her. 'I thought your granddad was dead?'

'No.' And Rosie told Amelia what Maggie had said about him.

Her aunt clicked her tongue against her teeth. 'It doesn't surprise me that he left her, though that doesn't help us now.'

'What do I do about tonight? Can Gran go to bed?'

'Best leave her where she is. She'll be quite comfy on the sofa if you bring down blankets and a pillow.' Amelia glanced at the clock on the mantelpiece. 'I'll stay here in case anything happens. You'd best get to bed.'

'We'll be going, Rosie. I'll call in tomorow and see if there's anything I can get you,' said Mrs Baxendale.

'Don't be worrying,' said Davey, lifting her hand and kissing it. 'And don't be forgetting her Sunday visitor.'

Rosie pressed her cheek against his hand a moment. Amelia stared at them, feeling an ache inside her.

When Rosie returned after seeing the Baxendales out, her aunt was making cocoa. 'Get this down you,' she said, 'then you can fetch the bedding. Bring a pillow and a blanket for me. I'll sleep down here.'

'What about Uncle Pete?' said Rosie. 'What's he going to say about you staying out all night?'

'He'll understand when I tell him,' said Amelia, making her voice light.

Rosie drank her cocoa and went upstairs. Maggie seemed to be sleeping and hardly made a murmur as they fixed her up. Both were certain they would not be able to sleep, but Rosie went off almost immediately.

But Amelia was wide awake in the unfamiliar surroundings, thinking at first about Maggie. It was a turn-up for the book that her husband was still alive, but were they still married? Amelia sighed. What did it matter anyway? This Sunday visitor was likely to be of more help to them. She eased her back, trying to get more comfortable, and began to brood over the quarrel with Peter. He would surely agree to an annulment if he believed what he said about the marriage being a mistake. It was a sad thing to admit, just when they had appeared to be getting on better. The trouble was that both of them had considered sacrosanct the plea of a dying woman and had not given enough thought to their own needs. Believing that a little self-sacrifice for the children's sake would be enough to make everything work out when it was not nearly enough after all.

Something more was needed to make all the sacrifice worthwhile. She turned the thought over and over in her mind most of that long, uncomfortable night as she recalled the past few months. It was only when a grey light filtered through the curtains into the kitchen that Amelia at last slipped into unconsciousness.

'Aunt Amelia, wake up!'

'What?' she muttered sleepily, wondering what Rosie was doing in her dream.

'Gran's up! She's smashed a cup and she's walking all funny and talking double Dutch again!'

Amelia shot up, wincing as she banged one elbow on the arm of the chair. She forced her eyelids open and saw the ceiling first where clothes hung from a rack. She struggled up and took in Rosie's anxious face, remembering the events of yesterday evening. 'Where is she?' she muttered, pushing the other chair away with her bare feet and throwing back the blanket.

There was the sound of something hitting the floor. 'She's in the shop,' said Rosie.

Amelia followed her out, face expressionless when she saw the sticky pool of jam and spilt dried peas on the floor, though her heart sank. She pitied her niece, having experienced this kind of thing herself with her father. 'It's going to be one of those days, Rosie,' she warned, and stretched herself and yawned.

'Tell me something I don't know,' said the girl grimly, stepping carefully over the mess on the floor.

Maggie swung round, her right arm coming down heavily on the counter, and threw a string of unintelligible words at the girl.

'You're not coming over loud and clear, Gran,' said Rosie.

'I waka go slavtry,' shrieked the old woman, banging on the counter. Then suddenly she dropped her arm to clutch her crotch. There was a pitter-patter on the floor and Rosie groaned.

'Too late,' said Amelia, pulling a face. 'You get the mop and bucket. I'll get the dustpan and brush if you'll tell me where they are. And some newspaper to wipe up the jam. We don't want Mrs Kilshaw slipping and breaking a leg into the bargain. Then we'll see to her together.'

Rosie stared. 'But you don't even like her. Why are you doing this? Why did you stay?'

Amelia's eyebrows arched delicately. 'I'd see to the cat if he'd made a mess. Your gran is human. Now let's get cracking. It's gone nine and I'm going to be late as it is. I'll have to go into the shop.'

It was gone eleven by the time Amelia arrived in Kensington. Mr Brown, who seldom got flustered, was looking harassed. 'Your niece hasn't come in and what with your being late, Mrs Hudson, I've been rushed off my feet! You wouldn't believe the people coming down with coughs and colds. Far more than usual. I hope we're not in for a 'flu epidemic.'

'We always have loads of colds at this time of year. It's good for business, Brownie,' she said, trying to make light of things, glad to put on an overall over her creased, slept-in clothes. 'Rosie won't be in, by the way. Her grandmother's had a stroke.' She explained what had happened.

'How are we going to manage?' he said. 'Perhaps we should look for someone extra to serve in the shop? It would give you more time to be at home looking after your family, Mrs Hudson, when Rosie is able to come back . . .'

Amelia felt a headache coming on. 'Perhaps,' she murmured, feeling like saying, *Don't you start!* 'But let's give it a week and see how things go.'

Nothing more was said as a couple of customers came in and Mr Brown vanished into the dispensing room.

It was not until lunchtime that Amelia had a chance to sit down. Mr Brown went off home and she put on the kettle and found the biscuit tin which contained a few broken biscuits. It was not much of a lunch but it was better than nothing, she decided, thinking she would have to make time to slip out that afternoon to collect her bread from the baker's. She had phoned the butcher's and he had promised her some liver and a couple of sausages, but there were more important things on her mind than food. She bit into another broken Nice biscuit, thinking about Peter and wondering how Rosie was getting on with her grandmother, only to be disturbed by a hammering at the door.

'Go away,' she called wearily.

The hammering persisted so she rose and went to open the door, thinking that maybe it was an emergency.

'I thought you'd be here,' said Peter, pushing his way in as soon as she had the door open. 'Where the hell were you last night?' He pushed back his trilby and in the process rumpled his hair, making him look younger than his thirty-six years, and more vulnerable somehow. 'I hardly slept a wink.'

'I can explain. And don't start shouting, please! I hardly slept a wink either,' she retorted, bolting the door behind him.

'You had us all worried. The twins and Dotty heard us arguing . . . heard the door slam. I didn't know what to tell them.' He threw his hat on to the counter, pushing back his unbuttoned overcoat and digging his hands into his trouser pockets. 'Well?'

Guilt mingled with anger. The kids again! They were all he cared about. She folded her arms across her breasts, hugging herself. 'I couldn't leave Rosie. Her grandmother had a stroke.' She tossed the words at him. 'And I know what you're going to say – that it was my fault for writing that note.'

'I wasn't going to say anything of the sort.' He frowned. 'So don't go jumping in before I get a chance to speak.'

'What's there to say? Our marriage was a mistake, as you said. The only answer is an annulment. It hasn't been consummated so we should have no difficulty.'

'And that's your answer?' There was a pinched look about his nose and mouth. 'If I'm not mistaken, you'd have to provide medical evidence to that fact. Do you fancy that?' His laughter was hollow.

'If needs must.' She pressed her lips tightly together and turned her back on him. Of course she hadn't thought about that and the idea filled her not only with acute embarrassment but mortification as well.

'Marvellous! I can just imagine the gossip.' His voice shook.

She whirled round. 'Is that all you care about? What people will say?'

'Don't you?' His angry eyes met hers and he grabbed her by the shoulders. She was surprised by a thrill of excitement. 'You who've always been so prim and proper. You'd be making a holy show of us! It would be so wrong to destroy this marriage just because we fell out over your sister coming to live with us.'

'It's not just that and you know it,' she retorted. 'It's the children! I'm always having to think about *them*. There seems to be no time for anything else.'

'But you must have known what it would be like when you took the job on?' He shook her slightly, his expression softening. 'And what have I been saying these past months about you giving up the shop so you could have more time to yourself?'

'I know. But that's out of the question now. Didn't you hear what I said?' Her tone was milder. 'Rosie's gran's had a stroke. Rosie's going to have to stay at home for a while and look after her.'

'I'm sorry. Sorry for Rosie too. But couldn't you – I – we—'

'What?' She gazed up at him and suddenly it was as if she had never seen him properly before. How long that moment lasted while they just looked at each other she had no idea but her bones felt as if they were melting. With a great effort he cleared his throat and she tried to remember what was the last thing said.

'If Iris comes . . .' he murmured, rubbing a hand up and down her arm.

'Yes?'

Peter hesitated. 'I was thinking – we could share a room and Iris could have mine. Babs could bunk in with Dotty, and Harry with the boys. I know it would be a bit crowded but—'

'That sounds sensible.' Amelia lowered her eyes, tracing the black and white pattern on the tiled floor with the toe of her shoe.

'Sensible. Yes.' His voice sounded odd.

She cleared her throat which felt as if it had a fish bone stuck in it. 'You see married couples in twin beds all the time in American films.'

'Do you?'

'Yes.'

'Then we'll do that, shall we? It would be a step in the right direction.'

'Yes.' There was no need for her to ask which direction that was. She sensed that he, like she, was unsure just how and when they should make certain moves. It was less than a year since Tess had died. Her presence was still very real to Amelia, and she felt sure it must be the same for him.

Peter dropped his hands. 'Will you be in when I get home this evening?'

'I should go and see if Rosie and her grandmother are OK.'

He nodded. 'You do that. But why don't you knock off a little earlier and come home first so the kids will know everything's all right between us?'

'Of course. That's a good idea. I'll do that.' Even to herself Amelia thought her voice sounded terribly polite and she remembered what he had said about that.

'Right.' He summoned up a smile.

Amelia smiled too. 'I don't like being out of friends,' she said.

'Me neither.' He reached out and took her hand, fingering her wedding ring. 'It's six months.'

'I know.'

He raised her hand to his lips and kissed it. She felt the breath catch in her throat, wanting to reach out and touch his face and bring it closer to hers. The moment was fraught with possibilities but she just could not do it. Why? She did not know but the opportunity had passed now and he left.

By the time Amelia arrived at Maggie's house, Rosie was drooping. She stripped off her gloves and gave Rosie her orders. 'Go and get some fresh air. I'll make a pot of tea and stay with your gran.'

A smile flooded Rosie's peaky face. 'What about Uncle Pete? Does he know you're here?'

'Of course he knows I'm here,' she said briskly. 'I've spoken to him and everything's OK.'

'I think I'll slip over and see Davey then, if you don't mind?'

'As long as you don't let yourself get too serious about him,' said Amelia lightly. 'This is only a temporary setback. You'll be back in that dispensing room in no time, you'll see.'

Rosie was silent, grabbing her coat and leaving the house.

Amelia sat next to Maggie, who sat slumped in a chair. 'How are you feeling?' she said loudly.

'Sheiam mussh betcher.'

Amelia agreed she was looking much better but thought here too it was early days. She watched Maggie fall asleep in front of her, then rose and reached for the old woman's handbag. Perhaps she would find the address of the Sunday visitor in there. She rifled through the bulging bag's contents and came across a couple of letters that interested her greatly. She smiled and when Rosie returned told her she would come again on Sunday and see how things were.

Over the next couple of days, Maggie's condition improved marginally. She had little movement in her left arm but was able to walk down the yard with Rosie's help. On Sunday Amelia arrived, accompanied by Dotty. Rosie was glad to see the pair of them but when her sister went up close to her grandmother, gazing at her intently and saying, 'She looks smaller than I remember. Is she still talking double Dutch?' Rosie was vexed with her.

'She's not deaf, you know. It's really frustrating for her, being the way she is.'

'Sorry!' said Dotty, pouting. 'I didn't mean to upset her.'

'Why don't you two go out?' said Amelia, sensing Rosie really needed a break from the house and her grand-mother. 'I'll hold the fort.'

Dotty looked relieved but Rosie said, 'You'll have to see to the shop too. People still come on Sundays.'

Amelia gave no sign of disapproving of the Sabbath being desecrated in such a way, only saying in a dry voice, 'I think I can manage.'

Still Rosie was not satisfied. 'People get things on tick. There's a book on a string attached to the counter.'

'Get out, girl!' Her aunt pushed her towards the door, half laughing. 'The day'll be over before you've been anywhere. I think, after running my own place, I can manage this.'

Once rid of her nieces, she took out a large slice of
the carrot cake she had made last evening and cut it in
half. She gave a piece to Maggie and made a pot of tea.
Amelia switched on the wireless, watching her charge fall
asleep. She had done some hard thinking and now settled
down to wait.

It was not long before she heard the back gate opening
and heavy footsteps in the yard. She looked out of the
window before walking into the shop and was behind the
counter when the door opened.

The man was elderly with vivid blue eyes, which
showed surprise on seeing her. He removed his checked
flat cap, placing it on the counter. He had a thick crop of
greying sandy hair and was still a good-looking man for
his age. 'Who are you? And where's Maggie?' he said
gruffly.

'Who are you?' she retorted promptly.

He hesitated, tapping his fingers on the counter. 'You
answer my question first. Where's Maggie?'

'She's had a stroke.'

'Bloody hell!' He looked stunned for a minute, then
he coloured. 'Pardon me language but you gave me a
shock. When did that happen?'

'The day after Boxing Day.'

He leaned against the counter, shaking his head. 'I
knew we shouldn't have played cards. She always was a
lousy loser.'

'Was that on Boxing Day?'

'Naw! She was seeing friends from her old street then.
I dropped in the day after.'

Amelia's conscience lightened a little. 'I see. Did she get all worked up?'

'You can say that again! Stubborn ol' faggot.' He took a pipe and leather pouch from a pocket, blue eyes still on Amelia's face. 'But what business is it of yours? Yer still haven't told me who yer are, queen?'

'I'm Amelia Hudson, née Needham. But I don't suppose that'll mean anything to you?' She paused but he did not flicker an eyelid.

'Nice to meet yer.' He put down his pipe and held out a hand. 'Not from round here, are yer?'

'West Derby.' They shook hands, Amelia quite liking the look of him.

'Had an uncle who lived out that way. So how is Maggie? I take it she's not dead or yer'd have told me.' He picked up his pipe again, packing shreds of tobacco into the tortoiseshell bowl with stubby fingers.

'No. And I'm hoping she'll make a good recovery. At the moment, though, she needs help. It's my niece who's doing that. She lives here with her grandmother.'

He blinked. 'Who the hell's your niece and who's her grandmother? I thought only Maggie lived here.'

'Rosie Kilshaw. Mrs Kilshaw's her grandmother.'

His jaw dropped. 'What are yer saying? Maggie hasn't got any grandchildren.' He looked aggrieved. 'And I should know, queen. I'm her husband!'

Amelia was delighted to hear it. 'That is good news. We thought you were dead!'

'Yeah! That's what she probably wanted people to think,' he said grimly. 'She's got some explaining to do.

Not one word has she mentioned about us have a granddaughter.'

'You have several grandchildren,' said Amelia, enjoying the moment. 'They're Joe's, of course.'

'The owld bitch! Begging your pardon for my French.' His bushy eyebrows met in a frown and he took the still unlit pipe out of his mouth. 'I've always liked kids. Me one big regret when I left was leaving our Joe behind, but she was a hard woman to live with and that's a fact. I would have taken him with me but I were a sailor and it wouldn't have been fair on the lad.' He looked sad.

'You do know Joe's dead?' she said gently.

He nodded, shoulders slumping. 'She told me last February. I was real upset. She would never let me see him when he was a kid, yer know? Moved house. Said I upset him. I'd see her on her pitch and ask after him. I even followed her once but she twigged and led me a merry old dance before I lost her. I gave up in the end and didn't see her for years.'

'But you've been coming here every Sunday recently?'

Unexpectedly, he grinned, showing a mouth of strong-looking if yellow teeth. 'I got a letter about a year ago saying she was going in for an operation and would I come and see her?'

'How did she know where to get in touch if you hadn't been seeing each other?'

'A mutual friend who still lives down Great Homer Street. "Walter," she writes, "I wants to make me peace before meeting me Maker." Which surprised me, I can tell yer, because she never was one for churchgoing. So I visits her in hossie and I've been coming most Sundays ever since.' He paused to light his pipe, puffing busily to get it going. 'So where is she? Hossie?'

Amelia caught the sound of movement in the kitchen. 'No.' She smiled. 'If I'm not mistaken, she's just woken up. Would you like to see her? Although you probably won't understand a word she says.'

'Right yer are! But I'm downright annoyed with her and I'm not pretending otherwise.' He followed Amelia into the kitchen.

'Whoshish?' said Maggie, eyes fixing on Walter.

'Yer know me, yer stupid woman,' he said, shaking his head. 'I'm yer husband.'

Maggie's expression was wistful. 'Hanshum.'

'Bloody hell!' Walter's face was a picture. 'Has she lost her marbles an' all? She hasn't called me handsome since we went to Morecambe for our honeymoon and that was before the Great War.'

'Strokes do affect the brain,' said Amelia, trying not to laugh.

He flashed her a keen glance. 'Yer seem to know something about it. Are yer some kind of nurse?'

'No. Although I own a chemist's shop and I've seen some sights. But my father had a stroke and I nursed him.' Amelia sat down and waved him to a chair. 'You said you liked children, Mr Kilshaw?'

'Course,' he said with a touch of scorn. 'Help down at the boys' club, don't I? Teach them a bit of ju-jitsu and table tennis.' He put his pipe back in his mouth and drew on it. 'Where are these grandchildren of mine then? Can I see them? How many are there?'

Amelia glanced at Maggie, who had not taken her eyes off Walter the whole time he had been talking, and wondered how much the old woman was taking in. She turned back to Walter and began to explain.

When she had finished he shook his head, gazing at Maggie and muttering, 'Yer owld bitch! Why didn't yer let me know? Jealous, I bet. Yer never were any good at sharing.' He glanced at Amelia. 'Always had a temper, yer know. Threw a knife at me once. Didn't like me giving anyone else any attention.' He fell silent, puffing at his pipe.

'Right now she doesn't look like she could say boo to a goose,' murmured Amelia.

'Not herself, is she, though?' he grunted. 'Once she's back to normal, she'll be just as bad.'

'She might never get back to normal,' said Amelia, leaning closer to him. 'And in the meantime Rosie is going to have her work cut out looking after her. It's a lot for a girl who isn't yet seventeen and has just started training for a secondary certificate in pharmacy. She's a bright girl, Mr Kilshaw, and she's working for me. I have high hopes for her, but how can they be fulfilled if she's stuck here day after day, looking after your wife and working in that apology for a shop?'

His eyes were wary. 'Why are yer saying all this? Yer not thinking me and Maggie can get together again, are yer? Cos I'm telling yer now, queen, it's not on! She wouldn't like it and neither would I. Things aren't that simple.'

'Nothing ever is as simple as we would like it to be,' said Amelia. 'But you don't work any more, do you?'

'That's right. Gave up the sea just before war broke out. But I don't sit round twiddling me thumbs. I go down the Pierhead and watch the ships. Told yer about the boys' club. And I meet me old mates in the park and have a chinwag. I feed the birds and go to the library and read the papers . . .'

'You look like a man who keeps himself on the go.' She allowed a note of admiration to creep into her voice.

Walter's chest swelled. 'No, I'm not one to be lazing about. Might as well cock up me toes and die. Keep busy, that's what I say.'

'You're like your wife in that if Rosie's anything to go by. By the way, why did you carry on coming to see her, once you knew she wasn't going to die, if the pair of you don't get on?'

He drew on his pipe, not looking directly at Amelia. 'Still me wife, isn't she? Only separated – never divorced. Although I did ask her once about that but she wouldn't hear of it. So I stopped bothering.'

'Then you do care what happens to her?'

His bright blue eyes fixed on hers. 'Yer could say that. But I'm not coming to live here, I told yer.'

Amelia was not about to give up. She leant towards him. 'Then what about helping out so Rosie can go to work?' He kept silent but she persisted. 'Just until Maggie can cope on her own. You'd be doing your granddaughter a real favour, Mr Kilshaw, so think about it. You owe it to Joe.'

There was a long silence before he said, 'Where is she now?'

'I sent her and Dotty out for some fresh air. They'll be back in an hour or so.'

'Tell me more about them?' he said, settling back in the chair. 'And I wouldn't mind a cup of char.'

'Why not?' said Amelia, hopes high, and put on the kettle.

By the time the sisters returned, Amelia had done her work well. The sight of a spry but elderly gentleman reading the Sunday newspaper aloud to Maggie was enough to convince Rosie that here was just the right person to help her.

'Rosie, Dotty!' said their aunt. 'This is your granddad, Walter Kilshaw.'

Rosie stared at him. 'But . . . I thought you'd gone for good!' She darted a glance at her grandmother.

'Naw, queen. That was her wishful thinking at one time.' He bounced to his feet and seized both her hands. 'I'm downright pleased to meet yer!'

'And I'm pleased to meet you, too,' said Rosie, scarcely able to believe what was happening. 'But I don't understand. How did you know to come right now?' She gazed into his moist blue eyes and caught a glimpse of her father. It gave her a warm feeling but also filled her with sadness and regret.

'I've been visiting here for the past year, girl, but I never knew you existed until today.'

'Not at all?' said Dotty.

'Not at all, queen.' He took her hand and squeezed it hard. 'I'm bloo—blinking angry about that. But there, we've met now.'

Rosie remembered how Maggie had chased her out every Sunday. Why had she done it? What had happened to turn her into the kind of person who didn't want her husband to meet his own grandchildren?

There was a brief silence and then Dotty made them laugh by saying, 'What do granddads do?'

'That's a funny question,' said Walter, a twinkle in his eye. 'What would you like me to do?'

'Be here, I suppose,' said Rosie hesitantly.

His expression changed, became suddenly sober. 'Now that's not on, queen.' He rested one gnarled hand on her shoulder. 'But your aunt's been telling me how well yer doing at her shop so I've said I'll be around when yer need me.'

She took his measure. 'What's that mean exactly?'

'That I'll spend some time here during the day, to look after your gran. Your aunt said some woman—' He paused, trying to remember the name.

'Mrs Baxendale,' supplied Amelia.

'Will put in an hour or two keeping her company as well. Together we should be able to manage while you're at work.'

Rosie could not have been more grateful. Here was the answer to her prayers. But God had sent not just any old body. He had sent a granddad who appeared to be kind and, unlike some old men she had seen, even clean. It was a miracle and she told him so. At that they all laughed, hearts much lighter than they had been a few hours ago.

Chapter Fourteen

Rosie watched Amelia remove her overall. It had been a quiet day even before the fog had come down, and now, at three o'clock, it was a peasouper. Her aunt had started knocking off work at this time since Rosie's return to the shop. 'Perhaps there'll be a letter when you get home,' she said.

'I hope so.' Amelia frowned. 'I'd just like to know where we are. Whether they're coming or not. It's almost two months since Iris last wrote. It's funny that you haven't heard from Babs either.'

'It is worrying.' Rosie wrinkled her nose. 'They couldn't be dead, could they?'

Amelia smiled fainty. 'I think we'd have heard. The trouble is, after you lose someone you keep expecting the worst to happen to other people you care about.'

'Perhaps their letters have gone missing?'

'But we've both written again so they'd know we haven't received them.' Amelia put on her coat and wrapped a green patterned scarf round her neck. 'You haven't mentioned the possibility of Babs and Harry living with you to your grandmother again?'

Rosie shook her head, thinking how Maggie's condition had improved over the last few weeks. She was walking unaided and could feed herself if someone cut up her meat for her. Dressing unaided was still beyond her but at Walter's insistence Rosie had returned to work a few weeks ago. 'I have mentioned it to Granddad, hoping he might come and live with us. But he says his landlady's been good to him and he can't just leave her in the lurch. Apparently she's the mother of an old Army mate of his from the first war who was killed.'

'It's nice to think he's so caring,' murmured Amelia. 'But carry on working on him. You're his grandchildren and you have a greater claim on him.'

She opened the door and a swirl of fog entered the shop. Quickly she closed it behind her and hurried along the pavement to the tram stop, thinking now of Peter. Since he had mentioned moving into her room, she had not been able to get the idea out of her head. She thought about it every day. Indeed she had visions of herself, clad in a satin negligee (flesh-coloured), lounging seductively on her bed, and of him covering the space between his and hers in one leap. He would smother her face and throat with kisses and . . . But she never got further than that. Somehow imagination failed her at the necessary moment. Amelia often wondered if it had anything to do with her being a virgin and Bernard's having tried it on only once.

She was still undecided about the reason for her own lack of imagination when she arrived home. She was so distracted that she trod on a letter before realising it. Hastily she peeled it off her shoe and recognised the stamp as Canadian. Hurriedly she slit the envelope with her finger, walking into the kitchen as she did so. She drew out a flimsy sheet of paper and read swiftly before allowing it to flutter to the floor.

She went over to the window and gazed out, but the fog was a grey wall shutting her in with her dismal thoughts. Now that Iris had finally made her decision, where did that leave her and Peter and the move into her room? Would everything go on just the same as always?

'They're not coming.'

'Who's not coming?' Peter glanced up at her. He was hunched over the fire, accounts book on his knee.

'Iris and the kids, of course!' She drummed her fingers on the mantelshelf. 'Would you believe they're going to America! Probably there now. She's sold her share of the factory and has decided to head south. I can't understand her! A woman on her own with two kids who aren't even hers. It's not like her.'

'How black did you paint Liverpool?' said Peter, leaning back in the chair and closing his eyes.

'I painted it sky-blue pink with a finny haddy border! What do you think?' she said crossly. 'Home, that's what Liverpool should be to her, Pete. And no matter how humble, there's supposed to be nowhere like it.'

'She must think differently.' His voice sounded husky.

Amelia peered down at him and thought he looked flushed. 'Have you got a sore throat?'

His eyelids fluttered and he stroked his neck and jaw. 'It hurts there. It's been a hell of a week, with women and kids coming in all the time, coughing and sneezing.'

'Tell me about it,' she said, smiling and touching his forehead with the back of her hand. She frowned. 'You are hot! I'll get you a couple of Aspirin. And keep away from the boys in case it's 'flu.'

She went into the hall. Chris was out again and the twins were playing darts. The board hung on the cupboard door under the stairs. Amelia had had visions of there being hundreds of holes where they had missed their aim but they weren't that bad. Besides, Peter had said they had to have somewhere to play indoors, holes in walls or no.

She came back with the Aspirins and a glass of water. 'I'm not sure if you should go to work tomorrow.' She felt his forehead again. 'In fact, I think you should stay home.'

He gave a faint smile. 'You're a bossy woman.'

'Some men need to be told.' She flushed, removing the accounts book from his lap, hoping that whatever it was would not go right through the family.

By morning, Peter was complaining of being burning hot but had dressed and was planning to go into work.

'You're stupid,' said Amelia, shaking her head in disbelief. 'You'll give half of Tuebrook your germs instead of keeping them to yourself.'

He squinted at her from red-rimmed eyes. 'They gave them to me in the first place.'

'No need to take your revenge. Have a day off. Take two.'

'OK.' He sounded tired. 'Any more and I'll have to see the Post Office doctor. Will you still be going to the shop?'

Amelia touched the curl that always seemed to hang loose at the nape of her neck, and sighed. 'I need to see Rosie. Why? Do you think you need a nurse?'

He swallowed painfully. 'My ears hurt. Couldn't you afford to pay someone else to help Rosie? I mean, you spoke of compensation the other month.'

'Most of it's in a trust until they're either twenty-one or marry,' she said, rapidly clearing their plates away. Peter had not eaten anything, she noticed. 'I never got as far as telling you that. I thought it could be of more use to them when they're older.'

'You're crazy,' he said hoarsely. 'Surely some of that money was meant to help with their keep?'

'I told you, there's a little for emergencies but your having a cold isn't that.'

'What if it's 'flu?' He rested one flushed cheek on his hand. 'I'm not happy about you going into the shop any more. And if you don't need that money, then you could afford to pay someone in your stead.'

She shifted uncomfortably. 'I'll think about it. But not now.'

He ran a hand over his tawny hair and rasped, 'I should be supporting you and we both know it!'

'If that's how you feel, I'll do something about it,' she said emphatically. 'Next week, perhaps. Now get back to bed. I'd best get the twins ready.'

Peter pushed himself up. 'Hi ho, hi ho, off to work you go. See you when you get back – if I'm still alive.'

'You're not going to die just because I won't be here, fetching cups of tea and supplying Aspirin.' She smiled but felt guilty nevertheless at the thought of leaving him to fend for himself.

*

'What do you feel about them not coming?' said Rosie, as soon as Amelia entered the shop.

'So you got a letter, too?' She sighed. 'I'm really disappointed. I can't understand our Iris going to America. She never had any time for the Yanks.'

Rosie looked pensive as she put some change in the till. 'She didn't mention Sam in her letter to you, did she?'

'Sam who?' said Amelia absently, her mind having gone off at a tangent, wondering how Peter was.

'It doesn't matter,' said Rosie. 'Out of sight, out of mind. I suppose we can't blame them. What have we got to bring them back for, after all? A battered old city and hardly anything in the way of the little extras that make life better.'

'True,' murmured Amelia. 'Still, we're all in the same boat. Have you remembered you're going into town this morning?'

Rosie brightened up. 'No! Will I go now?'

'Why not? Thomas's at the back of Duke Street. That's where you're going.'

'Right!' Happily Rosie took off her overall.

'And don't be all morning,' called Amelia, turning the sign on the door. 'I want to leave early. Your Uncle Pete's not well.'

'What's he got?'

'A temperature and a sore throat. On top of that he wants me to give up the shop.'

Rosie dropped her handbag and bent to pick it up. 'You mean, sell it? But I'm only in my first year's apprenticeship!'

'No. He's talking of me getting someone in to help you.' She smiled. 'My father started this business. I couldn't get rid of it. Pete just wants me at home soothing his fevered brow like the rest of them.'

'So what are you going to do? Give up and let him take over? Just think, Aunt Amelia, you could be a lady of leisure.'

Amelia gave a sharp laugh. 'You haven't lived in our household as it is now. The only difference if I wasn't coming here is that the floors would get washed more often and I'd catch up on the ironing and washing and still have a chance to breathe! Now get going, Rosie.'

She experienced a moment's pleasurable excitement at the thought of going into town. 'I'm going.' She paused in the doorway. 'Are the twins all right, by the way?'

'Full of beans,' sighed Amelia.

'Pity!' She grinned. 'There was a woman in here the other day who said mumps was going round. That'd stop their gallop!'

'They've had it. They looked like they'd loaded their mouths with gobstoppers,' said Amelia, opening a box of soaps. 'Now go!'

Rosie went.

Seated on the tram, she rubbed a circle in the condensation on a window and peered out. She had not been into town since before Christmas when Lewis's and Blackler's, still bearing the scars of the Blitz, had done their best to make it look festive. In other parts of the city there were acres of wasteland where once there had been shops, offices and homes. It made her feel sad, seeing places so derelict, wondering how long it would be before rebuilding really got going. She doubted, though, that Liverpool would ever be its old self again.

Rosie got off the tram in Church Street and hurried up Hanover Street to Thomas's drug company. It was lovely being out among the bustling crowds. A year ago, the war was still on and the atmosphere had been completely different. Battles were still being fought; men, women and children were still dying. Davey would surely stand a better chance of surviving his call-up now than he would have twelve months ago.

It was on the return trip that Rosie thought she saw her granddad and waved to catch his attention. He did not appear to see her. It was then that she realised he was not alone but arm in arm with a woman. She decided to take a closer look, pushing her way through the crowds, but the couple had crossed into Clayton Square before she could catch up with them.

She followed them, getting glimpses of the woman every now and again. She was taller than Granddad, with brassy sausage curls showing beneath a red felt hat. Rosie almost caught up with them outside St John's Market but a woman came hurrying out with a pram and Rosie only just managed to stop herself from falling over it. The woman apologised. Rosie smiled and brushed away her words and hurried on, past Kendall's the umbrella shop and round the corner into Lime Street. There was no sign of the couple. It was as if a genie had magicked them away.

*

'You're late!' said Amelia from her place in the window.

'Sorry.' Rosie had walked the whole length of Lime Street, peeking into the doorway of the Washington Hotel, O'Connell's pub, even the railway station, but had not been able to spot Walter and his companion. 'What are you doing?'

'Never mind what I'm doing,' retorted Amelia. 'You're supposed to be working here, my girl. Now get into the dispensing room and give that box to Brownie. It's almost lunch hour.'

Rosie went.

Amelia wiped the neck of a carboy filled with coloured water in the display and gazed through the window. Movement on the other side of the road caught her attention. A man was standing outside the tobacconist's staring in her direction. Suddenly, she realised who it was and with unsteady fingers bent and arranged packets of Amami shampoo in the shape of a fan, surreptitiously watching him.

He was coming over! She dropped a packet, stepping down from the window and racing behind the counter, knowing she would feel safer with a barrier between them.

The door opened and Bernard Rossiter stooped to enter. He was well over six feet and as he stared at her for a moment, Amelia felt like a mouse mesmerised by an owl.

'Good day, Amy.'

'Mr Rossiter.' She inclined her head, hoping she appeared calmer than she felt. Her heart was thudding like an engine that had already got up steam and was about to chug away.

He moved towards her with all the grace of a large cat. His dark hair was greying at the temples and he sported a pencil moustache, reminding her of Ronald Colman in *The Prisoner of Zenda*. He had broadened over the years so that the pinstripe material of what was obviously his demob suit stretched tightly across his chest.

He rested one elbow on the counter. 'Why so formal? I've forgiven you. Surely you can forgive me?'

She knew from his eyes he was lying. He hated her and in a way she didn't blame him. Men and their pride! She had jilted him and he had never accepted her reason for doing so, seemingly unable to believe that ending their engagement was as painful to her as it had been to him. 'Are you here on business?' Her voice was cool.

'What else?' He brought his hand down over hers, resting on the glass-topped counter. 'Nothing seems to have changed here,' he added, glancing around.

'Everything's changed.' She kept control of her voice, pretending to ignore the pressure bearing down on her hand. 'Father's dead.'

'I heard. Too late for us, though, isn't it? If only he'd died earlier.'

'I loved my father.' She made to withdraw her hand but he pressed down on it even harder. Her eyes glinted. 'I think you're forgetting yourself, Mr Rossiter. Please take your hand away or I'll have to call for help.'

A corner of his mouth curled. 'Brownie? Now there's a joke!' He removed his hand. 'How's business?'

'The sick are always with us,' she said, moving away from the counter to lean against the rows of small drawers behind her.

'I was sick and ye did not visit me.' His mouth curled into a sneer. 'How did that match up to your sense of duty?'

'Your bad chest didn't stop you getting into the Army.'

'Never left old Blighty, though, sweetie.'

'I'm not a dolly mixture.'

'You were sweet on me once.'

'Those days are gone, and besides you soon married someone else.' She folded her arms. 'How is your wife, by the way?'

'Sick.' He took a piece of paper from his pocket and threw it on the counter. 'Here's her prescription. She was bombed out during the Blitz and had to move in with my mother. Her nerves are bad. I hear you've married?' There was that curl to his mouth again.

Amelia's heart jolted in her breast. She hoped whoever had told him had not mentioned to whom, but she hoped in vain.

There was that look of smouldering hatred back in his eyes again. 'Peter Hudson, I believe. Tess hardly cold in her grave and you tie the knot? Suspicious.'

'She had been ill for years, you know that.' There was a tremor in her voice despite all Amelia's attempts to keep calm.

'Even so, for the pair of you to marry so quickly . . . Some of us with nasty minds might think there'd been hanky-panky going on for years. I've never forgotten his interference in something that was none of his bloody business!'

'I was thankful for his interference,' said Amelia hotly, remembering that day Bernard had followed her. 'And please don't use that language in my shop. Now, if you'll excuse me, I'll take this prescription through to Mr Brown.'

She was glad to get away and seriously thought of knocking off work there and then and letting Rosie deal with him. But almost immediately she decided against it. Bernard would think he had put the wind up her and Amelia wasn't having that. Fortunately, when she returned there were a couple of other customers waiting and he was over by the door, gazing out. It was not until Rosie popped out of the back with his wife's tablets that he came over to the counter again.

'You'll be seeing more of me, Amy,' he said, barely glancing at the girl. Amelia made no comment, taking his money and handing over the tablets. 'Yes.' He flung back his head. 'I'm going back to my old job, working for Evans, Lescher & Webb. I'm sure you won't let the past affect any orders you might give me, Mrs Hudson?' There was a definite challenge in the way he threw the words at her.

'Business is business, Mr Rossiter,' she said coldly. 'Good day.'

He walked out of the shop. Rosie's eyes followed him. 'Who's he?'

'Just an old sales rep back from the war,' said Amelia, turning the sign on the door to CLOSED. 'But you need to watch him. He has the gift of the gab. I'm going home, Rosie. I want to see how Peter is.'

'OK.' For a moment, the girl looked as if she was going to say something more. Amelia did not want her asking any awkward questions about Bernard. She put on her coat and hat and hurried out.

As soon as she closed the front door and set foot in the house, Peter called down, asking who it was. Amelia hurried upstairs, knocking gently on his door before going in. The room was cold and all she could see of him was the crown of his head.

'Are you OK?' she whispered.

He lowered the covers and elbowed himself up.

She stared at him and the exchange with Bernard was completely forgotten. The left half of his face and jawline was swollen and his skin was a fiery red. 'You look awful!'

'I feel awful,' he groaned.

'Oh, dear!' She bit on her lower lip and sat on the bed. 'I don't think it's 'flu, Pete.'

'I know.' He sighed heavily. 'I haven't been sneezing but I've got a damned awful earache. Can you give me something? And can I have a drink?'

'Yes to both. But I think you'd better see the Post Office doctor after all. I think you've got mumps.'

He peered at her resentfully from beneath heavy eyelids. 'That's not funny.'

'It's going the rounds, and honestly—' She said no more, only smiling sympathetically.

His expression was so horrified it was almost comical. 'You're serious!' he croaked.

'Sorry.' She gripped her lower lip between her teeth to prevent herself from laughing.

'But I'm grown up! This can't be happening to me!'

Amelia repeated, 'Sorry.'

'You're enjoying this,' he groaned, burying himself beneath the bedcovers. 'And get off my feet. You're no Skinny Melink, you know!'

'I'm no Two Ton Tess either,' she retorted, getting up. 'I'll get you that cup of tea.'

'Yeah. And a bottle of Aspirin.' His words were muffled.

She patted his hunched shoulder and left the room, feeling like dancing because there was no question of her returning to the shop in the next few days. She was going to have enough on her plate to cope with here without having to deal with Bernard and his snide insinuations if he came into the shop again. She would have to warn Brownie about him, though.

By the time the twins arrived back, Amelia had been in touch not only with the doctor and Mr Brown but had called at St Vincent's as well. 'Do you want a visit from your sons?' she said cheerfully to Peter.

'Too full of bounce. I don't want to see anyone,' he muttered, turning over on to his stomach and burying his hot face in the pillow.

Her eyes twinkled. 'I'll remember that when you want someone to mop your fevered brow.'

' "For better, for worse, in sickness and in health," ' he reminded her.

She could just about catch the words. 'You don't have to tell me that,' she said, thinking mumps was not exactly what she had expected to cope with when she made her marriage vows. 'Then you don't want visitors?' she asked again.

He shook his head and she left the bleak little room, wondering if she was being heartless abandoning him in his misery.

The next morning, he seemed fractionally worse and the other side of his jaw had swelled up. The doctor still had not called. 'I'd best ring him again,' said Amelia, sitting on his bed in her pyjamas.

'No, I'll go to him,' croaked Peter, struggling to sit up.

She raised her eyebrows. 'Don't be stupid! You're not fit.'

His mouth set stubbornly as he attempted to throw back the bedcovers. 'I'm not having him visit me in this box. What's he going to think?'

'That you're a sick man, I shouldn't wonder,' she said as patiently as she could. 'And that you're in quarantine.'

'From my wife?' He stood up on obviously wobbly legs.

She scowled at him. 'Lie down before you fall down. What do you suggest? That we move you?'

'Yes!' He glared at her. 'We planned to anyway. I could have a fire in your room,' he said mournfully. 'It would make me feel more cheerful.'

He noticed her reaction to this only because they were sitting so close. 'You'll be safe! I couldn't do anything to anyone at the moment,' he said, gingerly touching his jaw. 'I'll stick to the letter of what we agreed.'

'Did I say anything? I'm just hoping you don't give it to me. I'll rouse the twins and get them to help move the bed.'

Faced with that challenge and a father they had never known ill before, the twins behaved sensibly and even chopped some wood and fetched some coal. Soon a fire crackled in the fireplace in the large front room.

'That's better,' said Peter with a satisfied sigh, eyes on the flames, propped up by pillows.

Amelia agreed that there was something about being in bed, watching a fire burn brightly while rain lashed against the windows. Going one step further in her mind she thought how nice it would be if they were both in the bed. But now was not the moment. She went downstairs to make him a drink.

The first night Peter spent in her room, Amelia was convinced she would lie awake, listening to his breathing and waiting for something to happen, but she was asleep in minutes, tired out with all she had done that day.

The next few nights were just the same and she began to get used not only to Peter's presence in her room but also to the change in her routine as she continued to leave the shop in Mr Brown's and Rosie's capable hands. The twins seemed happier, too. She did not know how Chris felt because she had seen little of him.

But a week after Peter had gone down with the mumps, when Amelia was pegging out the last shirt in the washing basket, she heard a bike being wheeled up the front path. Chris came through the back gate. She smiled at him. 'I didn't expect to see you at this time of day.'

'I thought I'd drop in and see how Dad is. He's not infectious now, is he? It's my lunch hour so I can't stay long.'

'I think he's a little better. Go up and see him but don't get too close.' Amelia went into the kitchen and then remembered something Peter had asked for so slipped into the parlour. It was quiet downstairs and she was immediately aware of raised voices overhead. She was surprised because father and son seldom argued.

When she heard feet thundering on the stairs, she hurried into the hall. 'Is everything OK, Chris?' she asked, worried.

There was a strained expression on his face. He rubbed his eyebrow. 'I didn't know! I thought—' He stopped, his Adam's apple jerking.

'Didn't know what?'

He looked away. 'It doesn't matter.'

Of course it did, she thought. He was upset. 'Stay and have a cup of tea with me,' she coaxed, taking his arm. 'It's not often we have a chance to talk. You're always at work, playing football or at the pictures.'

He hesitated, rubbed his eyebrow again, then blurted out, 'No, I've got to go.'

'But you've hardly been here five minutes. Have a warm drink.'

'I'm OK!' he shouted, yanking open the front door and slamming it behind him.

Amelia could not believe Chris had behaved in such a way and ran upstairs, tapping on the bedroom door before opening it.

'You don't have to do that,' said Peter, tawny hair dark with sweat. 'This is your room.' He sounded vexed.

'And yours. I brought you these.' She placed the book and pencils on the bedcover. 'What's up with Chris?'

He reached for the exercise book as a drowning man clutches a rope. 'He hadn't realised I'd moved in here.

He doesn't like it. Says I've betrayed his mother's memory. Have you ever heard such rubbish?'

She hesitated. 'Didn't you tell him why you've moved in here?'

Peter's expression hardened. 'I've told him as much as he needs to know. I'm not having him dictating to me. It's none of his business what goes on between us. I'll never forget Tess and he should know that.'

Amelia's heart sank as she sat on the bed but she tried to sound sensible and reasonable. 'It's not so long since the anniversary of her death. That probably opened the wound again. They became very close while you were away. And don't forget, he found her body. It was a shock and it takes time to get over these things.'

Peter scowled. 'Don't be so bloody understanding, Lee! I'm not having him speak to me that way. You don't know—' His voice faltered and he sank back against the pillows. 'Go away,' he said weakly. 'I'm not fit company. Leave me alone. You don't know it all.' He closed his eyes.

For a moment, she gazed down at him, feeling the pain of failure all over again. Then she went downstairs and sank on to a chair, determined not to think about Tess or Bernard again. She yawned, wistfully remembering the days when her mother had had an all-purpose maid to help her with household tasks. But the maid had gone even before the war when domestics had left for the factories or the Forces.

The cat miaowed, reminding her none of them had had lunch. She went into the kitchen and scraped butter on to bread, poured lentil soup into bowls, made tea and took it upstairs. Peter's eyes were closed and, thinking he was still asleep, she went to creep out, only to be stopped by the sound of his voice. 'Don't go!'

She turned and their eyes met. She knew he was sorry for being cross. 'I didn't mean to wake you but I thought you might be hungry,' she said softly.

'I was waiting for you to come up. I must have just dozed off a minute. I was thinking about my being in here and whether you were unhappy about it. I don't want you to be, Lee.' His eyes searched her face, seeming to plead with her. 'If you want me to move out again when I'm better, I will.'

She put down the tray and sat on his bed, unsure how to answer. 'Would you like something light to read? There's a comic in the lavatory downstairs. It has a picture of a German soldier and a flying officer on the front, wrestling with one another.'

He laughed. 'No, thanks. I told you the kind of stories I like.'

'So you are having a go? Of course you are,' she mumbled, pleating the cotton bedspread. 'I've seen you writing. You mustn't overdo it, though. Isn't that what the doctor said?'

'Yes. Mumps can cause complications in a man.' He took the cup from the tray and drank thirstily.

Amelia picked up a slice of bread and butter and dunked it into one of the bowls of soup, remembering reading about those complications in one of her father's medical books.

'Not that it matters in our case,' said Peter softly. 'But at least you've got a good excuse to give to the priest if he asks you why he hasn't heard the patter of tiny feet yet.'

'I've already told him that God has decreed I can't have children,' she responded.

Peter drew in his breath sharply. 'I didn't think he'd be that quick asking. Why did you tell him that?'

'Because it's true.' She avoided his eyes, glancing round the room, feeling the colour rise in her cheeks. 'It does happen that women can't have children.' She got up from the bed. 'If there's anything else you want, just bang on the floor with the tray. I'll leave you in peace now.'

She did not wait for his response but picked up one of the bowls and scooted out of the room. As she went downstairs, she could hardly believe she'd come out with it like that. Her periods came and then often did not come again for three or four months. A doctor had told her it would make having babies difficult to say the least, so she had not really told the priest or Peter a lie. But, as he said, infertility was hardly going to make any difference to them.

Chapter Fifteen

'How is Uncle Pete today? And when d'you think you'll be back?' said Rosie.

Amelia placed a wad of cotton wool in the wicker basket, which already contained toilet rolls, Brylcreem, shampoo, soap, olive oil and Aspirin. 'I think that's everything,' she murmured.

'Did you hear what I said?'

'Yes. I don't know. Perhaps not properly ever again.'

Her answer almost took Rosie's mind off the letter. 'You mean that?'

Amelia squeezed the packet of cotton wool. 'Your Uncle Pete *really* wants and needs me at home and I see the sense in that now. What news have you got? How are you getting on with you grandfather?'

Rosie almost told her about the fancy woman but changed her mind and said instead, 'Fine. I've had a letter from Babs.'

Amelia's eyebrows rose. 'It's more than I've had from Iris. What does she say?'

'They're in Chicago. And guess who they've met up with?' Rosie leant across the counter, eyes sparkling. 'Sam!'

'Who?'

'Sam the Yank,' she said patiently. 'He wrote to them in Canada and now they're staying with his family.'

Amelia put the basket on the counter, resting her chin on her hand. She gazed thoughtfully at Rosie. 'You're behind this. Did you give him their address?'

'Anything wrong with that?' said the girl as casually as she could, running a finger along the edge of the counter.

'No. But what was the thinking behind it?'

Rosie grinned. 'Daft, really. I thought he would go and visit them and persuade them to come home. Tell them how much we're missing them. I didn't realise how far away it was. Hundreds and hundreds of miles. England could easily fit into one of their lakes.'

'So they went to him,' murmured Amelia, lifting the basket. 'I wonder—'

'I know!'

'I think you've been watching too many films,' said Amelia dryly. 'But I'm glad you're not unhappy any more about them being over there.'

'That's because one day I plan to visit them,' said Rosie promptly. 'I'm saving as much as I can.'

Amelia nodded. 'Understandable. Anyway, I'd best be going. I've loads to do.'

'Whoah, Aunt Amelia!' Rosie reached across the counter and seized her shoulder. 'You can't go without telling me what's going to happen here. Are you selling the shop?'

Amelia's eyebrows lifted in that familiar supercilious way. 'Of course not, I've told you that before. But I am thinking of finding someone to help you out. I'll put in a few hours a week to do the ordering and that. Keep my eye on what's going on.'

'What about Uncle Pete taking charge here? Did you ask him? It would be the perfect solution. Keep it in the family.'

Amelia's expression altered and for a moment Rosie thought she looked positively shifty. 'He's in no fit state to do anything right now, although he's determined to go back to work on Monday. Men!' Her mouth softened.

Rosie thought, *So she does care for him.* 'Have you told him he's not fit?'

'D'you think he'd listen to me? I've told him he looks a funny colour and frankly he's got me worried. He's finding it really hard to throw this off, although he's not contagious any more. Drop in if you've time after you've finished here. Dotty's home for the weekend. She'll enjoy seeing you.'

Amelia made for the door and Rosie hurried to open it for her. 'Thanks, I'll do that,' she said warmly, thinking she needed to talk to someone about Granddad, and her sister was probably the right person.

Rosie met Dotty as she was coming out of the newsagent's on Eaton Road with that evening's *Echo*. She linked arms with her, telling her about Babs's letter before mentioning Walter and his fancy woman.

'You're joking?' said Dotty, eyes looking enormous behind her metal-rimmed spectacles.

'I tell you, I've actually seen her. Real brassy blonde and sexy with it. I followed him home the other day and saw them come out of the house half an hour later. I don't know what his landlady thinks.'

'Perhaps they're related?' said Dotty.

'Who? Her and the landlady?'

'Yes. Or maybe she's his sister?'

Rosie shook her head. 'Granddad's never mentioned having a sister. If he had one, I'm sure he would have said. He told me about Great-grandmother having been a milliner and about his younger brother emigrating to Australia in the twenties.'

Dotty looked perplexed, then her face brightened. 'How about going to the house and asking the landlady who she is?'

'It's a thought.' Rosie screwed up her face. 'Perhaps I'll go tomorrow when he's with Gran. I'll say I'm going to visit Dad's grave. I haven't been there for ages.'

'Did you go to Mam's on the anniversary?' asked Dotty, changing the subject. 'I wasn't able to but Chris went to his mam's on hers.'

'You two still friends then?' said Rosie with a smile.

'He's OK.' Dotty flushed. 'He was telling me Uncle Pete's always swearing, at the moment. He swears at the chairs, at the wireless, at the cats. I haven't heard him myself but—'

'Cats? You've only got one.'

'We've two now. One's a stray and Uncle Pete took pity on it. He said it looked as down in the mouth as he felt. Chris said Aunt Amelia wasn't pleased, said they had enough mouths to feed and if he felt that bad he should be in bed. That he was a fool.'

'She called him that in front of Chris?' said Rosie, startled.

Dotty nodded. 'She's been flaring up a lot lately.'

'What did he say?'

'That fools were prized in the old days and she should read *Hamlet*.'

Rosie stifled a laugh. 'And what did she say to that?'

'That he was a Smart Alec. And then he collapsed.'

'What?' The smile was wiped from Rosie's face. 'Aunt Amelia didn't tell me that!'

'It only happened this afternoon. The doctor's been and says Uncle Pete's got something called pancreatitis. One thing's for sure – he won't be going back to work on Monday and neither will Aunt Amelia. She's got him exactly where she wants him, Chris said, in a bed in her room.'

Rosie stared at her.

Dotty smirked. 'That's surprised you, hasn't it? They're in single beds but even so Chris doesn't like it. Says he thinks Uncle Pete and Aunt Amelia have fancied each other for years and are glad his mother's dead. That as soon as Uncle Pete's better, he wouldn't be surprised if they tried to get a double bed.'

'You talk to each other about things like that?' said Rosie, even more surprised.

Dotty's eyes avoided hers. 'He's got to talk to someone.'

'Well, it shouldn't be you,' said Rosie firmly. 'You're too young. Anyway, I don't believe all that he said. They married because it was convenient. Aunt Amelia had that other fella, Bernard whatshisname, years ago.'

Dotty pouted, pushing open the gate to 'Eden'. 'I don't know whatshisname. Anyway, Uncle Pete could have lied to Chris about it being a marriage of convenience to put him off the scent. His mam died from taking too many pills. And who provided them?'

Rosie had thought a few things about her aunt but never that. 'Don't be daft! She couldn't force them down her throat!' Irritated, Rosie slammed the gate behind her.

'How do we know?' said Dotty with a sniff.

'She was with us, dummy! Chris's mam died a couple of days after ours.' Rosie's tone was scathing.

'But she could have given her extra strong sleeping pills,' cried Dotty defiantly. 'And with his mam being half blind . . .' She stopped at the look on her sister's face. 'Anyway, if not that, his mam could have suspected they felt something for each other and that thought drove her to commit suicide. Chris says—'

'I don't care what he says!' said Rosie, walking up the path behind her sister. 'And if he had any sense, he'd keep his mouth shut. Where's his sense of loyalty? Aunt Amelia's provided him with a roof over his head. He should be grateful.'

'No need to blow your top,' said Dotty, looking offended. 'I'm surprised to hear you defending her. There was a time when you didn't have a good word to say about her.'

'Well, I know her better now. And I know old Brownie doesn't make mistakes and it's him who'd have made up the pills.'

'OK, OK!' muttered Dotty. 'But Chris isn't the only suspicious person round here. *You* think Granddad's up to something.'

'That's different. I've seen the evidence. Anyway, I'm not against him. He and Gran have been living apart for years. He was probably lonely and needed a woman to look after him. Not that I agree with him having a fancy one, of course!'

'I should hope not,' said Dotty in a hoity-toity voice. 'It's a mortal sin.'

'So what?' said Rosie crossly, wishing she had kept her mouth shut.

The next day, Rosie made her excuses to her grandparents but was completely unprepared when Maggie said, 'I'd like to come with yer, girl. I've been wanting to visit our Joe's grave for ages but I didn't know where it was.'

'I'd like to come too,' said Walter, nodding. 'Pay me respects, like. Me and your gran mightn't have been together when he went, but I think he'd like it that we're sort of together in his death.'

Maggie beamed at him. 'Yer right. We'll get some flowers when we reach the cemmie.' And with that she linked her arm through Walter's and walked out with him.

Rosie could not help being moved when the three of them stood by the graveside in Anfield Cemetery. 'I hope Dad does somehow know we're all here together,' she said, clearing her throat. Then she decided to make the most of this moment. 'But wouldn't it be lovely if we could live together as well?' She hugged Walter's arm, forgiving him his duplicity. 'You're not getting any younger, Granddad. Won't you come and stay, please?'

'I've explained, queen,' he said, looking uncomfortable. 'Me landlady's old man did me a good turn when I was at sea. Saved me life.'

'I thought you said it was her son you knew?' said Rosie, fixing him with a steady eye.

'I knew them both,' he said hastily, taking his pipe from his pocket and ramming it in his mouth.

'Doesn't she have any other lodgers?' said Rosie, determined to push him into telling the truth.

'No, no room, only me.' He sucked his pipe then patted his pockets and brought out a baccy pouch.

'Don't go on about it, girl,' said Maggie, taking Rosie's free hand and tapping it. 'Men hate women who nag.'

'I'm not nagging, Gran,' cried Rosie. 'But the way housing is she'd have no trouble finding another lodger. She really needs a woman, anyway, if she's that decrepit. Perhaps I should go home with you, Granddad, and suggest it to her?'

'Hey, hey! There's no need for that. You're taking too much on yerself, queen. You listen to yer gran,' he said, fingers quivering as he packed the bowl of his pipe. 'Anyway, it's time I was going,' he mumbled. 'She'll have me tea ready.'

'She's not too decrepit to cook?' said Rosie, an innocent expression on her face.

'She's determined to struggle on,' said Walter, pecking Maggie's cheek and then Rosie's before hurrying off.

His words and actions only served to make Rosie more determined to get rid of that woman and have him living with them. As she and Maggie sat on a tram rattling along Sleepers Hill, Rosie listened with only half an ear to what her grandmother was saying.

'I did him a great wrong, girl, as I did my poor lad.' The head on the fox fur she wore round her neck bobbed towards Rosie. 'I should have been a better wife and mother, but he was a good few years younger than me and I'd known him since he was in short pants. It wasn't good for our Joe and it wasn't good for me. I thought I could always have me own way.' She sighed gustily, and the fox's head rose again. 'When I goes, will yous and Walt see I'm buried with me lad?' She dug Rosie hard with one elbow. 'Are yous hearing me, girl?'

'Yes, Gran.' Rosie gathered her thoughts together. 'But you're better now. You'll live to ninety.'

'Maybe I will and maybe I won't,' said Maggie, looking sad. 'It's not often yous gets a second chance in life. But the unexpected – yer never know when it's going to happen.'

'You're right, Gran,' said Rosie, a tremor in her voice. It was a comment she felt sure Davey would appreciate. The unexpected happening unexpectedly. Well, perhaps she could make it happen?

'You're mad,' said Davey when they met the following evening. He clasped Rosie's cold hand tightly in his and shoved them both into his pocket to keep them warm. 'Why can't you leave things as they are? Your gran's happy. Your granddad's happy. It might all go wrong if they start living together again.'

'But they should be together,' said Rosie, rubbing her cheek against his shoulder as they walked past Barker & Dobson's sweet factory. 'Marriage is about facing things together and being a support to each other.' She lifted her head and gazed at him. 'Come with me? It'll be easier for me if you're there.'

He kissed the tip of her cold nose. 'I'd rather go to the flicks and sit on the back row. It'll be comfy cosy there.'

She agreed that that was a much nicer idea and, standing on tiptoe, brushed his lips with hers.

He pulled her against him. 'Then let's have no more arguing,' he whispered against her mouth.

'Who's arguing? I've said I'll go to the flicks, haven't I?' She toyed with a button on his jacket. 'But I'll go on my own to that house if I have to. I mightn't always be able to be there for Gran. Especially if she lives to be ninety. I could be in America.'

'America!'

That made him sit up and take notice, thought Rosie, smiling. She told him about Babs's letter.

'They're staying with that Yank?' Davey scowled. 'And you want to go out there? Is *he* the attraction?'

'Don't be daft,' said Rosie, frowning. 'What are you thinking? He's my stepfather. He was married to Mam!'

'Then why go?' said Davey moodily. 'What about us? I'll be getting my call-up papers this year. I want to see as much of you as I can.'

'I won't be going yet. I haven't the money. I'm talking about in a few years' time. After you've done your National Service and I've finished my training. I want to see Babs and Harry and I thought you might want to come as well?'

'And what about Ma?' His voice was tight and his dark brows hooded his eyes so that she could only imagine their expression. 'What is it you're suggesting exactly? Us getting married and living there?'

'Don't you want to marry me?' she said, removing her hand from his. 'I thought you—'

'Loved you? I think I do. But that doesn't mean I can forget about Ma and go and live thousands of miles away just because you want to be with Babs and Harry.'

'So you'd put your mother before me?'

'I'm not saying that. But what's the difference between me doing that and you wanting to be near Babs and Harry? If they lived the other end of the country, yeah, that would be OK. I'd be willing. But to be divided by an ocean – I couldn't do it to Ma permanently. It's bad enough me doing my National Service. I'm all she's got! And what about your Aunt Amelia? Does she know you're planning on living out there?'

'She knows I want us Kilshaws to be together. But OK, OK! I get the message,' said Rosie, meeting his gaze squarely. 'If I go, it'll have to be while you're away, and you'd want me to come back.' She stared at him. 'You would, wouldn't you?'

He said with an intensity that thrilled her, 'Need you ask?' Reaching out, he caught her to him, pressing her body so hard against his that she knew just how much he wanted her. 'I do love you. If you're not here when I return, I'll come over there and drag you back by the hair.'

He kissed her passionately and she responded just as passionately. But at the back of her mind was the thought that she still wanted to go to America and had to persuade Granddad to come and live with them when that time came. She was just beginning to realise how difficult it must have been for her aunt to put duty first and give up her fiancé.

Amelia lay awake, tortured by what Peter had told her. The evening Rosie had visited, he had overheard the girls talking on the path below and been so stunned he'd had to tell her. Amelia could still scarcely take it in. She was shocked that Chris believed she could have wanted to kill Tess. He couldn't be thinking straight. Grief had twisted his mind. But even worse than his believing such a thing of her was that he had expressed his beliefs to Dotty. Worse still was the thought that Peter's fears when they'd married had seeded themselves in his son. How could Chris believe they could have driven Tess into an early grave? *Oh, God!* she thought, pressing her fists against her cheeks. How many other people had thought that, even for a moment?

Bernard, for one, said a voice in her head.

Amelia glanced across at Peter and wondered what he was feeling right now. Her heart ached with longing to be able to be honest with him, to give in to her emotions, but at the moment that was impossible. It might drive

Chris into doing something even more stupid than confiding in her besotted young niece. She had to keep up with the play-acting.

As if sensing her eyes upon him, Peter's hunched shape shifted and he turned in her direction. 'Can't you sleep?'

'No,' she sighed.

'I shouldn't have told you.' He sounded annoyed with himself.

'You were right to tell me.'

'At least you know Rosie believes the whole idea's ridiculous.'

'I'm coming round to really liking Rosie,' said Amelia, a warm feeling inside. Her niece's defence of her had touched her deeply.

Peter made a noise in his throat that sounded like a chuckle. 'She's worried about her granddad being up to something with someone!'

Amelia pushed herself up on an elbow. 'You didn't tell me that.'

'I've only just remembered. Dotty said he was committing a mortal sin. You're the Catholic so what d'you make of that?'

She was silenced, mind hopping around like a frog on a lily pad, thinking of sexual sins in connection with herself now. Surely Chris could not have believed she and Peter had gone that far? No. They would have seized the double bed in the other room for themselves immediately they had married if they had secretly loved each other for years. She flopped down again, mind drifting, forming images that filled her with aching dissatisfaction.

Peter's voice brought her back to reality again. 'Rosie thought her granddad must have been lonely living all these years apart from her granny and that's why he has someone,' he murmured. 'Understanding for her age.'

'Rosie? Yes.' Amelia sat up, hugging her knees. 'You don't think the neighbours heard the girls?'

'I worried about that at the time but what are the odds? I was up in the bedroom with nothing better to do than lie there feeling ill. Anyway, we both know it's ridiculous.'

A thought suddenly struck Amelia. 'You never once believed I could have done it?'

He laughed. 'You're worse than the kids! The pills were prescribed by the doctor and made up by Mr Brown. How could you?'

Her panic subsided and she lay down again. 'Are you going to speak to Chris?'

'Yeah. When I feel up to it. He'll get all tight-lipped but I can't let him get away with saying such things to an impressionable girl like Dotty.'

'Rosie would have put him in his place.'

'Some girls mature earlier than others.'

Amelia lay down again, thinking now of Rosie and her relationship with Davey. Thinking also of Rosie's suggestion that Peter run the shop. It made sense but she could not risk him and Bernard meeting again. She should have banned Bernard from the shop, but she had never been able to rid herself of the feeling that in rejecting him she had damaged him somehow and changed him for the worse. Next she thought about Rosie's granddad. If he was committing a mortal sin, did that make him the best kind of man to live under the same roof as her niece? She would have to have a word with Rosie the next time she saw her.

Rosie had put on her Sunday best coat, given to her by Amelia last Christmas. It was royal-blue and she wore a navy-blue beret and gloves to match. She looked up at the house. It was three storeys high and had a metal hand rail and steps leading up to the front door from the pavement. She remembered what her granddad had said and knew he had lied. There was definitely room inside for more than two people.

She ran up the steps, aware of being watched. The lace curtain had moved slightly in the window next door and a group of kids noisily gathered beneath a lamp post also had their eye on her. She almost wished she had not come, but there was no backing down now. She was here so she would do it. She raised her hand and rat-tatted on the brown front door.

She heard the sound of slippered feet approaching and then the door opened. A woman Rosie immediately recognised stood before her. She was wearing a green and white spotted frock beneath a capacious pinafore, and although most of her hair was hidden by a tartan turban, her face was fully made up. Eyebrows had been plucked and lines drawn in their place, cheeks were rouged, and a cigarette dangled from full lips painted scarlet. The girl reckoned the woman was sixty if she was a day.

'Yeah! What d'yer want?' Her expression was unfriendly.

'I'm looking for my granddad.' That was untrue because Rosie knew exactly where Walter was.

'And who would he be when he's at home?' The cigarette somehow managed to cling to her lower lip as the woman spoke.

'Walter Kilshaw.'

The woman caught the cigarette as it fell. Leaning towards Rosie, she poked her with a long fingernail. 'I'm not very good with jokes. Shove off!'

'It's not a joke.' Rosie frowned, rubbing her upper right breast. 'I'd like to speak to his landlady, please?'

'I'm his landlady and I don't want to speak to you. So shove off like I said.' As her hand shot out, Rosie moved swiftly down a step. She tilted her chin. 'I don't want to shove off. I'm his granddaughter and I want to know what you are to him.'

The woman's expression turned ugly. She stubbed out the cigarette on the hand rail and placed it in her pocket. 'Who sent yer here? What are yer after? Money? Joe get yer mother into trouble, did he? Well, I tell yer, girl, yer granddad hasn't two brass farthings to rub together – so beat it!'

Rosie laughed. 'I'm not after his money! And my mother's dead so I live with Gran.'

'Yer gran?' The woman's eyes started in her head.

'Maggie Kilshaw. Don't you know about her?'

The woman pressed her lips together, measuring Rosie up. Then she stepped down and poked her in the chest again. 'Of course I do. We were at school together. Yer'll take me to her. Show me where she lives – now!'

'Don't poke me!' said Rosie, flaring up. 'It blinking hurts!'

'I'm upset!' The woman folded her arms, glaring down at her. 'Real upset. He never told me about you. As for the owld cow . . . made his life a misery, she did.'

'She's changed.'

'Ha!' exclaimed the woman, turning and going inside. 'You wait!' she called over her shoulder.

Rosie decided she was not going to do any such thing. She had found out what she wanted and it proved she just could not trust her granddad to be honest. She clattered down the steps and walked up the street but had barely turned the corner when the woman caught up with her.

'The name's Vera McIver,' she said. 'And yer granddad's been lodging with me for more than twenty-five years – and it's the first I've heard tell he had a granddaughter. I hate kids, he knows that. Are yer sure yer not telling me lies?'

'Why should I?' said Rosie, wishing Vera would go away. 'And there's more than one of us. In fact,' she added, giving vent to her imagination and the devil inside, 'there's ten of us.'

'Ten? Holy Mary!' Vera crossed herself. 'Has he known about you all these years?'

'He was at the christenings. There's Josephine, Bernadette, Mary, Dorothy, Iris, Amelia, Babs, Eileen, Veronica and me.' Rosie's eyes glinted wickedly. 'You just can't trust men to tell you the truth, can you?'

Vera looked outraged. 'I don't know how he had the nerve! I suppose that woman was at the christenings as well?'

'Gran wouldn't miss out on a christening,' said Rosie, enjoying herself. 'She mightn't believe in going to church, but give her the chance to wear a decent hat and she's in there with the best of them.'

'Wait 'til I see him,' said Vera wrathfully, taking a grip on her umbrella. 'He'll rue the day he was born.' There was the rattle of a tram and her head turned. 'Is this yours?'

Rosie could see there was no stopping her so did not bother lying. Vera sat on the seat behind Rosie and she realised her grandfather's fancy woman had no intention of letting her out of her sight. The girl could hear her muttering beneath her breath and tried not to think about what was going to happen when they reached Gran's. She only hoped Maggie did not have another stroke.

Rosie prayed she would be asleep and that Walter could whisk his fancy woman away before Gran woke up. She decided it would be best to go in the back way. If her grandfather was behind the counter and there was a customer, things might work out. Then she could really get to work on him to give up this woman, make him feel guilty and a no-good adulterer.

Unfortunately, both her grandparents were in the shop, bagging sugar.

'Yer late, girl. Where've yous been?' said Maggie, smiling at Rosie as she came through the door in a rush.

The girl did not get a chance to speak. Vera pushed past her yelling, 'Yer swine!'

Walter's pipe fell out of his mouth as he ducked behind the counter.

'It's no good hiding!' cried Vera, rushing round the side. She picked up a pound weight from the scales and was about to throw it at him when Rosie grabbed her arm.

'Leave him alone – he's an old man!'

'What's going on?' said Maggie, looking bewildered.

'I'll tell you what's going on,' said a struggling Vera, almost choking on the words. 'Walt's had two of us on the go. He's been promising me marriage for the last year but yer still here!'

'What d'yer expect me to do?' said Walter, bobbing up from behind the counter, pipe clamped between his teeth. 'She's tough as old boots!'

'To behave like a gentleman!' yelled Vera, still struggling. 'But I should have listened to me sister. She had yer measure! Said yer were too good to be true. Helping at the boys' club. Always keeping yer room nice and tidy and yerself clean – and all the time yer've been living a double life. *Ten* granddaughters! She won't have any money over from that lot when she kicks the bucket.'

'*She's* the cat's mother,' said Maggie, eyes intent on Vera's face. 'But who are you?'

'She's ranting, Mag. Take no notice of her,' said Walter.

'I'm his landlady. Or should I say *was*!' said Vera, dropping the weight.

'But yous have all yer faculties,' said Maggie, apparently bewildered.

Rosie thought, *You're not so daft, Gran!*

A knowing expression came over Maggie's face. 'How old are yous?'

Vera smoothed her sleeve. 'None of yer business.' She glared at Rosie. 'Has she got a slate loose?'

'She's had a stroke.' Rosie could barely stop herself from giggling. Perhaps, she thought, she did owe Vera the truth. 'Granddad's only been helping us for the last few months. I want him to live here. I don't have ten sisters, only two, and one brother.'

Vera stiffened and her eyes went as hard as stone. 'Then yer've got yer way, haven't yer, queen? Because I don't want him now. The lying sod!'

'Yes. Shall I see you out?' said Rosie politely.

'I can do that meself.' Vera turned a scathing look on Walter. 'As for you, don't you be showing yer face round my place again.'

He looked even more alarmed. 'Hey! What about me clothes?'

Vera walked towards the door before answering, 'I'll give them to the ragman.'

'Hey, Vera, yer can't do that!' he said, hurrying after her. He reached the door and a tin of peas hit the wall next to him.

'Tart!' bellowed Maggie.

Walter ducked. A bag of sugar followed the peas.

Vera scurried into the yard as Walter fielded a second bag of sugar. 'Maggie, think of the profits!' he said.

Rosie doubled up over the counter.

'Maggie, calm down,' said Walter, waving his arms at her. 'It's not good for yer!'

Her only response was to throw another pound of sugar.

Later, when Rosie had control of herself, Maggie stopped throwing things and a pot of tea was made. Walter grovelled before them, saying how much he had wanted to be with them but how difficult it had been for him.

'I'm not speaking to you,' said Maggie, then her face crumpled and she began to cry.

'Oh, Lor'!' said Rosie, putting an arm round her. 'I'm sorry, Gran. I did it all wrong. I didn't want it to come out like this.'

'Not your fault,' said Walter gloomily. 'I should have told yer the truth. I wanted to but I thought you wouldn't want to know me.'

'You're my granddad,' said Rosie, pacified. 'We all do wrong things.'

'What about me?' wailed Maggie, lifting a tear-blotched face.

Walter gazed at her and his knees cracked as he got down on to them. 'Forgive me, Mag. I've made a real muck of things. Let me make it up to yer? Let me come and look after yer properly?'

There was a silence which seemed to go on for ever, and Rosie could see her granddad was finding it difficult to keep his pose. Then Maggie said in a disgruntled voice, 'I'm a fool to meself but I'll give yer a fortnight. No monkeying about and thinking yer can get yer hands on me money, though.'

'Mag, I'm not after yer money, queen! How many times do I have to tell yer? Honest!' He sounded distressed.

'A hundred times and I still wouldn't believe yous,' she said. 'But I do believe you care about this girl of ours and I want her to have all me jewellery. D'yer hear me, girl? Yous is my witness.'

Rosie could scarcely believe it. 'That's good of you, Gran. But I hope it won't be for years yet.'

Maggie smiled. 'Aye, well, we'll see. Yous just carry on looking after me and I might survive that long.'

'We'll do that, won't we, Rosie?' said Walter, eagerly struggling to his feet and wincing as he did so. 'I can hear someone coming up the yard. Will I see to them, Mag?'

She scowled at him. 'No, Rosie can go. I don't want you sticking yer fingers in me till.'

He looked hurt. 'You haven't got a till, and I wouldn't anyway. You've got to trust me or me living here won't work.'

Maggie gave him a look that said it all. 'A fancy woman with a feather in her hat taken from some poor dumb bird,' she growled. 'Well, I'm no dumb cluck, Walter Kilshaw, so don't be thinking yer can bleat on about how hard done by yous are. Yous broke the seventh commandment and yer being punished for it now.'

She *would* punish him, too, thought Rosie, feeling sorry for him and thinking that maybe she and Davey could go and pick up his clothes. She thought of Joe and felt sure he would have approved of her actions and that maybe he was laughing somewhere.

Chapter Sixteen

' "Clang, clang, clang went the trolley," ' sang Rosie, slamming shut the till.

'Someone sounds cheerful.'

Rosie spun round. 'Good morning, Aunt Amelia. I didn't expect to see you here today, it not being Friday.'

'I've been to TJ's. They advertised underwear so I've been queuing up.' She placed her shopping basket on the counter and nodded in the direction of Irene, the new shop assistant, before addressing Rosie again. 'Everything still OK at your grandmother's?'

'Fine. Although Gran seems to be reverting to her old self.' Rosie grinned, thinking that Maggie had Walter under her thumb now. It was just over four months since he had come to stay, and if it had not been for Davey's mam having hung on to her husband's clothes, he would only have had those he stood up in, because Vera had given his stuff to the ragman as she had threatened. They had been lucky to get his ration book. 'Gran has him doing his whack. Although he does manage to skive off sometimes.'

'Let's hope it lasts,' murmured Amelia. 'Did you put up that notice on saving soap?'

'Over there,' said Rosie, coming out from behind the counter to show her. 'Who'd ever have thought soap would be rationed?'

'The twins think it's a good excuse not to wash.'

'How is Uncle Pete?'

'Still not A1 but he's back at the Post Office and says he's OK.' Amelia avoided her eyes, reading again about skewering soaps and hanging them on a string to dry and harden. Her mind was elsewhere, thinking of how strained the atmosphere was at home since Peter had had it out with Chris. Amelia had received an apology of sorts, but since then her stepson's manner had been downright insolent; not that he said much, it was just his manner. Peter had no time for such behaviour and had threatened that if Chris did not change his ways, he would be out on his ear. She had tried to reason with them both but it had only led to more arguments.

'Won't Uncle Pete be having his holiday week soon?' said Rosie.

'Yes, I'm hoping he'll paint the house.'

'You could do with a proper holiday away together,' said Rosie, elbows on the counter.

Amelia gave a wry smile. 'Chance would be a fine thing. But maybe we'll manage a day trip to Chester. Everything OK here? No awkward customers? Salesmen?' Her tone was casual.

Rosie smiled. 'I hand them over to Mr Brown.'

'Sensible girl.' Amelia touched her shoulder and left.

Ten minutes later, Bernard breezed into the shop, giving Rosie a wink, and as usual asked if the boss was in.

'Too late, Mr Rossiter.' Rosie gave him a friendly smile. 'You've just missed her.'

'Story of my life. I'm always missing out.' He lifted Rosie's hand to his lips and planted a kiss on it. 'You're looking as luscious as ever.'

'Flattery won't get you anywhere.' Her eyes twinkled. 'You try it on with Mr Brown.'

He groaned. 'The man would chase me. Has no sense of humour.'

'But it's him you have to get around, not me.'

'Pity. See you later, Rosie.' He dropped her hand and hurried towards the dispensing room.

Rosie watched him go, thinking that her aunt had been right when she said he had the gift of the gab, but that was what a good salesman needed, in her opinion. He breezed out as swiftly as he'd come in and she soon forgot about him, looking forward to the weekend, when she would see Davey.

'And where d'you think you're going, all dolled up?' said Maggie.

'I told you, Gran!' Rosie's skimpy skirts fluttered as she whirled away from the mirror. 'Davey's expecting his call-up papers any day now and then I won't see him for eighteen months.'

'Humph! Well, that's one thing I won't miss. His ugly mug.'

'He probably feels the same about you, Gran. Only he wouldn't say it,' said Rosie, turning back to the mirror and applying lipstick. 'But I think he's dead good-looking and you aren't so bad when you forget to put on your hard-done-by act with Granddad. You don't want to lose him again, do you?'

She put an arm round Maggie's shoulders, thinking she had no chance of getting to America if her grandmother changed her mind about leaving her all her worldly goods. And she did *so* much want to see Harry and Babs.

'Why should I care?' sniffed Maggie. 'I did without him for years. Anyway, never mind him. It's you and that lad we're talking about. I'm telling yer, girl, there better hadn't be any shenanigans between the pair of yous. Yous keep yerself pure for when someone better comes along.'

'He's the one I want, Gran.' Rosie blew her a kiss and left her grandmother moaning to herself about Walt teaching lads cricket when her legs were giving her gyp.

Rosie's heart seemed to swell inside her at the sight of Davey waiting on the corner of the street. His dark hair was ruffled by the breeze and his face and throat had already caught the sun. He appeared devastatingly handsome to her. 'Hi, Davey!' She felt breathless and her voice came out all husky. 'How's tricks?'

'Terrible 'til I caught sight of you.' He whirled her around before pulling her close and kissing her. 'I've had my call-up papers.'

'Oh, no!' Her spirits plummeted.

'God only knows where they'll send me once I've had my training. It could be thousands of miles away.'

She gazed at him in dismay. The war might be over but only the other day the Archbishop of York had called on British Jews to condemn the violence against British

servicemen in Palestine, and in India there had been kill-
ings in New Delhi. 'I don't want you to go,' she said,
clinging to the front of his shirt.

'Me neither. But I have no choice,' he said miserably,
arms tightening about her. 'You will wait for me, won't you?'

'What do you think?' she said lovingly.

'And you'll write?'

'Let them try and stop me.'

They held each other, swaying slightly. 'I wish we could
get married now,' he said, brushing her hair with his lips.

'Aunt Amelia wouldn't allow it. But when you get
back, I'll be eighteen and maybe she'll think it a good
way to get rid of me.'

'Ma won't say no. She's always liked you.'

'And I've always liked her.' Rosie avoided mentioning
America.

They kissed.

'Do you two mind?' said a scandalised voice. 'You
shouldn't be canoodling in a public place. It was bad
enough when the Yanks were here.'

Rosie and Davey glanced at the prim-faced middle-
aged woman and drew apart. They smiled at each other,
settling for holding hands but determined to make the best
of the day.

They went to the Pierhead, catching the ferry to New
Brighton. They stood shoulder to shoulder, gazing down
at the oily khaki-coloured waters as a seaman cast off.

'Dotty, look!'

Rosie's head turned at the sound of the voice but
the deck was too crowded for her to see if it was her

sister. She gave her attention once more to watching the widening gap between boat and landing stage, feeling a thrill of excitement. Water foamed as the screw whirled and the ship swung round, heading towards the estuary where the Mersey spilt out into the Irish Sea.

There were plenty of other ships to watch: tankers, cargo boats, liners, and the dredgers that helped to keep the channels between the sandbanks from silting up.

Rosie breathed deeply of the salty air, arm linked through Davey's as they strolled the upper deck, whispering sweet nothings to each other and planning their future. The breeze lifted their hair and gulls swooped and screeched overhead. 'Isn't it lovely?' she said, holding her face up to the sun. 'I'd forgotten there could be days like this away from everything. Wouldn't it be smashing if—'

'Rosie!'

She whirled round and this time saw one of the twins, waving madly to her. The other was hanging over the ship's rail and all she could see was his rear end. Tom, probably, she thought to herself grimly.

She pulled on Davey's arm. 'Get down from there!' she yelled, hurrying over to the rails. She seized the twin by the collar of his shirt and the seat of his pants and dragged him down. Not a whit put out, Tom beamed up at them. 'Hi, Rosie! Hi, Davey!'

'Never mind the pleasantries,' she said. 'Who's supposed to be looking after you? Aunt Amelia and Uncle Pete must be mad, letting you loose on the ferry on your own. Where are they?'

'They haven't come. Our Chris and Dotty are with us,' chorused the twins.

Rosie glanced round. 'Invisible, are they?'

'They're somewhere,' said Tom, drawing a circle in the air with one arm. 'But never mind them. Tell me, what's this thing in the water?'

Davey and Rosie peered over the side. Not so long ago there had been an article in the newspaper about the danger of floating mines. Both of them let out a sigh of relief when they recognised the 'thing' as a buoy.

'There's lots of them around, marking where ships went down,' said Davey.

'Davey's dad was a river pilot,' Rosie informed them, hugging his arm. 'I remember there were all these charts in the parlour and he used to let us look at them.'

'Those charts were magic,' said Davey, face rapt with nostalgia. 'Remember, Rosie, we used to pretend they were treasure maps? You were Jim Hawkins.'

'And you were Long John Silver,' she laughed. 'You broke your mam's brush pole using it for a crutch.'

'I got a clout for doing that.'

Just then Dotty and Chris made an appearance.

'Where've you two been?' said Rosie, frowning. 'You could have lost a twin overboard. They need watching.'

'What business is it of yours?' Chris scowled. 'You're always putting your oar in.'

'Don't you speak to her like that,' said Davey, clenching his fists. 'She cares what happens to them, which is obviously more than you two do.'

'And who are you?' Chris thrust one bony shoulder almost in Davey's face.

'Stop that!' said Rosie, attempting to push him away. Davey removed her hand. 'Keep out of it, Rosie. I can handle him.'

'What's going on?' said Dotty, squinting in her sister's direction.

'What have you been telling him?' said Rosie. 'And where's your glasses? You haven't broken them, have you?'

Her sister pouted. 'I don't have to wear them all the time. Chris is here to look after me. And anyway, I look prettier without them.'

'And there was me thinking he was supposed to be keeping an eye on his brothers,' said Rosie, grabbing Dotty's arm and drawing her aside. 'I want a word with you, little sister. What d'you think you're doing, mooning over him?' she hissed.

'I'm not mooning,' said Dotty indignantly. 'Anyway, you're with Davey. You've no right to talk!'

'I'm older than you. Old enough to know what I'm about with a fella. So what are you doing here?'

Dotty smoothed her hair and smiled. 'Uncle Pete chased us out. He and Aunt Amelia were having a row.'

'You surprise me.'

'No, honestly. They were going at it hammer and tongs. Chris reckons they've fallen out, like thieves after a crime.'

Rosie groaned. 'He's crazy. What were they arguing about?'

'They were just picking at each other, like you pick at me. Over us kids and money and things.'

Rosie shrugged. 'I'm not surprised. It can't be easy taking someone else's kids on.'

Dotty brought her mouth up close to Rosie's ear. 'I think Chris is wrong and they don't fancy each other,' she whispered. 'She wears pyjamas, you know. When we left she was in bed with a headache. She wears striped ones, not a bit glamorous. When I start earning money, I'm going to wear négligés in satin and lace.'

Rosie raised her eyes skywards. 'Bully for you! I'm going back to Davey.'

'Don't go without me,' said Dotty in alarm, grabbing her arm. 'I'll be bumping into people.'

'Get your glasses on then and don't be so stupid.' She hauled her sister over to where Davey and Chris were still standing bristling at each other, held back by a twin apiece.

'Come on,' said Rosie, grabbing Davey's arm. 'This is our last day. We don't want to be bothered with them.'

By now the boat was approaching New Brighton pier and Davey allowed himself to be dragged away. Rosie scanned the water. 'I remember Dad telling me there used to be a one-legged bloke who dived off the pier here for pennies.'

'Mine too,' said Davey. 'His name was Bernie and he lost a leg in the Great War. The guts some people have, hey, Rosie?'

'Not half,' she said, thinking what were any of their problems compared to losing a leg and then plunging into the cold Mersey to earn coppers?

Even so she felt uneasy about Dotty being in Chris's company. What had Uncle Pete been thinking of? There was something not quite right about what her sister had told her . . .

*

'How's the head?' asked Peter.

'It's still there.' Amelia's voice was muffled by the bedclothes.

'Why don't you try one of your own remedies? What is it? Feverfew leaf sandwiches?'

'Perhaps later.'

There was silence but she knew he had not gone, could sense his presence. She wanted to reach out and touch him but was too unsure of how he would react so kept her hands firmly beneath the covers. The silence stretched. She cleared her throat. 'I thought you were going to start painting the house?'

'I haven't the heart for it.' He sounded weary. 'And I want to get on with my writing.'

'Leave it then.'

'I think I will.' She felt the mattress give and knew he had sat down on the edge of the bed. 'I hate all this arguing between us.'

Amelia turned over and lowered the bedclothes but could barely make out his features in the darkened room. 'You didn't like it when we were being polite either. Not that I enjoy the arguing any more than you do. So why do we do it?'

'I suppose it's a way of communicating when other ways seem to have failed. I spent a couple of years arguing with Tess until I decided it was a waste of time and less tiring if I didn't argue back. In the end we barely spoke to each other.'

'Long silences,' murmured Amelia, remembering Tess's letter.

'You knew? She told you?'

Amelia took a deep breath. 'In her letter.'

'What else did she say?'

'I'd rather not say.' Her fingers curled over the edge of the covers.

'I can imagine.' His voice was flat. 'That she didn't love me. That she had never loved me but felt guilty about it because I had loved her and been good to her.'

Amelia sat up. 'How did you know?'

He laughed. 'I know because she said pretty much the same in her letter to me. But I already knew. You can tell when someone cares about you.' Their eyes met. 'I know you care, despite the arguments,' he said softly.

She was silent, almost scared to admit it. But her heart had begun to hammer.

'I'm not going to talk about being in love,' said Peter, slipping an arm round her waist. 'I'm not sure I trust those words. But I admire you, Lee, and I like the person you are.' He kissed her gently at first then exerted more pressure as she clung to him like a limpet.

From somewhere deep inside there was an eruption of feelings long suppressed. There was no holding back now. If he wanted her then he could have her. She returned his kisses with a passion that was intensely satisfying. Like eating strawberries and cream when you hadn't had such scrumptiousness for ages. He was out of his clothes before she had even taken off her pyjama jacket and then he was tearing it off her too, kissing her breasts as if starved, kicking down the covers as he did so.

She gasped with surprised pleasure, never having thought it would be like this. His hands were undoing her bottoms and rolling them down over her hips. Then he

was inside her, tearing her with a brutality that was unexpected. Her body shuddered with the force of his invasion.
'Sorry,' he whispered, gripping her hips as he slowed
down. 'I don't want to hurt you but there's no other way.
Next time it won't be so bad.'

'It's all right! Carry on.' She wrapped her legs around
him and held him.

'God, that was good!' he gasped, collapsing on top of
her.

Despite the pain, she was aware of a deep satisfaction.
They had done it. And if he liked it so much they would
do it again and again. She kissed his collar-bone and in
turn felt his lips against her neck. 'I'm sorry I hurt you,'
he said earnestly.

'Forget it. I half expected it.' She loosened her grip on
him and stretched her legs. He slid off her but curled up
against her side, placing his arm across her. She lifted his
hand and kissed the palm and left him there while she
went to the bathroom. When she returned, he was obviously asleep. She lay beside him, pulling the covers up
and snuggling against him. There was not much room in
the single bed but she did not want to leave him. She was
so glad he had sent the kids out.

She was wakened by something tickling her. She
reached down and her hand came into contact with firm
flesh. Hastily she twisted in his arms and gazed into his
face. Before she could speak, he kissed her. She held his
face between her hands and kissed him back forcibly. He
rolled on to his back, taking her with him so that she lay
on top of him, breast to chest. He brought her face down

to his so their mouths joined again. Then his body began
to move slowly from side to side in a rocking motion. The
movement was hypnotic, soothing, sensual, exciting. She
rubbed against him and desire erupted again. Frantically
they kissed and touched and caressed until, gasping, they
joined again. She panted over him like a tiger having
pinned down its prey until a scream escaped her. 'More!'
she cried, astonishing not only herself but him as well.

Peter shut off the sound with his mouth, rolling her
over and finishing it.

'Ohhh,' she sighed, gazing up at him.

'What?' He smiled down at her.

'I didn't expect it to be so nice,' she said with a hint
of embarrassment.

'You complaining?'

'No.' She stretched out her arms, aware of a content-
ment never experienced before. 'No,' she repeated.

'You're a surprising woman, Amelia Hudson,' he said,
pressing his lips against her naked shoulder.

'I didn't know I had all that in me,' she responded. 'It
must have been buried deep for years.'

'Waiting for Prince Charm—' Peter stopped.

Amelia had heard it, too. She gave him a push. 'You'd
better get downstairs,' she whispered.

He just stopped himself from falling out of bed. 'This
is ridiculous,' he hissed. 'Why can't we be honest, for
God's sake? Married people do go to bed together.'

'Not us,' she said, placing the flat of her hands against
his chest. 'You must go now. We don't want Chris
thinking—'

'Sod Chris! He already thinks it so why shouldn't we do it? I never told you, but after the twins were born, Tess and I never made love again. And she never, never asked for more.'

More fool her, thought Amelia, bones melting just thinking about it. 'I'm sorry,' she whispered, touching his cheek with her hand. 'But he believed his mother loved him. He's still trying to come to terms with what she did.'

'Do you think I don't know that?' hissed Peter. 'Tess was great at rejection. You didn't know that, did you? But you do know Chris isn't mine?' He pressed his lips against Amelia's hand before rolling off the bed.

'Yes. But I didn't know you knew that I knew.' She stared at him as he fumbled for his trousers. 'Did Tess put that in her last letter?'

'Yep. It was yet another bloody thing she wanted me to forgive her for.' He found his trousers and struggled into them.

Amelia could scarcely believe it. 'The father?'

His laughter contained a bitter note. 'She threw out hints.' He straightened and met Amelia's eyes. 'She didn't tell you so I guess she didn't want you knowing.'

'But why should it matter if I know?'

He did not answer, shoving his flapping shirt inside his trousers as he walked towards the door. 'I'll say you've still got a headache, shall I?'

'Yes, OK! But, Pete, who do you think it was?'

He shrugged. 'Let's put it behind us. Not one thing with her was as good as it's been with you.' He blew her a kiss, opened the door and closed it quietly behind him.

Amelia could not forget, though. She lay down, arms behind her head, gazing up at the ceiling, trying to remember who had interested Tess besides Peter. But she could not think. Hearing the children's voices from below, she decided she was not going to allow the past to affect the here and now. Today was a day she would never forget, but would she and Pete ever be able to live like a normal married couple and not always be worrying about someone else's children?

'We're going to need more of your homemade herbicide,' called Rosie, stepping down into the garden, eyes red-rimmed from weeping, having just waved Davey off at the station. She had not wanted to go home to Maggie just yet, so on impulse had come to see her aunt.

Amelia had been pulling up lettuce and only now saw her close up. 'Are you OK?'

'Davey's gone.' Rosie swallowed the lump in her throat.

Sympathy welled up inside Amelia and she placed an arm around her niece's shoulders. 'Work. That's the best panacea for an aching heart. How are things at the shop?'

Rosie took a deep breath. 'Fine. Due to the heatwave we're selling a lot of camomile lotion and Nivea cream.'

'What about the old ladies? Eau de cologne?'

Rosie nodded. 'And rosewater. And the gardeners are demanding Paraquat. We also had a sales rep in asking after you, by the way. In fact, he always asks is the boss in.'

'Which one?'

'Mr Rossiter.'

There was a pause in which Amelia's mouth tightened. 'Bernie. He's still coming in then?'

The girl looked at her, remembering Davey mentioning Bernie, the one-legged diver, on their last day out, and how the name had touched a chord. Now she made the connection. *Bernie* Rossiter had been her aunt's fiancé. She realised Amelia was staring at her and said quickly, 'You know him, of course. You were right about him. He has got the gift of the gab.'

'Does he know you're my niece?'

'I haven't told him. He'd probably try and get round me even more if he knew. He kisses my hand but I tell him it won't wash.'

'You carry on saying that,' said Amelia, entering the house through the French windows. 'I'll go and put the kettle on.'

Rosie sat down, glancing about the tidy room and wondering where the twins were. Maybe Bernie Rossiter was the cause of the rows Uncle Pete and Aunt Amelia were having now?

Her aunt entered the room, carrying a plate. Rosie longed to ask about Bernard but guessed Amelia might go all prickly on her if she started prying.

'I made a cake today. You're lucky there's actually a piece over. I've never known anyone eat like the twins.'

Rosie took the plate from her and watched her go out of the room again, seeing her with new eyes. Amelia really was quite attractive for her age. There was a bloom about her that had not been there a few weeks ago. Could it be because Mr Rossiter had returned? Although she had not sounded that pleased about his coming into the shop. Rosie bit into the cake, not wanting to believe her aunt could still be in love with the man. He was a charmer, but even so he was married and so was she.

'I had a letter from Iris,' said Amelia, pouring out the tea. 'She's renting a house and Babs has found a job in a store, Harry's made new friends, so they're all OK.'

'Babs hasn't written. And Aunt Iris didn't mention Sam?'

'Not in any significant way.'

Rosie pulled a face. 'Pity. I was hoping something might come of their meeting.'

Amelia smiled. 'I told you, you watch too many films. At least you must be glad Harry's OK?'

Rosie nodded. 'I still miss him, though.'

'It would be unnatural if you didn't. I still miss Iris.'

Amelia changed the subject. 'The twins told me you met them on the ferry. How did Chris and Dotty seem to you?'

Rosie said cautiously, 'In what way?'

'Do you think she's happier now? Do you think she'll be able to cope with a job?'

Rosie gnawed at her lip. 'I think she's happier than she was. As for managing when she leaves St Vincent's, I'm sure she could if she puts her mind to it. The trouble is, she likes having someone to look after her.'

'And at the moment that's Chris,' murmured Amelia. 'Maybe she could help you in the shop? You could keep your eye on her there.'

'If that's what you want,' murmured Rosie, not relishing the idea. 'You're the boss. But it won't be for a while,

will it?' She polished off the cake then said she would
have to be going.

'D'you want me to carry that Paraquat in tomorrow? It's
my early Saturday,' said Peter, teeth biting into some toast.

'Yes . . . no!' His offer took Amelia by surprise. She
made the herbicide in the shed at the bottom of the garden
to an old formula of her father's. 'I'll manage. You still
need to get your strength back.' She was thinking, what
if Bernard should just happen to come into the shop while
Pete was there? Her husband certainly wouldn't like it.

'I thought I'd proved I'd got my strength back?' He
got up and kissed the nape of her neck.

Amelia seized his hand and pulled his arm round her.
'Save it then for next time.' She felt a possessiveness
towards him that grew inside her every time they made
love. 'You get on with writing that book that's going to
make us rich.'

'It's nice you've faith in me.' He hugged her. 'What
about Chris carrying the Paraquat?'

She stared at him, a thought occurring to her, and paled.
She had been wondering why Tess wouldn't have wanted
her to know who the boy's father was and suddenly she
thought she knew.

He frowned. 'Don't look like that. We've got to treat
him just the same as we always have.'

'Of course,' she said, clearing her throat. 'He's lost his
mother at a difficult age in terrible circumstances.'

'He could do it in his lunch hour.'

'I don't want him thinking I'm putting on him.'

'OK.' Peter dropped a kiss on her head and sighed.

Amelia changed the subject swiftly. 'My lodger over the shop is having a baby. The newspapers reckon there'll be a baby boom next year.'

He stood in the doorway, leaning against the door jamb. 'What are you saying?'

'I don't know.' She sighed. 'I'm not a woman who cries for the moon.'

'Then why mention it? I'll never understand women.'

She got up and linked her arm through his. 'You're not supposed to. But lately I can't help thinking every time we make love how I'd like to have your baby. Although last night I thought you'd forgotten how.'

'I was remembering how Tess made excuses for Bernard Rossiter that time he went for you.'

'I know she did.' Her heart missed a beat. They had talked about old times, of her broken engagement. She wished she had told Peter then about Bernard's coming back into the shop; wanted to tell him now; hated keeping secrets from him. But her nerve failed her, just as it had last night. Scared that what they had now might be spoilt. Besides, she did not want Peter getting hurt, especially when physically he was not at his peak. She hoped he would forget about the Paraquat.

She saw him out, relieved that he saw little of Rosie nowadays; the girl just might mention Bernie without thinking. Perhaps in a few months time, when she felt more secure, she would tell him about Bernard.

Chapter Seventeen

'That looks nice,' said Irene, watching Rosie decorate the shop window with tinsel. 'Let's hope it brings the customers in for something other than a bottle of Black Magic. I hate them coughing and spluttering all over the place. It's a wonder we stay so fit.'

'Speak for yourself,' said Rosie, putting on a cough and climbing down from the ladder. 'We won't see many of them this afternoon anyway. I think this weather's on for the day.'

Irene opened the door and a swirl of fog came in. 'I feel sorry for them Russians,' she said. 'Their coalfields are frozen.'

'Shut that door! It's cold enough in here.' Rosie tucked her scarf more snugly down the front of her overall and thought of Davey sweltering in Palestine.

Irene made to shut the door but it was pushed from the other side. 'That's not very welcoming,' said a voice both of them recognised. 'Where's your Christmas spirit, girls?'

'Hello, Mr Rossiter. What can we do for you?' Irene beamed at him.

'Came with a prescription for the wife and to introduce my son to you.' Bernard ducked his head as he came through the doorway, calling over his shoulder, 'Come in, Eddie, and meet Rosie and Irene.'

A youth followed him inside, closing the door after him. He was tall and lanky but the overcoat he wore was short in the sleeve as if he had shot up since it had been bought for him. 'Hiya!' He eyed the girls boldly from beneath the brim of a tilted trilby which gave him a rakish appearance.

'He's joining the business,' said Bernard, flashing a smile. 'What d'you think, girls? Does he have his old man's style?'

'Never!' said Irene, but nevertheless eyed Eddie with interest.

Rosie smiled and put down the fact that he looked vaguely familiar to his being Bernard's son. She took the prescription from the older man. 'How is Mrs Rossiter?'

'Just the same. Lives on her nerves and has a bit of a dicky heart. You'll know that from the medicine she has to take.' He indicated the prescription, resting one arm on top of a glass display cabinet. 'How are things with you and how's the boyfriend? Still dodging bullets?'

'That's right,' she said with a bright smile, wishing he would not talk in such a way of something that terrified her, but the only thing she could do was to joke back. 'At least he's getting a suntan while we're all freezing.'

'Hmmm!' He looked around. 'Is the boss in?'

'No. And before you ask, she's fine as far as I know.' She filled in the book and took the prescription in to Mr Brown.

When she returned, to her surprise Amelia was in the shop and immediately Rosie sensed tension in the air. Her aunt's face was set as she stared at Eddie, and Bernard's expression as he looked in her own direction contained a hint of menace. He loomed over her and a shiver rippled down her spine. 'Why didn't you tell me Amy was your aunt?' he said softly.

The question took her aback. 'Amy? You mean, Aunt Amelia? I never thought about it.'

'Seems strange to me you didn't,' he sneered. 'You'll be Violet's girl, I take it?'

'That's right,' said Amelia, coming to life and moving to Rosie's side. 'My sister died nearly two years ago.'

'She was a looker. And so are you, girl.' Bernard's voice was silky as he leaned over and, before Rosie could prevent him, traced the line of her cheek with one probing finger.

Amelia's arm shot out to push his hand away. 'Don't do that!'

'My, we are protective.' There was a sneer on his face. 'You surprise me, Amy. I never thought you'd care about one of Violet's kids.'

'Shows you've something to learn then about family feelings, doesn't it? That was something you never understood,' she said fiercely. 'How's your wife, by the way?'

'Oh, we're like two turtle doves. Isn't that right, Eddie?' He glanced over his shoulder at his son.

The youth looked startled and said hastily, 'That's right. Turtle doves. Those things that coo.'

'I'm so glad,' said Amelia, smiling sweetly as she took Rosie's arm. 'A word, love, in the back. Irene, you'll see to Mr Rossiter, won't you?'

'Yes, Mrs Hudson,' said the shop assistant, a mystified expression on her chubby face.

There was a fluttering in the region of Amelia's heart as she hurried Rosie away. How she wished she had not chosen today of all days to come into the shop. That Eddie! He was almost the spitting image . . . Had Rosie noticed the likeness? She hoped not.

'What's the problem?' said her niece as they entered the stockroom. 'I know to be on my guard with him.'

'I just wanted us both away from him. He's trouble.'

The girl nodded. 'I *felt* it today. In the past he's always been as nice as apple pie to me. Can't you get Uncle Pete to warn him off?'

'Let's keep Peter out of this.'

'Would he be jealous?'

Amelia leant against some shelving, wondering how much to tell her niece. God knew she needed someone to talk to about it.

'Mr Rossiter isn't always a very nice man,' she said in a low voice. 'After I ended our engagement, he started sending me letters, pleading ones. As well as that he would cause trouble here in the shop on the days I was in and took to following me home. One sunny afternoon, he caught up with me in an entry and lost control.' She paused, feeling a sudden tightness in her chest and beads of sweat forming on her forehead and the palms of her hands. The unexpected violence was as real to her today as on that far-off day. She took a shuddering breath. 'Fortunately or unfortunately,' she murmured, 'Peter came along and there was a fight. It was a sheer fluke that Bernard was knocked cold. He's a big fella, as you'll have noticed, but he tripped over my foot and hit his head on a wall.'

'Lucky,' said Rosie, thinking, *Just fell over her foot, my eye! Maybe Chris was right and there was something between her and Uncle Pete. But years ago, not once he was married.*

'Bernard was never the same after that fall. His personality changed and I've always wondered if it was down to the bang on the head.'

'It was nice that Uncle Pete should fight for you,' Rosie murmured.

Amelia frowned. 'Tess was my best friend. He did it because of our friendship. But he got pretty knocked about and I wouldn't like anything like that to happen again. If he knew Bernard was coming into the shop, there could be trouble. So you mustn't say anything about this to Dotty. She'd tell Chris and then God knows what he'd say to Peter.'

'You can take my word for it, I won't be telling them anything. But surely you don't really think they'd fight again? They're grown men.'

'You never know. A man can be like a dog if another dog tries to take his bone.' Amelia gave a twisted smile, hugging herself. 'Bernard thinks Peter knocked him out. Now he knows you're my niece, I want you to be on your guard against him.'

'I will be, but you don't really think he'd try and get back at you through me?'

'I don't know. Anyway, I've said enough.' Her aunt's expression was distant. 'Let's hope he's gone by now. Maybe it's time I stopped ordering from him. Time I stopped feeling guilty and thinking if I hadn't broken off our engagement—'

'If Mam hadn't met Dad,' said Rosie.

Their eyes met and Amelia gave a faint smile. 'There's a lot of ifs in life, Rosie. You're here because they did meet and I'm glad of that now.' She squeezed the girl's shoulder and went into the dispensing room.

Rosie had a lot to think about that evening when she went home, but there was a surprise waiting for her which temporarily drove all that had happened that day to the back of her mind.

'A parcel's come for yer from Canada,' said Maggie from her seat in front of the fire. 'And there's a letter from *him*!'

Knowing that *him* meant Davey, Rosie pocketed the letter, preferring to read that when she was alone. The parcel was different. She lifted the box on to the table and began painstakingly to undo the string in order to save it. Food wasn't the only thing in short supply.

'What d'yer think it is, queen?' said Walter, peering over her shoulder while puffing on his pipe.

'It'll be something we can all enjoy, I'm sure of that,' said Rosie. And she was right. It was a box of goodies which put a smile even on Maggie's face. But it was the enclosed letter that was just as welcome to Rosie, although she read its contents with mixed feelings. According to Babs, Sam and Iris were no longer seeing each other.

She says it's because not everybody wants to take on someone else's children, but I don't believe that. I think it's her. He isn't as rich as Uncle Bill was. So I don't know what's going to happen, whether we'll stay here or move on. Aunt Iris has mentioned California but me and Harry are feeling homesick. She holds the purse strings, though, so we'll have to go where she says. But I'll be keeping in touch with Sam's youngest cousin Wilbur. He's a nice guy but Aunt Iris says it's only puppy love. A lot she knows! Maybe she'll change her mind. She is inclined to do that and then you'll be seeing us in the New Year. Do you think the grandparents would put up with us?

Rosie determined to get to work on them once Christmas was over. She folded the note and left Maggie and Walter putting the box's contents away while she went into the parlour to read Davey's letter. She could almost hear his voice whispering the words of love. She longed to see him. He never mentioned snipers and terrorists but she knew from the newspapers and wireless that although it was almost Christmas, there was no peace and goodwill to all men in the Holy Land. Instead there were curfews and a call for more British troops. What if Davey was killed? How would she cope?

Suddenly, life seemed dark and it was not only the thought of losing him which made her feel like that. Despite the end of the war, on every side there were strikes and shortages and the threat of more power cuts. Even bread was now on ration. She wondered what they would have lived on as children if it had been rationed during the war. Jam butties, chip butties, conny onny butties had filled their hungry little stomachs. Rosie thought of her mother and found herself remembering that last evening in their old home when Violet had click-clacked into the kitchen with a bag of fish and chips and Harry's birthday present. She had looked so happy. Her mother's voice seemed to speak in Rosie's head.

Stop worrying, girl. You should have more faith. Go out and enjoy yourself! What good are you doing Davey, moping around and imagining the worst? Think of all the songs telling you to smile even though your heart is aching! That's how I managed. You can do it too.

Rosie managed a smile, thinking, yes, that had been her mother's way of doing things. Crush the dark thoughts down and go out and have fun. There never had been a job working for the government after Joe died. She'd bet a pound to a shilling Violet had been a hostess or waitress in a place where servicemen had gone to relax, and that's where she had met Sam.

It was a year since Rosie had met him in the cemetery. Instantly, she decided to go there again tomorrow. She would drop in at 'Eden', too, and see how things were between Aunt Amelia and Uncle Pete, and invite Dotty along to the pantomime next week. *Dick Whittington* was on at the Empire this year. It was time they both had a bit more fun in their lives and it wouldn't be a bad thing if her sister saw less of Chris.

On Sunday morning, it was as if the whole world agreed with Rosie that everyone needed a bit of sunshine in their lives. The fog had gone and a pale yellow sun flooded the kitchen with a brightness that made her sing along with the carols on the wireless as she cooked her grandmother's salt fish.

'I don't know what yous have got to be so cheerful about,' grumbled Maggie.

'It's almost Christmas, Gran.' Rosie put an arm round her and planted a smacking kiss on her wrinkled cheek.

'Gerroff,' she said, scrubbing at her face. 'What are yous after?'

'It's the sunshine. I'm going out to visit Mam's grave and see our Dotty.'

'I thought yer might have put up some deccies for me in the shop, yous and Walt,' mumbled Maggie. 'Liven it up for the customers. I'm feeling knackered and yer said yous'd be home today.'

'Let the girl go and visit her ma's grave. It shows respect,' said Walter, jabbing the air with his pipe. 'If you're not feeling too good, yer can go back to bed. If you've crêpe paper, I'll cut up some deccies and see to the shop.'

'Maybe I will and maybe I won't,' muttered Maggie, wincing and moving her head as if it pained her. 'The only time my mam took to her bed during the day was when they carried her out feet first.'

'You'll outlive us all, Gran,' said Rosie, wondering how she was ever to persuade her to have her other grandchildren living with her. Maybe singing Babs's praises would be the best. Saying what a good little worker she was. And Maggie was going to need someone to take her own place when she married Davey. As for Harry, she felt sure he'd be able to charm his way into his grandparents' hearts. Having decided that, Rosie got on with things, thinking too that maybe she and Dotty could find some holly in the fields around West Derby and bring it here so the place would look even more festive once her grandfather had done his bit.

Walter snipped and twisted and soon the shop was looking a lot more cheerful with red, white and blue streamers (left over from the VJ celebrations) as well as green and yellow ones. They criss-crossed the smoke-grimed ceiling in the kitchen as well, but Maggie had yet to see them. She had gone up to bed with a hot water bottle and he had not heard a peep out of her since. Now it was time for him to surprise her by taking her up a cup of tea. On the stove bubbled a pan of scouse for their Sunday dinner.

He found Maggie asleep, fully clothed with just the eiderdown over her, lying in a pool of sunlight, the sun having worked its way round to the front of the house. He thought how much better she looked like that, peaceful, almost friendly with her mouth shut.

He crept downstairs and ladled himself out a bowl of scouse. After wiping the plate clean with a round of bread, he switched on the wireless, fiddling with the knobs to get rid of the static. He lit his pipe and settled back to listen to some music, wishing Rosie was there. She was good company, his granddaughter, knew when to be quiet, a bit of a thinker like her dad. Before long the old man had dozed off.

Walter woke, not knowing how long he had been asleep. It was still light, though, so he decided it had not been that long. Someone was banging on the yard window so he stumbled to his feet and hurried into the shop to open the back door, which Maggie must have locked.

He dealt with the woman, who said she hadn't got a leaf of tea in the house or sugar either and went on adding this and that to her bill, asking after Maggie and Rosie and complaining about her kids. Once she sniffed and asked could he smell smoke, but his sense of smell was not all it should be since a bang on the nose a few years back.

At last he got rid of her and went straight upstairs to check whether Maggie was awake and wanting her dinner. All was quiet and he stood for a moment in front of the window overlooking the street where a couple of neighbours were gossiping in the afternoon sunshine. Some lads were kicking a ball and he watched them for a moment, reaching into his pocket for his pipe. But it was not there. Must have left it on the counter, he thought, and went downstairs, thinking to listen to the shipping forecast, a habit he had picked up from his years at sea.

He pushed open the door only to step back swiftly. 'Bloody hell!' he whispered, heart in his mouth, eyes starting in his head as they took in the burning armchair and curtains. Even as he watched, the linoleum burst into flames as did some of the decorations.

Taking a deep breath, he dashed over to the sink and turned on the tap. Water gushed into the washing-up bowl but even as he turned to throw it on the flames, he saw that the shelf on which the wireless stood had caught fire and the edge of the wooden mantelpiece was beginning to smoulder.

'Oh, hell, she'll murder me,' he groaned, hurrying out of the room and clambering upstairs, shouting, 'Maggie, get out of bed! The house is on fire!'

His wife was still asleep, which surprised him. 'Maggie, come on, queen,' he implored, shaking her roughly. 'Wake up! Wake up! D'yer wanna end up like a cinder, girl?'

'Wha'? What's going on?' Her eyelids fluttered open. 'Walt, what are yer doing in here?' She sat up slowly. 'Now listen, melad. Don't yous be thinking yer getting in my bed. Yer still on trial.'

'Shut up, yer stupid woman!' he gasped. 'The bloody house is on fire! And if yer don't stir yer stumps, we're both dead!'

Her button eyes fixed on him. 'The house? *My* house! Hows the bloody hell did that happen?'

'Never mind that, girl. Let's get out!' He seized her by the arm and dragged her out of the bed, but she was so heavy she fell on to the floor. He pulled her up but she brushed off his arm and clung on to the bedstead. She slapped his hand away. 'Hang on, hang on! Let me think!'

'There's no time to think,' he wailed, wringing his hands.

'Stop whingeing! I'm not going without me jewellery.'

He dropped his hands, expression alert. 'Where is it?'

She told him and watched as he lifted the floorboards, while she clawed beneath the eiderdown for her handbag.

Walter weighed the soft chamois bag he had taken out of the box on the palm of his hand. He had thought she kept everything in her handbag but he had been wrong. 'I'll carry these, queen.'

She reached across the bed as if to snatch the bag out of his hand. Then unexpectedly she sank on to the floor, looking bewildered.

Walter pocketed the bag and dragged her up, gasping as he forced her over to the door. But as soon as he opened it, he had to shut it again, both of them coughing as the smoke caught them by the throat. He wondered what the hell he was going to do now.

Rosie's day had not turned out quite as she'd expected. First she had found Aunt Amelia and Dotty at the grave before her, they having remembered it was Violet's birthday too. Then, instead of Amelia's asking her back to the house, she had suggested that Rosie take Dotty home with her, saying it was a long time since she had seen her grandparents and if they weren't going to see her on Christmas Day, it would be nice for them to see her today. On the way home, Dotty, who had seemed reasonably keen to see her grandfather at least, suggested they drop in on Mrs Baxendale, of whom she had always been fond.

Davey's mother had made them welcome, inviting them to share her dinner, saying there was plenty because her lodger had told her at the last minute she had been invited out. Gwen had made so much fuss of them both that they had stayed far too long, talking of Christmasses past.

So it was getting on for late afternoon when they finally made their way to Maggie's house. As they turned the corner, Rosie saw that a crowd had gathered and it took only seconds for her to realise what was happening. 'Hell and damnation, the blinking house is on fire!' She gripped Dotty's hand and ran.

Smoke was billowing out of the parlour window where the glass had shattered and seeping through the letter box and cracks round the front door. 'Yer gran and granddad are in there!' shouted a neighbour.

Immediately, Rosie made a dash for the door, but a woman dragged her back. 'Don't be daft, girl! Yer can't go in that way. Besides, look!' She pointed upwards.

Rosie's eyes followed her finger and she saw her grand-father's face at the bedroom window. Even as she watched, Walter pushed up the lower sash.

'Granddad, how are you going to get down?' she yelled.

'Has someone phoned for the fire brigade?' he said in a tremulous voice. 'And we need an ambulance. Your grandma's not too good.'

Rosie turned to the crowd. Those next door to Maggie were standing on their own steps, having already brought out some of their possessions in case the fire spread. 'Has someone—?'

'They should be here any minute, luv,' said the woman who had stopped Rosie going into the house.

As if on cue, there came the clanging of bells and a fire engine came tearing round the corner, followed by another.

'Ah! Aren't they a lovely bunch of men?' said Gertie, who was a regular customer of Maggie's. She was wearing curlers, headscarf and a thin winter coat. 'Although I feel sorry for the one that's got to carry old Maggie down the ladder.'

'Fireman's lift, luv,' said the woman next to her. 'Those men know exactly how to get a grip on a girl!'

Rosie gnawed on her lower lip, watching impatiently as a hose snaked along the ground as a fireman connected it to the nearest water hydrant. Another two had already set about getting a ladder up to the bedroom window.

A trembling Dotty clung to Rosie's hand. 'What's happening? What's happening? I can't see clearly.'

'A fireman's started to climb the ladder,' Rosie informed her, her gaze on the bedroom window where Walter appeared to be trying to persuade Maggie to get her leg over the sill and give up her handbag, but she was struggling with him, determined to hang on to it.

'The fireman's there now,' said Rosie. He was saying something to the old couple. Then, not without a struggle, Maggie was hoisted firmly over the fireman's shoulder. 'He's bringing Gran down.'

It was halfway down that it happened. Maggie stopped struggling and seemed to go limp. The handbag which swung from her wrist slid off and disappeared in the billowing smoke.

'Phone for an ambulance,' panted the fireman as soon as he reached the ground.

'It's done, mate,' said someone else.

Rosie dragged Dotty over to where Maggie lay and searched for a pulse. Minutes later her granddad joined them, having descended the ladder unaided. 'Is she OK? Stubborn old faggot,' he said fretfully.

'She looks proper poorly,' said a woman. 'And you don't look too good either, mate,' she added to Walter. 'Here!' She seized his arm. 'Best come over to my place and sit down and I'll make you a nice cup of char.'

'I can't leave Maggie,' he gulped, face blackened by smoke. 'Is she still breathing, Rosie girl?'

Rosie shook her head, too upset to speak.

'Now don't you fret yourself, Rosie luv.' A woman helped her to her feet. 'She'd had a good innings.'

Rosie nodded but could not help remembering her mother lying on the ground, dying. Tears filled her eyes and she put an arm round Dotty.

'Where's her handbag?' said Walter.

'She dropped it,' said Gertie. 'It disappeared through the smoke.'

'Bloody hell! They say He works in mysterious ways,' said Walter faintly, then his legs buckled under him and he would have fallen if Rosie had not moved swiftly and eased him down on to the pavement. 'Don't you die on me too,' she said unsteadily.

He clung to her but his gaze was elsewhere, on the house where the firemen fought the flames, thinking it was amazing the damage one small pipe could do.

'What are we going to do?' said Rosie, sitting on the kerb at the bottom of the garden opposite, staring at the still smouldering building, gloved hands cupped round a steaming enamelled mug. 'We've lost everything. All my letters from Davey and my present from America.'

'Ration books?' said Dotty.

'No. Fortunately I had mine with me in my handbag. I planned on nipping into town in my lunch hour tomorrow.'

'Yer gran's handbag held all her wealth,' said Walter, looking wretched. 'It's all my fault. If I hadn't been having a smoke and fallen asleep.'

'It's just one of those things, Granddad,' sighed Dotty. 'What's more important is, where are you going to sleep tonight? I think you'll have to come back with me to Aunt Amelia's and Uncle Pete's. They'll make room for you.'

'I can't do that,' he said glumly, chin in hands. 'I hardly know them.'

'Of course you can,' said Rosie, knowing Amelia would see it as her duty to take them in.

'Well, just for tonight, queen,' he said, struggling to his feet. 'Then tomorrow we'll have to see.'

'Tomorrow's Christmas Eve,' said Dotty with a touch of excitement in her voice. 'You won't be able to go looking for somewhere else to live until after the holiday.'

It's going to be some Christmas, thought Rosie. Another funeral to face. And how were they going to pay for it with all Gran's worldly wealth gone? So much for her inheritance.

Chapter Eighteen

Their footsteps rang on the frosty pavement as they passed Beech Farm and the chemist's on the corner, hurrying to get in out of the cold – only to collide with Peter as they turned into Honey's Green Lane.

'What's happened?' he said immediately, staring at Rosie.

'Something terrible,' said Dotty with a barely suppressed shudder. 'Gran's dead and the house has burnt down!'

Peter looked flabbergasted. 'You are joking?'

'Honest to God,' she said sadly. 'It was terrible.'

'I am sorry,' he told her. 'I take it you're the girls' grandfather?' he addressed Walter.

'That's right,' said the old man lugubriously, holding out a hand. 'How d'yer do? You must be their Uncle Peter.'

'Yes.' His brow creased sympathetically. 'It's a helluva thing to happen.'

'They've nowhere to live,' said Dotty, eyes bright. 'I said you'd put them up.'

'Of course we'll put them up,' said Peter without hesitation.

'Only for the one night,' said Walter hastily. 'I'll find meself somewhere else tomorrow. It's different for Rosie, though.'

'How's it different? We've got to stick together,' she said, linking her arm through her granddad's.

'Can't always do that, queen,' he said with a sigh. 'I can stay places that wouldn't be suitable for you.'

'Why not?'

Walter looked lost for words so Peter butted in. 'Why don't you discuss this later? You're not going to find anywhere until after Christmas anyway. Let's get on home. You all look freezing.'

'Gran dropped her handbag into the fire!' said Dotty melodramatically as they hurried along. 'They've got no money.'

'Shut up, Dotty,' said Rosie. 'We might be able to salvage something. I mean, how does fire affect metal and precious stones?'

'It'll melt and shatter them, me lovely,' said Walter, limping beside her. 'I think yer going to have to accept her jewellery's gone.'

But Rosie was not convinced. As soon as she had the chance, she was determined to go and search the ruins for Maggie's treasure.

Amelia could hardly believe her eyes when they all trooped in and told their tale. At any other time she would have been pleased to have her niece living with them but right now, when Bernard and Chris were so much on her mind, it was the last thing she wanted. Yet she had no choice but to make Rosie and her granddad welcome. She ushered them into the sitting room, where the fire still glowed, before going into the kitchen with Peter to discuss where to put them and to make a hot drink.

'We'll have to have a move around,' he said, putting on the kettle.

Amelia delved into the box Iris had sent her and brought out a tin of spam. 'We can't do it right now.'

'Tomorrow then. Chris'll have to move back in with the twins and they can top and tail in my single bed. We'll move the double into our room and Walter can have your bed. Rosie and Dotty will have to top and tail too.'

'You've worked that out quickly,' she said, unable to prevent a smile. 'But you can guess what Chris'll think of us sleeping in the double.'

'Who cares? But if you'd rather top and tail in a single . . .' he murmured, winking at her as he opened the spam.

Amelia flushed. 'It would be fun and games, knowing you, but the double's more sensible. I hope he doesn't get a face on him, though. Things are going to be upsetting enough for Rosie and her granddad. I don't count Dotty because she had little to do with her grandmother.'

Peter frowned. 'You worry too much about Chris. He's not a kid any more. It's time he grew up and learnt to thank his lucky stars we've been so patient with him. It's almost two years since Tess went and look how well the twins are doing.'

'You're right. I won't mention him again.' She put on the frying pan.

'Good! It's time you started thinking more about yourself.'

'It won't be easy. I wasn't brought up to it,' she murmured.

'Try!'

There was silence.

He took a jug of milk from the pantry and changed the subject. 'Think you'll manage with a full house?'

'I'll have to, won't I?' She placed slices of spam in the pan and stepped back as they sizzled. 'We couldn't say there was no room at the inn. Not at Christmas.'

'I wish I didn't have to mess you about,' said Rosie, climbing into the other end of Dotty's bed, clad in a pair of her aunt's pyjamas.

'It's not your fault,' said Amelia, forcing a smile. 'I'm sorry about your grandmother. We didn't always see eye to eye but she took you in and did her best by you.'

Rosie tucked her knees under her chin. 'I grew fond of her over time, even though she was an old misery. Do you think some people are just born that way?'

'I don't know. At least she got her husband back in the end, which must have given her some satisfaction.'

Rosie thought of Vera and how it had been with Maggie and Walter at the end, but decided some things were best unsaid. She snuggled down, trying to remember just what the box Maggie had kept her jewels in had looked like, determined not to be put off by Granddad telling her it was a waste of time. Come Boxing Day she was going to be at the house looking for it and the handbag.

*

'Can we come with you?' The twins stood in front of Rosie, feet apart, hands clasped behind their backs, and two pairs of beguiling eyes appealing to her better nature.

She glanced at Peter. 'What d'you think? Should I take them?'

'You don't need to ask,' said Amelia promptly, spreading homemade plum jam on toast. 'Be our guest.'

'Great,' murmured Rosie, pulling a face. She glanced round the table. 'Anyone seen Granddad?'

'He went out earlier,' said Chris sullenly. He was not feeling too happy with life, having lost his bedroom to Walter. What annoyed him just as much, though, was the discovery that Amelia and Peter now had the double bed. 'Just the excuse they wanted,' he had said to Dotty on Christmas Eve.

Rosie had been passing at the time and had given him a look that had made him feel like a worm. He wished her to Timbuctoo. Dotty was different. She looked up to him and he felt all protective towards her because like his mother she had bad eyesight, and like his mother she expected him to be big and brave.

'Did he say where he was going?' said Rosie, looking at Chris rubbing his eyebrow.

'Why should he tell me?' he muttered. 'I'm not his keeper.'

'No,' said Rosie dryly. 'You could have been more welcoming, though.' She pushed back her chair, thinking he would be a much nicer person if he got rid of the chip on his shoulder, because he wasn't the only one who had lost a mother. He was damned lucky he still had a father.

'He said something about going to see someone who might put him up,' said Chris.

'Thanks.' Rosie bent over him. 'See, it wasn't so hard, was it?' She plonked a kiss on his cheek and left the room, followed by the twins.

The sight of the charred beams, blackened walls and shattered windows of the house depressed Rosie but the twins were thrilled. 'It's a real ruin,' they said, and immediately climbed over the window sill.

Rosie behaved with more decorum and went through the open doorway, picking her way over rubble in the lobby. The staircase was a wreck and she knew she would never get upstairs. In the parlour, part of the ceiling had fallen in and what was left of the furniture was filthy beyond redemption. 'What a mess!' she said.

'What are we looking for?' called the twins.

'A large handbag. Black. And a carved wooden box – that big.' She indicated its size with her hands. 'It might just have fallen through the ceiling and survived.'

The three of them began to poke around and surprisingly quickly Jimmy found the handbag beneath a charred length of curtain. Rosie took it from him with hands that trembled and undid the clasp. She could scarcely believe it when she found everything inside was intact: identity card, ration books, marriage lines, purse. She opened it and inside there was money.

Rosie smiled at Jimmy. 'Good lad!' She gave both boys a penny apiece from the purse and told them to carry on looking for the box while she went and searched in the shop.

But there the fire had blazed its fiercest and although the scales and weights were still recognisable, there was no sign of the old cash tin. As for the book with the names of customers owing money, that had gone for ever. At least some mothers would have a happy New Year knowing their debts had been wiped away, thought Rosie.

She returned to the twins, who had had no luck. 'Let's go home,' she said, trying to sound cheerful, thinking that at least there had been a fair amount of money in the purse.

As soon as Rosie saw Walter, she forgave him for going off without her and handed him the purse. 'What's this?' he said, the blue eyes so like her father's wide with surprise.

She smiled at him. 'I found Gran's handbag, so you don't have to worry about finding the money for her funeral now. There should be enough in there.'

He stared at her and for several seconds seemed to have difficulty getting his words out. At last he cleared his throat. 'I wasn't worried, queen. I've been paying into a Friendly Society for years. I mean, she was me wife and I wasn't to know she'd done all right for herself, was I?'

'Oh!' Rosie felt quite deflated. 'I didn't realise. But the money will come in useful, won't it? I mean you – we – we've only the clothes we're standing up in.'

'Yer right there,' he said hastily. 'You're going to need a whole new wardrobe, girl. And we could do with giving your aunt something for our keep.'

'Don't forget yourself, Granddad,' said Rosie, smiling.

Again Walter seemed to have difficulty in controlling his emotions and noisily cleared his throat once more. 'I – well, I don't need as much as you at my age.' He opened her hand and closed her fingers round the purse. 'Maggie would have wanted you to have this. You keep it.'

'But—'

Walter chucked her under the chin. 'Now, no arguments, sweetheart. It's yours. There'll be a bit over from the insurance, no doubt, for my needs.'

Rosie was so affected by his generosity that she forgot to ask him where he had been that day. Instead she kissed his rosy cheek and then went to speak to her aunt.

'A pound'll do for now,' said Amelia. 'And you don't have to give me any more for a couple of weeks. You'll need to buy yourself a few things. How did your granddad get on with looking for new digs, by the way?'

The pleasure Rosie felt in finding the money faded. She did not doubt that if he could, Walter would settle for any old hovel so that he was not beholden to anyone. 'I forgot to ask him. I'll go and see.' She hurried out of the kitchen into the sitting room where he was playing dominoes with the twins.

She put her question to him, aware he was avoiding looking at her, supposedly concentrating on the game. He sucked at a licorice torpedo furiously, not having smoked a pipe since the fire. She knew then it was just as she'd thought.

'Yer wouldn't like it, queen, so I'm not telling you. It looks promising but yer can't come with me. There's no room.'

'Couldn't we find somewhere else where we can be together?' asked Rosie, kneeling on the rug in front of him, elbow on his knee. 'I want us to be together, Granddad. I don't like the thought of you being on your own.'

'I'll be fine.' He touched the smooth curve of her cheek. 'Yer growing into a fine young lady. You've got to think of yerself and Davey. He'll be wanting to marry yer, no doubt, when he comes home. So yer not to worry about me.'

'But I do worry about you,' she said, touched. 'You're the only grandfather I've got.'

Walter was visibly moved and cleared his throat, almost choking on a sliver of licorice. Rosie got up and thumped him between the shoulder-blades. 'Enough, enough,' he gasped. 'I'll come and visit yer, don't you worry.'

'Promise?' she said firmly. 'Promise you won't disappear from my life again?'

'I promise,' he gasped.

With that she had to be satisfied.

Her granddad had filled her mind with thoughts of marriage again and so she went in search of Peter, whom she found in the parlour with a writing pad on his knee. 'What can I do for you, Rosie?' He gave her a smile that warmed her and she thought, not for the first time, how like him the twins were. Chris must take after his mother.

Rosie sat on the piano stool and told Peter about the money. 'Could you open a savings account for me in the Post Office? I want to put ten pounds in.'

'I think you're being very sensible.' He took the money from her and placed it in the pocket of the jacket he was wearing because it was cold in the parlour. 'Saving for anything in particular?'

'Marriage,' she said, firmly. 'When Davey comes home I'll be eighteen. We'll want to get married as soon as we can then.'

He put down his fountain pen. 'Have you spoken to your aunt about this?'

'Not yet.' She smiled ruefully. 'But I thought she'd be glad to be rid of me. She has enough to do with the boys and Dotty, and if she was to have a ba—' She stopped and took a deep breath. 'Anyway, I want to be with Davey, and if our Harry and Babs stay with Aunt Iris, I don't see anything to stop us getting married.'

He stared at her thoughtfully. 'Your aunt mightn't be too pleased about you getting married so young. Won't you be starting college in September? She really wants you to get your diploma.'

Rosie's brows drew together and her teeth worried her lower lip. 'I want to get it, too . . . but I want to be with Davey as well. I've really missed him.'

Peter smiled. 'If I were you, Rosie, I wouldn't mention this to your aunt yet,' he said gently. 'Besides her having enough on her plate at the moment, you might find that when Davey comes home the pair of you have changed. Give things time.'

Nothing will have changed between us, she thought, but did not say that to Peter.

On New Year's Eve, Maggie was buried as she had requested in the same grave as her son Joe. It was a much more elaborate funeral than Rosie had expected with a fancy carriage and black horses with plumes to draw it. Even so, it was a relief when it was all over and life could get back to normal.

But in the early months of 1947, nothing felt normal. Snow and hard frost held the country in an iron grip, numbing noses and toes and fingers, even indoors. There were continuing coal shortages which led to ever-growing queues for fuel and to power cuts. Even potatoes were in short supply, which made feeding the family even more difficult for Amelia.

Rosie worried about her granddad when he did not visit, especially as day after day people came into the chemist's for bottles of this cough mixture or that linctus, for tonics or chilblain ointment. Some brought with them news of elderly neighbours or parents dying of pneumonia or bronchitis. Of Mr Rossiter she saw no sign, only his son Eddie, who flirted with Irene, and whom she tried to ignore.

It was after one of their eldest customers died that Rosie decided to find out where her granddad was and to visit him. It was not going to be easy because he had not given her any clue as to where he would be staying. It was while she thought about his reluctance to give her his address that it struck Rosie just how strange that was. She worried about it, telling herself that if he was ill he would have sent a message to her. The more she thought, the more uneasy and suspicious she became. Until one cold bleak February Sunday she caught a tram which would take her along Westminster Road. She was half hoping she was wrong and would soon be home again.

*

'Rosie still not in?' Peter glanced at the clock on the mantelshelf, the hands of which stood at five past nine as he entered the sitting room.

'She might have gone to the pictures,' said Amelia, looking up from her darning and smiling at him.

'It's not like her not to say where she's going,' he said, turning down the wireless. 'She should be in by now.' He stood in front of the fire, gazing down at Amelia. 'Who would she go to the pictures with? She doesn't know any other lads but Davey, does she?'

'Not that I know of.'

'Then who's she out with?' His frown deepened. 'She's our responsibility, Lee. What if there was a power cut and something happened to her out there in the dark?'

'It's no worse than during the Blitz and we all coped then.' This concern he had for her nieces was nothing new and she knew she should be glad because it meant he was trying to fill a space in their lives, but Rosie was growing more and more like Violet and the likeness was unnerving in some ways, reminding her of the past and the trouble her sister had caused then. She knew it was stupid thinking like this but at least it took her mind off Chris and Tess and Bernard. Although Rosie had told her her former fiancé had not been in the shop for weeks. Perhaps he had taken over another area? The thought made her feel a lot better. She put down her darning. 'I'll get my things and go and walk to the tram stop. She could be coming now.'

'No!' Peter bent and kissed her. 'I'd be no happier with you out there on your own. The fog's coming down.' He walked out of the room and a few moments later Amelia heard the front door open and close.

A cinder fell in the grate and the coals in the miserable little fire shifted. The room became quiet again. Amelia sat, hands still in her lap, wondering where Rosie could be. The twins were in bed and Dotty had gone up, too. The girl had now finished at St Vincent's and although she had the opportunity of helping out there or in their workshop, Amelia was considering allowing her to work in her own shop. Irene was a caring girl and would watch over her and she would be a help when Rosie started college. Where Chris was she had no idea, thinking it best not to enquire too closely into his whereabouts during the evenings.

Suddenly, Amelia became aware that someone was tinkling on the piano. Getting up, she left the room. She pushed open the parlour door but the room was in darkness and, reaching for the switch, she flooded it with light.

On the piano stool sat Dotty and Chris, looking slightly dishevelled. 'What are the pair of you doing here in the dark?' said Amelia in astonishment.

For a moment, neither of them spoke. Then Chris, with an insolent curl to his mouth, said, 'Playing the piano.'

'Very funny,' she said, annoyed. 'But it's not a good enough answer.' She jerked her thumb. 'Out!'

They both rose and Dotty hurried into the hall ahead of him. Amelia said, 'Dotty, you can go straight to bed. Chris, I want a word with you.'

The girl whirled around. 'We haven't done anything wrong! Honestly, Aunt Amelia.'

'Then you've nothing to worry about, have you?' said her aunt quietly. 'Now upstairs and no nonsense out of you.'

'Don't you bully her!' said Chris loudly, moving swiftly to stand in front of Dotty.

'Don't be silly, Chris,' said Amelia wearily. And seizing his shoulder, she made to move him.

He stood rock-firm, glaring at her. 'You think you can have your own way all the time. Well, you're not our mother!'

'Don't, Chris,' whispered Dotty, pulling on his sleeve. 'She'll tell your dad.'

'You can take that as a promise,' said Amelia, exacerbated. 'Dotty, go to bed!'

The girl's eyes met hers briefly, then she turned and fled upstairs.

'I could do without this,' said Amelia, folding her arms and trying to hold on to her temper.

'I don't know what you mean,' said Chris sullenly, resting one elbow on the newel post.

'Oh, yes you do. So don't waste time trying to persuade me butter wouldn't melt in your mouth. I'm not going to have any shenanigans under my roof. You keep your distance from Dotty, or else.'

'Or else you'll tell your husband and he'll have my hide?'

'Exactly! And you'll deserve it if you've done anything to that girl.'

His face flooded with crimson. 'I wouldn't! It's just your dirty mind, you – you tart!'

'I beg your pardon?' Amelia stared at him in amazement.

'You wormed your way into his favour,' said Chris in a virulent voice, face twisted with hatred. 'And now he has no time for me!'

'That's not true.' Amelia unfolded her arms and clenched her fists.

'Oh, yes it is!' he shouted. 'You don't want me around here, I can tell.'

'I definitely don't want you around when you're rude and ungrateful. It's time you appreciated the home you've got,' she said, pushing him back against the stairs.

He managed to catch his balance and thrust out his hand, catching her in the chest. 'Home? *This* isn't my home,' he said in a choking voice. 'Home was where Mam was. I've had enough! I'm getting out.' He turned and raced upstairs, taking them two at a time.

Amelia lost her temper then and was about to fly after him when the front door opened and Rosie entered with Peter.

'What the hell's going on?' he said. 'I could hear your voices outside.'

Amelia whirled to face him. 'Chris has just called me a tart! And besides that I found him alone in the dark with Dotty in the parlour.'

Peter's eyes glinted. 'Where is he?'

She jerked her head in the direction of the stairs and he ran up them.

Amelia turned to Rosie. 'And where the hell have you been?'

'I don't want to talk about it. And I'm going to marry Davey whatever you say, so there!' snapped the girl. She too thudded up the stairs so that the whole house vibrated with the noise.

Amelia was so dumfounded that for a moment she did not know what to do. Then she ran upstairs and into her bedroom. She sat down on the bed and stared at the wall. *Kids!* She'd had them up to here. She was fed up. She had had enough. She wanted out. She wanted a peaceful life again when she did not have to worry about feeding them, about keeping the peace, about what they were up to or whether Peter was going to find out about Bernard and all that might lead to.

She jumped to her feet and flung open the wardrobe, beginning to drag things out and toss them on to the bed. Then she stopped, aware of raised voices and crying. She sank on to the bed, putting her hands over her ears.

The door was flung open and Rosie entered. She knelt in front of Amelia and pulled her hands away. 'What's going on? What's happened? Chris has slammed out of the house and Dotty's crying that much, I can't get any sense out of her. Did Chris do something to her?'

'He said not,' said Amelia, rubbing her eyes with the back of her hand. 'Where's Peter?' Her voice was unsteady.

'Trying to get the twins to go back to sleep, but they're kicking up a fuss.'

'Damn!' muttered her aunt, getting wearily off the bed. 'What should I do?'

'About the twins, Dotty, Chris or me?'

'I must get Peter to go after him . . .'

Rosie laughed. 'You're crazy! This whole house has gone crazy! But our Dotty might get some sense into her head if Chris isn't here, and you and Uncle Peter can settle down too. He certainly didn't want you two happy.'

'I know. But—'

'Let him go,' insisted Rosie, grabbing her arm. 'It's the only way he'll realise how good you two have been to him.'

Amelia stared at her, wondering how much her niece knew or at least guessed. Had she seen that likeness? Amelia took a deep breath. 'We'll see. What about you? Why were you all het up when you came in?'

Rosie dropped her arm and went over to the window, moving the curtain aside to gaze out. 'I found out where Granddad was living. He's moved back in with that Vera. I went to check and there he was.'

Amelia had to think before she could remember who Vera was. 'What did he have to say?'

'Excuses, excuses. I shouted at him. Couldn't believe he could do such a thing. Then she came out all smirks, and showed me a ring he had given her and I recognised it as one of Gran's.' Rosie faced Amelia, tears in her eyes. 'That was the final straw. I really blew my top then. He had her jewellery all the time and never told me! He offered me Gran's pearls but I threw them at him and told him I never wanted to see him again.' Her voice broke.

Amelia forgot everything else and went over to her. 'Poor Rosie.' She put her arms round her.

'I still love him, that's the trouble,' said the girl, a tiny sob in her voice. 'He's my granddad after all and there's a lot I liked about him. That's why it hurts so much.'

'I know. I liked him too,' said Amelia soothingly against her hair. 'He was good with the twins – started to teach them ju-jitsu as well as play dominoes with them.'

There was silence for a moment.

'How did he try and explain it away?' asked Amelia after a few moments.

Rosie lifted her head. 'He said he couldn't stay here and Vera's place was the only one he could think of. He needed the jewellery to buy his way back in with her and pay for the funeral. It was a fib about the Friendly Society. He stopped paying it when he left Gran.'

Amelia smoothed back her hair. 'He's known this woman a long time. I know that doesn't make it right, but – are they going to get married?'

'She said so. He said nothing. I don't know what to do now.' Rosie sniffed back her tears.

'Do nothing.' A faint smile lifted the corners of Amelia's mouth. 'That's what I was advised once. When in doubt, don't. Time works many things out.'

Rosie nodded, giving her aunt a hug before leaving her.

Peter entered a few moments later, looking thunderous. 'I've smacked the pair of them and they're packing a pillowcase each.'

Amelia glanced down at the clothes on the bed and did not know whether to laugh or cry. 'I was doing the same thing myself. I'd had enough. I wanted to run away.'

He looked stunned, picking up an armful of clothes and throwing them on to the floor. He sank on to the bed, shoulders drooping, head in his hands.

She picked up a frock and hung it back in the wardrobe.

'Do you wish you hadn't married me?' he said in a muffled voice.

She did not answer, couldn't because she might burst into tears.

She heard him sigh. 'I wonder if this is how Tess planned it. Chris hating us both and you hating me.'

'I don't hate you, you must know that?' Her fingers shook as she slotted another frock, the oatmeal one which had been Violet's, on to the rail. It reminded her of how long it had been since she had dressed up to go out with him. Every spare moment he was working on that darn book; not that he had much free time.

'Chris hates me,' he stated.

'No! It's me he hates. He's jealous, wants Tess back. Rosie said to let him go and then we could settle down and be happy.' Amelia went and sat on the bed beside her husband. 'Do you believe that?'

He put an arm round her shoulders. 'It's possible. He's going to have to grovel if he wants to live here again.' Amelia put both arms around him, loving him but wondering how long it might be before he regretted those words. He had treated Chris as a son for so long, despite everything.

'Let's go to bed,' said Peter wearily. 'I've had enough of young love for a month.'

'Me too, But what about the twins?'

'Can you see them going anywhere on a night like tonight? Besides, Rosie's with them. She'll talk them out of it.'

They undressed and snuggled beneath the bedclothes. The mattress dipped in the middle and the springs twanged. They did not move or speak for a long time. Then Peter said, 'Cosier than two singles, isn't it?'

'Mmmm,' said Amelia, thinking he was only a touch away, a breath! She wanted to make love, not only because she still found the act exciting but comforting as well. *But maybe he wasn't in the mood with all that had gone on this evening?*

Reluctantly, she turned over, twanging the springs and poking Peter in the back with an elbow. 'Sorry,' she murmured.

'That's OK. If we're going to apologise every time we touch or kick each other, we'll be at it all night.'

'I won't say sorry then.'

'Only if it's deliberate,' he said. 'Say if you kick me because you're really fed up with me. Or think I'm a bully for clouting Chris and the twins.'

'I pushed him and I wanted to smack Dotty. But if I kick you, it will be an accident.'

He twisted and said against her ear, 'We're both bound to turn over in our sleep. I believe it's a fact of life. But I'd hate you to think I was up to something.'

She could tell he was smiling, and lifting her head she caught him under the chin. 'Sorry! I didn't expect you to be there.'

'Liar.' He pulled her against him, burying his face against her neck. For a moment, they just held each other.

'Do you have many love scenes in this book of yours?' she murmured.

'Of course. Why d'you ask?'

'I thought you might want to run through them? Act them out?'

There was silence and she held her breath. 'That's not a bad idea. Can you imagine me in full regimentals, scarlet coat, the lot?'

'It's not how I want to imagine you in bed.'

He smiled as they kissed. She felt herself relaxing, limbs turning to water as he began to make love to her. There was silence then except for the occasional twanging of springs.

Afterwards, Amelia lay for a while, feet tucked beneath his legs, wondering if Rosie and Dotty and the twins had heard those terrible springs. Whatever they thought, it was a noise they were going to have to get used to. With Chris gone, there was no longer any need to pretend they were together just for the children's sake. Yet for all her bravado, the guilt was still there.

Chapter Nineteen

Water dripped from gutters and gurgled down drains. The thaw had come at last and suddenly it felt as if spring was just round the corner. Scarves, hats and gloves were discarded and the milkman from Brook Farm whistled as he delivered the milk. But Dotty went round with a face on her, refusing to eat. For days after Chris left, she had wept buckets.

Amelia had enquired at the estate farm, only to be told Chris had given his notice and they were unable to say where he had gone. That news only made Dotty more moody. Rosie had no time for such behaviour. She was missing Davey and her granddad but knew she just had to get on with things.

'You're a right tragedy queen,' she told her sister. 'Why don't you grow up? One thing's for sure, Chris is best away from you until you do.'

'It's OK for you to talk,' said Dotty sulkily. 'You know Davey will be coming home to you.'

Rosie leant across the bed, bringing her face close to her sister's. 'How do I know that? He could be killed! So stop making all our lives a misery and take some of the blame for what happened. Buck your ideas up. You shouldn't have been canoodling in the dark.'

'He only kissed me once,' said Dotty gloomily, sinking on to the bed and hugging herself. 'But that's not why I'm feeling so miserable. I saw him outside the chemist's on the corner the other day and he ignored me.'

'You what?' Rosie gave her a wrathful look. 'And you didn't tell Aunt Amelia, when you know she's worried about him, with his mother committing suicide!'

Dotty removed her spectacles and rubbed her eyes. 'What was the point? He didn't speak to me. And anyway, I don't think he's the type to commit suicide.'

'How do you know what kind of people kill themselves? Still, if you've seen him it means he's OK. He probably didn't speak to you because Uncle Pete warned him to stay away from you. Maybe Chris has some sense in his head at last.'

'That's not fair on me, though, is it?'

Rosie realised it was no use saying their uncle and aunt were trying to protect her, because knowing Dotty she wouldn't see it like that. She'd just say they were picking on her. Still, she took pity on her sister, deciding she needed taking out of herself. 'If you promise not to mope, I'll take you to the flicks,' she said loudly. 'And maybe, if you buck up your ideas, Aunt Amelia'll let you come and help out in the shop.'

Dotty put on her spectacles and gazed at her. 'You really think so? Could I cope? Are my eyes good enough? What if I made a mistake? A life and death mistake?' she added with a certain relish.

'You can see OK for at least six feet, can't you? And as I've said before, it's not that easy to make mistakes. Anyway, let's see what Aunt Amelia has to say.'

Amelia, who had convinced herself Dotty would spend the next few months sullen and uncooperative, greeted the suggestion with relief, having had second thoughts about her working in the shop because of her closeness to Chris. But she told herself that Rosie would keep her eye on her sister and gave the OK. Dotty, who seldom had a penny to bless herself with, realised she would be paid a wage and almost stopped feeling sorry for herself.

The next day she went into the shop with Rosie.

She wrinkled her nose, glancing round at her new surroundings. 'Why couldn't Aunt Amelia have had a sweet shop? This has got a hospitally smell.'

'No, it hasn't,' protested Rosie, taking a deep breath and closing her eyes, almost in ecstasy. 'It smells lovely – of soap and perfume, shampoos and creams. It's a little bit medicinal, I'll give you that, but what d'you expect of a chemist's shop?'

She ushered her sister into the back and plucked an overall from a hook. 'This was Aunt Amelia's. It'll probably be a bit big on you but it'll have to do.'

'She never works in the shop now, does she?' said Dotty, eyes magnified by the thick lenses of her glasses, reminding Rosie of Mr Magoo, the cartoon character.

'She comes in once a week to collect the books and see how the stock is. Maybe she'll come in more often when I start college in September.' Rosie shrugged herself into her own overall.

'What about when Davey comes home? You won't be working if you get married.'

'Nothing's settled,' murmured Rosie. 'Aunt Amelia mightn't give her permission. So, you see, you're not the only one who can't have what she wants right away.' She whirled round as Irene entered the stockroom and introduced the two girls to each other, telling her sister to take note of what the assistant said and did. 'She knows the customers as well as I do and it's them we're here to please.'

Dotty nodded and followed Irene into the shop, feeling important and grown up in the overall. She picked up things and sniffed them, listening with half an ear to all that Irene said, thinking of Chris and of boys in general. 'D'you have many lads coming into the shop?' she interrupted Irene in mid-explanation of the workings of the large brass till.

Irene looked startled, then she chuckled. 'That's not a question I've ever been asked before in here. Like the fellas, do you?'

Dotty flushed. 'I have been kissed. Do you have a boyfriend?'

'More than one.' Irene winked. 'Keep them guessing, that's my motto. But if you're looking to find one in here, you haven't much chance. More women and girls come in. Then there's the old men with ailments and the odd married man who gets all embarrassed and asks to see Mr Brown.'

'Why do they get embarrassed?' said Dotty.

Irene grinned. 'That'd be telling! You just pass any difficult ones on to me. Oh, and there's the salesmen. But you won't be having anything to do with them.' She was about to add something more when a couple of customers came into the shop, one with a child on leading strings. 'She'll want Farley's rusks and Virol,' hissed Irene. 'You can deal with her.'

Dotty stepped forward with an important air to serve her very first customer.

'So how did you get on?' said Amelia when the sisters got home that evening.

'I enjoyed it,' said Dotty, flopping on to the sofa and kicking off her shoes. 'But my feet hurt with standing all day.'

'You'll get used to that,' said Rosie, sitting next to Jimmy, who was sorting out cigarette cards on an occasional table.

'I'm not complaining,' said Dotty.

Peter glanced up. 'You *do* surprise me. If I'd known all we had to do to hear those words was send you out to work, I'd have done it earlier! Let's hope it lasts,' he added without much conviction.

To his and Amelia's relief, the next few weeks passed without any complaints or Dotty getting the sulks. She chattered about different customers but made no mention of the sales reps. Something Amelia was thankful for. She began to believe all her worrying had been unnecessary.

Dotty was fairly content with her job. She had discovered like Rosie that life did go on, and although she could not get Chris completely out of her mind and her heart, began to make the best of things. She was earning money and getting out and about with her sister and Irene, going to the pictures, the theatre and the occasional dance at the church hall. But she did not meet anyone she liked half as much as Chris.

Rosie's eighteenth birthday came round, bringing letters from America and Palestine, as well as a registered parcel.

'Open the parcel first,' said Tom eagerly, as they sat round the breakfast table. 'I've never had a parcel delivered on my birthday. Dad's were always late.'

Neither had Rosie. She tore at the wrappings to reveal a narrow oblong box. It contained Maggie's pearls. She fingered each glowing orb, knowing the eyes of the whole family were on her. Then she picked up the accompanying card, although she knew already it was from her granddad. She read it, then glanced at Amelia. 'What do I do?' Uncertainty shadowed her eyes.

'Keep them, of course,' said her aunt without a shadow of a doubt. 'Your gran intended you to have them, didn't she?'

'You're a lucky duck,' said Dotty, looking sulky. 'I bet I never get anything half as nice as that in my life.'

'You might,' said Rosie. 'Anyway, what if he's gone and married that Vera? If he has, I don't want to accept anything from him. I can't forgive him for lying to me and decking that woman out in Gran's jewels. She would have had a fit.'

'What does he say in his card?' said Amelia patiently.

'That he wants me to have them and hopes we're all keeping well. Nothing about coming to see me.'

'Probably nervous,' said Peter. '"Hell hath no fury"!
You threw everything at him but the kitchen sink when
you last saw him.'

'I did not,' she said indignantly.

'Words can hurt just as much as a rolling pin,' he said,
smiling. 'Why don't you go and see him? Then you'll
know if you've got a stepgranny or not.'

Rosie shuddered at the thought. That Vera was so tarty
and full of herself, having got her claws back into Walter,
that Rosie could not bear it. 'I'll think about it,' she said
loftily, putting the pearls to one side.

'You could write to him,' suggested Amelia. 'You
should anyway to thank him for the present. He didn't
have to send them to you, after all.'

'I suppose I could do that,' said Rosie, grudgingly,
reaching next for the letter from America. She read it
swiftly, letting out an exclamation. 'They're coming
home!'

'Who? What! You mean, our Iris and the kids?' said
Amelia, starting to her feet.

Peter, who had been halfway through the door, came
back. 'What's that?'

Rosie's dark eyes shone with excitement and she tapped
the letter with her finger. 'It says right here *they're coming
home!*'

Peter and Amelia exchanged glances.

'When?' Amelia demanded.

Rosie read the contents of the letter again. 'Doesn't
give an exact date but Babs says Aunt Iris has almost run
out of money.'

'Great,' muttered Peter.

Amelia shot him a look.

He tapped a fingernail against his teeth. 'They haven't booked their passage then?'

'She doesn't say so.' Rosie turned over the card. 'There's an extra bit here. Babs says Aunt Iris will be writing to you, Aunt Amelia.' She handed over the letter. 'Read it for yourself. I'll have to get to work.' She picked up Davey's letter and left the house with Dotty.

It was another beautiful day with clear blue skies and real heat in the sun. Rosie felt a moment of pure happiness as they caught the tram, visualising the arrival of Harry and Babs. She made herself comfortable and told Dotty to stop nattering on as she opened Davey's letter. Hungrily, she read his declarations of undying love and best wishes for her birthday. Then two items of news seemed to fly off the page and hit her between the eyes. One was that her granddad had been to visit Davey's mother. The other, more importantly, was that Davey had been promoted, was now a lance-corporal and seriously considering staying on in the Army when he finished his National Service!

Rosie could scarcely take it in. She read the words again and again, then folded the letter and placed it in her handbag.

'What does Davey have to say?' asked Dotty. 'When's he coming home?'

'Doesn't say. But it won't be earlier than New Year,' murmured Rosie, gazing out of the window, the short crisp sentences drumming in her head. They did not seem real somehow. Never had she given a thought to Davey's being a real soldier. What was he thinking of? How did this news fit in with their plans to get married? She gnawed on her lip, trying to think sensibly, but all she could see was that he had changed as Peter had warned he might, and she did not know how she was going to cope with it.

'What's wrong with your face?' said Amelia in a teasing voice as Rosie entered the house that evening. 'What's happened to our smiling birthday girl?'

'She's been like this all day,' said Dotty. 'In another world since she read Davey's letter.'

Rosie paused in the act of taking off her jacket. 'He's been promoted.'

Amelia stared at her intently. 'Isn't that good news?'

Rosie shook her head, dark hair flying about her flushed cheeks, strands sticking to her damp skin. 'It's gone to his head!' she said in a strangled voice. 'He's talking about staying on in the Army. Says that *they* think he shows initiative and is proficient in his job.' Her voice rose several octaves. 'And you know what else?'

'What else?' said Amelia, understanding the turmoil her niece was in.

'Granddad's been to see Davey's mother! Apparently he thought I might have been to visit her and wanted to know how I was.'

'No mention of marriage to Vera, I take it?' said Amelia.

'Davey didn't say.' Rosie sank on to the stairs, resting her head on her knees. 'What am I going to do?'

'I'd go and see Davey's mother,' said Amelia. 'Walter and she used to enjoy a good gossip when your grandmother couldn't hold a conversation. As well as that, Davey's bound to have written and told her about his promotion. You could see what she thinks.'

Rosie nodded slowly. 'Perhaps together we can persuade him to change his mind.' She attempted a smile. 'Now I just want to put me feet up and have a sit in the garden.'

'That's a relief, because I've made you a cake and there's a few candles to blow out.'

Rosie was overcome. 'You've made me a cake?' she stammered. 'I've never had a birthday cake in my life.'

Amelia smiled. 'So I've done something right for once? It took some scrounging to get the ingredients but I managed it. We'll get Peter to take a picture of you with his box Brownie and you can send a photo to Davey. The lad will see just what he's missing then. Although it mightn't be a bad idea if the pair of you waited a while before rushing into marriage . . .'

Rosie remembered shouting that she was going to marry him the night Chris had left. She flushed but said nothing, hurrying upstairs to change out of her working clothes.

Dotty followed her, feeling a bit put out, wondering if she would get a cake when it was her birthday. But she bet they'd forget about hers in all the excitement of Harry and Babs coming home. She thought of Chris and how he used to make a fuss of her. Why hadn't he been in touch? Was it really as Rosie had said and he was scared of his dad? But who'd have told him they'd spoken? Not her. If he really cared for her, he'd do something to get in touch with her. But maybe, like Davey, leaving home had proved more exciting to him and she would never see him again.

Having made up her mind to visit Davey's mother, Rosie went there the following evening. She found Gwen on the front step gossiping with her next-door neighbour, keeping her eye on the kids playing rounders, her kerb being the base.

'Hello, lovey!' she said, beaming at Rosie. 'I was just talking about you. Telling Mavis about old times. She was asking about your granddad. Did you know he came to visit me?'

'Davey mentioned it in his letter.' She pulled a face. 'He also mentioned something else.'

Gwen's smile faded. 'Aye! I thought he'd want to be out of the Army in a flash but I was obviously wrong. Come in, lovey, and we'll talk about it. Have you come straight from work? Perhaps you'd like something to eat? Looks to me like you've lost weight.'

'It's this heat,' said Rosie, following her up the lobby.

'And worrying about our Davey, no doubt. Did you read in the papers about those Arabs not agreeing to the settlement with the Jews? When's all the sniping at our lads going to end? It's not that I blame the Jews for wanting their own country but our lads are only trying to keep the peace.' She pressed Rosie into the best armchair and asked would she like a drink of homemade lemonade?

'That'd be lovely. It's been too hot in work today.'

'A real scorcher. I haven't even lit the fire. I've settled for cold food for once.' Gwen bustled out into the back kitchen but returned in minutes with two glasses and a chipped white jug. 'You'll have a butty,' she said. 'Got a nice bit of brawn. You don't want to lose any more weight, lovey.'

Rosie smiled her thanks, enjoying being cosseted and feeling at ease. Mrs Baxendale mothered her in a way Amelia never could, which was nice now and again. 'Granddad,' said Rosie, wanting that subject out of the way so she could spend more time talking about Davey.

'He's having trouble with that Vera,' said Gwen, handing her a doorstep-sized butty.

'You know about her?' exclaimed Rosie.

Gwen snorted. 'Course I do. Our Davey told me all about her and your granddad. Silly man! She's taking him to the cleaners, she is. It's just like the story in the Bible. The one about the Prodigal Son who went off with loads of money and ended up with nowt because his mates were only after one thing. She'll have everything off him if she can.'

'I knew it!' said Rosie, biting savagely into the sandwich. 'He hasn't gone and married her, has he?' she added with her mouth full.

'No. But I reckon it's only because of you that he's dithering. It's just a matter of time, though. Unless we do something.'

'We?' said Rosie.

'Of course. I have an eye to him myself. Now my lodger's leaving to get married and our Davey's wanting to stay in the Army, I'm looking for someone and Walter would do me nicely. As well as that, he needs saving.'

'From Vera?' said Rosie, amazed, thinking she obviously wasn't going to get any help from Davey's mam in persuading him not to stay in the Army. She'd made plans which didn't include him.

'No! From the devil, lovey.' Gwen shook her head and tutted. 'He's living in sin and he's a thief to boot. He told me those jewels really belonged to you.'

Rosie could not believe it and wanted to laugh at the seeming craziness of it all. 'He's told you all this?'

'Confession's good for the soul, lovey. Besides, your gran told me she was leaving them to you. I just happened to mention that to Walter and he spilt the beans. I know he hadn't given you any of them because our Davey wrote me saying how hurt you were about it.'

'You amaze me,' said Rosie, shaking her head from side to side, a smile on her face. 'I thought you'd be down on Granddad for what he's done.'

'I don't approve.' Gwen pursed her lips as she filled their glasses again. 'I aim to get him to church and then the Lord'll do the rest. He's already got saving graces. He's good with kids and he's clean. We could do with someone like him helping with the Boys' Brigade.'

'Right!' said Rosie, picking up her glass. 'Here's to you, Mrs Baxendale. That you'll be able to save Granddad from Vera's clutches.'

Gwen winked at her. 'I'll do it, lovey. But I'll need your help. Can I tell him you'll see him? You can meet here.'

'Yes. And you can tell him something else that might tip the balance our way: Harry and Babs are coming home. His grandson's going to need him.'

'Right!' said Gwen, clinking glasses with her. 'Now our other problem – our Davey. I don't suppose he'll always be out in Palestine, even if he stays in the Army.'

'No. But he could be sent abroad. Germany. Aden. India even. I can't understand it. Davey was never ambitious.'

'Ah, that was because he didn't get the chance. He never told anybody but he won a scholarship to the Collegiate but wouldn't take it up because he knew I had no money. He said he didn't want me slaving me guts out scrubbing floors and the like. He knew that to make it worthwhile he'd have to stay on at school until he was sixteen, like you. Not that he ever said any of this to me. Just that he wanted to stay with his friends.'

Rosie put her chin in her hand and said pensively, 'Now he's got the chance to make something of himself and I bet he expects us to be against it.'

'You always did have a good head on your shoulders,' said Gwen. 'So what do we say to him?'

'I should think you'd say, "Well done, son!"'

Gwen nodded, tears in her eyes. 'And you?'

Rosie swallowed the lump in her throat. '"I'm proud of you. Keep up the good work."'

'Aye,' said Gwen clearing her throat. 'That'll do. But what about getting married, lovey, and this certificate you're doing?'

'I think we're just going to have to wait and see. In the meantime, we'll concentrate on Granddad. As soon as Harry and Babs are home, I'll have them here to meet him. You must tell him not to do anything until he's seen them. He owes us that, for Dad's sake. And if he marries that woman, I'll never have anything to do with him again.'

Chapter Twenty

'What do you think? Where are they going to sleep?' asked Dotty, helping Rosie dress the window.

'Aunt Amelia will sort it out,' she murmured. 'Anyway, they won't be here for another three weeks.'

'Babs'll have to find a job.'

'Hmmm. She can always work here while I'm at college. Save Aunt Amelia coming in.' Rosie gazed out of the window and froze. 'Now what the heck is he doing back here?' she murmured.

'Who?' asked Dotty, trying to spot who her sister was talking about amongst the shoppers out on the pavements but unable to distinguish faces from that distance.

'Nobody you know,' said Rosie firmly, seizing her shoulder and dragging her out of the window. 'Go into the stockroom and put the kettle on. And stay out there.'

'Why?' said a struggling Dotty, glancing over her shoulder.

'Because I told you!' said Rosie in a voice that brooked no argument. She pushed her sister into the room and closed the door before hurrying behind the counter. Irene was on a week's holiday at the new holiday camp which a resourceful Mr Butlin had developed from a naval training site in Pwllheli. So there was nothing for it but for her to deal with Eddie and his father.

'Good afternoon,' she said, to all outward appearance in complete control of the situation. 'It's been some time since we've seen you, Mr Rossiter. Your wife well?'

'Dead. She died last week,' said Bernard, tersely.

It was the kind of news Rosie heard quite often but even so it came as a shock. He looked quite grey, which surprised her somehow. 'I am sorry,' she said sincerely.

'Why should you be? You didn't know her.' His voice had an edge to it. 'Anyway, I'm not here to make small talk. Is Mr Brown in? I believe there was some mistake in an order my son took.'

'That's right.' She looked at Eddie, whose expression was strained. 'Nothing that can't be put right, though,' she said reassuringly.

'Come on, Eddie. Don't let's waste time,' said his father.

Rosie watched them go into the dispensing room then hurried to the stockroom and had to force the door open. 'What were you doing right behind there?' she said to Dotty.

'Nothing!' said her sister in a muffled voice, clutching her nose. 'Who's that with Mr Brown?'

'Only salesmen. Nobody you know. How's the tea coming along?'

Before Dotty could answer, the shop door opened and Rosie went back out again. Dotty appeared a few minutes later carrying a steaming cup. 'Will I take Mr Brown's in to him?' she asked.

'No! Why don't you nip up the road and get us a bun each? I'm starving.' Rosie reached into her overall pocket where she knew she had a shilling.

Dotty regarded her suspiciously. 'You're not trying to get rid of me, are you?'

Rosie smiled. 'Of course I am. I'm madly in love with a salesman and don't want Davey to know. Here, buns!' She threw Dotty the shilling. 'Take your time.'

Five minutes later, the Rossiters left the shop, much to Rosie's relief. But not a minute later Dotty entered in a rush. 'I've just seen Chris!' she cried.

'Oh?' Rosie tried to act normal. 'Where?'

'Just outside.' Dotty was trembling as she pulled on Rosie's arm. 'Come on! You'll be able to catch up with him.'

'You didn't speak to him?' said Rosie, taking her time.

'I didn't get a chance. He looked right through me as if he didn't know me. Just like that last time on the corner of Honey's Green Lane.'

'Are you sure it was him? You know your eyesight.'

'I could *see* him!' said Dotty indignantly. 'I was that close.'

'But he didn't seem to know you?'

'No.' Her bottom lip trembled.

'It must have been his double then,' said Rosie cheerfully. 'They say everyone has one.'

'I was really pleased to see him too,' said Dotty forlornly, taking off her spectacles and polishing them on her overall. 'It shows I must still like him a lot.'

Rosie was silent, thinking she had said enough.

*

'Do you believe everybody has a double, Uncle Pete?' said Dotty across the dining table that evening.

He paused, potato on a fork halfway to his mouth. 'What makes you ask?'

'Because I said it,' said Rosie swiftly, wishing her sister had kept her mouth shut. She glanced at her aunt. 'Dotty thought she saw Chris outside the shop, but you know her eyes.'

'It really looked like him,' said her sister fiercely. 'Only Rosie said it couldn't be because he ignored me.'

'How did he look?' said Peter.

'Just like himself only smarter. He was wearing a tie,' said Dotty.

'You didn't see him, Rosie?' said Peter.

'I didn't see Chris, no.' She avoided meeting his eyes.

'Pity,' he murmured. 'You should have been quicker off the mark and then we'd have known for sure if he was still alive and kicking.'

Dotty paled. 'You make it sound as if you think he could be dead!'

'I don't think that!' he said harshly. 'I'm just as worried about him as you are, that's all. I'll kill him when I get my hands on him.' He dropped his fork, which clanged against his plate. The noise sounded loud in the room because everything had suddenly gone quiet. He pushed back his chair and walked out.

Amelia waited a few moments then went after him. She found him lying on their bed, gazing up at the ceiling. 'What was that all about?'

'You tell me,' he said angrily. 'Doubles! Why should Rosie think it wasn't Chris but a double?'

'You heard Dotty. He gave no sign of recognising her.'

'That could have been an act and Dotty might not have recognised it as such.' He sat up abruptly. 'I can't understand why Rosie didn't act more swiftly.'

'The shop might have been busy.'

'No excuse! We're talking about a member of the family who's gone missing. She should have cared more. She's a caring girl. It doesn't make sense.' His brows drew together, hooding his eyes. 'Why would she think it wasn't Chris?'

There was silence. Amelia had run out of excuses.

'Bernard Rossiter,' said Peter.

It was so unexpected that she almost jumped out of her skin. 'I don't know why I did that,' she said crossly.

'Guilty conscience?'

She flushed. 'I've nothing to be guilty about.'

'I'm glad to hear it.' He continued to stare at her. 'Did you know he was back?'

'Back from the war, you mean?'

'You could say that.' He smiled grimly, sliding his legs over the edge of the bed and getting to his feet. 'Although I doubt he ever set eyes on a German. Richie's seen him in the chemist's here on the corner.'

Amelia felt faint. 'I've never seen him around here,' she whispered.

'But you *have* seen him?'

She knew it was time for honesty. 'Yes, over a year ago. He came into the shop.'

'Why didn't you tell me?'

She reached out for the bed post to steady herself. 'I was scared what you might do. I didn't want the two of you meeting again.'

His laughter seared her. 'What are you frightened of?' He seized her wrist. 'You can't still care for him?'

'Of course not. You're hurting me!'

He stared at her for what felt like hours but was only seconds then released her. 'I'll tell you something, Lee. If I meet him round here, I'll knock his block off. As God is my witness, that's a promise. He's not going to destroy this marriage like he did my last. I'd see him dead first!'

Amelia could only wonder what Peter knew about Bernard's relationship with Tess, but most of all she realised her husband had to be reassured before he did something stupid. 'If he had set foot in this house, I'd have been tempted to put Paraquat in his tea,' she said rapidly. 'You still don't know me if you think I'd take up with him again. Like you, I've tried my best to make the children feel secure and reasonably happy. Do you think I'd risk spoiling that? We've only failed with Chris, and maybe that's not our fault.'

'Maybe not.' Peter looked less tense. 'If only he'd get in touch! I keep telling myself he's not my son, but part of me still finds that difficult to accept.'

'I know.' She sank on to the bed, feeling drained, wishing she could tell him the whole truth, but then he would be even angrier.

He stared at her pale face and instantly went down on his knees in front of her. He took one of her hands between his. 'I'm sorry. I should have known better, but I've had trouble thinking straight lately. Are you OK?'

'I felt faint for a moment. It's passing now.'

He looked relieved. 'You have a rest and I'll bring you up a cup of tea.'

Amelia did not argue but stretched out on the bed. She felt exhausted and could quite happily have slept the clock around.

'His wife's dead, you know,' said Rosie.

It was a fortnight later and she was due to start college that morning.

'Whose wife?' Amelia's mind had been a thousand miles away. To be precise, in the middle of the Atlantic on the liner bringing her sister, niece and nephew to Liverpool.

'Mr Rossiter's.'

There was a pause while Amelia gathered her wits. 'You've seen him recently?'

'The day Dotty thought she saw Chris, he came into the shop with his son.'

Amelia stared at her. 'Thanks for telling me. I'd guessed as much. He's been seen round here but I suppose that's not so strange. I mean, he works for a drugs firm and there's Miss Scott's on the corner.'

Rosie nodded, picking up the briefcase which had been a birthday present from her aunt and uncle. 'I thought you'd like to know because of Dotty. I'll be on my way now. See you later.'

'Have a good day.'

Half an hour later, Amelia caught a tram to Kensington. For the next week or so she had decided to go into the shop for at least part of the day. If Bernard came in, she was going to have a talk with him, although she had not yet made up her mind exactly what she was going to say.

But he did not come that day, nor the next, and the day after that Amelia had to go down to the docks to meet the liner from America bringing Iris, Babs and Harry home.

For a while, as she stood on the quayside amongst the milling crowds, she forgot her worries in the excitement of the moment. She craned her neck, gaze scanning the people lining the rails of the ship. Then she saw Iris and a young woman she barely recognised as Babs, and squashed between them caught the gleam of Harry's golden hair. She waved vigorously, calling their names, and somehow above all the noise they heard her. They waved but it was to be another half hour or so before they were through Customs.

The sisters flew into each other's arms, hugging and kissing before each held the other at arm's length. 'Oh, it's so good to see you,' cried Amelia. 'You look so smart! You can tell rationing hasn't hit you over there.'

'Don't remind me,' said Iris, laughing. She was wearing a navy-blue and cream checked suit and a wide-brimmed hat. She looked lovely. 'But I can't say the same for you, dear sister. You look drawn. Life tough, is it?'

Amelia shrugged. 'It could be worse. I've a lot to tell you.'

'Me too, when we can get a moment's peace,' said Iris, pulling a face.

Amelia turned to Babs and Harry. 'And how are you two? Glad to be home?'

'Where's Rosie?' said Harry with a hint of an American accent, gazing about him as if expecting his sister to materialise out of thin air.

'At college. But you'll see her later. Come on now! Grab the smallest of the suitcases and let's get home.'

Babs and Harry met Rosie at the door that evening. 'I can't believe you're actually here,' she said, eyes sparkling as she hugged them both. 'It seems for ever since I last saw you.'

'More than two years,' said Babs gravely.

'Your ringlets have gone,' sighed Rosie. 'You've got a pageboy and you've really filled out. I like the frock. That neckline.'

'It's a sweetheart. We're all grown up now,' said Babs, linking her arm through her sister's. 'We'll soon be old and grey. And talking about old and grey, when are we going to meet this granddad of ours?'

'As soon as I can arrange it with Davey's mother.'

'How is Davey?'

'Fine as far as I know.'

'I think I'll be a soldier too,' said Harry.

Rosie shook her head at him, taking in his sturdy body and cherubic features. 'You're back in Liverpool, my lad. You stick to the sea if you want to travel. I think you'll be safer there.' She hugged him again.

'God help the Navy in that case,' said a voice Rosie had not heard for a long time. 'He's a right scallywag!'

Rosie gazed at Iris and could not speak for a moment. She had never realised just how like her mother Aunt Iris was. Maybe her hair was a shade darker and the brown eyes less luminous but the likeness was there in the bones of her face just as they were in Rosie's. She could not help wondering what Sam had made of that likeness. She held out a hand. 'Hello, Aunt Iris. It's nice to have you home.'

'It's nice to be home. Although I think we're going to be a little bit overcrowded.' Her handshake was brief. 'No wonder our Lee's looking ready to collapse.'

'I help her as much as I can.'

'I'm sure you do, honey, but she was never very good with kids. It's a miracle to me how she's managed. But there you are. Lee always was one to do her duty.'

Rosie realised she had not heard that word on Amelia's lips for a long time now but said no more, believing it was more than duty that drove her to do what she did.

One of the twins stuck his head through the morning-room door. 'Tea's ready. Hurry up, we're starving! But we can't sit down 'til you're ready, Rosie. Dotty arrived home early.'

Rosie raced upstairs, washed her hands and face and hurried into the morning room. There was a noisy dragging out of chairs and jostling for places from the boys. 'Stop that!' rapped Peter, flicking Tom across the cheek with his finger. 'It's not feeding time at the zoo.'

Immediately, Harry made cheetah-like noises, scratching his armpits and snuffling. 'See what I mean?' said Iris, her smile not quite reaching her eyes. 'A scallywag!'

'Harry, if you carry on like that you can go outside and eat off the cat's plate,' said Amelia, shaking her head at him. 'That's where animals eat.'

'Lovely grub,' he said, smacking his lips.

Peter picked up his plate and headed for the door. Harry's grin vanished. 'Sorry!' he called, scrambling down from his chair and going after his uncle. 'Sorry.'

'Perhaps all he needs is a man's touch. I remember he used to behave for Bill,' drawled Iris, flicking ash from her cigarette into a cut-glass bon-bon dish.

'He'll behave for me or it'll be bread and water for the rest of the week,' said Peter, putting the plate back on the table.

'I'm an angel,' said Harry, putting his hands together in an attitude of prayer, and started to sing 'Ave Maria' in a piercingly sweet voice.

Everyone except Babs and Iris stared at him. 'Since when did you start singing like that?' said Rosie, a thrill running through her.

'Since a music teacher discovered I had a voice,' Harry said, throwing out his chest.

'It's cissy,' said Tom, elbows on the table, eyes narrowed as he stared at his step-cousin.

Harry's chin jutted. 'No, it's not. It's a gift from God.'

'Which has gone to your head,' said Jimmy.

'Quiet!' thundered their father.

The silence was immediate but Babs had an expression on her face which caused Amelia, remembering how the twins had once tormented Harry, a moment's disquiet. She could see trouble ahead if they reverted to their old tricks. Hopefully, they wouldn't.

She put it out of her mind and listened to Iris talking in an animated manner about the people she had met in

America and on the trip home. Suddenly, it occurred to
her that her sister might find it difficult to settle down here.

'So how was America?' said Rosie, as soon as she and
Dotty were alone with Babs. A camp bed had been
squeezed in alongside their single bed. 'I wrote to you,'
said Babs, yawning and wriggling into the sleeping bag
bought from the Army and Navy store.

Rosie pushed Dotty's foot out of her face. 'Of course
you did, but you can't tell everything in a letter. It's like
I never got to tell you about Granddad's fancy woman or
about Davey being made lance-corporal and wanting to
stay on in the Army.'

'Does he?' Babs let out a low whistle. 'How d'you
feel about that?'

'How d'you imagine I feel?'

'Pretty lousy, I guess.' She hesitated. 'I got pretty fond
of Willy, Sam's cousin. I think I mentioned him, didn't I?'

'Were you in love with him?' said Dotty, turning over
and digging a knee into Rosie's back.

'I guess so. But I'm not pining away or anything. What
would be the point?' She sighed. 'Aunt Iris wanted to get
away from the Dixons. I don't think he loved her anyway.
It was just that she was so like Mam. They are alike,
aren't they? Aunt Amelia's one on her own.'

'She's OK is Aunt Amelia,' said Rosie.

Babs laughed. '*You've* changed your tune. You used to
hate her.'

'I know. We get on much better now, though. Do you
think Aunt Iris and Sam – whether it was too soon after
her husband died?'

'No. She's just a flirt,' said Babs firmly. 'Everywhere we went there was some guy or other who'd take her out. On the ship coming home there were several.'

'No one special, though?'

Babs pursed her lips. 'There was Derek who she said was a real bright spark. I think she had a pash on him. They used to dance the night away.'

'Shipboard romance,' said Dotty dreamily. 'Didn't you get to smooch with anyone under the stars? I'd love to be on a ship with Chris.'

'Chance would have been a fine thing,' said Babs dryly, meeting Rosie's glance and rolling her eyes. 'I was stuck in the cabin most evenings looking after Harry. I got the distinct impression we cramped her style.' She shrugged. 'Anyway, we're home now and it'll be interesting to see what she does. She likes her comfort and I don't think she's going to find much of that here.'

Rosie frowned. 'You don't think she'll stay?'

Babs rolled her eyes again. 'You want me to tell you what I really think?' she drawled.

They nodded.

'She'll be off like a shot.'

'You won't be going with her, though, will you?' said Dotty, pouting.

'No way,' said Babs firmly. 'Now fill me in on your news, Dotty. You never did write to me.'

'I won't be stopping, Lee.' Iris lit a cigarette, gazing over the flame of the platinum lighter into her sister's face. 'I think you've enough on your plate without me adding to the workload.'

Amelia paused in mid-stitch as she turned a sheet outer edges in, aware Peter had stopped pencilling in figures in the accounts book. 'I thought you'd be helping me with the workload? I've been looking forward to having you here,' she said quietly.

Iris did not speak for a moment, then she sighed. 'I've met someone. He has his own import-export business down in London and he suggested I go work for him. I told him all about Bill and the canning factory and the experience I've had there, and he thinks I'd be a real asset. The only thing is—'

'You don't want to take Babs and Harry,' murmured Peter.

'It's not don't want,' said Iris swiftly, smiling at him. 'More a case of can't, really.' Even more swiftly she added, 'I don't expect you to look after them. After all, Babs is seventeen, Rosie's eighteen and Dotty's hardly a kid any more. They're old enough to find somewhere and look after Harry themselves.'

'You can tell you've been away from Liverpool for a while,' said Peter. 'You've no idea what the housing situation is like since the Blitz, have you?'

'Rebuilding must have started, surely? The Americans are loaning money, aren't they?'

'The Marshall Aid Plan?' grunted Peter. 'It hasn't really got going yet.'

'He's right,' said Amelia, putting down the sheet. 'There's hundreds of newlyweds wanting to set up home. What chance do three young girls with a seven-year-old brother have of finding somewhere?'

'What about the grandfather?' said Iris, drawing on her cigarette. 'Couldn't he help?'

Amelia gave one of her basilisk stares. 'Are you joking? He needs to get his love life sorted out first. Besides, I'd hate them to think they're not wanted here.'

Iris shrugged her shoulders. 'I know they've suffered, poor things. But haven't we all? We lost Father and then I lost Bill. Peter lost Tess. It hasn't been easy for any of us. But at least you two are all right together and the children have each other. I have no one of my own really.'

'You have us. You're part of the family,' said Amelia, deeply wounded. 'Isn't that right, Peter?'

'If Iris is in love, then we mustn't try and hold on to her,' he said mildly.

Amelia frowned at him. 'Is she in love? She didn't say she was in love.'

'Of course I'm in love!' Iris seized on the words. 'You've no idea what it's like being in love all over again.' She stubbed out her cigarette and stood up. 'Well, I don't think it's worth me unpacking, do you? I'll see about getting a ticket tomorrow. I don't want to delay in case he finds someone else. You do see that, don't you?'

'We see,' said Peter, carrying on totting up figures. 'You going to bed?'

'Yes. I want to be up early in the morning.' She blew them a kiss and left the room.

'Bitch!' said Peter savagely, not looking at his wife. 'She's a selfish—'

'You don't have to say it,' said Amelia. 'It's been a rapid lesson but I've already worked that out for myself. We're just going to have to manage without her.'

He nodded, certain they would get on better without Iris. His only worry was that it was going to be more work for Amelia.

She, though, did not doubt that somehow she would manage and was more concerned about Bernard, his son and Dotty. So she put her energies into working out a solution to that particular problem. She had to keep Dotty and Eddie from meeting again. Babs had only met Chris once so the chances were she would not make the connection.

By morning, Amelia had it all worked out, but she had to see Miss Scott first before putting it to the girls. Iris went out early and Amelia presumed she was making travel arrangements for London. She still felt hurt about the whole thing but decided there was nothing she could do, so went to call on Miss Scott in the chemist's on the corner. Amelia had noticed only the other day that there was a card in the window advertising for a shop assistant. She was pinning her hopes on Bernard's son not covering this area any longer now he was back covering hers.

'So you've arranged for me to work for Miss Scott?' said Dotty when Amelia broached the subject that evening. 'Why?' Her pale delicate face was bewildered.

'I don't need you *and* Babs in the shop,' said Amelia briskly. 'And you're trained now. Miss Scott jumped at the chance of having you. Besides, it's not as far for you to go so it'll be easier.'

Dotty could see that and decided that although she would miss Irene's company, at least she would be able to come home for lunch and would save on tram fares. She never had enough money for what she wanted. 'OK!' she said. 'I'll do it.'

Babs shot a glance at Rosie and winked. 'I can't wait to get started myself,' she said cheerfully. 'I haven't a penny to bless myself with. You are going to pay me something, aren't you, Aunt Amelia? I'm not doing it for my keep, am I?'

'I'll pay you what you're worth,' she said with a smile. 'So you'd better work hard.'

'So you're another one of them?' said Irene, taking in Babs's smart appearance in a grey suit with a red pinstripe.

'That's right! Barbara Kilshaw, at your service.' Babs gave her a curtsey.

Irene chuckled. 'You don't look like either of your sisters. Where did you get that suit?'

'The States.' She did a twirl. 'And, no, I don't. We're all different.'

'I'd heard you'd been to America,' said Irene eagerly. 'What d'yer think of the Yanks?'

'Friendly, most of them. Why?'

'Me mum wouldn't let me near them when they were over here. She said I was too young,' said Irene, sounding exasperated. 'They had money to burn, so my mate's sister said. Not like our blokes.' She sighed. 'Anyway, I'd better show you the ropes and I hope yer listen better than that younger sister of yours. Head in the clouds, her, half the time.'

Babs was prepared to work hard. She liked people and was ready to help them.

Two days later, she came face to face with Eddie Rossiter, and as nobody had warned her about him, she was willing to be friendly with him, too.

'Who are you?' he said, eyeing her up and down as she reached up to get something off a high shelf, revealing a couple of inches of deliciously rounded thigh in the process.

She glanced down. 'Babs Kilshaw. Who are you?'

He told her. 'You got a boyfriend?'

She laughed. 'You're a quick worker. No, as it happens. Why? Are you asking me out?'

He grinned. 'Why not, if you're willing? What about the flicks? Believe there's a good film on at the Kennie. One of those American musicals.'

'Sounds fun.'

'Tomorrow night?'

'I'll meet you outside straight from work,' she said.

He blew her a kiss and went on into the dispensing room.

Babs watched him go, tapping the tin of National Dried Milk against her teeth. He wasn't Willy, she thought, but he looked nice enough.

When Babs got home that evening, it was to discover the bedroom Iris had vacated had been given to Harry. Peter, having found the three boys fighting, had decided he would be better separated from the twins. Babs was pretty easygoing but thought she had more right to the room than her brother did. 'A camp bed in that tiny room is no joke, Uncle Pete,' she said severely.

'We're doing our best,' he said, shaking open the evening paper. 'If you have a better suggestion, let me know.'

'Why can't us girls have the twins' room and they have ours?' she said promptly.

'Because Chris might come back and then he'd have to share with them.'

Babs said nothing else until she was alone with Rosie and Dotty. 'You might be prepared to sacrifice your comfort but I'm not,' she told them firmly. 'I got used to better in America.'

'I agree with you,' said Dotty immediately. 'It's not right, the twins having that big room to themselves. Chris might never come back. Uncle Pete's putting his own before us. It's not fair.'

'It's not fair but it's natural,' said Rosie patiently. 'And at least he accepts that putting Harry in with them isn't the best thing for him.'

'But it's boys against girls and the boys win every time,' said Babs, tidying a ragged fingernail on a scrap of sandpaper. 'You're the eldest, Rosie. You should *do* something. You went on and on when Mam died about getting a job and us all being together. Perhaps now's the time to do it?'

'You want me to leave college, do you?' she said, starting to get irritated.

'No, but surely you can do something?' said Babs. 'I know it's not easy with Aunt Amelia paying your college fees but can't you think of something?'

There was silence. Then Dotty dug her elbow into Rosie's chest.

'Do you mind?' she said. 'I'm thinking.'

'It was an accident,' said Dotty. 'But you can see what our Babs means. Now they're back we're overcrowded.'

'OK! Perhaps I can think of something,' said Rosie, remembering she had arranged for them to meet their grandfather at Davey's mother's on Sunday. 'There just might be someone who can help us.' She turned over and pulled the covers over her head.

Babs and Dotty looked at each other, wondering who on earth she meant.

'Oh, isn't it nice to be back!' said Babs, hugging Dotty's and Rosie's arms as they shivered in the cold wind that blew up the street of soot-grimed terraced houses where they had spent their childhood. Despite the cold, there were some lads playing ollies in the gutter and a couple of others were kicking a ball about. There were several girls playing hopscotch and another one was skipping, reciting breathlessly, 'Salt, pepper, mustard, vinegar.'

'That takes me back,' said Babs, a nostalgic expression on her plump face. 'The street might be scruffier and the houses smaller than I remember, but it still gives me a warm feeling right here.' She put a hand to her breast.

'You *are* waxing lyrical,' said Rosie, eyes twinkling. 'What about you, Harry? Do you remember the street?'

He wrinkled his nose. 'Not really.'

'But this is our old house,' said Babs, releasing her hold on Rosie and seizing her brother's arm. 'Don't you remember splashing in the gutter outside in your wellies, and Mam telling you off for getting the hem of your coat wet? Don't you remember sitting on the step almost strangling the cat because you wanted to carry it everywhere with you?'

He shook his head, chin jutting. 'I'm younger than you. Anyway, I wanna see Granddad.'

'And hopefully you shall!' said Rosie, marching up the neighbouring steps and rapping the front door with her knuckles.

There was the sound of hurrying footsteps. 'So you've arrived at last,' said Gwen. 'Well, it really is lovely to see you all.' She beamed down at them. Having discarded her pinny and released her hair from pipe-cleaner curlers, she looked quite attractive for her age, thought Rosie, and said so.

'Thank you kindly,' said Gwen. 'Come on in! Your granddad's here. He'll be that pleased to see you. Walter, visitors!' she called as they went up the lobby.

He was looking very much at home, even down to wearing a pair of old slippers and smoking a pipe. He took it out of his mouth and rose hastily to his feet, trembling slightly as he looked at Rosie. She took a deep breath and decided there was nothing for it but to forgive him; even if he didn't fall in with her plan. She went over and kissed him and the others trailed after her.

'You're my granddad?' said Harry, gazing up at him.

Walter stared down as his grandson. 'Good God!' he said, almost reverently, blue eyes suspiciously bright. 'You're our Joe reincarnated.'

'What's that mean? And are you crying?' said Harry with a note of disgust in his voice.

'Naw!' said Walter, brushing away a tear, then sweeping the boy off his feet and hoisting him up against his chest. 'What's there to cry about when this is the happiest day of my life?'

'So you won't be going back to her then?' said Rosie.

Gwen shushed her and gave her a look. 'Vera's in the past,' she whispered against Rosie's ear, passing her to put the kettle on. In a loud voice Davey's mother added, 'What do you say? Cocoa all around, kids?'

There was a chorus of agreement and they all sat down, starting to talk at once. Harry, on Walter's knee, was telling him all about America. It was not until later that Rosie got the chance to explain to Gwen and Walter how things were at 'Eden'.

'So what do yer want me to do?' said her granddad. 'Is it money yer want, queen? I know I owe yer.'

'Not only me,' said Rosie. 'I think we're all owed something.' She hesitated. 'But it's not money as such I'm after. It's lodgings for Babs and Harry.'

'They could come and live here,' said Gwen, without hesitation. 'Don't you agree, Walt? I mean, we are getting married, aren't we?'

He looked startled but then the moment passed and he nodded. 'Anything you say, Gwennie. I'd have to have lost all me marbles to refuse such an offer.'

Harry gave a whoop. 'I've got away from those twins!' And he began to perform an Indian war dance.

Babs winked at Rosie. 'Nice going, big sister.'

Chapter Twenty-One

Rosie did not say anything to Amelia that evening when they arrived home, but the next morning she was up early, intending to have a good talk with her aunt before going to college. Even so, someone had beaten her to the lavatory. Inside she could hear someone being noisily sick. She crept back into the bedroom and put her eye to a crack in the door, eventually seeing Amelia vacate the toilet, looking washed out. Instantly she drew her own conclusions, deciding her aunt might be relieved at her having taken things into her own hands.

'Why didn't you tell me what you were planning?' said Amelia, nibbling an arrowroot biscuit and watching Rosie put on the kettle.

'It mightn't have worked out. As it is, it has and I'm glad because I didn't want to fall out with you and Uncle Peter. I've got fond of the twins but I'd be bound to take Harry's side if they started their tricks.'

Amelia understood that and was relieved. 'When will they go?'

'As soon as they can pack. Babs is pleased about it. It's nearer to the shop.'

'And how does Dotty feel about not being included?'

Rosie shrugged. 'I didn't ask her. She's hoping you'll let her have Chris's room.'

Amelia said quietly, 'Why not? He's been gone months. He might never come back.'

Rosie was not so sure. During those months, Chris would have had time to think and realise how difficult life could be out there on your own without a family. If he had friends, Dotty had never mentioned them and they'd never been to the house. Sooner or later, Rosie felt certain, they would hear from him again.

In the meantime, she helped Babs and Harry move in with Davey's mother. Davey had sent his blessings, saying not to wait for him to come home because he wasn't sure when that would be. So just before Christmas, Gwen and Walter were married in a quiet ceremony at St John's. There was just enough money left over from the sale of Maggie's jewellery for Walter to buy a wedding ring, a gas cooker and a bottle each of port and sherry. The couple were both amazed and gratified when Amelia gave them fifty pounds, saying she hoped it would go some way towards helping with their expenses with Harry and Babs in the coming year.

It was just after Christmas when Dotty was leaving Scott's the chemist's that she was seized by the arm and pulled into the doorway of the newsagent's next door.

'Do you mi—?' She stopped and gazed up into the young man's face. 'Chris?' she said hesitantly.

'Hello, Dotty!' He smiled down at her, gripping both her hands tightly. 'How are you?'

'You can't care when you haven't been in touch for months,' she said with a rush of hurt and anger, wrenching her hands free. 'There've been times when I've thought you were dead, just like your mother!'

His smile vanished. 'Who put that idea into your head?'

'Uncle Pete. We were all worried sick about you.'

'But not now?' he said, eyes bleak.

She did not answer immediately. Then she said, 'They don't talk about you any more. And last time your name was mentioned, Uncle Pete said he'd kill you when he saw you.'

Chris leant against the wall. 'I suppose that shouldn't surprise me. When was this?'

'A few months back, when I thought I saw you.'

He frowned. 'You couldn't have. I left the area, went down to Kent. I've only just got back.'

'So it was your double, just like Rosie said.'

'I've got a double?' he said, an interested expression on his bony face.

Dotty shrugged her shoulders. 'Rosie reckons we've all got doubles.'

'Where did you see this one?' His gaze was intent.

'Outside Miss Scott's here, and then outside Aunt Amelia's shop.'

'Two chemists,' said Chris thoughtfully.

She stared at him. 'You're right! I never thought of that. Queer, isn't it?'

He was silent, gazing absently into space.

She pouted, touching his arm. 'Haven't you anything more to say to me? You haven't seen me for months and when you do you go into a trance. I thought you liked me. I cried for days after you left.'

Chris shook his head as if to rid himself of his thoughts and said seriously, 'I was in a state then.' He took hold of one of her hands and squeezed it, seeming to come to a decision. 'I never told you but Mam sent me a letter just before she killed herself.'

Dotty's eyes were wide, eyelashes fluttering like moths behind the thick lenses. 'You're joking?'

'I wish I was. It seemed she had to get everything off her chest before she went.' He paused, rubbing his eyebrow with his free hand, expression uncertain.

Dotty could see that he was really wondering whether to tell her what had been in the letter. 'You might as well tell me,' she said in a low voice, 'or how can we ever trust each other? I mean, why did you come back and pounce on me the way you did if you don't care for me just a little?'

'Of course I care for you,' he said vehemently, lowering his head and kissing her hard on the mouth.

'So what's your secret?'

'Your Uncle Pete's not my father.'

Dotty's mouth opened but no words came out.

'Bad, isn't it?' His expression was strained. 'I'm a bastard. I kept thinking it couldn't be true. It's no wonder *they* don't want me, is it?'

Dotty did not have to ask who *they* were. 'You think they know?' she stammered.

'Of course they do!' His face turned ugly. 'If Mam was driven to confess and told me, she'd have told them too. I worked that out while I was away.'

'Did she tell you who your father is?'

'Yeah.' He toyed with her fingers. 'Some bloke called Bernard Rossiter. Mam and Aunt Lee both knew him. In fact, Aunt Lee was engaged to him at one time but broke it off.'

'Because she found out?'

'No! It happened after that. But Mam did think Da—I mean, Pete, had a soft spot for Aunt Lee when they were young. He was all sympathetic when she finished with this Bernie.'

'Then why did he marry your mother?'

'They were engaged. It seems it was OK for women to break it off but it wasn't the done thing for a man. But she didn't think of all this at the time. It wasn't until later, after she was seduced by this Bernie bloke - he was a bit of a charmer, apparently – and was having me, that she realised the mess she was in. So she just went through with the wedding to Pete.'

'Golly, who'd believe it?' exclaimed Dotty, eyes round.

'Anyway, it's all in the past now. But I wanted to come and see you one last time before I leave, and explain everything,' said Chris, dropping her hand and looking down at the ground, scuffing a sweet wrapper with the toe of his shoe.

Dotty stared at him in dismay. 'What do you mean?' she stammered. 'Where are you going?'

'To America. I've signed up on a cargo ship to work my passage. It leaves this evening.'

'I'll never see you again!' Tears welled up in her eyes and spilled over.

'Don't cry,' he whispered.

'What do you expect me to do? I love you and now you tell me you're going away for ever!' Her voice broke. 'You'll meet someone else out there and forget all about me.' The tears were coming thick and fast now, so that her spectacles slid down her nose. 'I need you,' she sobbed.

'Don't! Don't say that.'

'Take me with you?'

'I can't.' He sounded desperate. 'We couldn't get married, Dotty. You're not sixteen yet. I love you but—'

'I could lie about my age.'

'I can't do it.'

She removed her spectacles and wiped her eyes. 'If you don't take me, I'll stowaway on a ship to America. I'll search all over there until I find you.'

'Don't be crazy,' he said shakily, gazing down at her and thinking how lovely she looked, even though she had been crying.

'It's not crazy,' she said passionately. 'I know exactly what I'll do. I'll go to Sam. I'm sure his family will take me in. After all, he is my stepfather. Then, when I'm sixteen, we can get married.'

Chris stared at her in astonishment. He'd never have thought she had the brains to think up such a scheme. 'Perhaps you're not so crazy.'

Dotty clung to the front of his jacket. 'Then smuggle me aboard your ship? If you leave me here, I'll kill myself because I'll never love anyone the way I love you,' she said dramatically.

He looked stricken. 'How can you say that, knowing Mam—'

'How can you leave me if you say you love me?' She pressed herself against him. 'Please, Chris? I've been so miserable without you. Please take me?'

He was silent for a long while. Then he said, 'Let's go and get some chips from the chippy. I'm starving. We'll eat them while we walk and discuss things.'

Dotty slipped her arm through his, determined he would soon see things her way.

'Dotty said she'd take us to the pictures this evening but we can't find her anywhere,' said Jimmy, entering the shed where Amelia was tying bunches of herbs to the rafters.

She paused in her task. 'Have you looked in her room?'

'We looked there first,' said Tom with a touch of scorn.

Amelia stared at him. 'Don't you speak to me in that tone. Perhaps she's slipped out for a minute and will be back soon?'

'If she's not back in the next five minutes, we'll miss the beginning of the first picture,' said Jimmy, kicking the leg of the bench.

'Don't do that,' said Amelia automatically. 'Go back into the house, I'll be with you in a second. If she's not back soon, your dad and I will take you. Perhaps she's forgotten and gone with Rosie to see Babs?'

'She's no right to forget,' said Tom, brows knitted, strolling out.

As there was still no sign of Dotty when Amelia went into the house, the four of them went off the to Carlton cinema. When they returned, Peter went upstairs with the twins and Amelia went into the living room where Rosie was sitting, listening to the radio. 'Where's Dotty?' she said.

Rosie turned a surprised face to her. 'I thought she'd gone to the pictures with the twins?'

Amelia frowned. 'I wonder where she's got to?'

'Perhaps she's gone to bed? I never thought of looking.'

'Well, go and look, please. It's not like her to go out on her own.'

Rosie left her book and went upstairs.

Dotty's room was in darkness. Rosie whispered her sister's name but there was no response and she felt sure the room was empty. She switched on the light. It was not only empty, it was tidy, which was a miracle in itself. Dotty was never tidy.

Rosie did not know what led her to do it but she opened the tallboy to find it empty. She pulled out a drawer and that was empty, too. Her heart began to beat fast. Where had her sister's clothes gone? What was this all about? Had somebody said something to upset Dotty?

Rosie searched the rest of the room, even looking under the bed, and there she found an encyclopaedia which fell open in her hands to reveal a sheet of paper tucked between its pages. She read it and raced downstairs.

'Chris! Scotland?' Amelia's mind seemed not to be focusing but had gone completely blank.

Peter snatched the letter from her hand, read it and swore. Both women stared at him. 'It says here they've eloped! That's clear enough.'

'I know, but I can't believe it,' said Amelia.

'What do we do?' said Rosie, tense as a coiled spring. 'They can't have had much of a start.'

'That depends on when they left,' said Peter, face darkening, clenching his fists. 'One thing's for sure, we're not going to get to Gretna Green tonight. We'll have to bring in the police.'

'She's underage. Chris could be sent to prison,' said Amelia.

'Did you see what she wrote?' said Rosie wrathfully. 'She's snaffled Babs's birth certificate and is going to go under her name. When did she do that? I could kill her!'

'It's Wednesday afternoon. Early closing. But what do they think they're going to live on?' said Amelia, exasperated. 'And how could they believe they could get away with it?'

'She probably hasn't thought it through,' said Peter.

'I don't know,' said Rosie, shaking her head. 'If she's thought of taking Babs's birth certificate, she'll have thought about the rest.'

'I never thought she had it in her,' said Amelia. 'I think we'd better all check our rooms.'

'You do it. I'll go and phone the police,' said Peter.

'No. Wait,' said Amelia, gazing at him. 'Do we want Chris arrested? Imagine the scandal.'

He hesitated. 'Perhaps I should go up there?'

Amelia nodded. 'If they've got that far.'

'I can't understand why she left the letter,' muttered Rosie, treading heavily on each stair as she went upstairs to search her room. She did not really believe her sister would steal from her but changed her mind when she discovered her jet beads were missing and in their place was a pawn ticket and another letter.

Rosie was so angry she rushed into Amelia's bedroom. 'Is Uncle Pete going to go after them? Because if he is, I want to be there when he confronts them,' she said, fuming. 'I'll have her hide for this!' she said, brandishing the pawn ticket and the letter which said Dotty had never thought it fair that Rosie should be given some of Gran's jewellery when she had got nothing.

'I wonder what happened to the nervous, retiring girl she was a few years ago?' said Amelia, sinking on to the bed. 'When I said I thought she should be more independent, I never meant this!'

'Dotty's not so dotty after all,' said Peter.

'No,' said Rosie in a hard voice. 'Perhaps she never was. Perhaps she learnt her lessons from Mam only too well.'

Peter turned to Amelia. 'What do you want me to do? Go racing after them? They can't get married yet. They have to live in the area for three weeks before they're allowed to get hitched over the anvil.'

'We'll both go,' she said, fearing what her husband might do when he caught them.

Rosie sat down next to Amelia. 'They must know that if she read it up in that encyclopaedia.'

'What are you saying?' said Peter, eyes narrowing.

'That they might be sending you on a wild goose chase.'

'And be somewhere else completely?' said Amelia, eyebrows raised.

Rosie nodded. 'Where, though? That's the thing. They could be anywhere.'

There was silence. For a moment, the three of them could not think what to do next.

'By the time we find them it's going to be too late,' said Peter heavily.

'They'll have spent the night together, you're saying,' said Rosie, drooping against Amelia, who slipped her arm around her.

He nodded.

She got to her feet, feeling angry, frustrated and a complete failure. Somewhere along the line she had let down her sister. 'I'm going to bed,' she said.

'You might as well,' said Peter, a grim expression on his face. 'But I think I might go and have a word with the police.'

Rosie left them.

'I should have suspected something,' said Amelia, feeling worn out. 'I've failed our Violet.'

Peter took her in his arms. 'How were you to know? You couldn't be watching her every minute of the day. She kept it quiet, though, about Chris coming back, didn't she? It's obvious he doesn't want anything to do with us.'

Amelia nodded, snuggling up to him. 'I wonder what she told him about us?'

'Does it matter? They've gone. And why is it I have a feeling we're never going to see them again?'

She made no answer, fearful all of a sudden that the runaways might have made a suicide pact. God only knew what was going on in Chris's head! Then she thought, *I'm not thinking straight. Why take the birth certificate and money?* Still, they had to be found.

Rosie did not have the heart to go into college the next day and went to the shop instead to tell Babs what had happened.

She was flabbergasted. 'The nerve of her, rooting through my stuff!' she squealed. 'I know what I'd like to do to her.'

'The police have been brought in and alerted those up north just in case they've gone to Gretna Green.'

'If she's been crafty enough to keep this whole thing a secret then she's not going to make it easy for you to find them,' said Babs, frowning in thought. She tapped a pencil against her teeth. 'I don't think she's there. She might be in London. You could get lost there easily. How's Aunt Amelia coping with it all?'

'She's blaming herself.' Rosie grimaced, fiddling with a card of hairslides on the counter. 'One thing she said was that when we two decide to marry, we must tell them, even if the fellas have green hair and wear earrings.'

'I'll remember that,' said Babs, smiling as she turned to deal with a customer.

When Rosie returned to the house she told Amelia what Babs had said about London but her aunt shook her head. 'Who's going to take them in without a marriage certificate?'

'They could pretend to be brother and sister.'

It was a thought that Amelia passed on to the police.

By this time, the twins knew that Dotty had run away but not the whole story. They were torn between admiration and surprise that whinging Dotty, as they called her, had actually done anything so adventurous.

'We know what we'd do if we ran away,' said Tom to Rosie as she ladled soup into bowls.

'What?' she said in a vague voice, having received a letter from Davey in the afternoon post saying he would be back in England in a fortnight. She was desperate to see him, needing to know that their feelings had not changed.

'We'd stowaway on a ship,' said Jimmy.

'In a lifeboat,' said Tom. 'It was in the *Echo* a few weeks ago about some lads from Bootle doing that. I'd go to America and become a cowboy.'

'We'd shoot all the redskins and stop them scalping people,' said the twin.

'They don't do that now,' said Rosie absently.

Jimmy made a disappointed face. 'But we could still stowaway.'

Rosie's hand stilled and soup dripped on to the table-cloth. 'Stowaway, stowaway,' she murmured, putting down the pan.

Without another word to the twins, she hurried upstairs. Amelia was having a lie-down but listened as Rosie told her what the twins had said. 'I don't know why we didn't think of it,' she said, sitting up against the pillows. 'But I'm sure the police will have done.'

'Not if they think they're in Gretna Green or London,' said Rosie ruefully, perching on the side of the bed.

Amelia nodded and got up. 'It's going to take some time, checking all the liners that left Liverpool round about then, but I'm sure they can do it.'

*

Amelia had been right about it taking some time and they all decided there was nothing for it in the meantime but to try and put the runaways out of their minds and get on with their lives. It was not easy but they went through the motions.

Rosie decided it was time she and Babs took Harry to a pantomime and called in at the shop on the way home to suggest it to her sister. But Babs was not there, having been sent on a message by Mr Brown.

'You'll be lucky to get her to go out with you one night,' said Irene, smiling. 'I asked her out but she was seeing her boyfriend.'

Rosie laughed. 'Which one's this? I thought she had several.'

'I think she's played the field a bit since she's been home but she seems to be sticking with Eddie more than the rest,' said Irene.

'Which Eddie's this? Do I know him?'

'Of course you do. Eddie Rossiter! He works at the drug firm she's gone to visit. They've been seeing each other on and off since she's worked here.' Irene rested her elbows on the counter and brought her head closer to Rosie's. 'In fact, she was only saying to me today that she was taking him to see your aunt this evening. Meeting him somewhere in town first . . . She's decided it's time they got engaged.'

'No! She can't do that,' said Rosie, gazing helplessly at Irene. 'Where's her commonsense? Besides— I've got to warn her,' she gulped, and rushed out.

Rosie was in luck and caught a tram straight away. She hurried into the house and was just about to take off her

coat when the letter box rattled. She opened the door immediately. On the step stood Babs and Eddie. 'You can't come
in,' said Rosie, closing the door behind her. 'You've got to
give each other up,' she said, getting straight to the point.

'You're joking?' said Babs, laughing.

'No, I'm not. There's no way Aunt Amelia and Uncle
Pete will allow you to get engaged to Eddie.' Rosie stared
at him. 'You know who my aunt is?'

'Sure I do. She's Mrs Hudson.'

'You know Babs is my sister?'

'Sure, but—'

'You won't know, though, that your father and Aunt
Amelia went out together and she jilted him. There was
a lot of bad feeling. I don't think there's any way your
father and my aunt will allow you two to get married.'

'Hang on here,' said Babs, frowning. 'That's all in the
past.'

'Not to his father, it isn't. He's never forgiven Aunt
Amelia. So it's not going to happen, is it, Eddie?' said
Rosie, not taking her eyes off his face.

'No,' he said unhappily. 'Dad wouldn't allow it.'

'Never mind your dad,' cried Babs, poking him in the
chest. 'What about me? Don't you love me?'

'Of course I love you, but me dad – you don't know
him.' Eddie's face crumpled. 'Since Mam died, he's been
terrible. All hell would be let loose.'

'I don't care,' said Babs, grabbing him by the hand.
'I'll speak to him. He'll soon see that it's stupid to keep
an old feud going.'

'It's not a feud exactly,' said Eddie.

She said firmly, 'If I say it's a feud, it's a feud. Just like in *Romeo and Juliet*. Well, they're not keeping us apart. Come on! We're going to see your dad.'

Rosie just wanted her off the step so gave her a push in the right direction. 'You go and visit his dad then – and see if he'll make you welcome.'

They went and Rosie sagged against the door jamb.

'What's going on?' It was Amelia. 'I thought I heard Babs's voice.'

Rosie sighed. 'It's Eddie. Babs brought him here, talking about getting engaged. I told her to forget it.'

Amelia looked as if she was going to faint. 'Don't mention this to Peter! What next with you girls? Where've they gone?'

Rosie hesitated. 'To see his father.'

Amelia put a hand to her head. 'I don't believe this. What does Babs know?'

'Only that you and Eddie's dad were engaged once.'

'Right. Don't let them into this house if they come back,' said Amelia, reaching for her coat.

She was hardly out of the door when Peter came into the hall. He stared at Rosie, who by now was wondering whether she should have gone with her aunt. 'What's up with you?' he said. 'Where's Amelia? You look like you've had a shock.'

'It was only Babs and her boyfriend. They came and went,' she babbled.

'So where's Amelia?'

Rosie's heart seemed to stop beating for a moment. 'Er – I don't know.'

'What? Why don't you try telling me the truth. Has she gone with them?'

'Er, I wouldn't say that exactly.'

Peter's eyes did not shift from her face. 'You're hiding something. What's wrong with the boyfriend. Eddie, isn't it?'

'You know him?' gasped Rosie.

'Mr Brown mentioned Babs was seeing some young salesman when I called in there for the books to save Lee's legs. The shock over Dotty is taking a lot out of her.'

Rosie breathed more easily. 'So you've never met him?'

'No. That's a pleasure I haven't had yet,' he said dryly. 'But I think I might remedy that.'

Rosie gnawed on her lip. 'What are you going to do?'

He hesitated then seemed to come to a decision, opened the front door and went out.

Peter hurried and caught up with Amelia just by Brook Farm. He seized her arm. 'Where d'you think you're going? Rosie was just telling me about Babs and her boyfriend, Eddie the young salesman. Where are they? I'd like to meet him.'

The colour drained from her face and she clutched at his jacket. 'What did Rosie tell you?' she whispered.

'Nothing much,' he rasped. 'She's very loyal to you. But you'd better tell me what's going on or I'll think the worst: that you've been carrying on with Bernard and she's found out.'

'You couldn't possibly believe that?' said Amelia, shocked. 'I told you, I haven't seen him for ages.'

'I don't want to believe it. But I know his wife's dead and you've always had a misplaced compassion for him. I only have your word for it you haven't been giving him tea and sympathy.'

She gasped. 'I can't believe you've just said that.'

'Tell me what's going on then?'

Only for a moment did she hesitate, then with a sigh she said, 'Babs has been seeing Bernard's son. They want to get engaged. I can't allow that and Rosie told Babs I wouldn't. But she's as determined as Dotty to have her own way so she's gone to Bernard.'

Peter smiled and said sarcastically, 'He's really going to make her welcome.'

Amelia released her grip on his jacket, smoothing it as she did so. 'I'll have to go. I'm wasting time. God only knows what he'll say to her.'

'You know where he lives?'

She hesitated.

'Come on, Lee!' He scowled at her. 'It's you that's wasting time now. And you're stupid if you think I'd let you go there alone. Do they have to get a tram?'

'No. He lives with his mother. His wife moved in with her after being bombed out of her own house.'

'That close!' Peter's face darkened and his hand tightened on her arms. 'You go home, I'll handle this.'

'No!' she said fiercely. 'You might fight him and then God knows what he might do. He hates you and I couldn't bear it if anything happened to you.'

Peter stared at her. Then he kissed her gently on the lips. 'We'll have a talk when we get back. You're not to worry. I don't think it's good for you in your condition.'

Her mouth opened but no words came out. He turned her round and patted her gently on the bottom, pushing her in the direction of home. Then he strode on, past Moor's Hay deliverers, along Eaton Road in the direction of Knotty Ash.

Bernard was slumped in an easy chair, a glass of beer in his hand. He had chased his mother out, telling her to get him some cigarettes, and now through narrowed disdainful eyes was taking in Babs's well-rounded appearance. 'So you're another of Amy's nieces and you want to marry my son?' he said.

'That's right,' she said, keeping a tight hold on Eddie's hand. He had argued against this meeting all the way here, saying she had no idea what his father was like. Now she had seen him, she was not impressed.

'What does your aunt have to say about it?'

Babs hesitated. 'My sister seems to think she wouldn't approve because you and she were once engaged. I don't think that's much of a reason. After all, you did both go on to marry someone else. I love Eddie and he loves me and that's all that matters.'

'Is it?' Bernard let out a bark of laughter. 'You're not like your aunt, are you? Family duty! That's what came first with her. I'm almost tempted to give you my blessing. That would be one in the eye for Lee.'

Babs stared at him with interest. 'You still feel like that after all these years?'

His smile faded and he did not answer her, saying instead, 'And what does Mr Hudson have to say about all this?'

'I don't see why he should say anything,' said Babs, tilting her chin. 'It's Aunt Amelia who's my guardian.'

'Then you're mistaken. She's not going to go against his wishes.'

For the first time since she had set out, Babs felt a moment's doubt about getting her own way. It was in those few seconds that there was a rat-a-tat at the door.

Eddie went to open it. Peter stared at him. There was no mistaking the likeness to Chris and he waited for the anger that he had felt realising the person Dotty had mistaken Chris for was Bernie's son, but nothing happened. 'Your father in?'

'Yeah, who are you?'

'He knows me.' Peter brushed past him.

Bernard stared at Peter as he entered the kitchen. 'I take it this isn't a social call?' he sneered.

'Too right it isn't. Babs, out!' ordered Peter with a jerk of the head. 'Mr Rossiter and I have things to say to each other.'

'If it's about us, I want to hear,' she said defiantly.

Peter gave her an exasperated glance and at that moment there was another rat-a-tat on the door. He took advantage of it to hustle her out of the room. She struggled but he was stronger than her. He opened the front door and on the step stood Amelia. 'No!' he yelled before she could open her mouth, and thrust Babs at her, closing the door.

He returned to the kitchen. 'I've only one thing to say to you, Bernie, and that's – keep away from my family. I'm not having you hurting Lee more than she's already been hurt. That's it.' He turned and walked out of the kitchen.

He did not get far before Bernard lumbered to his feet and came after him. Peter spun round, arm raised, fists clenched.

Bernard parried the blow. 'Will you stop it?' he growled. 'I'm not looking for a fight. I've something to say myself.'

'I don't want to hear your excuses,' said Peter, tight-lipped.

'You're not going to. We both made mistakes years ago. Come back in.'

Peter hesitated but his old adversary looked so drawn that he reconsidered. Eddie was standing with his back against a wall, like a fox preparing to hold a hound at bay.

'Go in the garden, Eddie,' said Bernard roughly.

His son did not need to be told twice.

Peter felt a momentary pain at the lad's likeness to Chris but it passed. 'Say what you've got to say,' he said tersely.

'You already knew about the boy?' said Bernard. 'I never thought she'd tell you.'

'She named no names but dropped enough hints. Maybe actually writing "Bernard Rossiter" was too much even for her at the end.'

'Maybe. But it was my fault. I seduced her to punish you for interfering between me and Amy.' Bernard drew cigarette smoke into his lungs. 'You're bloody lucky getting a second chance. I married my wife on the rebound and spent most of our married life treating her like rubbish. It wasn't until she died that I realised my mistake. She was a good woman and now it's too late to make amends. I really miss her.'

There was a long silence as the two men stared at each other.

'Is that supposed to make me feel sorry for you?' said Peter harshly.

Bernard shrugged. 'Think what you want. You might like to know I'm moving to Wales. Making a fresh start.'

'That'll go some way to making amends,' said Peter. He gave a sharp nod and left.

He found Amelia waiting for him on the corner of the road. 'Where's Babs?' he said.

'Stormed off. I feel sorry for her.'

Peter put his arm round his wife. 'Well?' she said.

'He's leaving the area.'

Amelia sighed with relief. 'Then everything's OK.'

'As long as you stop putting other people first all the time and take care of yourself. I was pretty sure Chris was Bernard's son when Dotty mistook him for someone she kept seeing outside chemist shops. Besides, Tess threw out enough hints; I just didn't want to believe it. I reckon she didn't tell you because she thought even you would have found that too much; your best friend having gone with him.'

'You're probably right. I didn't tell you of my suspicions when I saw him because I didn't want *you* hurt.'

Peter hugged her to him, pressing his lips against her temple. 'The damage she caused Chris I find hard to forgive. But fortunately the twins don't seem to have come out of it too badly.'

Amelia frowned. 'You don't think she told Chris?'

He shrugged. 'Who knows? It would explain a lot, wouldn't it?'

Amelia nodded. If that were true, she would find it hard to forgive Tess too. Surely they would all have been better off never knowing?

'I tell you something, love,' murmured Peter against her ear. 'If Rosie wants to marry Davey as soon as he comes home, then we're not stopping them. I've had enough of trying to protect your nieces from themselves.'

Amelia wondered how he would feel if he had a daughter of his own, deciding it was time for her to tell him about the baby, which still seemed a miracle to her. Although she felt certain from what he had said earlier that he had already guessed.

Chapter Twenty-Two

As soon as Rosie saw Davey, she knew where her future lay. They went into each other's arms without hesitation, gazing greedily into each other's face. 'God, I've missed you,' he said unsteadily.

'Me too.' Her voice was husky and there were tears in her eyes as, with trembling fingers, she touched his mouth and brought his head down to hers so their lips met. They kissed long and deep and when at last they drew apart, he said, 'We have to get married soon.'

'Yes.'

'You don't think you'll have any trouble getting permission from your Aunt Amelia?' His blue eyes were intent on her face.

'No.' She laughed. 'Although I did say a while ago I wouldn't be rushing into marriage, so she might dig in her heels and say wait.'

'I don't want to wait,' he said, nibbling her ear. 'I want you now. I'd marry you today if I could. I want to spend as much time as I can with you before I have to leave again.'

'Me too. Although I don't want you to leave.' She pressed against him. 'Are you sure about staying on in the Army?'

He lifted his head and stared at her. 'I enjoy the life, Rosie. I feel like I'm a round peg in a round hole. But if you don't want me to—'

'No. Whatever you decide, I'm with you. I want you to be happy.'

'I want you to be happy too.'

'I will be so long as you are.' He hugged her tightly.

'Aren't we soppy?' she said happily. 'Almost as soppy as Dotty's letter.'

'What letter?' Davey held her away from him. 'You never mentioned any letter last time you wrote?'

'That's because I only got it yesterday. They're in America. Dotty's staying with Sam's mother, who's written to Aunt Amelia.'

Davey let out a whistle. 'So what's going to happen? Where's Chris?'

'Working on a farm, saving up so they can get married. According to Dotty, he never touched her. She says that she's still a virgin,' murmured Rosie, staring up at him. 'I want to believe it.'

'Believe it then,' he said promptly. 'Thousands wouldn't but – I mean, it's not going to make any difference to our lives. What does your Aunt Amelia say?'

'That Uncle Pete had a big say in Chris's upbringing and left it at that. She's going to let them marry when Dotty's sixteen. Otherwise, she says, the strain might prove too much.'

Davey grinned. 'I always knew your Aunt Amelia was a sensible woman. How's Babs? Has she got over Eddie yet?'

'I think so. She said yesterday he'd proved a bit of a disappointment. I believe she might still feel something for Sam's cousin but he's in the American Air Force now so there's no point her saving money to go over there.'

'So there's just you and me to think about?' said Davey, planting kisses all over her face, much to her delight.

'Let's go and see Aunt Amelia,' she said, after returning every one of his kisses. So they went.

'I'd say wait until you're older,' said Amelia. 'But I don't want you two running off as well,' she added with a twinkle. 'Where will you live?'

Rosie hesitated. 'I'd like to stay here until we can get married quarters.'

'But that might not be for a while,' said Davey. 'Is that OK?'

Amelia glanced at Peter for confirmation. 'It's fine. Plenty of room with only the twins at the moment.'

'The wedding?' said Amelia.

'We haven't much money,' said Rosie.

'I don't think you need worry about money,' said her aunt. 'You've got some coming to you, Rosie.' And she explained about the compensation.

Rosie stared at her, hardly able to believe what her aunt was saying. 'You're not kidding me?' she stammered.

'Would I?' said Amelia, twitching an eyebrow and looking stern. 'It should pay for the wedding, a honeymoon, a few sticks of furniture and a decent frock. Unless you want to borrow your grandmother's wedding gown?'

In her mind's eye, Rosie saw Amelia sweeping down the aisle like a queen and gracefully accepted.

So Rosie and Davey were married in style on the last Saturday in February. Her granddad gave her away and she wore Maggie's pearls and her maternal grandmother's wedding gown.

'If he feels the way I felt after I saw you in that dress,' said Peter, after they had seen the newlyweds off in a taxi, 'it's going to be some steamy honeymoon.'

Amelia squeezed his arm. 'You really felt like that about me then?'

'I fancied you like crazy but I was fighting it.'

'Me too,' she said, thinking that maybe it was time to forgive Tess and Violet for all the pain they had caused. If it had not been for their children, she would still be full of resentment and regret. She was happy now in a way she had never thought possible. 'Let's go home,' she said softly.

Peter called the twins, who were swinging from a lamp post, and together they went to catch the tram.

'Did you notice,' said Amelia, 'that Babs caught the bouquet?'

Peter said thankfully, 'Not our worry, love.' And slipping his hand into hers, carried on walking.

Epilogue

Amelia picked up the envelope from the doormat and gazed at the London postmark. She held it up to the light, wishing she had X-ray eyes, and even thought of steaming it open. Filled with hope and excitement, she hurried into the morning room where her daughter sat banging a spoon on an upturned empty eggshell. 'This,' she said, waving the letter under Daisy's dainty nose, 'is just what Daddy has been waiting for.'

'Dad-da! Dad-da!' Daisy gave her mother a toothless grin.

Amelia's heart felt fit to burst with love as she scooped her up out of the high chair, kissed her eggy cheek and went upstairs. She would take it to him, she thought, as she washed her daughter's face. Surely if the publishers had turned the book down they would have returned the manuscript? It had to be good news and she could not wait to see Peter's expression when he opened the letter. It would make up for the ones he had never received from Chris.

She was halfway downstairs when the doorbell rang. *Oh, no!* she thought. *Don't let it be a vacuum cleaner salesman right now, please, please!* She opened the door with Daisy balanced on one hip but the words died on her lips at the sight of the man in uniform standing on the doorstep.

'Mrs Hudson?'

'Yes?'

He removed his cap. 'Excuse me, ma'am, but I wonder if you could help me?' he drawled. 'My name's Willy Dixon an'—'

'So the Yanks are back at Burtonwood?' Amelia smiled in delight and, seizing his sleeve, drew him inside. 'You want to see Babs, of course,' she added, not giving him a chance to speak. 'Well, you're in luck, Mr Dixon, because I'm just on my way to the shop.'

'Shop, ma'am?' he said, looking bewildered.

'The family chemist's where she works. I have to see my husband. Hopefully I've good news for him. If you'll wait a moment while I put Daisy's coat on, you can come with me.'

'Yes, ma'am!' he said, expression changing to one of relief. He almost came to attention. 'And I've a letter for Mr Hudson, ma'am, from Chris.'

Her mouth fell open. 'I can't believe it! This must be our lovely day, as the song goes. But there's no need for "ma'am".' Her eyes twinkled into his and she thought what a nice face he had, not exactly good-looking but with kind eyes. She fancied he was a trustworthy boy. 'You can call me Aunt Amelia,' she said firmly. 'With you being related to Sam, I feel you're part of the family.'

She thrust Daisy at him and crammed a spare nappy, a feeding bottle, her purse and the precious letter inside a shopping bag. 'We'll catch a tram just up the road,' she said. 'Follow me.'

As if in a daze, Willy fell in behind her.

'Rosie, could you try and keep your mind on the job?' said Peter, putting the top on his fountain pen and closing the prescription book. He had been in charge at the shop for the last six months and was in the throes of extending the business. 'I know it isn't easy for you with the Russians blockading Berlin, but Davey will be OK, believe me! The Yanks have said they're going to lift the blockade.'

'I know,' she said moodily, taking a swipe at a fly with a toilet roll. 'But I've always been lousy at waiting.'

'Hey!' Irene, who had been out getting pies for their lunch, burst through the doorway, grinning from ear to ear. 'Guess what? The Yanks are back at Burtonwood! They've come to airlift aid into Berlin.'

'What?' cried Babs, thrusting a paper bag with bandages and Germoline at a customer. 'Where did you hear that?'

'In the bread shop. Let the good times roll!' said Irene, doing a jig.

Rosie and Babs stared at each other and delighted smiles lit their faces. They flung their arms round each other. 'Yippee!' they cried in unison.

Peter and the two old ladies in the shop smiled indulgently. 'I remember a Yank from the Great War,' said one. 'Black as the hobs of hell but he gave my Sadie a toffee.'

'Oh, I can't wait,' sighed Irene, a dreamy expression on her face. 'Chocolate, nylons, dancing and smooching.' She swayed as if in time to music.

The others watched her, barely aware of the shop door opening.

'So this is what you get up to when I'm not around,' said Amelia, smiling at them all as she entered.

'Willy!' cried Babs and flung herself at him.

'That's quick work,' said Peter, flashing his wife a quizzical smile.

'Isn't it just?' she said, handing Daisy over to Rosie and drawing him aside. 'I've got something nice for you too,' she whispered, ticking his nose with the envelope. 'London postmark.'

He took a deep breath and took the envelope from her, hesitating before slitting it open. Amelia watched him read it. 'Well?' she demanded, unable to contain her impatience any longer. He lifted shining eyes to her face and there was no need for him to say a word. 'My husband's going to be a famous author,' she breathed. 'We'll have to share the running of the shop.'

Peter cleared his throat. 'A published author. I don't know about famous. They want me to go down to London and have lunch with them, discuss the book and any other ideas I might have for another.'

'Great!' said Rosie, who had been listening. 'You'll have to go with him, Aunt Amelia. You can stay with Aunt Iris. We'll hold the fort.'

'Too right,' said Amelia, linking an arm through her husband's. 'I'll do just that and on the way we'll decide the plot of your next story.'

'I could tell them I've a great idea for a family saga.'

'It's got to have a happy ending,' said Amelia positively.

'Of course,' he said, brushing her lips with his. 'They're the best kind.'

'How about this then?' she said, eyes sparkling, handing him the letter from Chris.

He stared at her, then opened it and began to read. She read along with him. *Dear Dad*, it began.